Anne Baker trained as a nurse at Birkenhead General Hospital, but after her marriage went to live first in Libya and then in Nigeria. She eventually returned to her native Birkenhead where she worked as a Health Visitor for over ten years. She now lives with her husband on a ninety-acre sheep farm in North Wales. Anne Baker's other Merseyside sagas, *Mersey Maids*, *A Mersey Duet*, *Moonlight on the Mersey*, *Merseyside Girls*, *Nobody's Child*, *Legacy of Sins*, *Paradise Parade* and *Like Father, Like Daughter*, are also available from Headline and have been highly praised:

'A stirring tale of romance and passion, poverty and ambition . . . everything from seduction to murder, from forbidden love to revenge'

Liverpool Echo

'Highly observant writing style . . . a compelling book that you just don't want to put down'

Southport Visitor

'A gentle tale with all the right ingredients for a heart-warming novel'

Huddersfield Daily Examiner

'Another nostalgic story oozing with atmosphere and charm'

Liverpool Echo

Also by Anne Baker

A Liverpool Lullaby

Anne Baker

HEADLINE

First published in 1998 by
HEADLINE BOOK PUBLISHING

First published in paperback in 1998 by
HEADLINE BOOK PUBLISHING

20 19 18 17 16

ISBN 0 7472 5533 4

Typeset by Avon Dataset Ltd, Bidford-on-Avon, Warks

Printed and bound in Great Britain by
Clays Ltd, St Ives plc

HEADLINE BOOK PUBLISHING
A division of Hodder Headline PLC
338 Euston Road
London NW1 3BH

A Liverpool Lullaby

Book One

1909–1914

CHAPTER ONE

June 1909

For Evie Hobson, Thursday morning started like any other, except that she couldn't help but notice the woman peering through the shop door at her. She seemed fearful, her nervous eyes following Evie up and down the counter. Evie saw her lips move and was sure she wanted to tell her something. She looked ill and pitifully weak, but then so did many of their customers.

Evie's father, Joseph Hobson, chemist and druggist, kept one of the busiest shops in Birkenhead. It occupied a premier position at the end of a small parade; it was bigger than its neighbours, square in shape with double doors set across one corner.

Evie sold a packet of hairpins from the front counter. There were two counters, and she was always conscious of her father working behind her on the back one that he called the drug run. His voice reached every corner, reverberating off the high cabinets that screened him from her view. On his side was a series of small mahogany drawers each with a Latin label. On hers were high shelves holding huge ointment jars.

'Painful piles?' Her father sounded irritable; his voice dropped slightly as a token to customer embarrassment but was still audible to everyone in the shop.

'Oak bark is what you need. Boil it in water for an hour. Then take your trousers off and sit over the steam until it cools. That should ease you. I'll give

3

you enough for three applications.'

Evie had heard it all before and no longer blushed. She was used to her father giving advice of an intimate nature. He was in one of his bad moods this morning. He'd had to give Johnny Simms, his senior apprentice, a day off, because last evening he'd dislocated his shoulder playing in a cricket match. As Johnny did much of the dispensing, this meant her father had more work to do.

Joseph prided himself on always being in control of his shop. He'd placed mirrors so he could see exactly what was going on in every corner. Evie knew they allowed him to watch her, his assistants and his customers. But likewise, in the mirror over the door she could see the back of the shop and him too when he came to speak to his customers.

'A packet of Pine Liptus throat lozenges, please.'

Evie moved down the counter to get them. From here she could see herself in one of the mirrors. She looked pale and the freckles across her nose seemed to stand out. Her dark hair was gathered up in a loose bun on top of her head. It looked insecure; several strands had broken free to hang down beside her chin. She tried to tuck them in. Her father was always telling her she looked untidy.

'A stick of shaving soap, please.'

The front counter had glass cases on top to display all manner of cosmetics and soaps. To reach the shaving soap, Evie had to ease herself past Miss Lister, the senior assistant, who had presided over the front counter for twenty years. She was in her late thirties but looked much older because she was so stout.

It was a dark morning, muggy and close, and thunder seemed to threaten. Her father's voice came again, crackling with ill temper.

'More of that sleeping draught I gave your baby? You

can't expect him to sleep night and day, you k.
mustn't give him too much.'

Joseph Hobson behaved as though he had the pov.r
of life and death over his customers. Evie reflected that he
treated her and those who worked for him in the same
way, and it made them all nervous. She heard the pages of
the prescription book being flipped over to find the date
of his original prescription. Joseph was meticulous in
everything he did and expected the same standard from
everybody working for him.

He reckoned he didn't get it from Bertie Pugh, the junior
apprentice, and was always at his throat. Bertie was only
nine months into his five years of training and was made to
spend a good deal of his time dusting and polishing.

'The best way to find out where everything is kept,'
Joseph was in the habit of telling him. Bertie also helped
out at the front counter when they were busy. Today, with
Johnny off nursing his injured shoulder, he was working
on the back counter.

Bertie had a problem with acne. When he'd first started
his apprenticeship, his face had been a mass of pustules
and spots. Joseph had prescribed a lotion and informed
him confidently that he'd soon have it cleared up. It had
not improved one iota, though Bertie had appealed to
him for further remedies and had applied them all
conscientiously. Evie thought her father showed less
patience with him as a result.

The succession of customers seemed never-ending.
Evie sold two flypapers and then had a moment to look
up. Her counter faced the window fronting on Argyle
Street – it was filled with bedpans and feeding cups,
crutches and splints. The woman she'd seen earlier was
still there, watching her. Something about her drew Evie's
sympathy.

She almost went out to speak to her, though Father forbade her to leave the counter without permission, but at that moment another customer was asking for rhubarb and ginger for his bowels.

The other shop window faced into the side street. It held four magnificent onion-shaped glass carboys filled with coloured water, the traditional symbol of the four elements of the alchemist adopted by all apothecaries: red for fire, green for earth, blue for water and yellow for air.

Evie caught a glimpse of the woman's pallid, waxy face between the coloured carboys and straightened up in surprise. Why was she hanging about? It was almost as though she had to find the courage to come in. She took a closer look. The woman was bent nearly double and had a matted black shawl pulled close about her head. It was only her manner that singled her out from their other customers. Evie could almost feel the intensity of her gaze. She decided she must speak to her, and on the spur of the moment she went to the door. The bell pinged as she opened it.

'Evie?' Her father's voice boomed through the shop, halting her in her tracks. 'Where do you think you're going?'

'Just to have a word . . .'.

'Not now. There are customers waiting to be served.'

Evie glanced hastily outside, but the woman had disappeared. Obediently, she returned to the counter and sold a jar of Virol and a bottle of embrocation.

The shop seemed to fill with customers all at once; three came together to the counter in front of her. She was looking for lip salve for one when the doorbell clanged again and the woman lurched inside at last. She edged forward, holding Evie's gaze with feverish eyes, and seemed to be offering her a bag. Then, in the crush, one of the waiting customers stepped back against her, knocking her off balance and making her drop the bag and spill its contents. Bertie Pugh happened to be passing close enough to prevent her falling.

'You want to consult Mr Hobson, ma'am?' he asked as he collected up her possessions and put them back in her bag.

Evie thought she heard the woman say, 'No.' She was sure it was to her she wanted to speak.

'You need to sit down, ma'am,' Bertie was saying, and in truth she seemed to sag as he guided her to the wooden bench provided for customers who were waiting their turn to consult Joseph.

She'd been there only a few minutes when Joseph called: 'Next, please.' It was a refrain that punctuated the day. Now, with greater impatience, he shouted: 'Who's next?'

Evie looked up into the mirror. It was the woman's turn. She was making an attempt to stand but fell back on the bench. Joseph went towards her. When his voice came again, he sounded shocked, horrified even.

'Helen! It is you? What brings you here?'

Evie couldn't move. They were all attuned to her father's moods. His tension was immediately theirs. It was awe and fear that made them like this. Everything in the shop came to a standstill.

'I didn't think you'd ever come near here again.'

Evie couldn't take her eyes from the woman. She was very frail and her shabby black dress was spattered with mud up to the knees. Evie had thought her a stranger, and yet her father had called her by her given name and seemed to know her well. Every eye in the shop watched them. His voice was colder now.

7

'Why can't you leave me in peace? Do you want to ruin what I have left?' He was angry and at his most hurtful.

'It's Evie I want . . .'

'You leave her alone. I don't want you here. Didn't I tell you never to set foot in my shop again?'

Everybody saw the woman stare at him in horror and then slowly slump against him.

'Pugh,' he shouted, 'help me put this woman in the dental chair.' Joseph was aware that he should show concern for his customers, and occasionally he tried. 'She can recover there in peace.'

To Evie his concern sounded false, a front he had assumed for the benefit of listening customers. She was sure he didn't feel compassion. Not for anybody. Bertie had once whispered that he was a dry stick of a man and there wasn't an ounce of sympathy in him. She watched them half carry the woman between them, her chin on her chest, her head escaping now from the shawl, grey-haired and unkempt.

The dentist's room opened immediately off the shop. Many years ago, when he'd first come here, Joseph Hobson had pulled teeth too. Now he rented his room to a travelling dentist who came two days each week. Miss Lister took appointments for him.

Evie felt overwhelmed with curiosity. She'd never known a customer to be put in the dental room before. She was afraid the woman must be very ill.

'Sal volatile,' her father's voice boomed, and Bertie Pugh rushed to get it from the drug run. 'She's fainted.'

'Who is she?' Bertie whispered to Evie as he passed.

Evie wished she knew. Another customer was demanding her attention by rapping on the counter with a coin.

'I want something to cure the biddies. Can you get it for me? Or do I have to wait for your father?'

'Head lice, do you mean, Mrs Stott?' Her father was coming from the dentist's room with a face like thunder. 'Sassafras oil, Evie. Do you have a toothcomb?'

'Yes, you sold me one last time. Pick 'em up at school, they do.'

'Use vinegar and water to loosen the nits from the hair.'

'I do,' the woman said. 'You told me that last time.'

Bertie Pugh was coming out of the dentist's room. 'She's coming round,' he said.

'Leave her be. She can rest there for a while,' Joseph said crossly.

Joseph Hobson was below average height and slight in build. His head was thickly covered with steel-grey bristles. His brows were like miniature coils of barbed wire, drawn tightly together over a large nose. That, and the granite line of his chin, gave him a permanently angry expression.

Evie knew he thought himself a cut above his neighbours because he was an apothecary, a professional man who had his own business.

They were all kept busy for the rest of the morning. Evie sold hairnets and nail brushes and bottles of Matron Milly's Infallible Female Mixture. The rush only died down when there was a rumble or two of thunder, the heavens opened and rain started to come down in sheets. Evie went to the end of the drug run. Her father was writing in his prescription book and Bertie Pugh was washing out medicine bottles.

'Father, did that poor woman say she wanted to speak to me?'

'No! Why should she?'

'I thought I heard her.'

'You thought wrong.'

'Shall I see if she needs anything?' Nobody had been near the woman for an hour and a half.

'No,' he barked. 'You stay away from her.'

Evie hesitated, but her curiosity got the better of her. 'Who is she, Father?'

'Better if you keep your mind on your work.' The doorbell pinged again. 'Here's a customer for you to attend to.'

It didn't escape Evie's notice that he went to see the woman himself five minutes later. He was only in the room for seconds and looked a changed man when he came out. He was supporting himself against the door jamb.

'Mr Pugh?' His voice lacked its usual confidence. 'Go and fetch the policeman on crossing duty. By Central Station.'

Bertie Pugh stared at him as though he'd taken leave of his senses.

'Do what I say. A customer has died on our premises.'

'Died!' Bertie's eyes were out on sticks.

Evie felt the blood rush to her face. 'That woman's dead?'

'I've said so, haven't I?'

Her father seemed suddenly as bent as the woman had been. The habitual blue tinge to his chin was more pronounced.

'Get along with you, Mr Pugh. I want her out of here as soon as possible.'

Bertie shot out into the rain without his coat. Evie's hand covered her mouth as she remembered that Mr Tennant the dentist would be here this afternoon.

Another customer came in and her father attended to him as though nothing had happened. Evie felt in a turmoil. It was only when she saw that Miss Lister had cheeks the colour of paste and was clutching the edge of the counter for support that she collected herself and ran for the sal volatile for her.

A few moments later, Mr Pugh was bringing in the policeman.

'In here.' Her father hurried to join them in the dentist's room, his lips set in a thin straight line.

'Passed away on your premises, has she, Mr Hobson?' the policeman was asking. Raindrops were dripping from his cape.

'Yes.'

'Do you have any idea who she is?'

Joseph closed the door with a firm click and Evie could hear no more. Moments later, it opened again as Bertie Pugh came out.

'I know who she is.' She could see that Bertie was bursting to tell her. His face shone with the latest balm he'd been prescribed for his spots. 'She's a relative of yours.'

'Who then?' Evie asked. She knew of no such relative. By what name had her father called her?

'Your father said her name was Helen Katherine Hobson.'

'What?' She couldn't believe her ears. 'No. Can't be. That was my mother's name.'

'It's your mother?' Bertie's mouth opened in amazement.

'No, course not,' Evie said. 'She died when I was six years old.'

'Another relative with the same name?' he asked, frowning in concentration.

'No!' Evie had never heard of any.

The shop closed for an hour at twelve thirty. Usually they all went upstairs then, apart from Miss Lister, to eat the hot dinner that Matilda, their cook-general, prepared for them. Evie went up with Bertie.

'Shall I dish up?' Matilda wanted to know. 'Or had we better wait for your father to come to the table?' He was still closeted in the dentist's room.

Evie said: 'We'd better wait.'

Her mind was on fire. Her father had recognised the woman. 'It is you?' he'd asked. Could it be that her mother had not . . . ?

She swung on her heel and ran back downstairs. This was something she had to know now or she'd have nightmares. She flung open the door of the dentist's room. The policeman was just closing his notebook.

Her father's eyes met hers. 'Leave us, Evie, if you please. I don't want you upset.'

She was determined to stand her ground. 'I won't be upset.'

The policeman said: 'There'll have to be a post-mortem, sir. I'll arrange for her to go to the mortuary.'

'As soon as you can. I can't have her here. The dentist is due this afternoon. Two o'clock in this room.'

Evie demanded: 'Who is she?' She risked a glance. The shawl now covered the woman's face.

The policeman was moving towards the door. 'I'll be on my way then.'

'Thank you. As soon as you can then?'

'Yes, sir, I'll do my best.'

As soon as they were alone Joseph seemed to crumble. He leaned against the back of the chair and took out a large handkerchief to blow his hawk-nose.

'Who is she?' Evie persisted.

'Never you mind.' His face was drained of colour. His hand showed a slight tremor. He was more shaken by this than she'd first supposed.

'She's my mother, isn't she? Why did you tell me she was dead?'

She saw her father moisten his lips. Anger was boiling up inside her.

'Do you know what that did to me? I cried myself to

sleep for months. I missed her dreadfully.'

Joseph straightened up. 'And what about me? Do you think I didn't miss her? She ran off with another man. She didn't want either of us.'

'But you lied . . .'

'Better for you to think she'd died than that she was guilty of that. I didn't want to spoil your memories of her. She walked out and left you too, don't forget. She didn't care what happened to either of us.'

Evie was turned to stone. She felt sick.

'Remember it was me that brought you up. You'd have had precious little if you'd had to rely on her. I did my duty by you. I've kept a roof over your head all these years. I've fed you, clothed you and educated you.'

There was a lump in Evie's throat the size of an orange. Duty! Oh yes, everyone could rely on Father doing his duty. He'd shown her no love and precious little affection. Gently she lifted the shawl from the woman's face.

'Undernourished,' her father said.

The woman looked as though she'd been ill for a long time. There was nothing of her but skin and bone. Not undernourished, more wasted away. She looked pathetic.

'She ran away to have a better life, but she didn't get it.' There was contempt in Joseph's voice.

'Is that what she said? She was looking for a better life?'

'She told me she was in love with someone else. A flashy fellow. Looks as though he dumped her in the way she dumped us.' He sighed. 'We'll never know now.'

Evie could barely see the body. Her eyes kept misting over. She told herself it was an empty shell, not anybody now. It didn't seem like her mother. She could feel nothing for her except shivers. This was the first dead person she'd ever seen.

13

'Leave her be, Evie. We'd better go up and have our dinner.'

'Dinner!' Evie felt another wave of nausea. The lump in her throat was bigger than ever. 'I don't want . . .'

'You must. Put this out of your mind and come up and eat. How do you expect to work and stay healthy if you don't refuel your body? You'll feel better if you eat something. Believe me.'

'She was my mother! She wanted to speak to me, I know she did. I could see her looking at me. She wanted to explain . . . You shouldn't have lied, told me she was dead.'

He pulled at her arm. The shawl fell back over the dead face and Evie allowed herself to be led away. 'I grieved for her.'

'Better that than to expect her to come back. You were six years old, for goodness' sake. What else could I tell you?'

'All those lies about a road accident . . .' She'd never understand why he'd told her such a story. He'd said her mother had slipped when she'd got off at the back of one of those old two-horse omnibuses at Charing Cross, and fallen in front of a governess cart, frightening that horse. It had kicked her before she could get up.

It was such a cruel thing to say if it wasn't true. It had given Evie terrible nightmares. She had very definite memories of her mother. She remembered the care she'd taken when brushing her daughter's hair. The way she used to sit Evié on the table to fasten all those little buttons on the leather gaiters she used to wear in winter.

Her mother used to give out love. She remembered her voice as she sang; her laugh as she'd taught her nursery rhymes. The feel of her soft body as she cuddled her close. Her good-night kisses.

14

Her mother had played with her and read stories to her. She'd taken her to school every day. She remembered a soft blue dress and the petticoats that swished as she walked. She'd had soft brown hair piled high on her head. But she couldn't remember her face. Not the way she'd looked.

She'd been woken one night by her father's voice. It had been wild with anger but she'd never known why. Only that the anger was directed at her mother. Then the next day she'd been gone, and Father had told Evie about an accident in which her mother had been killed.

The sun had gone from her world. The change in her life was fundamental. There had been no more school. Father thought it better if he and Aunt Agatha saw to her education. Nobody played with her after that, nobody laughed or joked.

Matilda had been kind, but Evie had recognised a change even in her. She was afraid. If Father came near and found them talking, Matilda would hurry away to some suddenly remembered task. There was an atmosphere of oppression in the household after that.

CHAPTER TWO

Evie found herself seated at the table with a plate of steaming red beef in front of her. Matilda always sat down with them for meals, as did Johnny Simms, who lodged with them. Bertie ate his dinners with them but his home was nearby and he lived out. The events of the morning cast a cloud. Nobody had much to say. Nobody ate much.

'Pull yourself together,' her father told her coldly. 'Come on, eat up.'

Evie had never felt this mutinous before. 'You're fond of telling everybody what they should do.'

'I know the human body. I know what's best for you.'

Evie put the food in her mouth and tried to swallow. Her mind raced with memories. Other things her father had said when she was six.

'Aunt Agatha will come and take care of us. We'll manage very well with her.'

Aunt Agatha was his older sister and very like him to look at. She had the same hawk-nose and darting grey eyes that missed nothing. The same wiry hair but with more grey in it, drawn back severely into a tight roll at the nape of her stringy neck. Agatha was a spinster with strict ideas about child-rearing. She shared with her brother an iron self-discipline, and together they did their best to instill that trait into Evie.

Agatha was efficient and thrifty in every aspect of home care and cookery. She could serve in the shop and act as dispenser. She wasn't qualified to prescribe as her brother was – he didn't believe women should be. He'd taught

17

her just enough to make her useful to him on the back counter.

That was to be Evie's lot too. Joseph had been articled to an apothecary from the age of thirteen and saw no reason why Evie shouldn't learn to make herself useful in the shop in the way he'd had to. From the age of eight she was responsible for washing out all the medicine bottles returned by customers to collect the penny charged on them.

It was Aunt Agatha who decided that Evie's hair should always be drawn back into tight plaits. She chose the black boots that laced up over her ankles, similar to Agatha's own. She asked the local dressmaker to run up Evie's dresses, always from the same pattern and always in dark greys and browns. She ordered serviceable serge for winter and plain cotton for summer. Evie felt a frump and pleaded for lighter colours, but was not allowed them.

'They'll need washing twice as often,' she was told. 'What's the sense in making work?'

Joseph believed in an early bedtime. Evie was fourteen before she was allowed to stay up after eight o'clock at night. He also believed in early rising and liked to have breakfast over and see her opening her lesson books by half past seven. He gave her lessons in herbalism and Latin.

Aunt Agatha was in charge of her general education and saw to it that she was kept busy every minute of the day. Sewing and housekeeping skills were not neglected. On Sundays, she was taken to church and Sunday school, and taught the scriptures.

Agatha chose books of instruction for her to read, or stories written from a strong moral viewpoint. Reading for pleasure was not allowed until the evening meal had been eaten and cleared away.

Evie was not allowed to play with other children, and

on no account was she to encourage them to come to the shop. She was given to understand that the local children were not of her class. And anyway, Joseph Hobson believed in keeping himself to himself.

If she was ill, Father took her down to the pharmacy when it was closed. Evie remembered sitting on the bench provided for customers and being questioned about her stomach aches. Then he'd prescribe some remedy, and pound up the herbs with his mortar and pestle. For her, he'd make the powders, which she understood tasted horrible, into sugar-coated pills. That was the mark of her father's love.

Evie had also been taught the value of money by having to work for it. She'd been taking out the babies from the baker's shop next door every afternoon for the past five years; ever since she was thirteen and considered old enough. The older ones were in school now, but there was always a new baby needing her attention. This served as a means to get her out in the fresh air, learn re-sponsibility for others and earn her own pocket money. All necessary lessons for a girl, in Joseph Hobson's view.

He told her that what she earned in this way was hers to keep. But it must be put into her money box, which was kept on the living-room mantelpiece. It stood on a small cash book, into which she was trained to enter all sums added or withdrawn, so that there was a running balance. Father checked on this regularly. Every Sunday, she must withdraw twopence, a penny for the church collection box at each service. She was told she needed prior approval to withdraw money for anything else.

She knew she disappointed both her father and her aunt. There were always red ink corrections scrawled across her lesson books. Her efforts in housework and shop work didn't please either. She saw Aunt Agatha as a jailor who never left her side. She felt caged.

She was fifteen, and had been told it was time to wear her plaits pinned up round her head, when George Appleby started to attend the same church. Evie felt an immediate change in her aunt, who seemed more cheerful and less constrained by duty. Joseph, on the other hand, seemed more morose. Evie only understood why when Aunt Agatha announced her intention of getting married. She found it hard to believe. Her aunt seemed too old.

Agatha said stiffly: 'Mr Appleby's asked me and I've said I would.'

Evie felt uplifted by the news; joy spread through her like a warm tide. There was nothing she wanted more, and it couldn't come soon enough for her. Mr Appleby was a missionary and a widower, whose first wife had succumbed to the unhealthy climate of central Africa.

'I don't think it's safe for you to go out there,' Joseph told his sister resentfully. 'The same fate could befall you.'

'I shall look after myself. Mr Appleby wants me to run the Sunday school and teach the native children their letters.'

Evie was delighted that the children of Africa rather than her would benefit from Agatha's discipline. The future suddenly seemed more rosy.

Before leaving, Aunt Agatha said: 'You'll have to look after the house for your father now, Evie. You're old enough and you've been well trained.' Her smile had been frosty. 'You'll manage well enough, I'm sure.'

Well trained or not, Evie was afraid she'd fall short of Agatha's standards.

'I'll not have that much time,' she'd faltered. 'Not to do everything you do.'

'Perhaps it's time you stopped taking next-door's

children out,' Father suggested, lifting his eyebrows of twisted wire-like hairs. 'That would give you another couple of hours every day and save your energy for more important things.'

That was the last thing Evie wanted. She never mentioned it again.

Her father didn't want Agatha to go. He was very tight-lipped about it. As soon as she had gone, he began to carp at Evie's efforts. She must be more thrifty. The housekeeping was costing more and she was gossiping with Matilda and allowing her to get lazy. From then on, Father directed the housekeeping.

With her aunt gone, Evie wanted to ditch the drab dresses she'd chosen for her. She thought the ten shillings a week her father allowed her for working in the shop very generous and wanted to spend some of it on new clothes. He told her off harshly.

'You mustn't waste, Evie. There's plenty of wear left in the clothes you have. Waste not, want not is what I say. You'll live to rue the day if you don't.'

This year, she'd been allowed to buy one new dress. It was light blue, but blue had not been her first choice. Father had thought red wool quite unsuitable and had forbidden it. Red was for hoydens and women of the street.

Evie hated her hairstyle. One night she sat in front of her dressing-table mirror looking at the plaits pinned round her head. She thought them frumpish and more suited to the middle-aged. On the spur of the moment she took her nail scissors to them and sheared six inches off each. She piled what remained of her hair into a loose bun in the style of Lillie Langtry, except that on her it didn't look quite so elegant.

Father was very cross and said she was cheapening herself. That her hair was untidy and looked a mess, and why did she want to make such a fool of herself? Bertie Pugh whispered that she was not to listen to him, it looked wonderful.

Her hair was too fine and silky to stay in position, and strands seemed always to escape and hang down by her face. Bertie assured her that didn't matter. Johnny and Miss Lister approved too.

By the time their dinner plates were being cleared away, Evie realised that her father was making a mighty effort to appear his normal self. He was the only one to have eaten a hearty meal. He even had a second helping of the beef. Evie did feel better with hot food inside her. Not good, but better than she had.

'Get yourself out to the park. Some fresh air will do you good,' he said briskly. This morning's events must not be allowed to change their routine. It was time for her to take next-door's baby out.

'She'll be gone to the mortuary by the time you come back, and we'll all be able to put it behind us.'

Evie noticed that he couldn't bring himself to call her mother by her name. She'd had the feeling that there was some mystery about her for some time. Matilda had said in an unguarded moment last year:

'How like your mother you are.'

'Am I? What was she like, Matty? I'd love to know more about her. Tell me what you remember.'

'No!' Matilda's voice had sounded strangled and she'd turned back to battering cod with uncharacteristic speed.

'Why not?' Evie had asked. 'Why does nobody want to talk about my mother? Father's just the same.'

'He's still grieving.' Matty had recovered her wits. 'It upsets him to talk about her.'

'It upsets me that nobody ever has,' Evie retorted. 'Not

you, or Aunt Agatha. You can't all be so locked in grief that you can't bear to remember her. Not after all these years. Doesn't anybody have happy memories of her?' It really had upset her that that was the case.

Now Evie put on her hat and coat and went slowly downstairs, knowing that she wouldn't be able to go out without seeing her mother once more. If she didn't see her now, there might never be another chance. Slowly she turned the knob on the door to the dentist's room. It was always closed up and airless.

It was hard to accept, even now, that this inert figure was the mother she'd thought had died eleven years ago. Father had been very wrong to lie about that. Evie was sure she'd have grieved less if she'd known the truth. And now to be told her mother had lived many more years! She wouldn't have believed it if she wasn't here in front of her eyes. There were knots in her gut. She was numb and sick with the horror of it.

She folded back the matted wool shawl. It was a face that ought to be as familiar to her as her own. Grey and waxy as it was, it had the same neat nose and even features that she had. She tried to imprint it on her mind. The outline became hazy as tears misted her eyes. Her mother had come back to see her before she died. Surely that meant she had loved her?

She looked round for the bag her mother had been carrying when she'd come into the shop. A grey canvas shopping bag, but it was not here now. If only Father had told her who the woman was when he first saw her, Evie would have been able to talk to her. Her mother wouldn't have had to die alone.

Blinking hard, Evie slowly covered the still form, closed the door softly and let herself out of the shop.

★ ★ ★

When Evie returned at four o'clock, there were two patients waiting for the dentist's attention.

'It's all right,' Bertie whispered. 'Everything's back to normal.'

Evie felt nothing would ever be normal again. 'My mother's gone then? The hearse came in time?'

'A hand cart. They didn't send the horse hearse for her. They don't if they're going to the mortuary.'

Evie couldn't get the vision of that out of her mind either. She had a terrible night. She'd been unable to think of anything but her mother since yesterday morning. She felt in a state of shock.

At breakfast, her father flared up when his bacon and egg was put in front of him.

'Matilda, you've overcooked it again. Just look at this egg, it's all dried up. Why can't you cook things as I like them?'

'I'm sorry.' His complaints made Matty nervous and apologetic. 'It's me feet. Giving me gyp they are. I can hardly walk this morning.'

Matilda had a round face, and her large pale cheeks were mottled with broken veins. She was well padded and could be motherly if Joseph were not about. It was to her that Evie had turned for comfort when she'd been a child. This morning her brown eyes showed distress.

'Can Evie do a bit of shopping for me? Get a few things for dinner?'

'Of course I can,' Evie told her, hoping to calm things down. She felt they were all walking on eggshells.

But Johnny Simms upset her father further by taking off his shirt and showing his shoulder, now black and blue with bruising.

'Still very painful, sir. Didn't sleep. I think another day to recover?'

'Damn it, Simms! You ask for time off to play that confounded game. You come home with your shoulder put out, begging for help. I put it back for you, I give you embrocation and a day off, and now you want still more.'

Evie knew Johnny wanted to use the time to study, because his final exams, his majors, were not so far off now. He was rarely to be seen without his copy of *Materia Medica* sticking out of the pocket of his white coat.

'And it's Friday,' Joseph exploded. 'One of our busier days.'

'Not as busy as Saturday, sir. If I rest now, I shall feel much better by then.'

Johnny was a good-looking young man, with smooth fair hair swept straight back from his forehead. They were all in awe of Joseph Hobson, but everyone knew Johnny was Joseph's favourite and could get away with more than the rest of them.

'All right, but I shall expect you to pull your weight next week.'

'Of course, sir.'

Evie watched Joseph's eyes go round the table. She knew Bertie Pugh had not pleased him yesterday. She had heard him shout several times: 'Look lively, lad. Why are you so dozy? Keep your wits about you.'

By nine o'clock, when the shop was opening, Evie couldn't even think straight, and it seemed Bertie couldn't either. Within fifteen minutes, she'd heard Father tell him off twice. Then he committed the cardinal sin. He made out a packet of powders to the wrong customer. The error was discovered only because that customer was expecting a bottle of cough mixture.

'You aren't capable, Mr Pugh,' Joseph exploded. 'Sometimes I wonder whether you should be allowed to continue in this profession. Get out of my sight. Go and help on the front counter.

'Evie? You can come and help me in the drug run today.'

Evie's heart sank. Although she felt permanently under surveillance in the shop, to work to Father's instruction in the back was much worse. As Father saw it, it was a privilege to make herself useful by writing to his dictation in the prescription book, to wrap up his powders and lotions.

'Couldn't I learn to be a real chemist like you, Father?' she'd once asked. 'I could help you much more then.'

'No,' he'd said.

'If Bertie Pugh can do it, I'm sure I could.'

'You're a woman. It isn't possible for you. A woman's role in life is to support her father or her husband.'

'I could help you more if . . .'

'You're being silly, Evie. Don't argue.'

Evie had had to accept that she'd be taught to fetch and carry for her father, and no more.

Ned Collins's step was jaunty as he walked into the centre of Birkenhead. He paused outside the Argyle Theatre to look at the billboards. Harry Lauder was top of the bill tonight. Ned bounded across the road, in front of a brewer's dray, to post a letter at the General Post Office opposite, and then back to stride on down Argyle Street towards Hobson's the Chemist. Evie Hobson had caught his eye some time ago and had filled his mind ever since. He thought her the prettiest girl he'd ever seen.

He went past the shop as often as he could, hoping to catch a glimpse of her. If possible, he found some reason to go inside. On his last day off, he'd asked Joseph Hobson to prescribe a cure for a hangover. His brother had been very grateful for it and he'd been able to stand around the shop for ten or more minutes. Evie had been serving most of that time, but she'd noticed him and asked if there was anything she could get him.

He was pleased because today he had two commissions to fulfil. He'd be able to speak to her. Perhaps get her to say something to him; something more than the transaction called for.

He could see Evie now in his mind's eye. A slight figure in a drab dress that reached to her ankles. That was covered with a starched white apron with straps crossing between her shoulder blades and tying in a big bow in the small of her back, trailing streamers down her skirt. She had dark silky hair and thick eyelashes that threw shadows on her cheeks and a delightful dimple that came when she smiled. Her eyes were big and soft and brown and could look happy, but were more often wary or anxious.

Ned knew that a lot depended on her father's temper. He was a terrible tyrant, but all the same, many in the community preferred to put their trust in Joseph Hobson when they were ill. The poor came in droves because he charged only for the remedies he made up for them, while Dr Jones, who practised round the corner, charged one shilling and sixpence for a consultation and then exacted another payment for the medicines he handed out.

His own mother thought Joseph Hobson's powders, pills and lotions more effective, as well as being cheaper. Customers put up with his shortness of manner and volatile temper because they respected his skills. He had the reputation of being a hard man who would do his best for them. He saw that as his duty.

From the doorstep the shop looked busy. All the better as far as Ned was concerned. He didn't mind waiting around inside, not one bit. His brothers laughed at him.

'You're aiming a bit high, aren't you? The apothecary's

daughter? What would she see in you?'

The bell clanged as he went in. Straight away he felt the atmosphere. Tension crackled in the air. Things were more fraught than usual. His heart lurched with disappointment when he saw that Evie was not in her usual place.

Then he heard her voice and knew she was helping her father on the back counter. Mr Hobson's face was heavy with irritation. Ned went forward until he could see her. Evie's eyes were frightened and had mauve shadows beneath them. He wanted to take her hand. No, he wanted to take her in his arms and comfort her.

Evie could see the shop filling up with customers. She was doing her best to please her father. He was pounding herbs to fine powder with his mortar and pestle. She felt all thumbs as she folded the doses into tiny papers with the exact precision her father required.

'Look lively, Evie,' he growled, as he pushed another prescription alongside one she hadn't finished. 'Be careful you don't get them mixed up.'

It was for pills this time, thank goodness, so she'd be able to catch up. It took Father longer to roll his powders into pills and coat them with sugar. Most customers were prepared to put up with the bitter taste of the powders because it was the cheapest way to buy the remedies.

Evie scurried back to the prescription book to fill it in. Cough mixture this time, for Mrs Gertrude Collins. Then she had to wrap the bottle in white paper with meticulous care, seal it top and bottom with hot wax and write the dose and the name of the customer on the pleat she'd folded down the front.

'Do put a move on, Evie, you're falling behind again,' Joseph complained as she moved past him.

He had his back towards her. After what had happened yesterday, the sight of his narrow shoulders covered by his white coat was enough to frighten her. She shrank at being reprimanded in front of customers and staff. But worse than any fear was the feeling of shame that she couldn't cope with the simplest of tasks. He'd always sapped her confidence. He showed no fatherly affection. No affection for anybody or anything. Everybody but Johnny Simms was scared of him.

She went to the end of the drug run and called: 'Mrs Collins? That will be sixpence, please.'

Neither of the two elderly ladies waiting on the bench looked up. Evie felt a momentary misgiving: had she got the name right? Her fingers were cold and she felt numb with agony.

She knew Mrs Collins by sight, a stout middle-aged woman. Everybody round here knew the large Collins family. It consisted mostly of boys, grown to manhood now. They all came in from time to time, generally in search of a cure for a thumping head. Father said they all drank like fishes, their mother included.

Evie didn't know how she let it happen, but somehow the newly filled bottle of cough cure slid through her fingers. She made a desperate grab to save it. The sound of shattering glass brought her father off his high stool.

'For goodness' sake, girl!' His hawk-nose was screwing up in outrage. 'How can you be so careless?'

Evie could feel her heart thudding against her ribs. She'd never done such a thing before.

'Look at the mess!' Dark-brown syrupy fluid was leaking out of the package. She tried to pick it up but the sodden paper parted and let the glass tinkle on to the floor. The next second it was crunching under her feet.

There was a fit of coughing from the bench and a

querulous voice rasped: 'Was that my physic she dropped?'

'No, Mrs Smith. It was mine, or rather my mother's. She asked me to get it for her.'

Evie registered that it was one of the Collins boys who answered. She thought he'd been studying the scented soaps in the glass case on the front counter.

'I'll make up another bottle,' Joseph told him shortly. 'I'm sorry you've been kept waiting.'

To Evie, he said: 'Better get this glass brushed up, before it causes more trouble.'

She ran for a floor cloth, a dustpan and a brush. The smell of cough mixture was filling her nostrils; it was so strong she could taste it on her tongue. The heavy fumes were warming her throat, spreading down to her lungs. She breathed in deeply, trying to still her thudding heart.

Down on the floor she could see herself in the mirror advertising Proctor's Pine Liptus Pastilles. There were brown splashes now along the hem of her dress. Her face looked drawn with worry and almost as white as her apron.

Ned Collins was standing too close. She could see cough mixture all over his boots. He was reading the advertisement.

' "Pastilles for dusty roads and a tendency to catarrh. For chest, throat and voice. A boon to singers, speakers and travellers." Are they good?'

She looked at him then. He had a pleasant smile. 'We sell a lot. One and threepence a box.'

'Evie?' her father called. He was pushing another bottle of medicine towards her, already wrapped. 'At seventeen, you should be capable of handling a bottle of medicine without dropping it. Try again.'

'Sorry, Father.'

She took it to the end of the counter. 'That will be sixpence, Mr Collins, thank you.'

'And a couple of corn plasters.' His eyes seemed to be searching for hers. 'They're for my mother, too.'

Evie went to the front counter and reached into one of the glass cases.

'Two?' She knew her voice sounded strangled.

'How much are they?'

She turned one over, looking for some clue. 'Four a penny, I think.' She couldn't see her father, but she knew he was listening.

'Two a penny,' Joseph corrected. He was always close enough to monitor everything she did and said. As she took out two corn plasters, two more fell to the floor.

'Evie! What's the matter with you today? You've got to be more careful.' Her father had come to see what she'd let fall and couldn't hide his exasperation.

'No harm done,' the customer said mildly. 'No need to go for the poor girl.'

That made Evie look squarely at Ned Collins. He was a handsome young man in his early twenties, with a thatch of curly brown hair. His eyes smiled into hers. They seemed full of sympathy, as though he wanted to share and lighten her misery. She warmed towards him.

'Stay out of this,' Joseph barked. 'It has nothing to do with you.'

Ned Collins crashed his coins down on the counter, scooped up the corn plasters and left without another word. He let the shop door bang behind him so that the bell set up a frenzied clangour.

'Scum of the earth, those Collinses,' her father said contemptuously. 'Irish tinkers.' Evie could feel herself shaking. She couldn't stand any more of this. She glanced at the clock.

'Had I better do that shopping for Matilda next? She wants me to get something for dinner.'

'For all the good you're doing here, you might as well. Get her list and let me see what she wants. Tell her we'll have liver and onions for dinner.' Liver was a favourite of his; the rest of them didn't care for it.

To pull the shop door shut behind her and get out was always a high spot in Evie's day. She gulped at the fresh air. Joseph always had to know exactly where she was going.

She walked slowly past the baker's next door, sniffing at the scent of freshly baked bread. Past the barber's shop with its red striped pole. It was steamy inside from the kettle kept simmering on the gas ring to provide hot water for shaving. She could smell the scented soap and bay rum wafting from the door as she passed. A man sitting waiting his turn looked up from the *Liverpool Advertiser* he was reading.

She called in at the grocer's and bought the half-pound of fig biscuits her father had added to Matilda's list. She wouldn't let herself look at the Meadow Creams, which she much preferred.

Bentley's, the butcher's, was the last shop in the row. With the lamb's liver in her bag, she went back to Darty's, the baker's. She wouldn't look at the display of cakes either, because she was never allowed to buy any of them. Her father's tastes were austere; he didn't approve of shop cake. He expected Matilda to make everything they ate. She made big cut-and-come-again plain cakes when she had time.

'Hello again.' Ned Collins was standing at this counter now, his eyes sparkling down at her, as though he was pleased to see her. Not sympathetic eyes after all; he had laughing eyes. He was in the middle of making his choice from the luscious delicacies set out in the window.

'Two buns with pink icing and two with white, please,

Polly. And I'll take a couple of jam tarts and four apple tarts, if you haven't burned them today.'

'We never burn them,' Polly Darty chuckled. She knew when she was being teased. She was a middle-aged matron with a plump figure showing how much she appreciated her husband's baking.

'And a lardy cake. My mother loves those.'

'How is she, Ned?'

Evie could feel her mouth beginning to water. The shop was filled with heavenly scents. She found it hard to believe that the Collins family her father so looked down upon could indulge themselves in this fashion.

'Give me one of your pork pies too. I'll eat that on the way home.' Ned's manner was relaxed. Everything about him suggested he enjoyed the pleasures of this world.

He said to Evie: 'Your dad lets you out, then?'

'I've just come for bread. The usual please, Mrs Darty. A white tin.'

Ned bit into his pork pie. He was making no attempt to leave the shop before she did. She wanted him to stay. She wanted to know him better. He was the first person who had ever tried to support her against her father.

'He was giving you a very hard time.' The friendly brown eyes were searching her face.

She couldn't openly admit that. Not so close to home. Father would half kill her if he knew! Polly Darty knew what he was like.

Evie managed: 'That's the way he is.'

'He's a hard man. Bloody-minded and foul-tempered, so they say. Don't they, Polly?'

'Perhaps not the easiest to get along with.' Polly was carefully noncommittal too, and wouldn't look at Evie now.

They all heard the baby cry for attention in the back of the shop.

'There's Herbie waking up,' Evie said.

'Wants his dinner. You'll be back to take him out at two?'

'Of course.'

Ned followed her out and seemed reluctant to leave her. He kept her talking on the doorstep of the pharmacy.

'Walk a little way with me. You don't want to rush back to your father, do you?'

'I have to. We're busy and Johnny Simms has the day off.'

He looked disappointed. 'But you'll be taking the Darty baby out at two?'

'Yes, to the park.'

'Good.' His eyes beamed down at her. 'I mean, you've got to have a bit of fun, haven't you? What's life for if it's all work?'

Evie couldn't have agreed more. She felt starved of fun. Starved of life itself. Through the glass in the shop door, she saw her father striding towards them, his face like thunder.

'Goodbye,' she said hastily. 'I've got to go.'

Once inside, she felt the medicinal fug close round her again. Her father was furious.

'You stay away from those Collinses, do you hear? They're a bad lot. I don't want you keeping such company. Putting his oar in where it's not wanted. He should mind his own business.'

Evie's heart was thumping wildly as she scurried upstairs with the shopping. A few minutes later she could hear Joseph pounding his mortar and pestle with ill-tempered zeal.

34

CHAPTER THREE

As Evie unpacked the bag of shopping on the kitchen table, Matilda was peeling potatoes at the sink. She noticed for the first time that Matty's figure was not as well padded as it used to be. She had been a fixture in their household for as long as Evie could remember. Now she was looking older and not very well.

Evie did as much as she could to help with the housework, for she was afraid it was becoming too much for Matilda. She knew she worked long hours on her own; she'd rarely seen the older woman sit down. The nervous tremor of Matty's work-worn fingers was more marked today. When Father had turned on her, Evie had seen raw fear in her brown eyes.

It occurred to her now that Matilda must have known her mother well.

She said: 'A terrible thing, my mother coming back here to die.'

'Terrible. I can't get it out of my mind. I wanted to see her but your father wouldn't let me. Why did she come?'

'To see me. I think she wanted to tell me something.' Evie was getting used to the idea now. 'I feel so churned up . . .'

'It upset me too. I was right fond of your mother.'

Matilda wore her straight grey hair in a bun in the nape of her neck and covered most of it with a large, no-nonsense cotton cap. Like the shop assistants, she wore a large white starched apron. To show her lower station, Joseph insisted that instead of black she wear a print dress

of striped cotton which came down to her ankles. Instead
of boots, she wore incongruous red carpet slippers to ease
her painful bunions.

Evie had tried to talk to her about her mother before
but she'd never got much out of her. Matty had seemed
on edge the moment Evie mentioned her name. Evie was
in no doubt that Joseph had forbidden it.

'All these years . . .' Evie said. 'Did you think she was
dead?'

The brown eyes were troubled. 'That's what your father
said. He spoke of her as being in her grave, and you
thought she'd gone to heaven. I suppose I came to believe
. . . that perhaps she might have died.'

'That means you didn't.'

She saw Matilda swallow. 'You're a quick one. Determined too. You stand up to him better than she did. She
didn't dare.'

'You knew she wasn't dead?'

'She told me she was leaving, you see. And I never
heard of any funeral.'

Evie felt a surge of fear. She might dare, but that didn't
mean she wasn't terrified of Father. Her heart began to
hammer.

'She told you what was going on?'

The pounding from the drug run below ceased. They
both paused to listen in case Joseph should be coming
upstairs. Evie's voice dropped to a near whisper.

'It's all right . . .'

'He doesn't like me talking about her. Told me I
mustn't. Not one word.'

'To me?'

'To anyone. He'd be furious if he knew about this. He
threatened to sack me.'

'Please,' Evie pleaded. 'She told you she was leaving?'

'I knew she wanted to. There'd been an awful row.'

'Between Mother and Father?'

'She wanted to take you with her. She'd asked me to pack all your things.'

Evie's mouth felt dry. This was what Father was trying to keep from her. 'What happened?'

'She went to meet you as you came out of school. She was going to leave straight from there. But your father went too.

'She tried again the next day but he caught you both as you were going downstairs. Helen thought he'd be busy in the shop once it was open. That you'd both be out of the door before he could stop you.'

Evie caught her breath. Something stirred in the depths of her memory. She remembered clinging to Mother's coat. She was weeping and they were both hung about with bags and coats.

'Where was she taking me? Where did she go? You should have told me.'

'Look, lass, you were nobbut a child, and if your father said she was dead, it wasn't my place to say otherwise.'

'Matty!' Evie wanted to shake her. 'You've got to tell me everything now. Father stopped her taking me away with her. Then what happened?'

'She didn't know what to do, she was worried about you, distraught. She made me promise to look after you. See you was all right.'

'You did that, Matty. You were always kind. I used to come to you if I wanted a cuddle.'

'You came too often. Your father saw you and warned me off. He thought I was telling you things, but I wasn't. He said I must stop it anyway. I was spoiling you, softening you.'

Matty's voice dropped until Evie could hardly hear.

She held her hand in front of her mouth.

'Your mama gave me something to keep for you until you were old enough to understand. After what happened yesterday, I reckon that's now. Save my legs and run up to my room, Evie. There's a photograph of her in a frame.'

'Where? I've never seen it there. Never seen any photos of her.'

'Your father packed all her things away when she went. All those he could get his hands on.'

'Why? That's awful.'

Matilda was shaking her head. 'Not my place to question why. You'll find this one in the top drawer of my chest, at the back. I didn't want him to see it.'

Evie rushed up two flights of stairs to the attic where Matilda slept. The room was like a cell, plain and sparsely furnished. She had the framed picture in her hands in moments.

It made her gasp aloud. The eyes were so like her own. It was sepia and somewhat faded now, so it was hard to tell what her mother's colouring had been. She wore a high-necked Victorian blouse, all frills and furbelows. Evie feasted her eyes and was delighted to find a resemblance to herself. She took the photograph to her own bedroom and hid it in her bed before going back down to the shop to help her father.

'Where've you been until now? You know we're busy and you dawdle upstairs. You need to jump to it, young lady.' His wiry eyebrows were pulled down in a formidable frown.

At two o'clock, Evie steered the baby carriage out of the yard behind the bakery with one hand, and kept a firm hold on Herbie Darty's reins with the other. His plump arms reached up to the handle to push it too. At eighteen months, he was leaving babyhood behind.

This was her favourite time of day, when she could get away from her father and the shop for two whole hours. Yesterday's thunder had cleared and it was a cool summer's day. She lifted her face to the pale sun and tried to take pleasure from it. But today, she couldn't get her mother out of her mind.

She walked back along the parade of shops and looked both ways, wondering if Ned Collins would come. He'd said he would, but there was no sign of him. That disappointed her too.

Little Herbie was waddling on plump legs, already looking over-podgy from the buns he received to keep him quiet. Evie thought him a lovable child, full of energy and always happy. He cried only when he was hungry.

His father had to be up and in his bakehouse by four in the morning. By nine, he had the shop stocked with fresh bread and cakes and was ready to open. Evie had been told that he took a cup of tea and some fresh bread to Polly's bedside at seven, so that she could get dressed, get the children off to school and see to little Herbie.

They tended the shop between them during the morning, and after dinner at midday, Arthur Darty went to bed for a two-hour rest while his wife ran the shop on her own and Evie took the baby out for some fresh air.

Herbie was encouraged to take his nap before his dinner, and Evie's instructions were to keep him awake at all costs while he was out. He was to walk and run as much as possible and hopefully tire himself out, so that he could be put to bed and would sleep soon after having his tea.

There were not many places within walking distance that she could take him, and it depended upon the weather. For wet days, the best place was the big market hall. They could walk round there, up and down the aisles, and keep dry. She amused herself by pricing the goods on display: cotton and wool cloth, ready-made blouses, boots and shoes, hams and cheeses and pies, crockery, and fruit and vegetables. For better days, there was the recreation ground in Camden Street, but that could be commandeered by older boys playing rough games.

Evie loved to go up Grange Road, window-shopping in the fine shops, but it was a busy road and she dared not let her attention stray from Herbie there.

On warm days, Hamilton Square offered a bench for her to sit on and a bit of grass in the formal gardens, but much the nicest place for Herbie was Birkenhead Park, though it was also the furthest. There she could play games with him on the grass and he could run about freely. On such a fine day as today, it was the obvious place for her to go.

It took her about twenty minutes to push the perambulator there, but much longer if Herbie's stumpy legs were covering the distance too. She'd started up Conway Street when she heard feet thudding on the pavement behind her. She turned and found Ned Collins running after her.

'You went without me!' he accused, but his eyes danced with pleasure. He was puffed after his run. 'Didn't know whether you'd set out or not. Had to ask Polly Darty.'

'You asked her!'

Evie stopped, horrified. She knew exactly what her father would say. He'd see any boyfriend as a source of trouble, and he'd already warned her off the Collins family.

'It'll be all right. Told her not to mention it to your dad.'

Evie started to breathe again, hoping he was right.

'A bit strict, Polly said he was.' His brown eyes smiled down at her.

'Yes.'

Ned laughed. 'We're never going to reach the park at this rate. How do you stand this meandering?' He picked Herbie up and set him across his shoulders. The child chortled with delight. 'What a little roly-poly you are. You weigh a ton.'

After that, Evie had to skip along to keep pace with Ned's long stride. She told herself she wasn't going to worry about upsetting Father; she wasn't going to think about her mother either. She was going to enjoy Ned's company.

She kept stealing sideways glances at him. Trying to commit to memory the strong planes of his face, his curly brown hair blowing in the breeze and the spotted red kerchief round his neck.

They reached the park and went in through the grand entrance. Ned swung Herbie to the ground and let him walk between them, holding on to their hands. They were almost swinging him off his feet.

'The duck pond's the place,' Ned said.

'No,' she protested. 'I'm afraid he'll fall in, and he tried to paddle with his shoes on last month.'

There was a cricket match in progress. Ned paused to watch it for a moment. Herbie was crawling round. Evie unhooked his reins and sank to the grass beside him. He was safe enough just here.

Ned sat down beside her. There were so many things Evie wanted to know about him, but she didn't know how to ask. She'd never been alone with a man before. In the shop, her father was always within earshot.

She knew she was blurting it out: 'Don't you have to go to work?'

He smiled at her. 'I have got a job.'

'I know.'

'How?'

'All those cakes you bought.'

He laughed. 'I'm on the Isle of Man boats. Day off today.'

'Oh! A sailor . . .'

'Deck hand.'

Evie knew her father wouldn't approve of that either. He thought his position in life was considerably higher than that of a deck hand.

'Do you like it?'

'It's a job.'

'But the Isle of Man? I'd have thought you'd like to go further. You could see the world.' Evie could think of nothing she'd like better.

'No. Those who want to see the world are away for years. I did a three-year trip on a tramp steamer once. Nothing but work . . .'

'But you must have seen far-off places?'

'I saw a lot of docks. Whether it's New York or Cape Town, the docks don't look much different from those in this country. This way, I'm home regular, like. There and back in a day.'

His brown eyes were exploring hers. 'Do you want to get away from your dad? I would if he were mine. He's ferocious.'

She said nervously: 'He won't like me talking to you.'

'You're doing more than talking to me,' Ned laughed. 'You're here in the park with me. Keeping company.'

'You tagged on to me.'

'Course I tagged on to you. I liked the look of you. Besides, your dad was being horrible. Couldn't help feeling a bit . . . well, you know.'

'What?'

'I'd have liked to punch him on the nose.'

Evie couldn't hold it back any longer. 'I've always wanted a friend.'

'A boyfriend?'

'Any sort of a friend. Someone I could talk to.'

He took her hand in his. It felt comfortingly warm. 'Go on then,' he said. 'Talk to me. I'd like that.' She laughed but didn't know where to begin.

Ned was handsome. She liked the way he closed his eyes against the sun. She'd felt his support this morning when he'd stood up for her against her father. Ned was keeping an eye on Herbie now. He called out to him and obediently the child waddled back towards them.

She started to tell him how claustrophobic she found the pharmacy, how domineering her father was.

'He was in a terrible temper this morning. I still feel sick when I think about it.'

'Why?'

'Yesterday . . .'

It wasn't easy to talk about it. It sounded impossible, a nightmare. Evie swallowed hard. 'My father did a terrible thing. He told me my mother was killed when I was six years old. All these years I've believed she was dead.'

Ned's hand tightened on hers. Gently, then, he began drawing the whole story out of her.

'She died in the shop?' Even Ned shivered when she told him that.

'She was so near to speaking to me. Telling us where she'd been and what had happened to her. He said he hadn't heard from her from the day she left. She was terribly ill but he left her alone in the dentist's room, and I didn't even know who she was.'

Evie put her head down on the rough flannel of Ned's shirt. She felt his arm go round her shoulders and the tears start to her eyes.

'He forbade me think of her, but I can't stop.'

'Course you can't,' he comforted.

'He said she knew where I was and could have come back for me at any time. He said she didn't want anything to do with me.'

Ned's arm tightened across her shoulders, pulling her closer. 'That was cruel. A horrible thing to say.'

When Evie returned to the shop it was full of customers again. They were often busy in the late afternoon when people were leaving their work.

She took off her hat, tied on her apron and went behind the front counter, hoping her father would allow her to stay there. She sold a packet of Carter's Little Liver Pills and a jar of Eastern Foam Vanishing Cream.

Nothing seemed to have changed in the shop. Miss Lister and Bertie were trying to behave as if nothing out of the ordinary had happened. Her father's voice boomed out, full of impatience.

'What's that? Speak up, I can't hear you. Pain in your back?'

She knew from his brusque manner that he hadn't got over seeing her mother again. He wasn't usually this short with his customers, only with his staff. She felt better now she'd poured out her troubles to Ned. She felt comforted; it was a weight off her shoulders.

What bothered her now was that her father would notice how much higher her spirits were and guess the reason. She'd done what he'd forbidden and spent two hours with Ned Collins. That she'd dared to do it brought shivers of guilt. If Joseph found out, he'd be raving. He expected to control everything in her life, and it was the first time she'd ever disobeyed him.

She and her father usually went up to eat their tea at

five, leaving Johnny Simms in charge of the shop for half an hour. Today, Joseph sent Evie upstairs to find Johnny.

'Ask him to come down and relieve me,' he ordered. 'It won't hurt him to do that. He knows I can't trust Bertie Pugh to do it, not yet.'

Johnny's handsome eyes rolled up to the ceiling when she told him, but he put on his white coat and went straight down.

When she was alone with Father, sitting one each side of the table and eating their boiled eggs, he said:

'I've heard from the police. The post-mortem showed that your mother died of consumption. She was very far gone. Must have had it for years. There was nothing anyone could have done to help. The funeral's to be on Monday. I've told them I'll pay for that. Nobody need say my wife was a charge on the parish.'

'Will we go, Father?'

'I'll go because some might think it odd if I don't. There's no need for you.'

'I'd like to.' Evie moved egg round her mouth while her father thought it over.

'All right then. We'll both go. Though she hardly deserves it. She made her own bed, Evie. It's only right that she had to lie on it.'

Evie said nothing. It was safer to keep quiet.

'Your mother made bad friends. They led her astray. I don't want that to happen to you.'

She felt the hairs on the back of her neck stand up. It sounded as though he knew all about Ned. She must keep her friendship with him a secret whatever happened. Ned's brown eyes had laughed down at her when they'd parted this afternoon.

'I'll look out for you again when I have my next days

off,' he'd said. 'In about two weeks. Easy to spot you, pushing that big pram.'

Joseph went on: 'I've tried to bring you up properly. I don't want you to be tempted by the devil and come to the same sad end as your mother. I know I've been strict with you, but I've had to be.'

'I can't get it out of my mind,' she agonised. 'That my mother was living all these years and I didn't know.'

Joseph was clicking his tongue with impatience but she made herself ask:

'Do you have the bag she brought with her?'

'What bag?'

'A grey canvas shopping bag. I'd like to have it.'

His eyes were wide with outrage. 'She had nothing with her.'

'She did. It had books in it. She dropped them and Bertie picked them up. They might throw some light on where she's been all this time.' Evie sighed. 'If only I'd been able to speak to her, we might have found out about . . .'

'There's nothing to find out. Nothing that need concern you.'

She wasn't sure whether it was fear or nerves that was making Father so abrupt. 'I want no more of this nonsense. She's gone and that's the end of it.'

Evie's mind whirled. Clearly there was a lot to find out, but Father wanted to keep her in ignorance. It only served to whet her curiosity.

'Better if you forget all about your mother,' Joseph thundered. 'It's quite wrong to fill your mind with her affairs. She cut herself off from us years ago.'

Evie wanted to close her ears to such talk. 'I wish I could have told her how I felt. I wish there was some way I could find out where she's been . . .'

'Don't you try. Do you hear? I forbid it. She went back on her marriage vows, Evie. She didn't care what happened to me, or to you. I told her quite clearly that if she went she need never come back. I wouldn't have her. It's better that she's dead. Better for all of us. It finishes it now.'

Evie could feel the food sticking in her throat. She knew this would alter for ever how she thought of her father. She'd never felt close to him. Now an unbridgeable rift had opened up between them.

As Evie slid between her sheets that night, she found the framed photograph she'd hidden in her bedclothes. She pulled it out and studied her mother again by the light of her candle. She looked so pretty it was hard to equate her with the woman who had tried to talk to her in the shop and died so tragically soon afterwards in the dental chair.

Evie wondered how old her mother had been when the picture was taken. She turned the frame over, then opened the back to see if there was a date on the reverse of the picture. An envelope fell out on her eiderdown. She felt her heart turn over when she saw that it was addressed to Miss Evelina Hobson. A letter from her mother!

It slid through her nerveless fingers and fell to the floor. Evie swooped down after it. Within seconds she had the envelope open and began to read:

My darling Evie,
I feel torn in two by a trouble that is not of my making. Fate is making me choose between the two people I love best in all the world.

I can either stay here with you and abandon the man I love, or go to him and turn my back on my beautiful little daughter. It seems I cannot have both of you. Don't think because I choose to go that I love you any the less. I hate leaving you but there are other reasons that make it impossible for me to stay.

Try not to think ill of me. I do love you, dearest Evie. I shall think of you daily and hope you are growing up well and strong and happy.

Forgive me, please, and try to understand.

Evie felt the tears washing down her cheeks. She leapt out of bed, pushed her feet into her slippers and pulled on her dressing gown. Leaving her candle where it was, she crept quietly out on to the landing. She thought her father was still downstairs. She peeped over the banisters. She could see the light showing under the living-room door.

She crept up the attic stairs to Matilda's room as quietly as she could. She wanted to show her the letter. She wanted to find out more about what had happened to her mother. Matilda was in bed, but she hadn't doused her candle. She looked old and wizened with her nightcap on.

'You found her note? She had only a minute to scribble it.'

'Read it, Matty.'

'I can't see to read. Not by candlelight.'

'I'll read it to you.' Evie heard her voice shake as she did so. When she came to the end, there was a silence.

Matilda said at last: 'Your mother tried several times to take you with her. I heard your father shouting from the landing, "She's my flesh and blood too. If you take her, I'll follow you to the ends of the earth. You'll not take any daughter of mine. I'll get her back, I won't rest until I do." ' She sighed. 'He has looked after you, Evie, as your mam knew he would.'

'But I don't understand what happened. Why did she want to leave home?'

Evie was aware at that moment of footsteps pounding up the attic stairs. She went cold with horror and just had time to push the letter into the pocket of her dressing gown. Matty's bedroom door crashed back on its hinges, making them both jump.

Joseph stood in the doorway, quivering with rage, still holding his candlestick before him though the flame had blown out in his angry rush upstairs.

'I won't have it, Evelina. I won't have you sneaking up here to gossip about things that are not your concern.'

Evie took a deep breath and said quietly, 'They are my concern. I need to know, Father. About what happened. Matty knew my mother. I hoped she might be able to . . .'

He turned on Matty and bellowed: 'What have you told her?'

'Nothing yet,' Evie said.

'Then she better hadn't. How many times have I to tell you, I won't have you going on about what is none of your business.

'It's the last time I'll tell you, Matty. You'll go if I have any more of it. Do you think I can't hear you? Whispering up here together.'

Johnny Simms's bedroom was on the same landing. He came to the door in his nightshirt.

'What's all the noise about? What's going on?'

'Get back to your room,' Joseph thundered. 'It's indecent wandering round like that. And this has nothing to do with you either.

'Come down to your own bed, Evie. Then we can all get some sleep.'

He made Evie go down before him. She could hear him groping in the semi-darkness.

'Discussing family matters with servants. Have you no sense? I wish your mother had never come back. She's caused nothing but trouble. A right hornet's nest of it.

'I think perhaps, after all, it would be a mistake for you to come to her funeral. What you need to do is to put her right out of your mind.'

'No, Father, please . . . I want to.' Evie knew she must say no more in case he forbade that. 'I'm sorry, Father. I won't do it again.'

She shot into her own room and closed the door behind her. She knew she must be more careful. Matilda had been frightened and upset. She mustn't bring Father's wrath down on her head again. Poor Matty, threatening to dismiss her like that! She was too old to start again with another family now. Evie decided she'd try to find out what she needed to know some other way.

CHAPTER FOUR

For the funeral, Evie decided to wear her second-best grey coat. Aunt Agatha's influence had left her with plenty of clothes in sombre shades, and Father had said no new clothes must be bought.

Matilda, who had been refused permission to go, gave Evie a piece of black ribbon to sew on her sleeve as a mark of mourning. Joseph saw her doing it.

'Take that ridiculous band off,' he snapped. 'No need to draw attention to yourself.' Reluctantly, she did as she was told.

'Can I take some money from my money box?' she asked. 'To buy flowers.' She was afraid nobody else would.

'I've already spent enough on her funeral.' Her father's face was grim. 'No point in wasting good money.'

Bertie Pugh overheard that. 'I'll bring you some, Evie,' he told her. 'My mother won't mind if I pick a few for you from our garden.'

He'd arrived at the shop this morning with a great bunch of blue scabious and pink roses, and had even found some silver paper to wrap round their thorny stems. She carried them with her as she walked to church. Her father walked silently beside her, deep in his own thoughts.

The morning was dark and overcast; the church was gloomy inside. Evie thought it was empty, apart from the unadorned deal coffin on its stand, but then she heard the sound of hammering and found there were workmen repairing broken hinges on the door to the vestry.

She laid the flowers on top of the coffin before joining

51

Father in the pew. She knew Joseph had let it be known that he wanted no sightseers from the other shops along the parade.

'It's a private funeral,' he told everybody who asked. 'I want to keep it that way.' There were still only the two of them when the new curate came and conducted a brief service.

The rain that had threatened since dawn hurtled against the windows throughout. When the time came to go out to the grave for the interment, one of the workmen helped the curate trundle the stand with the coffin to the door. Evie felt the sting of tears as she followed with her father.

When they reached the porch the rain was drumming on the roof and bouncing off the flagstones outside. The waiting grave-diggers pressed back to shelter from the downpour.

'Perhaps we'll wait a moment,' the curate murmured nervously. Father was shuffling; Evie could feel his impatience. When, a few moments later, there was no sign of the downpour moderating, he said:

'We'll leave this to you, I think. We've done our duty. Yes, done our duty.' Evie was surprised and a little shocked to be pulled out into the rain and marched down the street.

'No point in standing by the grave to get soaked,' Father said as he towed her along. 'Besides, I need to get back to the shop. Don't like leaving young Simms in charge for too long. Not got his majors yet, after all.'

Evie was in her room when her tears came for the bleak and lonely burial.

Evie felt in limbo for a long time, but slowly the weeks began to pass. Johnny Simms's five-year apprenticeship came to an end. He passed his final exams and became a Licentiate of the Society of Apothecaries.

'There's no need for you to leave.' Joseph was in a good mood at breakfast the day Johnny received his results. 'My business is expanding.' He was smiling magnanimously round the table, as though about to bestow a great prize on Johnny.

'Plenty of work for two of us. I can offer you the job of assistant here. We've always got on well together, haven't we?'

Johnny's face went scarlet. 'I'm indebted, Mr Hobson. Most kind of you to say so.' Evie could feel his embarrassment, and it made her own toes curl up. She knew he couldn't wait to get away.

'But I've already had an offer and accepted it. A pharmacy in Liverpool.'

'You're going to leave? Just like that?' Joseph's attitude changed instantly. He looked incredulous.

'I thought you'd expect me to go. Apprenticeship completed . . .'

'You're very quick off the mark. I expected you to discuss your plans. Seek my advice.'

Evie met Johnny's gaze for a moment. He'd discussed his plans with everybody else. They were all envious that he was able to leave.

'Particularly when I've gone out of my way to help you learn. Allowed you the use of my books.'

Evie willed Johnny not to mention the times he'd been left to run the business on his own. Nor the number of nights he'd had to work until after ten.

'You have, sir. But I need to widen my experience now. Find out how another pharmacist . . .'

Joseph's cup crashed down on its saucer. As he leapt to his feet, his chair went back with such force it tipped over.

'You ungrateful boy! I don't know why I try so hard. After all I've done to help you make something of yourself.'

The dining-room door slammed shut and they heard his footsteps going up to his room.

'Thank goodness I'm going,' Johnny exclaimed, 'that's all I can say. Who'd want to stay and work for him if they had any choice?'

Matilda got up and started to collect the plates together. The colour had drained from her face.

'I can't stand all these upsets. I'd go myself if I wasn't so old. Nobody else would want me now. Not at my age.'

'Retire, Matilda?'

'I wish I could.'

'What would I do without you?' Evie wailed. 'Don't go, please.' When Johnny left there would be more pressure on her and Bertie to help in the drug run. She shivered at the thought.

'The man's half crazed,' Johnny said. 'Flying into a rage like that. Unreasonable behaviour, I call it. I'm going to pack my things and get out. He won't pay me if I work, not now I've said I'm leaving.'

Down in the shop, Evie whispered the news to Bertie Pugh. 'I dread the day you decide to go,' she told him.

'Can't help thinking I might be better going now,' he murmured.

Johnny's departure put Joseph in a terrible mood for a week. He advertised in the *Birkenhead News* for an assistant, and though he interviewed several pharmacists he ended up taking on another counter clerk instead.

It was exactly what Evie didn't want to happen. Bertha Lee was about thirty and unmarried. She'd worked in a chemist's shop before and soon got the hang of the work. As soon as she did, Evie had to work permanently in the drug run with her father.

Evie felt a nervous wreck. Father was always on her back

about some slip-up she'd made. She couldn't get her mother's fate out of her mind. The only thing that made life bearable was Ned. Over the following months, they met up on his days off when she took Herbie Darty to the park or round the market. There had also been a few evenings when it had been possible for them to see each other. Once she'd been baby-sitting the children next door when their parents went for a rare night out. She hadn't enjoyed that too much: she'd been on edge, afraid the older Darty children might hear them and come downstairs.

Little Herbie was late with his speech, but she was worried that sooner or later he'd convey to others that she was seeing Ned Collins regularly. Ned laughed at her.

'You're a real worry-guts. Polly Darty already knows. She can read the signs.'

Aunt Agatha had been keener on church-going than Joseph was: she'd attended both morning and evening services and taken Evie with her. While Father thought attending church once in a day was enough for himself, he continued to encourage Evie to go twice, as well as to Sunday school in the afternoon. On the rare Sunday when Ned was home, she met him instead. That they didn't have Herbie with them was a bonus.

She thought those Sundays utterly blissful. She could go out dressed in her best to meet Ned. But soon he wasn't satisfied; he wanted to see more of her.

'Tell your father you've been invited out to tea,' he urged. 'Then we can be together all afternoon and evening.'

Evie couldn't bring herself to do that. 'Nobody would invite me to tea on my own. Not without Father.'

'Somebody from Sunday school? Somebody he knows and approves of?'

She shook her head. 'It would make him suspicious. He'd wonder why they didn't seek his permission first and want to know all the ins and outs. Probably make a point of thanking them on my behalf next time he saw them.'

It meant she had to go home and eat her tea with Joseph and Matilda instead of staying with Ned, but even so they were blissful Sundays. Particularly the dark, cold evenings when they seemed to have the park to themselves. Ned could put his arms round her and kiss her, and there was nobody to see them do it.

She thought Ned was wonderful. It seemed a miracle when after a few weeks he said:

'You're very special, Evie. I've thought that for a long time.'

She smiled. 'From the moment I dropped your mother's cough mixture?'

'Long before then. Can't remember how many times I walked past your shop just to see you through the window. I used to beg my mother to let me go in and buy things for her.'

'You mean she didn't want that medicine?'

'Oh, yes. It did her good. But I encouraged her to keep taking it, so she'd empty the bottle and I could come for another.'

Evie stared at him in wonder.

'I'd try to talk to you, try to make you smile, just to see your dimple.'

'I don't remember you talking to me, I mean, not specially.'

'And you didn't often smile. How could you? Your father was always giving you the run-around. He bullies all of you. I'd hang back if Miss Lister was free to serve. Wait a bit until you were.'

She laughed.

'You're showing your dimple now. I've bought my shaving soap and razor blades from you for years. When you turned round to get them I'd see those apron strings tied in a big white bow in the small of your back.' He laughed with her. 'I wanted to pull them. Evie, I've been in love with you for ages.'

He gave her little gifts. She was thrilled with the silk stockings but she couldn't wear them in case her father should notice. She had lace handkerchiefs and a bottle of scent she dared not use either. She kept them hidden in her bedroom. She never spoke of him to anyone, not even Polly Darty. Ned didn't come near the parade of shops when she was likely to be about. As far as Evie was concerned, the fewer people who saw them together the better.

What she liked about him was that he seemed so happy; so contented with everything and everybody. He spoke of his family with affection and said: 'You must come home with me and meet them.'

One afternoon, he took her and Herbie to the Collinses' house, at the bottom of Jackson Street. It was within easy walking distance of the pharmacy but Evie had never been in that direction before. Father said that that area, caught between the gasworks and the railway lines, was a slum. He had lots of customers who lived there and he thought them a feckless lot. He said it was a dangerous and dirty place, and it was not safe for her to venture there.

Now, as Ned wheeled Herbie's carriage through the forbidden streets, she felt some trepidation. She always did when she disobeyed Father. It was the poorest part of town and the sight of heavy industry crowding close made it dreary. Ned's home was a two-up and two-down, and the front door stood open though it was a coolish day.

Evie tried not to look at the curtains, which were grey and torn.

His mother came out to meet them. She was short and stout and shapeless. Evie put out her hand, but she was gathered up in plump arms and kissed.

'Our Ned's so proud of you,' chortled Mrs Collins. 'Come on in.'

Evie was shocked to find how ramshackle their home was, and how poorly furnished. She tried not to notice the dust and the cobwebs. Aunt Agatha would have considered it in need of a good spring-clean. She would have said much the same of Gertie Collins: that a hot bath and some clean clothes would not go amiss. Gertie's hair may have been grey and lank with grease, but Evie felt the warmth of her welcome.

Gertie flung her bulk down on a sagging horsehair sofa and pulled Evie down beside her. Within seconds her hand was being cradled between two that were roughened by hard work. Evie saw it as a gesture of affection and support.

'Five lads I've got,' she had a hoarse, throaty chuckle, 'and Ned's the best of the lot. He'll make a good husband – not let you down.' That made Evie's heart beat faster. Ned had not mentioned marriage yet.

'I've gone through three husbands myself. A widow three times over. Would you believe such bad luck? Hope things are different for you, love.'

Ned made the tea, and with it Evie was offered cakes and biscuits of a standard considered luxurious and not to be indulged in at home. When later she told Ned this, he smiled.

'They're treats for us. Mam made an effort because she knew you were coming. She thinks you're posh, daughter of the apothecary.'

'She won't say anything to Father? When she comes to the shop?'

'I've warned her not to. And I've warned my brothers. They've promised to be careful. Not that they've been into the shop for ages. I've been getting what they want for them.'

Evie knew her father saw the Collinses as a rough lot. Even she thought Ned's brothers somewhat uncouth. Gertie made no secret of the fact they spent Saturday night at the local pub and usually brought a skinful home. But Ned was very different.

Evie knew that what she was doing was dangerous, that her father would be furious if he found out. Even more dangerous was the way she threw her arms round Ned and lifted her face to his. He was a passionate man who wanted more and more of her love and persuaded her to give it in the bushes in the park. But soon what they had wasn't enough for either of them. By Christmas, Ned was saying:

'I want to tell everybody you're my girl. I'm proud of you. I don't like this hole-in-the-corner business and I can't see enough of you. I want you to tell your father. Make it all above-board.'

'I can't!' Evie covered her face with her hands.

'But we can't make any progress unless you do. We can't change this.'

'You don't understand, he'll forbid me to see you. Then it'll be harder. He'll be watching me like a hawk.'

Ned laughed. 'He couldn't watch you more closely than he does already. Shall I come to the shop and tell him? Do it together, I mean.'

Evie's heart lurched at the thought, but she was also afraid that sooner or later somebody would see them together and tell Joseph. After all, Ned wanted to hold her arm as they walked down Conway Street. Sometimes he held her hand. To Evie, it felt like a time bomb ticking away. There were times when she felt sick with fear.

Spring came and the evenings grew lighter. There were more people about in the park when they went there on Sunday evenings. She knew that to be seen there alone with a man was a terrible risk. There were several thick shrubberies and Ned drew her deeper inside one or other of them, away from prying eyes. He also carried a macintosh to spread on the ground to protect their clothes. Evie grew more anxious. The risks she was taking seemed enormous.

'It's love I'm showing you,' he tried to explain. 'It's how I feel about you.'

'It's forbidden,' Evie breathed.

'It needn't be,' he insisted. 'Marry me, then it'll be the most normal thing in the world. Will you?'

Evie was in seventh heaven. Of course it was what she'd hoped for. Marriage followed courtship like night follows day, but for her, it seemed a huge and impossible step.

'Why not, Evie?' She could see Ned's love for her shining in his eyes. 'I love you and you say you love me.'

She smiled. 'You know I do.'

'All right then?'

She nodded, swept away by the thought of living openly with him, of being his wife. Nothing would give her greater pleasure. Ned's arms were crushing her against his strong, firm body. He was laughing with delight too.

'We'll do it. We'll get married as soon as we can.' Holding her close, he started making plans.

'We must look for rooms of our own. Won't be able to afford much to start with.'

Evie didn't care. Not even if the rooms were near his home.

He laughed again, excited at the prospect. 'But we'll manage. I've a bit put by. You won't be able to put off telling your father any longer.'

That came like a douche of cold water, but Evie knew Ned was right. She was seventeen, almost eighteen, but would still need her father's permission to marry. It was a sobering thought. She came down to earth with a bump.

'He won't allow it, I know he won't.'

'You'll have to ask him, Evie. Tell him about me. There's no way round that. Otherwise things have to stay as they are.'

She knew Ned had been growing restive because she'd been dragging her feet about this. For herself, she was being pulled both ways. Though she dreaded telling Father, she wanted to escape from the pharmacy, and even more, she wanted to marry Ned.

She made up her mind. 'I'll do it.'

'Do you want me to be there with you?'

She shook her head, afraid that the sight of Ned would infuriate Joseph before they had a chance to say anything.

'I'll have to choose the right moment. Wait until he's in a good mood.'

'Is he ever?'

'Well – he's not always in a bad one.' She knew she'd have to screw up her nerve to do it.

As she waited for the right moment, Evie went about her duties in the drug run feeling very much on edge. Both she and Bertie were improving with practice but it wasn't easy.

She rehearsed the words she would say to her father. She watched him, seeking some sign that he was in a better mood than usual.

The shop closed every night between seven and eight.

Last summer, it had often stayed open until ten, but Bertie wasn't considered competent to work alone. This meant that usually she had two hours alone with Father before bedtime.

After supper, Matilda always soaked her feet in a bowl of hot water, then climbed slowly and painfully up the steep stairs to her room in the attic. Evie sat on with her father, one each side of the empty grate in the austere sitting room directly over the shop. It was furnished with heavy Victorian furniture but there were no ornaments. Her father didn't care for ornamentation. She would watch him read, deep in his book, slowly turning the pages.

Every evening at supper, she'd will herself to do it that night, but the words remained unspoken. She couldn't find the courage.

Then came the day Evie had dreaded. She was walking back from the park with Ned. He was helping her push Herbie's baby carriage and his hand covered hers on the handle. He was laughing down at her, as he often did, when she caught sight of May Smart, wife of the barber who kept the shop further along the parade.

Evie pulled herself away but she knew it was too late. Mrs Smart had seen how things were between them. What made it worse was that she attended the same church – did the flowers there, in fact. Evie knew she'd have to tell her father now. He'd be even angrier if he heard it first from Mrs Smart.

'I'll come in with you now,' Ned said, squeezing her hand sympathetically. 'Get it over with.'

'No,' Evie quaked. 'Bertie will be there, and Miss Lister, and goodness knows how many customers. I couldn't, not in front of them. After supper is the best time. When I'm alone with him.'

'Promise?' He kissed her in the street then. If Mrs

Smart had seen that, it would surely have sent her straight round to the pharmacy. 'Promise you'll do it before my next days off?'

Evie had promised. But that evening her father had gone out after supper. She'd had to put it off the next day because he was in one of his moods. And all the time she dreaded seeing Mrs Smart come into the shop.

Time was going on, Ned's days off on Thursday and Friday were coming closer. She told herself she had to do it. She thought enviously of his lot, sailing backwards and forwards to the Isle of Man with no worries of his own.

By Wednesday, she felt she could delay no longer. But Bertha Lee had sent a message to say she was sick and had not turned up for work. That had made Joseph cross because Evie had had to take Bertha's place on the front counter. Then he had been made even more irritable when a customer said she couldn't afford the one and sixpence he wanted to charge for a prescription.

Even worse, just before they closed for dinner, Evie saw Mrs Smart come into the shop. She walked past to the drug run to consult her father. Evie didn't know where to put herself. She felt paralysed. Every second, she expected to hear him roar out her name.

A few minutes later, Mrs Smart was leaning against the front counter, smiling at her. 'I'll take a pot of cold cream, if you please.'

Evie's legs felt like lead. Had she by some miracle survived? When she turned back to the counter with it, Mrs Smart said:

'How fast you've grown up, Evie. It seems no time at all since you were a little girl; now I see you walking out with a young man.'

That took her breath away. Had Father heard? Certainly Miss Lister had. Evie's mouth was dry with panic. She must do it today! It would be a disaster if Father heard about Ned through a third person.

She was shaking when she sat down at the dinner table. She realised he'd not heard Mrs Smart, when he prodded his piece of fried fish and said affably:

'Nice bit of cod, Matilda.'

Evie felt heartened. He was in a good mood. Bertie and Matilda got up from the table as soon as possible – they always did. Her father sat on over a second cup of tea as usual. This was the moment. Evie closed her eyes and took a deep breath.

'Father,' she said. 'There's something I want to tell you.'

She found his cold grey eyes searching her face. 'What?'

'I want to get married.'

His cup crashed down on his saucer. She could see he was astounded. He ran his fingers through the steel-grey bristles on his head.

'Who to?' It was a bark of rage.

'Ned Collins.'

'Don't be silly! You can't possibly marry him!' He was glaring at her. 'You haven't been seeing him? Meeting him behind my back?'

Evie swallowed. She couldn't deny that.

'You fool!' Her father's face was savage, the line of his chin hardened. 'You've got yourself involved with one of those awful Collins boys?'

'I want to marry Ned.'

'I've never heard of anything so ridiculous. Absolutely not. He's quite unsuitable and you're only seventeen. Plenty of time for you to think about marriage when you're older. Much better that you learn something about dispensing first. I need you to help me.'

Evie could feel her heart pounding. She was stiff with tension.

Joseph flared up anew. 'When has all this been going on? Not while you've been taking out that baby from next door?'

Evie couldn't answer. There was no need to. It was the only time she wasn't in the shop.

'What are you thinking of?'

'I love him.'

'Nonsense! You don't know what you're talking about. Love, indeed! You'll not take that child out again.' His grey eyes glowered at her.

'I trusted you. I should have had more sense. Picking up men in the park when you've got babies with you. I'm disgusted with you, Evie. You've let me down. Going behind my back like this.'

'Father, please listen . . .'

'You'll not do it again. I'm going straight round to tell Polly Darty she can find herself another baby-minder. I'll put a stop to you carrying on with Ned Collins. I ought to tan your hide for you.'

He leapt up from the table and stamped downstairs. She heard the pharmacy door being unlocked and the shop bell clanging furiously as he went out.

Evie couldn't move. Mrs Darty would be expecting her to pick up Herbie in five minutes. Not to take him out seemed a terrible privation, but even worse, she'd not be allowed to see Ned again.

Minutes later, her father came racing back upstairs. He'd worked himself up into an even greater rage.

'You're too young to be walking out with men. Alone too. I wouldn't trust a fellow like Ned Collins.'

He came closer. Evie couldn't look at his face. She'd never seen it so twisted with anger.

He grabbed at the collar of her dress, screwing up the material, tightening it until it half choked her.

'Father . . . stop . . .'

'I told you to stay away from the likes of him, and you didn't.' He twisted the collar tighter until she could no longer breathe. The room was turning black and beginning to spin round her. Just when she felt she was passing out, he gave her a quick push backwards. Coughing and gasping for breath, Evie fell against a chair.

'You're just like your mother! Heading down the primrose path. It leads to hell, Evie. You saw what she was like when she came back. D'you want to end up like her?'

Evie's eyes were stinging. She could feel the tears on her cheeks. She'd expected him to fly into a rage, but this was awful, worse than she'd feared. His anger was boiling over, and how was she to meet Ned now?

'You'll stay where I can keep an eye on you after this. Those Collins boys are wild. You must know their reputation. It isn't safe for you to be alone with men like that.'

She was shaking. Her father was coming close again. She gulped for air, trying to fill her lungs, trying to be prepared this time.

'He hasn't touched you, has he?' His face was within three inches of her own. Dark with suspicion. 'Has he?' he bellowed.

'No, Father,' she choked. 'No.'

She had to tell that lie. She was terrified. A moment ago she'd really thought he meant to finish her. Her head still swam, she could still see black spots before her eyes. What would he do to her if she admitted the truth?

Evie didn't know how she got through the rest of the day. She had great red weals on her neck, and her throat was too sore to speak. She didn't know why she'd gone to such lengths to tell Father in private, because the staff all knew before teatime. He kept coming to the front counter to have another go at her, making no secret of it. Miss Lister patted her shoulder, Matty gave her a hug and Bertie offered her a humbug to console her.

'We thought he was going to kill you,' he said.

All evening, her father had kept on at her. She'd been glad to go to bed to get away from him. But sleep was impossible. When she did doze off at last, she had a nightmare. She could feel his fingers on her throat, throttling her again.

He was in a worse mood by breakfast and she had a thumping headache. In the shop, she hardly dared speak to the staff, in case he thought she was discussing her difficulties with them, and her hoarse voice riled him further. She was frightened and she could see no way out.

Her only comfort was to think of Ned. He'd be home now and expecting to see her with Herbie at two o'clock. The morning seemed interminable. Dinner was eaten in stony silence, with Bertie shooting sympathetic glances in her direction.

Then, instead of going out to meet Ned, she had to go back down to the shop. She watched the hands of the clock creep on. By now, Ned would be waiting for her to turn into Conway Street. Another fifteen minutes dragged by and he'd know that she wasn't coming.

She served a middle-aged lady a thick pink hairnet to sleep in. Sold some soap to another, Vaseline to a third. This time of the afternoon was never busy. She could hear her father in the drug run, clearing his throat and turning the pages of his newspaper with quick, angry movements. There wasn't a lot for him to do either.

The doorbell pinged. Evie went cold when she looked up and found that Ned had come in.

'Are you all right, Evie?'

She was nodding, unable to find words. Conscious that everything they said could be heard by her father. Her heart was pounding as, in the mirror, she saw Joseph come to the end of the drug run.

'I thought it was you I could hear,' he said. 'Get out, I don't want you anywhere near my daughter.'

'Mr Hobson,' Ned took off his cap politely and drew himself up to his full five foot ten, 'I need to speak to you, please hear me out. I want . . .'

'I know what you want. I've already told Evie she's to have no truck with you. Going behind my back, that's what you've been doing. I'll not even think of letting her marry the likes of you.'

Evie could see the colour running up Ned's cheeks, the look of stunned shock spreading across his face. She'd tried to tell him this might happen, but he'd said there was no other way, she had to ask her father's permission.

Ned tried again: 'Mr Hobson, I'll take great care of Evie. I've got a job, I can afford to keep a wife. I love her, I promise . . .'

'Get out of my shop and stay away from my daughter. Do you hear? That's my last word.'

'Father, please . . .' she began.

Joseph Hobson advanced on Ned menacingly.

'All right, Mr Hobson, I'll go. I don't want to make any trouble.'

The look Ned gave Evie was anguished, but he managed a smile and a wink before he went.

CHAPTER FIVE

Evie wished she hadn't opened her mouth. She should have kept her secret and the pleasure it brought. To lose Ned was to lose everything; she was left feeling sick with disappointment. She'd known what the likely outcome was and should never have let Ned persuade her otherwise. Now she felt like a prisoner. The only time Father wasn't at her side was when she went to Sunday school.

A week went by, the weals on her neck faded and her voice lost its hoarse note, but her nightmares continued and she felt shivers run down her spine each time Father turned on her in anger.

Then Bertha Lee sent word that she was not returning to work. She'd found another job.

'Good luck to her,' Bertie whispered. 'She's not bound to him like I am.'

Joseph was furious. There was no talking to him for days and they were short-handed in the shop. He said he might take another apprentice. She tried to look on the bright side. Another apprentice would mean she'd be back working on the front counter.

She missed Ned terribly but knew there would still be Sundays when they might be able to meet. It could take him a long time to arrange, because for the crew, a Sunday off was a popular option. Ned's turn didn't often come round, especially in summer, when a day out to the Isle of Man was within the pocket of many Merseysiders who could not afford a real holiday.

During the morning, Evie noticed a barefoot urchin

hanging back from the front counter when it was his turn to be served. She sold some razor blades to an elderly man and some Macassar hair oil to another. Her father's voice rose and fell behind her, exacting information from a customer suffering from aching varicose veins.

When Joseph turned back to the drug run to make up some ointment, the urchin crept up and said: 'Please, miss, can I have a halfpenny liquorice stick?'

His coin came across the counter with a note folded beneath it. Evie felt the blood rush to her cheeks as she read her name on it. She felt flustered with guilt and fear, and pushed it deep into her pocket before ringing up the till. The urchin was out of the shop in a flash.

Evie fingered the note all morning, knowing that it must be from Ned. It brought relief and happiness that he hadn't given up on her.

When dinnertime came, Joseph locked up the shop and led Evie and Bertie upstairs to the dining room. As a matter of habit he hung the keys on a keyboard at the top of the stairs.

Evie and Bertie had to pause for a moment behind him while he did this. They were close to the three framed photographs that hung alongside the keyboard. Joseph was pictured with his narrow chest bare, wearing tight leg-hugging breeches and looking incredibly young. In the first picture, he was holding up his Indian clubs. In the second, he was lifting heavy weights.

Joseph noticed Bertie studying the photographs and said: 'Exercise like that puts a man in control of his body, builds him up, allows him to do things he wouldn't otherwise be capable of doing.'

Evie understood that he kept these pastimes up. She heard him using the Indian clubs in his room sometimes, and she'd seen his weights there.

In the third picture, his face was clenched with determination and his bare fists were held up in a pugilistic stance.

'Were you a boxer, sir?' Bertie asked.

'In my youth.'

'What does it say?' In the gloom of the landing, Bertie was squinting at the lettering underneath. 'You won a title?'

'I won the regional lightweight title in 1881 and kept it for two years. Whatever I do, Mr Pugh, I aim to succeed at. I should have gone on, tried for a national title.'

'Rather a shame to give it up when you were winning.' There was a note of respect in Bertie's voice now. 'Why did you?'

'I was being pulled both ways. As a boxer I was punching to hurt, to cause cuts and bruises. It takes a certain attitude to go in the ring to win.'

'The killer instinct?'

Evie saw her father flinch. His grey eyes shone nervously. 'Perhaps. And in my work I was trying to heal human sicknesses and traumas.'

'You didn't want to inflict pain on others?'

'I was frightened of doing so. I was too good at boxing.'

As soon as dinner was over Evie ran upstairs to her bedroom, where she was safe from prying eyes. Her fingers were shaking as she opened the note.

My dearest Evie,

My next days off are Sunday and Monday the week after next. I'll see you in church at morning service. Give me a nod if you're still going alone to Sunday school. If so, I'll meet you in Conway Street at ten minutes to two.

71

Your father is a tyrant. Don't let him split us up. I couldn't bear it. I'm not giving up hope, you mustn't either. Run away from him, if that's the only way. I could rent a room for you, just say the word and I'll start looking. I'll look after you. I do love you. Always will.

Your ever-loving Ned.

The note gave Evie a feeling of warmth and support on one hand, but misgivings too. She loved Ned. All her instincts told her to trust him. What frightened her was that she would have to do what her mother had done.

The thought of being with Ned was heaven. To take a few of her things and walk out would not be impossible. She could leave Father a note saying she was sorry it had to be this way.

But the thought of doing it brought shivers of terror. What would Father do to her if something went wrong? If, after all, she didn't manage to get away? She decided to put off making any decision until she'd spoken to Ned again. She wanted to talk it through.

Evie was counting the days to that. At times it seemed Sunday would never come. When it did, it was a dark, overcast morning. She felt very much on edge as she walked to church with her father. She saw Ned immediately they went inside, his eager face telling her how pleased he was to see her again. He was not a member of the congregation and to see him there scared her. Father counted the Collinses as Irish, and everybody expected them to be Catholics.

Ned moved to another pew so that Joseph would not be sitting between them; so that she could look at him without turning too noticeably. She conveyed that she'd be able to meet him that afternoon. She could feel his eyes on her.

That brought little frissons of anxiety, she was so afraid Father might notice and demand to know what Ned was doing here. She was relieved when the service was over.

Then, as the vicar shook hands with his departing congregation at the door, causing a hold-up in the aisles, Father had time to talk to an acquaintance, a regular customer by the name of George Parry. Evie heard them discussing a book on church history and Mr Parry offered to lend it to Father.

'Will you be at evensong tonight?' he asked. 'I could bring it for you then.'

Evie froze in consternation.

Joseph hesitated. 'I don't usually come twice, but Evie always does. Perhaps you'd entrust it to her?'

Mr Parry's eyes met hers. 'Of course. I'll look out for you, Miss Hobson.'

Evie felt her spirits plummet. That meant she'd have to come to church. Her father would know if she didn't. Today of all days, when Ned was home. She turned to look for him. He was still near though the crowd was thinning. At the door, he mouthed the words 'Ten to two,' and walked away jauntily with his hands in his pockets.

By the time dinner was on the table, rain was coming down in torrents. The weather was so bad that Father actually suggested she might prefer to miss Sunday school.

'No sense in going out in this. And I'll come to church with you this evening. Collect that book Mr Parry promised me.'

That blighted Evie's expectations still further. It would deprive her of Ned's company on the walk there and back. Her stomach was churning with fear. She had to see him this afternoon.

She made herself say brightly: 'I'd like to go to Sunday school. This rain's too heavy to last.' Nothing must stop her going now. It would be her only chance to talk to Ned.

She put on her macintosh and borrowed Father's large umbrella. As she closed the pharmacy door and stepped out in the rain she was fizzing with anticipation. Ned was waiting for her. He held her arm tightly, hugging it to him.

'Where can I take you? We must get out of this rain or we'll be soaked.' His brown eyes were not laughing down at her as they usually did. He was in a sober and determined mood.

'A tram ride? That's it, a tram ride. Where would you like to go?'

'Anywhere.'

'You're shaking, Evie. I can feel you.'

'It's just the tension. Going behind Father's back. Coming to meet you and hiding it from him.'

His hand tightened on her arm. 'I brought trouble down on your head, didn't I? Asking you to tell him about me.'

'I thought he was going to kill me.' She told Ned how Joseph had twisted her collar until she'd nearly choked.

'I'm sorry. I knew he was strict. Harsh too, but I didn't think he'd treat you like that. Why?'

'He doesn't want me to leave home. Not ever. He has his plans for me – and everyone else in his little empire. None of us are allowed any choice.'

'It's power?'

'He wants to control us all, but particularly me.'

'You'll be a nervous wreck if you stay with him.'

'Sometimes I think I already am.'

'No. You haven't let him stop you so far. You've been doing what you want. You've still got the guts to get away from him.'

'I wish I was stronger. He's wearing me down.'

'He'd wear anyone down if they had to live and work with him.'

They got on the first tram that came along. It was going to the terminus at New Ferry. Ned sat close against her on the hard, narrow seat, holding her hand while the rain lashed against the windows.

'How am I going to get away?' Evie wanted to discuss all the possibilities sensibly. 'Father won't change his mind. He never does, once it's made up.'

'Do you want to wait?'

'What for?'

'Till you're twenty-one? I won't change my mind. Would you wait that long for me?'

'If I had to. But Father still wouldn't give his permission.'

'He wouldn't have to.'

'He won't accept you. Never will.' Evie tried to explain. 'I'd still have to run away from home.'

'I'll look after you if you do. I promise. We'll be married.'

'How?'

'We'll go to Gretna Green. I've heard it's possible.'

'We won't have that sort of money to spare, Ned.' She was trying to be practical. 'Not to go travelling round. All the way to Scotland.'

'Then we'll have to pretend you're already twenty-one. We'll get married somehow. Just walk out, Evie.'

'It's what my mother did,' she said with a shiver. 'I feel I'm following in her footsteps.'

When the tram reached the terminus, they stayed up on the top deck and then rode back to Woodside. The rain had eased a little but it was a cold, damp afternoon.

Ned took her arm and led her into Woodside Station, where they could stay under cover. They watched the London train arrive. Evie was keeping an eye on the station clock. Sunday school lasted only an hour. Add half an hour to walk both ways and perhaps another ten minutes could be spent chatting outside. She couldn't afford to be away from home much longer. The time was flying now she was with Ned.

'We won't be able to do this again tonight.' She told him that her father would be coming with her to church again, that it would be impossible. Ned walked her back towards Argyle Street but she was afraid to take him near the shop.

'Not a happy outing for you.' Ned was miserable when the time came to say goodbye. He kissed her cheek. It always made Evie uneasy that he kissed her so readily in the street. Anybody could be watching.

'Not happy for you either.'

'I'm always happy when I'm with you, you know that. I'll come to church tonight, just to see you.'

'No, Ned. We won't be able to say one word, and I'm afraid Father'll notice you and guess why you're there.'

'But I want to be with you. I love you. And I've no idea when I'll be able to get another Sunday off. Can't I see you tomorrow?'

Evie shook her head sadly.

'You still fetch your bread from Darty's?'

'Yes.'

'What time? I can be there.'

'I can't say. It depends on the shop, how busy we are.'

'Eleven o'clock?'

'I don't know. I'll try, but I won't be able to stay more than five minutes.'

'Even five minutes.' His soft brown eyes smiled down at her. 'It's better than nothing. I'll leave a message with Polly. About when I'll be home again. If you want to get in touch with me, she'll let me know.'

'Yes,' Evie agreed sadly. 'I'll have to go.'

Sitting at the tea table between Matilda and her father later that afternoon, Evie knew she'd settled nothing.

76

Either she had to stay here with Father, or she had to run away as her mother had done. The circumstances were different, of course, but she'd still be running away with the man she loved. Things could turn out as badly for her as they had done for her mother. She could slide down the primrose path to hell as Father had predicted. If she went, she could live to regret it. It made her flesh crawl with fear, but it was what she wanted to do.

She was going to have to pull herself together. Fight this panic and not let him dominate her. But all their church acquaintances and most of the customers would side with Father on this. It was very wrong for a girl like her to go against her father's wishes.

She managed to go for the bread at eleven the next morning and found that Ned had been waiting for her for some time. Polly was kind enough to push them into the living room behind the shop, where Herbie was asleep in his cot. They had ten minutes alone but for Evie Ned's kisses settled nothing.

Over the following days, there were times when Evie felt confident about going. She started to make preparations, sorting through her belongings to decide what to take with her. Then, at others, she thought of her mother's half-starved body and was terrified she'd suffer the same fate. The pros and cons went round in her mind until she felt quite unable to decide one way or the other.

Evie tried to keep her mind on Ned, but when she closed her eyes to sleep it was often her mother's ill and frightened face that came before her. She knew Father hadn't forgotten Helen either.

'You take after your mother,' he told Evie, his hawk-nose quivering with distaste.

Although Evie understood well enough that he wasn't

referring to her looks, she said: 'I've always known I must look like her. After all, I don't take after you.'

She was grateful not to have inherited his big nose. Hers was small and straight. Her nearly black hair, fair skin and dark-blue eyes didn't come from him either.

'Don't pretend you don't know what I mean! You've inherited her weak character. I should have expected trouble from you. Men were her undoing. She was easily led astray. You're already on that downward path. If you're not careful you'll end up the same way.'

Evie knew now that he was trying to keep something hidden from her, and that it must be important to him. She couldn't ask Matty again, for she'd already made enough trouble for her, and nobody in the shop had been here all those years ago.

Her father advertised that he had a place for another apprentice, and a tall, thin youth with glasses came by appointment to see him. Joseph told Evie that he thought Arthur Mitchell seemed keen, and that he'd be starting next week. That evening, he told Matilda to prepare a bedroom for the new apprentice.

Evie went to help her turn out the room Johnny Simms had used. Apart from that one and Matilda's, there were two other attic rooms up here, that were used to store household odds and ends. Evie had been wanting to have a good look through them for some time. To see if she could find her mother's belongings, particularly the grey canvas bag she'd seen her bring with her.

She helped Matilda make up the bed and sweep the floor. Then she went down to get some polish and a duster and saw that her father was reading in the living room. It seemed a good moment to make her search. She had a reason to be up on that floor.

The attic rooms were dusty and airless. She found

several boxes and an old cabin trunk full of clothes. She thought they might have belonged to her mother but she wasn't sure, and they didn't tell her what she wanted to know. Then she came across a wedding gown of white satin, packed carefully in a large box. Fingering the smooth cloth brought such a rush of emotion that she couldn't go on. She felt sure the dress must have been her mother's. Of the grey bag, there was no sign.

For the rest of the evening she could feel herself trembling inside. She was turning into a devious witch of a girl. Not a nice person at all. Going behind Father's back like this. But what else could she do, other than let him rule her life and dominate her totally?

The next day when she went for the bread and found the Darty bakery empty of customers, she asked Polly if she'd known her mother.

'No. Eleven years ago? I wasn't married then. It's only nine since we bought this business, but . . .' Polly's dark eyes darted towards the door.

'You do know something?' Evie said. 'Why did she suddenly leave home?'

'Only what Matty told me.'

'She talked to you? When? What did she say?' Evie leaned eagerly over the counter.

'She used to come in every day for the bread and a bit of a gossip. Well, who else did she have to talk to but a child? She'd stop for a natter at the butcher's and at the grocer's as well, and why not?

'Anyway, this day she happened to say you were still fretting for your mother, so I asked about her. I heard somebody else say there was something of a scandal at the time.'

'What d'you mean? What sort of a scandal?'

'Well, bigamy is what she said.' Polly put a hand in

front of her mouth to make sure the dreadful word went no further.

'My father? Committed bigamy? No!' Evie couldn't see him doing any such thing.

'No, your mother.'

Evie straightened up in disbelief. 'That's just gossip.'

'Well, I don't know. It's what Matty said. Then she really let her hair down and started going on about Agatha and all the other things that were happening at the time.

'It was a hot day and the shop door was propped open to let some air in. Your father was in with us before we saw him. He was dancing with rage, blue in the face with it. You know how he flares up.

' "I've caught you at it, Matilda. How many times have I got to tell you I won't have you spreading gossip about me? You deserve to be sacked for this. And you, Polly Darty, have a wagging tongue. Nosy parkers all of you."

'He glared round my shop. Jean from the barber's was here, and Connie from the paper shop.

' "I've enough trouble without you adding to it and spreading lies round the neighbourhood. I'll not have it, do you hear?

' "There's all sorts of rumours going round about me. I hear some of them, you know. That I've thrown my wife out, that she's run off with another man and all the takings from the business. All lies, as you very well know. You can all mind your own business, or I'll withdraw my trade."

'Well, Evie, you know how it is in trade. You must never insult a customer, never risk losing business. He put the fear of God into all of us, I can tell you. The women couldn't get out of my shop fast enough.'

'Polly, who would remember my mother? Connie and Jean, who were they?'

Polly was shaking her head. 'The butcher's has changed

hands and the paper shop too. It's a long time. The barber now, his father was running the shop then, but May Smart might be able to tell you more. She might have heard about it from her mother-in-law, though she won't be able to ask her now because she died last year.'

Evie was disappointed. The Smarts were on good terms with her father. He had his hair cut there; they met at church. She didn't think she'd dare ask Mrs Smart.

Polly rattled on: 'Matty always stood facing the shop door after that. She wasn't going to get caught again. Your dad told her she was to buy what was needed and come straight back. She wasn't to waste time gossiping. Matty said he timed her. She was scared of him, well, we all were. He can turn nasty in an instant.'

The first morning she felt sick, Evie put it down to the rich pork she'd eaten hot for lunch the day before and then again cold for supper. She said as much to her father, who prescribed Smith's tasteless dandelion anti-bilious pills. She'd heard him recommend them many times for queasy stomachs.

But when the following morning she awoke to the same feeling of nausea, and had in addition a feeling of heaviness in her breasts, she was overcome with terror. She'd heard the symptoms described to her father too many times to be in any doubt as to what they signified. She pulled the blankets over her head and stayed stiff with tension on her bed.

What wouldn't she give to have the dull future she'd foreseen. Nothing but work – it now seemed a luxury. Her fate was to be very much worse. She longed to lie still in bed and fight the nausea, but she dared not. Nor must she show any sign that might alert her father to her trouble.

She wished she'd not been so foolish as to ask him for the dandelion pills yesterday, though they had helped. She forced herself to sit at the breakfast table and eat bacon. Even look as though she was enjoying it.

With all the upset about her mother and the worry about asking Father's permission, she'd overlooked what should have happened. As soon as she went down to the shop, she consulted the calendar hanging in the drug run. Her dates had passed unnoticed. Evie felt a hot flush run up her cheeks. Father would kill her when he found out. What was she to do? She had palpitations every time she thought of it. She was sweating in panic, wanting to retch, but she dared not do other than act as she usually did. She helped herself to some more dandelion pills when nobody was looking.

This was another secret she had to keep from her father. She'd have to get in touch with Ned and then do what her mother had done. Now she had no choice.

That night in her bedroom, Evie wrote to Ned. She couldn't stop the anguish she felt from pouring out on the paper. She sealed it up carefully in an envelope and put it in her pocket. Next morning, when Matty asked her to run next door for a loaf, she hung around outside the baker's shop until there were no other customers, then gave her letter to Polly Darty.

'Will you hand this to Ned, please? Next time he comes in? It may not be for a while, he'll not have a day off until next week. You'll not forget?'

'He'll ask, Evie. I'll put it under the counter for him. He popped in last night on his way home. Bought some lardy cakes for his mother.'

Evie wished she'd brought the letter last night. She wanted him to know, wanted him to do something to help her. Goodness knows when he'd call in again. She felt desperate.

'Have you found somebody else to take Herbie out?'

'Yes, Gladys Pool wanted to do it. She seemed quite keen but she didn't turn up on Monday. Said she wasn't well. And she's never here on time. Can't rely on her in the way I could on you. I don't suppose your dad will relent?'

'Not a hope,' Evie sighed.

She went out into the sunlight. It seemed such a long time since she'd been out. She walked a few yards up the parade, wishing she could go further. From the placards outside the newsagent's, she saw that Birkenhead was arranging a big event in the park to celebrate the coronation of King George V and Queen Mary of Tek. There were to be massed children's choirs and a military brass band. Evie sighed again. She didn't feel in the mood for a celebration. And she had to go back to the shop or she'd be in more trouble.

As she folded paper round individual doses of her father's herbal cures, she tried to work out how she could take her belongings with her when she ran away.

Behind the shop was a cramped kitchen and a small store room. The staff lavatory was outside in the back yard. From the yard there was access to an entry, though the door was always kept locked for security reasons.

The store room was full of the winchesters, jars and wooden packing cases in which their stock arrived. Her father's herbs and poisons usually went straight into the drug run. Evie often worked here with Bertie, decanting the lotions from the winchesters into small phials and scooping ointment from the big jars to fill the one-ounce pots in which it was sold.

She found a few bars of scented soap remaining at the

bottom of a large wooden box. She made space for them in the display case on the front counter and pushed the box to the back of the room, well away from the other empties, which were stacked together. All their jars, boxes and crates were returned to the factories when empty, but Evie wanted to keep this one. She thought she could bring her things down a few at a time and pack them into it.

She dared not start too soon, in case they were discovered. Father took an active interest in every part of his business, including the store, even though Miss Lister was nominally in charge of that.

Evie decided to wait until she had some word from Ned. In the meantime, she sorted through her things in her room. There were no other preparations she could make.

Early the next morning, in the drug run, she was trying to hide her sickness and growing apprehension. Her father, opening the post, exclaimed with pleasure.

'I've been invited to the coronation celebrations in the park. As an official guest.'

'You're a prominent citizen, Mr Hobson,' a waiting customer told him. 'So you should be.'

'You're invited too, Evie.' Joseph passed the embossed card to her. She read that seats would be reserved for Mr Joseph P. Hobson and guest.

'I hear it's to be a big gala,' Bertie said. 'There'll be a tug-of-war for the men.'

'And a country-dancing display by schoolchildren,' Miss Lister added. 'You'll enjoy it.'

'I shall,' Evie said with as much enthusiasm as she could muster. The coronation was to be on 10 June, almost two weeks off. She hoped to be away before then.

CHAPTER SIX

When Evie went to get the bread that day, Polly Darty beamed across the counter at her.

'Ned called in last night and I gave him your letter. He brought one back for you this morning.'

Evie flushed with relief. Ned understood she was in a hurry to get things settled. She pushed his letter into her pocket and swept out of the shop. She couldn't wait until dinnertime to read it. She walked to the end of the parade of shops, turned the corner and leaned against the wall. He'd had no envelope; instead, he'd stuck the page together with a dab of glue.

> Dearest Evie,
>
> I'm sorry I'm giving you more trouble. Truly sorry. We must get married now. We've got to talk about it. I'll be in the back entry behind your shop tonight between half nine and ten. Try to come out for five minutes to see me. If you can't, leave a note with Polly Darty about when the best time would be. I've got a day off next Thursday and then I'm having Coronation Day.
>
> I'll look after you, Evie. Don't you worry yourself. Tell me if there's anything else you want me to do. I do love you.
>
> Your loving Ned.

Evie was desperate to talk to him. She wondered if she'd be able to get out to the back entry without her father noticing. It all depended on whether he went down to work in the shop after it closed. Sometimes he did, to stock-take or make up his books.

She watched him all day. He and Bertie were not very busy. She hoped Joseph would be able to do all he needed in his books before closing time. The shop shut punctually at eight. They ate supper with Matilda. Father was still full of the invitation he'd received.

'I hear a special stand is to be erected for prominent people. The Mayor and Mayoress will be there, and all the managers from Laird's and Beaufort's. A good job you've got that blue dress after all. Perhaps you should get a new hat to go with it? I'll get a hansom to pick us up.'

'Or a car?' Evie suggested breathlessly. She couldn't imagine Father doing any such thing. He was far too austere in his habits. She helped clear the table, and while Matty was clattering dishes in the sink, she said:

'Ought we not to take Matilda with us, Father? She's hardly been out of the house for months. Her feet are too bad to walk far these days. But with a carriage to the door, she'd enjoy it.'

His voice was suddenly forbidding. 'It's not an occasion to which I'd want to take my servants, Evie. Anyway, she's not been invited.'

'Not to a seat in the stand, but she'd like to come to the park and see it all, I'm sure.'

'We won't be taking Matilda with us. Definitely not. In fact, I've been thinking lately that she's getting too old. Her cooking isn't what it was. Perhaps we should look for someone younger?'

Evie was shocked. 'But where could she go? She's lived with us for twenty years.'

'Twenty-four. She'd manage, they all do.'

Evie felt cold inside. He didn't care what happened to anybody. If he had no further use for their services, he was ready to cast them off.

'But she won't have saved much. Won't have been able to.'

'There are workhouses for those who don't save for their own needs.'

Evie shuddered. She was afraid Matty was already in dread of going to the workhouse. She could hear her filling a bowl with hot water to soak her feet before going upstairs to bed. She did it every night.

'Do you still prescribe something for her feet, Father?'

'It's arthritis and old age. Hot water alone eases the discomfort.'

'It's pain, not discomfort. Surely there's something more you can give her that would help?'

'A little camphorated oil rubbed into the joints, perhaps.'

'Can I get some for her, Father?'

She looked at the clock on the sideboard. It was ten minutes past nine. Too early, Ned would not be there yet.

'You're very concerned about Matilda all of a sudden. Camphorated oil will not turn the clock back. She's never going to walk like a forty-year-old again.' Joseph himself was just turned forty.

'I know that. But can I get some for her?'

'If you want to.' Father had lost interest. He moved to a more comfortable chair and opened his newspaper.

'I'll see if she'd like some. She's to rub it into the joints?'

'I've said so, haven't I?' Father was losing patience too.

Evie checked the clock, it was nearly quarter past. She went to the kitchen and talked to Matilda about camphorated oil.

'I've tried it,' she said. 'Your father gave me a bottle,

but nothing does me much good any more.'

'But it helps?' Evie wasn't going to give up. Not now she'd got Father's permission to go down to the shop.

'I suppose everything helps.'

Evie stood talking about the weather, what they would eat for dinner tomorrow, anything. The hands of the clock had never moved so slowly.

It was almost nine thirty. Father's eyes watched her as she crossed the landing from the kitchen. She knew he'd listened to all she'd said.

At the top of the stairs, Evie silently unhooked the keys she needed from the keyboard. Once down in the shop, she whipped a bottle of camphorated oil out of the glass case on the front counter, slipped it into her pocket and then went softly to the back door. She turned the key in the lock and crept up the yard. She'd brought the key to the yard door too.

The lock was stiff and she had trouble turning it. She hoped Father wouldn't look out of the window. It was still light enough for her to be seen. Ned was waiting in the entry, his face anxious. Evie was filled with relief to see him. She felt his arms come round her.

'Oh, Evie, I'm sorry.' He pulled her against him in a comforting hug. He was whispering, though there was no one within earshot. 'I blame myself. I should never have done it. You must let me be with you when you tell your father. I'll say it was all my fault.'

'He'll not let you say much of anything. You know what he's like. He'll throw you out of the shop as he did last time.'

She saw Ned stiffen. 'Better if I'm with you. I can't let you do this on your own.'

Evie shook her head. 'I can't tell him.' Hadn't Joseph twisted her collar until she'd nearly choked the day she'd first told him about Ned? He'd forbidden her to go near him and she'd continued to disobey. 'He'll half kill me. I'm afraid.'

She felt Ned pull her closer still. 'What will we do then?'

'I'll just walk out.'

'You'll come with me?'

'Yes.' She was going to do what her mother was said to have done. Run away with the man she loved. She found it hard to believe what Polly had told her, that her mother had committed bigamy. Surely not bigamy?

'We'll need to get married now.' Ned was lifting her chin so that she had to look at him. His eyes were gentle with love. 'You still need your father's permission for that. He'll give it when he knows about the baby. He'll be glad to.'

Evie knew he'd feel forced to now, but it would put him in a savage rage.

'Be it on your own head,' he'd say. 'What sort of a life do you think you'll have? You'd be a lot better off with me than you will with Ned Collins, I can guarantee that.'

'I can't tell him. I can't face him with it.'

'All right, love. Whatever you say. What do you have in mind?'

Evie quaked at her own daring. 'You said you'd rent a room for us.'

'When I got your letter last night I had a quick look round. There's two rooms in Henry Street. A front living room with front bedroom above. We'll have to share the kitchen and there's no real bathroom . . . Not like you're used to, I'm afraid.'

'It'll do for a start.' Evie tried to smile. At least Henry Street wasn't caught in that triangle of heavy industry where Ned lived now.

'I'll see about it tomorrow then. Fix it up. I'm thrilled

it's happening, Evie, you know that. I just wish it didn't have to be this hard for you.'

She told him about the wooden box in the store room and how she planned to fill it with things she wanted to bring with her.

'Is it big? Too big for me to carry?'

She nodded. 'You'll need something with wheels to move it.'

'Have you seen the cart we use to collect coke from the gasworks?'

'Yes, and it's just the thing, the box would fit across that. We could tie it on.'

'I can bring it round whenever you say the word.'

'I'll have to go back,' she worried. 'I don't want him to come down to the shop looking for me.'

'Coronation Day. It's my next day off. I'll fix up the rooms for then.'

'Father's been invited to the celebrations in the park. I'm to go with him. He's been given seats on the stand with the Mayor and Mayoress.'

'So the shop will be closed?'

'Yes, in the afternoon.'

'That's the best time, then,' Ned said quietly. 'I'll find you in the park.'

'There'll be a big crowd . . .'

'There won't be that many with seats on the stand. I'll find you. Just slip away and come to me.'

Evie was gripping his arm. 'There'll be speeches. Father won't be able to leave his seat once it starts. Not without making a show of himself.'

'We'll come straight back here, pick up your things and be away. It'll be a while before he realises you've gone for good.'

'Yes.' Evie felt excitement spiral through her. She was

very much on edge. 'But I can't stay any longer. Not now.'

Ned pulled her closer and kissed her. 'Till Coronation Day, then.'

She shot into the yard, closed and locked the door as quietly as she could and sped indoors, locking up behind her as she went. On the first floor she slid the keys back into their places. Father lifted his eyes from his book as she reached the living-room door. She knew he'd left it open to keep an eye on her. Her heart was hammering against her ribs. He must realise she'd been a long time.

To explain it, she held up the camphorated oil bottle she'd brought. 'Needed to fill more bottles.'

'I hope this isn't just an excuse to gossip with Matilda?'

Her knees felt weak with relief. 'No, Father. I won't be long.'

She ran up two more flights to the attic and knocked on Matty's door.

Matty was already in bed but had kept the candle alight. Evie insisted on removing her bed socks and rubbing the camphorated oil into her misshapen feet. Then she came down one flight and went to her own room.

Her heart still raced, she was too frightened to sleep. She tossed and turned well into the night. She hated being sly and going behind Father's back like this. She wasn't cunning by nature, and she wished she didn't have to do it. It filled her with guilt and made her feel like a criminal, but she could think of no other way. She couldn't stop herself shivering at the thought of what Father would do if he knew.

But he didn't know. He'd have come bounding after her if he'd noticed anything amiss. He might be watching her like a cat watches a mouse, but she'd made her arrangements with Ned.

★ ★ ★

Everybody was talking about the coronation. The papers had been full of the preparations in Westminster Abbey and descriptions of the gowns and robes that would be worn and the fashions that foreign royalty were wearing as they assembled in London.

Evie was counting the days until she could be with Ned. Each time she went down from her bedroom to the shop, she took something with her and hid it in the box in the store room. It was June, a year since she'd dropped his mother's cough mixture on the floor.

The new apprentice had started, and had taken Evie's place in the drug run. She preferred the front counter but she was counting the days she'd spend there. Only three more, then two, then one.

The day before Coronation Day, Polly Darty handed her another note from Ned, saying he'd taken rooms for them, and that he'd be waiting near the stand in the park.

Then the newsagent's placards were proclaiming that today was Coronation Day and had been declared a public holiday. Some shops didn't open at all and those that did were to close at midday.

Business was slow in the morning. Evie could feel the ball of excitement growing inside her. When she went to fetch the bread from Polly Darty just before dinner, she heard that every schoolchild in the land had received four shining halfpennies. They'd been told to keep and treasure them as a memento of this occasion for the rest of their lives.

Matty cooked roast beef and Yorkshire pudding, a dinner such as they usually had only on Sundays. Evie couldn't eat. Her nausea had gone by late morning but today there were butterflies in her stomach. She changed quickly into her blue dress, remade her bun and fastened her new straw hat on top. It was the prettiest hat she'd ever owned, fashionably large, with the crown covered in blue velvet flowers. As she went downstairs, she folded her best winter coat over her arm.

At the shop door she hesitated. 'Will I be warm enough without a coat?'

'You won't need it,' Joseph said impatiently. 'Come along, the hansom is waiting.'

It was what she'd been expecting. She ran back and tossed her coat over the banisters at the bottom of the stairs, then hurried out after him.

She was so used to seeing her father in his white coat that he seemed almost a stranger in his new silk top hat and morning coat. She looked across the bouncing haunches of the chestnut mare and knew that at any other time she'd have thought it a great treat to be riding in a carriage. Today she could think of nothing else but that soon she would be with Ned for good.

Evie knew every step of the way to the park, she'd walked it so many times with little Herbie. Today there was a procession of carriages going there. Crowds were trailing up the pavements on both sides of Conway Street, with barefoot children racing between more sedate members of the public.

Bunting stretched across all the main streets. Evie could hear it flapping in the blustery breeze. The sun sparkled down from a clear blue sky. As they approached the park, she could hear the military band playing. At the handsome gothic main gate, Father had to show his invitation before his hansom was allowed inside. They bowled along the main avenue towards the stand.

Evie was keeping a sharp look-out for Ned. She'd never seen the park so full of people, and was afraid that in the crush she'd never meet up with him. But she saw him with a wide smile on his face, waiting close to where guests were alighting from their carriages. He lifted his straw boater in greeting and his brown curls fluttered in the breeze.

She was filled with triumph. What she'd planned was going to be possible. All she had to do now was to give Father the slip. As though he could read her thoughts, his hand came out to hold her arm. He was leading her forward to meet the line of civic dignitaries waiting to receive them. Evie smiled politely and shook the hands offered to her, but she was filled with a feeling of urgency. She had to get away. Would it be better if she did it before they found their seats?

On his way up the steps of the stand, Father paused to exchange a few words with the vicar of their church. His wife, who ran the Sunday school, was with him. Filled with guilt, Evie murmured, 'Excuse me a moment,' and ran back down the steps.

Moments later, Ned took her hand and led her into the crush. His brown eyes were laughing down into hers. He was trying to hurry but they were walking against the crowd surging towards the stand. When they reached the main gate, they heard the band strike up 'Land of Hope and Glory' and knew the gala had started.

'You're going to miss all the fun,' he teased.

Everything worked out as Evie had planned. Ned collected his coke cart from the Dartys' yard, while Evie went through the shop and opened up the store room. She made one quick trip upstairs, to take her money box and cash book from the living-room mantelpiece. She was propping a note of explanation to Father in its place when Matty hobbled to the door.

'Goodness, you gave me a fright. I thought we must have burglars. What are you doing back so soon?'

'I'm leaving for good, Matty. Running away. Wish me luck,' she laughed.

'Glory be! What will your father say?'

'I'll never know.' She laughed again, gave Matilda a kiss on her cheek and ran downstairs, snatching up her best coat from the banisters as she passed.

She clung to Ned's arm as she walked away from her secure home. For better or worse she'd cut herself off. She'd set her feet on what Father called the primrose path to hell. The wheels on the coke cart squeaked at every turn. She felt triumphant, swept along with the excitement of the day, relieved it had gone without a hitch. Ned felt the same way, she knew. The only time he stopped smiling was to break into a laugh. Evie laughed with him.

When they reached the rooms he'd rented, she was pleased with them. They were better than he'd led her to believe, though the furniture was shabby and the crockery chipped. She was introduced to her landlord and his wife. They seemed a dour couple and she wasn't sure that she'd like them.

Ned opened the cupboards and showed her the food he'd bought in readiness. She recognised Darty's bread and cakes. It brought the first misgivings.

'I hope Father won't be able to find me. I've not gone far.'

'I haven't told Polly anything, just in case. But once we're married, he won't be able to take you back.'

'How can we get married without his permission?'

'I've got to marry you, Evie.' Ned wasn't laughing now but deeply serious. 'I've talked you into running away from home and got you into the family way. You want to marry me, don't you?'

There was such a look of hope on his face that Evie was blinking hard.

'Of course I do. I just don't see how.'

'It'll have to be the register office. I've already been along there. To ask about what's needed, I mean. There's a certificate your father has to sign, to give permission. But my mother has a friend who'll pretend to be your father. He's said he'll come with us when we make the arrangements and sign for you.'

'Forge Father's signature? But he's well known, because of the shop. Think of all his customers. What if . . .' Evie's mind boggled at the risk.

'Perhaps we should go to Liverpool and get married there. Or Wallasey, if you like.'

'Doesn't it have to be the town where we live?'

'I don't know. I didn't ask that. But I've an older brother who's married and has rooms in New Brighton, we could give his address. Probably safer to do that, do you think?'

'Will we be legally married?'

'Yes, I think so. Nobody can undo the knot once it's tied.'

'There's only one other way, and that's to wait until I'm of age.'

'That's nearly three years off.' Ned was aghast.

'We'll do it your way,' Evie said. 'We have to, don't we, for the sake of the baby?'

Ned had also bought sticks and coal and laid a fire in readiness in the grate. Now he lit it.

'It'll seem more like home when it blazes up,' he said.

'It isn't cold.'

'We need it to cook on here, Evie.' He showed her the trivet that stood on the hearth and could be swung over the flames to support a pan or a kettle. 'We'll start with a cup of tea.'

Evie thought it was like playing at house and rather fun.

* * *

Evie felt happier now she was away from her father. She'd made her choice and was sure it was the right one. Ned and his mother continued to buy from Darty's bakery, though Evie didn't dare. It was too close. Polly reported that Matilda sometimes came for the bread, though if her feet were very bad, Bertie Pugh or Miss Lister were sent. All of them had told Polly that Joseph had gone berserk when he realised what Evie had done. He'd said he wouldn't have her back if she came on bended knee.

It was what Evie had expected, but it made her feel guilty. Apart from that, she had a wonderful summer and felt as free as air. On the days Ned went to work, she played at being a housewife and cleaned their rooms and made a meal for when Ned came home.

But it took three hours to sail to the Isle of Man and three to return. The trip gave passengers two hours in Douglas. On top of that Ned had to be on the boat half an hour before it sailed, and there was the time it took him to walk to Woodside and take the ferry over to the Liverpool landing stage.

Evie had him home every night, but he seemed to spend precious little time with her apart from that. He had two days off every fortnight, and she thought they were heaven.

By the end of July, they'd managed to arrange their wedding. Evie wore her blue dress and flowered hat. Ned's family gathered for the event. Gertie Collins looked stouter than ever in a floral print she'd bought for the occasion.

Evie hung on to Ned's arm as they all took the ferry to Liverpool Pier Head and then caught another ferry to Wallasey. The marriage ceremony went without a hitch, just as Ned had assured her it would. She was glad to have a wedding ring on her finger.

'He had to see you right,' Gertie Collins assured her,

pulling her close in a hug. Her rolls of flesh yielded like a soft cushion. The rest of the family were equally free with their affection. All four brothers and the sister-in-law kissed her and welcomed her to the family. Evie felt she'd never been kissed so much.

They had to catch the bus to Ned's brother Alfie's house, where a good lunch had been laid out in readiness. But the Collins brothers could never pass a pub, and what better way was there to celebrate such a match?

Evie had never been in a pub before but she was persuaded into the lounge. She'd never tasted strong drink, either. Father took a glass of sherry before his Sunday dinner, and sometimes a glass of whisky to help him sleep at night, but he hadn't approved of alcohol for her.

Evie sipped the port and lemon that was put into her hand. The Collins men drank ale, and seemed to be settling in for a good session. But after one drink Ned stood up, and the women did the same.

'We're going to our Alfie's for something to eat,' Gertie told her other sons. Evie was led off towards the bus stop, and Alfie came running after them rather shame-faced.

His home was two cramped rooms, but there was a good spread of ham and pickles and a big variety of jellies and cakes set out on the table. Tea was made for those who wanted it, and there was ale for the others.

When Ned said it was time for them to go, much of the food that hadn't been eaten was parcelled up so they could take it with them. His brothers opened more ale.

'I'm not like them,' Ned told her, as they hung over the rail of the ferry boat and watched the murky water of the Mersey foam against the bow. 'Any more than you're like your father.'

Evie felt truly blessed to have Ned's love. She felt nurtured and valued for the first time in her life. There was a warmth about Ned. He was always thinking of some little luxury she might enjoy. He'd spend his last threepence on a bunch of violets for her.

His eyes caressed her across the table when they sat down to meals. His love made him get up to kiss her or gently stroke her cheek. He had a special smile for her.

But she didn't find it easy to settle to her new and very different life. She was living within a few minutes' walk of her father's shop and knew she'd have felt safer with more distance between them. She was also afraid that what she'd done had been very wrong. Her family set great store by doing their duty. She'd been brought up to listen to her conscience.

'Your father's a tyrant,' Ned tried to soothe her fears. 'You were scared of him. You needed to get away, you mustn't worry.'

His days off were idyllic now that they could spend the whole time together. On one of them, they called in on his mother. Gertie Collins always made a fuss of her visitors, and gave them a big welcome. They were sitting in her back room drinking tea when they heard a loud rat-a-tat on her front door.

'Who could that be?' Gertie put down her cup and went to see, leaving the door open. 'Can't be the rent man, I've paid him . . .'

Evie heard a man's voice, stiff with formality, say: 'Are you Mrs Gertrude Alice Collins?'

'Yes.' She sounded suddenly wary. Ned was on his feet, peeping up the hall.

He turned to mouth the words: 'It's a bobby.'

'The police?' Evie was aghast. Ned turned with a finger against his lips, but the look on his face alone would have silenced her.

The official voice boomed up the narrow hall. 'I'd like a word with you, can I come in?'

'What's it about?' Gertie was even more wary, scared even.

'You have a son, Edward Collins?'

There was a nervous pause. 'Yes.'

'He lives here with you?'

'No, no.'

'Then would you be good enough to give me his address?'

Evie held her breath. Her heart was drumming so loud she thought the policeman would be able to hear.

'He's away at sea,' Gertie said. 'What d'you want to know for? What's he supposed to have done?'

'It's in regard to a missing person. We've reason to believe he might know her whereabouts.'

Evie saw the colour drain from Ned's face.

'You'd better come in,' his mother said. 'This way.' She was taking the bobby into the parlour at the front, which was hardly used. Instantly, Ned was feeling for Evie's hand and drawing her cautiously out to the hall. The parlour door wasn't completely closed. Gertie was leaning against it.

'Away at sea, you say? How long has he been away?'

'I can't remember exactly. A year or so now it must be.'

'What's the name of his ship, Mrs Collins?'

Ned was drawing Evie out to the scullery, moving as quietly as possible. A moment later they were tiptoeing down the yard and out into the back entry. He was hurrying her then, faster, until they were running. They didn't stop until they were back in their own rooms, and even then Evie didn't feel safe.

'It's Father! He's got the police looking for me.'

'Mam won't say anything. You heard her. She said I was away at sea.'

'But they'll find us some other way.'

'Nobody knows our address.'

'All your family do.'

'They'll keep their mouths shut.'

'We've made everybody tell lies for us. I've done it myself. Done all sorts of devious things.'

'We had to get married,' Ned told her. 'We have to protect ourselves now.'

'I've got the collywobbles.'

'You worry a lot. I blame your father for that.'

When Evie stopped shaking she was able to tell Ned about the prescription book in which her father wrote down the names and addresses of every customer he prescribed for. That was the law. That was how he knew Gertie's address.

'Of course he wants you back,' Gertie said a few days later. 'What father wouldn't? He's doing his best, but he won't find you. I gave nothing away.'

Ned said in reassuring tones: 'Anyway, you're a married woman now. He can't force you to go back if you don't want to go.'

It took Evie a while to recover, and even longer to put her fears behind her, but apart from that, the weeks were beginning to drift past very pleasantly. As far as the weather went, it was not a good summer, but she thought it the happiest of her life.

When the summer season came to an end, the day-trippers, who this year had not flocked in their usual numbers to take the boat to the Isle of Man, ceased to go at all. There were autumn gales in the Irish Sea and the number of sailings was suddenly cut back to a winter timetable. Many of the crew lost their jobs, and Ned was shocked to find he was amongst them. He hadn't been expecting it. He'd been kept on all last winter, but then last year, the weather had been better.

CHAPTER SEVEN

'I'll soon find another job,' Ned said confidently. 'On the dredgers, or something like that.'

'Don't hurry.' Evie smiled. 'It'll be lovely to have you home all day. We can afford a week or two to ourselves, can't we?'

She was a thrifty housekeeper, having been trained by Aunt Agatha, and they had a little money in hand. She'd also managed to buy her own pots and pans and household linen, all of a better quality than had been provided by the landlord, and had accumulated most of the layette she'd need for the coming baby.

But Ned saw himself as the provider and had to start looking for work straight away. He spent his mornings tramping round the port offices and the shipping lines, and studying the jobs advertised in the *Birkenhead News* and the *Liverpool Echo*. As the weeks passed and he wasn't offered another job, he began to lose heart.

'There's only deep-sea jobs,' he worried, 'and that means being away for months, maybe years. I want a job where I can be home with you every night.'

Evie knew he wouldn't settle until he'd found another job. Money was suddenly much tighter and they couldn't spend it on doing things together. She could now appreciate how very poor the people living round her were. Most, and that included Ned's family, had no savings to fall back on.

Eventually, Ned said: 'I'll have to go deep-sea, Evie. I've got to earn some money and it's the only thing going.

It'll mean leaving you on your own. I hate doing that.'

Evie was nervous of the prospect. She wanted him with her. Her baby was due after Christmas. She couldn't see how she'd be able to manage on her own then. Ned put off the decision for another week or two, but eventually he signed on to a rusty freighter loaded with machine tools bound for Genoa. He chose it because it was due back in Liverpool before Christmas.

'Just in case I'm held up, I've asked my mother to do what she can. I mean, if it comes early and I'm not here.'

Evie had never seen Ned look so downhearted. She shuddered and hoped that wouldn't happen, but it worried her. This was their first real setback and she prayed that it didn't mean she was following her mother's downward spiral. All the same, she felt as though she was on the slippery slope.

Ned provided an allotment out of his pay which she collected every Friday from the shipping office, but he was not earning as much as he had done, and she decided she'd have to be even more thrifty.

She was lonely on her own and she didn't feel safe in the rooms Ned had chosen, because the landlord leered at her every time she went to the kitchen or the yard. She thought she could organise things better now that they didn't have to live close to Woodside to make it easy for Ned to travel to Liverpool every day. And most of all, she wanted to get further away from the pharmacy.

She decided she'd look for a whole house that she could rent. Within a few days she found what she was looking for near the old priory. Birkenhead Priory had been one of the first to be seized by Henry VIII, its treasures taken and the monks turned out. The first ferry across the Mersey had been started by the monks in the fourteenth century. Now the ancient slipway was used as a coal stage and was trapped between Clovers Graving Docks and Birkenhead Iron Works, where shipbuilding was carried on.

Evie looked at the ruins of the priory, where rank grass grew knee-high. The chapter house still had a roof on and had been restored at some time. She could make out the crypt and the great hall, but it was all so neglected and dismal.

Industry had blighted the whole area. There were small factories and warehouses, wood yards and coal stacks everywhere. The racket made by riveters and giant hammers in the shipyards went on all day. Mean streets of small houses crowded close, built to house the dock workers in the middle of the last century. Leicester Street was one of the better ones. On either side of it were dark, narrow courts. It was further away from the pharmacy, though Evie would have liked it more distant still. But it was something of a backwater, and Joseph would have no reason to come anywhere near.

She picked out a plain two-up and two-down terraced house with flat sash windows. The front door opened straight off the pavement into a narrow hall that went from back to front and from which the stairs went up. Evie knew she'd have to rent off some of the rooms, and this would make all the difference to her comfort and that of her tenant.

She still had the money that she'd brought with her. Ned had not wanted her to spend it on living expenses. He thought it was his responsibility to provide those. That was her money and she must spend it on herself or the baby. Evie had thought of it as their nest egg. Now she used it to buy good second-hand furniture and make the house as comfortable as she could. She bought some paint and smartened the rooms up. She made curtains for the windows and spring-cleaned and polished until the whole place shone.

Then she put a card in the window of a nearby newsagent, offering to rent two rooms in a respectable house to a single woman. She showed two ladies round and was delighted when one of them, a Miss Pringle, wanted to move in. She came with good references.

Ida Pringle was a spinster on the wrong side of fifty, employed as a lady typist in a nearby office. She was a stout woman with a rather plain, good-natured face and tiny shoe-button eyes. She dressed very smartly to go to work. Evie thought they'd get on reasonably well and was pleased that most of her own rent was met by what she was charging her tenant. She could manage now on what Ned sent her.

The time was passing. Evie was feeling more tired and growing ungainly. She made a Christmas pudding and a decorated cake, just as Matilda used to. All her preparations for the coming baby were complete and she was beginning to feel excited about it. Her main worry was that Ned would not be back in time.

She received letters from him, but the names of the small ports meant nothing until she found an old atlas in a second-hand book shop. After that she could follow his progress. When she went to the shipping office to collect her weekly money, she always asked the whereabouts of the *Redeemer*. When she heard it was heading back across the Bay of Biscay she was delighted.

Ned arrived home two days before Christmas, looking suntanned and healthy. He'd brought back several little gifts for her – an ivory fan bought in the Spanish port of Tarragona, a brooch from Palma, a leather purse from Morocco, a bottle of sweet wine from Malaga, dates from Tunis – and many pictures of the places he'd been.

Evie pored over the pictures. 'So many exotic places. You must have enjoyed seeing them.'

'I was thinking of you wherever I went,' he grinned. 'Couldn't think of anything else. All I wanted was to get back to you.'

They kept the fire roaring up the chimney in the back room and went out only to visit Ned's family and deliver the presents he'd brought for them.

Miss Pringle stayed out of their way as much as possible now Ned was home. Evie had the impression that she preferred him to be away. But Ida liked a laugh, and Ned could make her rolls of flesh shake with mirth when he joked.

The baby arrived on New Year's Eve, and Ned was there to fetch the midwife and boil the kettles of water she said were needed. Evie hugged her baby son in a surge of mother love, and decided that nothing in the world would ever part her from him. He was a strong baby with soft, thick brown hair like his father's. He slept well and fed well and was easy to manage. Together they chose the name Robert for him.

Ned was overwhelmed, and spent hours watching him while he slept in his cot. He nicknamed him Bobby. Evie felt that all the difficulties had been well worthwhile. She'd never felt so surrounded by love.

Within days Ned was worrying about getting another ship. He tried half-heartedly for a job in port, but when it wasn't forthcoming he signed on on an old ship that had brought sugar cane and rum from Barbados and was loading salt and manufactured goods for the return journey.

When he was leaving, he said to Miss Pringle: 'I'm glad you're here. It's better for Evie to have someone with her.'

'I don't like being alone either,' Ida told him. 'Evie's very good to me.'

Evie felt down when Ned went. She told herself fiercely that she had a lot to be thankful for. Little Bobby was a beautiful baby. All her love turned on him now; he was reason enough for everything she did. She also had a comfortable home and was free to live as she wanted to.

She took Bobby to see Ned's mother quite often, understanding that she'd want to shower her grandson with love too. Gertie would turn up on Evie's doorstep even more frequently, and Evie would put the kettle on so that they could share a cup of tea. She found her mother-in-law a comfort when Ned was away. Gertie was always reaching out to touch her, a hand on her arm or her shoulder to signal support. Evie thought about her father. They had never touched each other, never kissed, never shown affection like this.

Miss Pringle was captivated by Bobby too. Evie began cooking an evening meal for her. It was more economical and no more difficult to cook for two than it was for one, and she was glad of adult company at the end of the day.

Miss Pringle was jolly and optimistic by nature. She set great store by horoscopes and believed she could foretell the future for herself and her friends by reading their tea cups.

Many evenings, when she and Evie had finished their meal, she insisted they both swirl the dregs of their tea round the sides of their cups and upturn them on their saucers. She successfully foretold from Evie's tea leaves that Ned would be home before Easter.

He was home again for a month later that summer. This time Evie was determined to enjoy his company. She wouldn't let him worry about getting another ship, nor allow him to go back to sea after two weeks, as he felt he should.

But when he'd gone again and her evenings with Miss Pringle resumed, she realised that this would be the pattern of her life from now on. A husband she loved but rarely saw. When they were together, they had such joyous times. Like their honeymoon all over again.

Evie didn't know what she'd have done when Ned went away if she hadn't had Miss Pringle's company. It was having Ida in the house that kept her going.

Ned's ship hadn't even reached New York when Ida saw another baby's face in her tea cup. Evie hardly believed her, but a week or so later she realised it was true. She was going to have another baby.

'And Bobby only a few months old!'

Evie didn't know whether Miss Pringle was shocked at the speed with which she'd conceived again, or delighted that she'd managed to predict it. For her own part, she would have preferred to delay it a little, but she wanted more than one child. She knew Ned would welcome it too, that he wanted a big family.

This time Evie wasn't lucky enough to have Ned with her when her baby was born. She happened to be visiting her mother-in-law when she felt the first pains, and it was one of Ned's brothers who was sent running for the midwife.

Everything was normal and went well. Evie had a little girl she named Victoria. She managed well enough during the lying-in period. For a couple of weeks, Miss Pringle did much more about the house. She cooked the evening meal when she returned home from the office.

Gertie offered to look after Bobby for a week, and she brought him round to see Evie and the new baby every day. She always brought something with her for their midday meal, which they ate together. Evie began to appreciate Gertie. Ned had told her he'd grown up in a loving home. His mother might fall very short of Aunt Agatha's standards of housekeeping and cleanliness but she had Ned's way of wrapping everyone in her love.

By the time the baby was eight days old, Evie was feeling more her old self. Gertie came round wearing for the eighth time the same green skirt with a torn hem.

'Take it off and let me mend it,' Evie said. 'I'm just sitting here watching you work. It'll do me good to keep my fingers busy.'

'Your fingers are busy enough, lass,' Gertie said, but Evie insisted.

'It's too long. Caught my boot in the hem.' It came off, revealing several layers of petticoats, red flannel, striped navy and white twill, and what had once been white lawn.

'Then I'll shorten it.'

Evie also insisted on sponging off the mud from round the bottom, and she made Gertie put a flat iron in the fire to press the new hem.

'You've made it like new, love,' Gertie said with pleasure when she put it on again.

The following morning when she came in, Gertie was bursting with news: 'Guess where we've been this morning?'

She had a bag of shopping and she took out some iced buns and set them out on the table.

'Darty's?' Evie felt a shiver of fear. 'You didn't take Bobby there?'

'I did, and there's no need for you to worry.'

'But Father's just next door. He might have seen you.'

'Not him. Had his head down behind the back counter, and the shop was full of customers. Polly Darty was so pleased to see Bobby. She swung him up in her arms and took him into the bakery to show Arthur. 'Evie's little boy,' she said. 'Isn't he lovely?'

'When I said you'd got another, a baby girl this time, she said she knew you'd make a good mother. You were lovely with little Herbie.'

'How is he?' Evie choked.

'He's fine. And Polly sends her love.'

Evie stared into the fire for a long time. 'How's Father?'

'We don't go in his shop now, none of us do. I told you that.' They went to a chemist near the station now, though Gertie said his physic wasn't so good.

'Didn't Polly say anything?'

'Only that he's more bad-tempered than ever.'

'I wonder if he's managing all right.'

'That I can't tell you. I don't suppose Polly could either.'

'I wonder if Matilda's still there. I don't suppose Polly said?'

'Didn't mention her. You'll have to go round yourself if you want to know that sort of thing. It wouldn't hurt after all this time. It's so much water under the bridge now.'

'No.' Evie suppressed a shudder. 'You didn't tell Polly where we lived?'

'She didn't ask, love. But Polly won't say a word. Don't you worry.'

But Evie did worry. The Collins family were frequent customers at the bakery and had been friendly with the Dartys for a long time. Father was a customer too, and only next door. It was only too easy to see how a connection might be made.

Evie felt guilty because she'd walked out on Joseph in the same way her mother had, and she knew just how much that would upset him. She hadn't been the dutiful daughter he'd wanted. Gertie was still trying to ease her mind.

'Your dad ain't all that popular round there. Thinks

himself a cut above his neighbours, he does. Anyway, everything's changed now. You're a married woman with two lovely children. You can hold your head up with the rest of them. He's the one losing out. You don't need him.'

When Ned returned home, he was thrilled with his new daughter. He cuddled her in his arms and called her Queenie, and somehow the nickname stuck.

'Victoria's too big a name for a tiny scrap like this,' he laughed. 'You named her after the old queen, didn't you?'

He opened his arms to his growing family and seemed to have love enough for them all. He talked of adding to it in the future.

Ida Pringle pulled her flannelette nightdress over her head and climbed into her bed. Tonight, she'd try to get to sleep quickly. She blew out her candle and closed her eyes. Having a man in the house changed everything.

Evie and her husband were coming upstairs now. Creeping quietly, whispering softly like two doves. A little laugh, the creak of the bedsprings as they climbed in, a gentle murmur and then silence.

Ida had been so pleased with these rooms when she'd moved in. She had the two best rooms in the house, the largest bedroom in the front and the sitting room beneath it. They were comfortably furnished and nicely decorated, and she'd really taken to Evie, who was very sweet and welcoming.

There was a hot dinner ready every evening when Ida came home from work. She enjoyed playing with little Bobby, bouncing him on her ample lap until he squealed with laughter. She loved the long evenings by the fire, just her and Evie, gossiping and reading their cups. Ida counted Evie as a friend now that she'd lived in her house for over a year.

A LIVERPOOL LULLABY

She wasn't so sure about Ned, though he seemed a nice enough fellow to talk to. Evie had married beneath her, that was obvious enough to anyone. Such silky hair that it was always escaping her bun to hang down beside her face in shining dark tendrils. Such a pretty girl to throw herself away on a husband like that.

The table was set for three in the evenings when he was home. He was always there between them, taking all Evie's attention. And after they'd eaten, he left Ida in no doubt that he expected her to go to her own lonely sitting room. She felt pushed out.

Oh, no! Ida listened, stiffening with distaste.

Ned didn't give anybody a chance to get to sleep. It was bad enough having him downstairs. He pawed Evie, always reaching out to touch her. She'd seen him kiss the nape of Evie's neck this evening. He made his needs so transparent.

Ida turned over in bed and pulled her blankets over her ears. She could still hear the rhythmic creak of the brass bedstead in the next bedroom. It was downright embarrassing to have to listen to such sounds through the wall. Great gusts and sighs and grunts too.

She'd felt sorry enough for Evie before he came home. There was something vulnerable about her. She really did have a lot to put up with. Every night, half an hour or less after they'd come up to bed, this started. He could make the marital bed rattle in earnest and it wasn't only at night. Sometimes she heard it in the morning too.

Still, he wouldn't be home for long. No doubt Evie was looking forward to his departure as much as Ida herself was. Really, men were disgusting creatures. There was only one thing they thought of.

Ida thanked God she'd managed to stay single. It had been touch and go when she was young, before she

113

realised; before her sister Kitty was married and had such a terrible time. She hoped Ned Collins wouldn't be staying home for very long.

Evie's days were filled with child care now, and when Ned went away she was so busy she had less time to think of him.

Queenie was not such an easy baby as Bobby had been. She slept less and was difficult to feed. For the first time, Evie would have liked to have her father's expertise and experience. Many young mothers took their infants to his shop, he was used to weighing them. He prescribed for sleeping and teething problems, made ointments for the babies' bottoms and advised on more food or less food or different food so that they'd thrive.

If she had to pass his shop Evie always did it on the opposite side of the road, keeping a close watch on it as trams and carts and carriages swished between them. Sometimes she'd see Miss Lister serving on the front counter. Once she saw Bertie Pugh, but she never caught even a glimpse of Father, though she knew he was there.

The years were passing pleasantly enough, but she longed to see more of Ned. He was away so much of the time. She was finding it a struggle again to manage on the money he was able to set aside from his wages. It wasn't Ned's fault. She knew he kept very little for his own use. Their family was a growing responsibility and it was difficult to meet all their needs from one wage packet.

'I wish I'd learned to type like you,' she told Miss Pringle enviously. She knew that Ida earned more than Ned, and didn't have to travel the world to do it.

'Wouldn't help you now.' Miss Pringle screwed up her podgy face in thought. 'They don't employ married ladies

114

as typists. Anyway, you have two babies. You have to stay home to take care of them.'

'Taking in washing is about the only way married women can earn a bit extra. There's at least two in this street that do it.'

'But you wouldn't want to, would you?'

'I've plenty of washing of my own,' Evie laughed. 'But it can be combined with looking after babies.'

'If you have bags of energy.'

'I do.' Evie counted herself lucky in that respect.

A month later, Miss Pringle came home bursting with news.

'Would you fancy an office cleaning job, Evie? That wouldn't be beneath you?'

Evie was dishing up stewed steak and dumplings.

'It's an early-morning job at the office where I work. Really early, I mean, five till half past seven. You could be home again before eight to get the children up for breakfast.'

Evie felt a surge of interest as she set the two plates on the table and pulled out her chair. 'But I'd have to leave the children . . .'

'They never need anything at that time of the morning, do they?' Ida's face shone with good intentions.

'No.' They never did. If Queenie was wakeful and crotchety it was always early in the night. Bobby slept like a top and was never any trouble.

'And I'm sleeping in the next room. If something out of the ordinary happens, I'll hear them and go in. They know me now and wouldn't be frightened.'

'Would you mind? I mean, it's awfully good of you.'

'If they wake up, I'll comfort them until you get back. You'll only be away for three hours or so, after all.'

'If you're willing . . .' Evie was hesitant. 'It's asking a lot.'

'No it's not. Shall I put your name forward? Do you want that?'

'Yes please.' Evie clasped her hands together. 'Oh, yes please. A job like that, the extra money would make all the difference.'

'Then I'll fix up for you to come in and have an interview. I've already had a word. I told the person who'd be your boss that you keep your house spotless. She's been having a spot of trouble with cleaners recently. There have been three in the last five months. I told her I thought you'd be reliable.'

'I will be,' Evie promised. She was trying to think. 'Henry Ball and Sons, you said the company was called? I've never understood, what exactly is their business?'

'I told you, they're West Africa merchants.'

'But what exactly is that?'

'Mr Ball has a fleet of ships that trade between Liverpool and West Africa. It's an old family business, been going for years.'

'Big business then?'

'Oh, yes.'

When they were having a cup of tea afterwards, Miss Pringle said: 'We must consult your tea leaves tonight, to see if you'll get the job.'

Evie sat back and smiled. She didn't really believe the tea leaves foretold anything, although Ida had been right once or twice. With the babies tucked up in bed, and a good fire burning in the grate, she saw it as a bit of fun.

'Come on,' Ida urged. 'Swill the last of your tea round the cup three times. Now upturn it on your saucer.'

Evie did as she was told and handed her cup over. 'Don't look for any more babies,' she said. 'We can't afford them. Dots are what I want, they signify gain by money, don't they?' She was learning the basic rules.

116

'There are dots. Well, just one or two.'

'That means a little more money?' Evie asked hopefully.

'Just a little. I can see a horse.'

'What does that mean?'

'A lover. There are dashes and clouds round him, which indicate he truly loves you, but there are difficulties he can't control keeping him away.'

'That must be Ned,' laughed Evie. 'No dots round him, I'm sure.'

'Oddly enough, there's a parasol too.' Miss Pringle's voice warmed with interest.

'What does that mean?'

'It's another sign for a lover. Your cup shows two.'

Evie laughed. 'I don't need another.'

'The dots are close to it. This one will have more money than Ned.'

'Just the money will do,' Evie sighed. 'What about the job?'

Miss Pringle said, 'It shows nothing. I don't know.'

Evie had seen the office of Henry Ball and Sons on Knox Street many times. It was just round the corner from her house. Nothing could be more convenient. It seemed an old-fashioned building, and somewhat run-down. She asked Gertie to look after the children for her when she went for the interview.

Feeling nervous, she went through the double doors into a vestibule. It had a floor of mosaic tiles and a mahogany counter. There was nobody about, but a notice near a brass bell told her to ring for service. Evie pressed her palm down on the spring plunger.

'Good morning.' A young clerk appeared immediately.

Evie said she'd come for a job interview, and the end of the counter was lifted to allow her in. The office seemed

117

an alien place. She counted eight men, each standing in front of a desk writing in a large ledger. Above each desk was a wire rack holding more ledgers. A young office boy was told to take her upstairs. The stone steps were steep and winding. Evie wondered if she would have to clean them too.

'This is the manager's secretary,' the boy said. 'He'll look after you.'

Evie had expected to see Miss Pringle. Instead, a gaunt, middle-aged man sat typing at a desk positioned in front of a door labelled 'Mr Byron Ball'.

'You found us all right then?' He offered her a chair. He wore a high, stiff collar, and Evie could see an angry red line where it was chafing his neck. 'He'll buzz when he's free to see you.' The man nodded towards the door. 'We're busy today. Have to get on.'

Every time he came to the end of a paragraph, he ran a finger inside his collar. Evie was interested in what he was doing. It seemed a very pleasant way of earning a living. She knew that more and more women were doing it now, Miss Pringle for one. It was not to be compared with taking in washing, or even shop work. After ten minutes she heard the buzzer. The secretary looked up.

'Just knock and go on in,' he told her.

Cautiously, she did so. Mr Ball had risen from the chair behind his desk and was on his way to meet her. He was well built, with powerful shoulders, and in his late thirties. He wore a formal chalk-striped suit with a stiff-collared shirt. His eyes seemed to question everything. He had a lot of straight brown hair.

'Come in, come in,' he urged, putting out his hand. His clasp was so firm it hurt a little. 'Have a seat. You've come about the vacancy we advertised?'

'Yes.' Evie tried to smile. She felt tense.

'What are your speeds?'

She was disconcerted. 'I work quite fast.'

'Quite fast?' His brow furrowed. 'Come on now, you'll need to be more exact than that.'

Evie wondered if she could claim to be very fast. 'Surely thoroughness is more important than speed,' she managed. 'I'm very thorough.'

Now he seemed at a loss. 'Miss Topping, isn't it? The lady typewriter?'

'No, no. I'm Mrs Collins, for the office cleaner's job.'

'Oh!' He was trying to control his smile. 'I'm afraid there's been a bit of a mix-up. You do look more like a lady typewriter.'

He laughed then, and his brown eyes met hers. There was nothing unkind about his gaze. It travelled from her face to her clothes. She was wearing her best winter coat with her straw hat, the one she'd bought for the coronation gala. It was still March, and the weather was chilly: a little early in the year for her hat.

'I only wish I could type.'

He laughed again. 'Miss Hooper looks after domestic matters. I leave that sort of thing to her. Somebody's got his lines crossed. Office cleaner, eh? You're very young for that. Our cleaning ladies are usually much older.' His eyes were assessing her again.

'The young have more energy,' she said.

He smiled again. 'Even very early in the morning?'

She told him about her two children and why those hours were the only ones that she could work. That Miss Pringle would listen for them while she was away.

'Our Miss Pringle?'

'Yes, she rents rooms from me. She said she'd speak for me. Recommend me.'

'Well, we'll give you a try. Have to. It would never do to

119

upset Miss Pringle. She's quite an institution here.'

He buzzed through to his secretary, who summoned Miss Hooper, a grey-haired lady nearing retirement age.

Miss Hooper frowned at Evie. 'I've been waiting for you. I thought you were late.'

'No, I was a little early. I'm a good timekeeper.'

'It seems the staff thought I should see her first,' Mr Ball put in, explaining the situation.

'I was surprised when you didn't come. Miss Pringle spoke very highly of you. She's sure you'll give satisfaction.'

'I'll do my best.'

'Since Mrs Collins comes so well recommended, I think we must give her a try,' Mr Ball put in. Evie warmed to him and tried to smile her thanks.

Miss Hooper was perspiring. 'You'd better come with me.'

'Goodbye.' Mr Ball was still smiling as she left.

When Miss Hooper got round to mentioning her wages, Evie thought them reasonably generous, and accepted gratefully. It was a job she was glad to have.

Her duties were explained to her and she was shown where the cleaning materials were kept. As Ida had told her, they were having problems with their cleaning and they needed someone to start straight away.

'Tomorrow morning, five o'clock,' Miss Hooper told her. 'There'll be someone with you for the first morning. To show you the ropes.'

Evie set her alarm clock for four thirty, blessing the forethought that had made her bring it with her. It had been a Christmas gift from her father and was a reliable one.

'Now you've no excuse to be late for breakfast,' Father had said, when she'd thanked him.

It seemed like the middle of the night when it went off. She silenced it as soon as she could, so as not to wake Miss Pringle or the children. She dressed quickly in the cold of pre-dawn, peeped into the back bedroom to reassure herself that her children were still asleep and set off.

The office was within easy walking distance, which was what had attracted Miss Pringle to her house in the first place. She was warm when she got there. It was not quite five o'clock and a middle-aged woman was unlocking the doors.

The woman started by lighting the gas mantles. 'So you're the new woman? You're just a slip of a girl. I hope you know what work is. You'll be on your own tomorrow.'

Evie found there was plenty to do. There were four grates which needed to be raked out and new fires laid, the tiled entrance hall to mop out and the brass knobs and knockers to polish. Then she had to swing something called a dummy, a great hinged polishing pad, over the wooden floors of the main office.

'You've got to move the desks every day and polish them regular. I do six each morning,' the woman advised. 'Different ones so they all get a turn.'

Then there were three smaller offices to clean, and countless waste-paper baskets to empty.

'Don't forget the lavvies out in the yard. There's a special mop kept out there and the ladies are very fussy about them.'

The time flew. When they were leaving, the sky was lighter in the east. Evie almost ran home to light her own fire and put on the pan of porridge to heat through. She was hungry and much in need of her breakfast.

Miss Pringle reported that the children had slept through and hadn't noticed her absence. All the same,

Evie felt it was wrong to leave them, and she played with them more than usual that morning. She loved them dearly.

Bobby was a bright-eyed miniature of his father. He was turned three now, and Ned was telling her it was time she dressed him in shorts. It was the fashion to clothe all infants, whether boys or girls, in skirts and pinafores. Queenie, a year younger, took after Ned too. They were both sturdy children with clear, healthy skin, brown eyes and brown curly hair.

After the children's dinner at midday, Evie put them down for a nap and took a rest herself. She went to bed an hour earlier than she used to, and found she could cope.

The money she earned made all the difference. She bought new shoes for both her children that week, and she looked forward to persuading Ned to stay home longer next time he came. To have him home for more than a week or two would be a wonderful treat for them all.

The years were passing. Evie thought she had everything she could possibly want and was content. Father had been wrong when he'd predicted she'd be in trouble if she married Ned. She thought of her mother often, and hoped life had been good for her during the years she'd been away from home.

Evie was so busy with her job and her family that when war fever gripped the nation it took her by surprise. Suddenly all the newspapers were full of the possibility of war. Everywhere she looked, there were posters saying 'England Needs You'.

Gertie Collins came round to see her in a terrible state. She said that her sons had taken leave of their senses. One had already signed up to join the army and another the navy, and the other two were talking of doing the same.

'I don't know what our Alfie's thinking of, a married man with three young sons. Where's the sense in him going?' She hoped his wife would be able to keep him at home.

'Afraid they'll miss the fun.' Gertie was scathing, but full of pride too that they wanted to fight for their country.

Book Two

1914–1919

CHAPTER EIGHT

That evening, as he was being driven home by his chauffeur, Byron Ball was thinking of Evie Collins. Such a pretty, well-spoken girl who'd seemed pathetically pleased to get the job of cleaning his offices. The only reason he could think of was that she'd made a disastrous marriage and had put herself in a position where she was in need of money. Yet she didn't give the impression of being unhappy with her lot.

Byron thought he knew all there was to know about disastrous marriages. And more than he wanted to about people who were dissatisfied with their circumstances. Being so dissatisfied with everything in his own life, he marvelled at Evie and saw her as a lesson to him.

It didn't help that nobody appreciated that he had difficulties. Since he was a lad, distant cousins, old aunts, other relatives and friends had all been saying to him:

'It's all right for you, Byron. You'll inherit the family business. Look what a success your father and grandfather made of it.

'Then there's Parkfield, the house you've always lived in, and goodness only knows what else they've managed to put by for you. A goodly pile, I'm sure. You're cushioned for life. You won't have to struggle to earn a crust like the rest of us.'

At one time, he too had thought himself very fortunate, but not any longer. Samuels swept the big open tourer through the gates of Parkfield and pulled up outside the front door. Grace, his twelve-year-old daughter, came hurtling round the side of the house to throw herself at him.

'Daddy, come and see Lulu, she's had four pups. They're absolutely beautiful. Just balls of fluff.'

Byron allowed himself to be led by the hand to what had once been the stables. It was Grace who looked after both Labradors, fed them and walked them. She was also keen on the cat and the tortoise, always bursting with enthusiasm for something new. He had countless things she'd made for him, leather bookmarks, boxes covered with shells, hand-stitched handkerchiefs and hand-knitted socks. He told himself he had Grace. Life hadn't dealt him a totally bad hand.

He had Norman too, but though he'd never admitted it to anyone, he didn't find him nearly so rewarding. He'd tried to interest his son in cricket, rowing and football, but he wasn't keen on outdoor sports, though Grace had taken them up with boundless energy. He'd introduced him to stamp-collecting and butterflies, and both had left Norman cold, though Grace had blown them up into a craze.

Byron had expected his son to be more like himself, but instead he'd clung to Veronica and the armchair near the fire. He felt there was no common ground between them on which he could make contact. Family life seemed a continual tug of war with Veronica, his wife of thirteen years, and Norman pulling on one end of the rope, and he and Grace on the other.

When they went indoors, Veronica met them in the hall, dressed up to the nines.

'What's the matter with you, Byron? I asked you to be home early and you're later than ever. You knew I wanted to go out, that I wanted Samuels and the car. I was worried you wouldn't have him here in time.'

'Aren't you having supper first?'

'I'm going to a dinner.' She belonged to a number of ladies' organisations. 'I told you last night.'

'Sorry.' He'd forgotten. 'He's here now. Run and tell him, Grace love.'

Veronica's face was lined, she had pale, bulging eyes and a permanently dissatisfied droop to her mouth. She was the most unrestful person he knew. She found it impossible to sit still, and she paced the hall now, waiting for the car to come round.

She bustled everywhere at great speed and was very involved with civic and church duties. She wanted status in the world and had come to the conclusion that Byron was not doing enough to provide it.

Byron poured himself a drink when she'd gone. He'd grown up in this rambling old house on Shrewsbury Road and had always loved it. He and Veronica had started married life in a small new house. He'd rented that, knowing that one day he'd inherit Parkfield and be able to move back. He'd looked forward to it as much as Veronica had.

But almost as soon as they moved in, Veronica had started complaining.

'You must do something about the draughts. It's freezing in here. Look at those gaps under the doors, and the windows don't fit properly. They rattle in the wind. It's quite an uncomfortable house, really.'

Byron had arranged for workmen to come in and have the doors rehung. Their foreman told him that the house was beginning to subside at the back. The floors had dropped, but to do anything about them would be a huge job. He bought draught excluders instead, which Veronica found ugly.

'We really do need central heating,' she went on. 'Everybody's having it put in.'

'The roof's more important,' Byron sighed. 'We lost another slate in the last gale.' The roof leaked like a sieve, but he kept putting that off because it seemed like throwing good money after bad.

'Carpets would help,' she went on. 'The house needs refurbishing from top to bottom. Your father neglected it.'

'He was old and ill and had lost interest.'

'For whatever reason, nothing's been done for the last twenty years.'

Parkfield also needed a large staff to run it. Fires had to be lit in every room. Byron was coming to the conclusion that he couldn't afford to run it. Anyway, they didn't need all this space. Nine bedrooms as well as servants' rooms.

Veronica's mouth began to develop a petulant droop, until nowadays it showed lines of permanent dissatisfaction. He knew she was disappointed. She'd wanted the status of living in a large house, of playing chatelaine. She was disenchanted with everything. Particularly with him.

Veronica had been an attractive girl thirteen years ago, tall, even a little taller than he was, and reed-slim. With her fair hair and coquettish ways, she'd swept him off his feet. She used to lift her pouting lips to be kissed, and her hands would be reaching out constantly to touch him. She wore low-necked dresses which displayed some of her heaving bosom. He'd been totally besotted with her. Their courtship had been rapid. With hindsight, Byron was afraid it had been too rapid.

As soon as she had his ring on her finger, she no longer seemed to welcome his attention. She very quickly told him that a nice man didn't bother his wife too often. She became pregnant with Grace far too quickly by her reckoning, and when she was expecting Norman two years

130

later, she moved out of Byron's bedroom and had never returned. She complained that he was making too many demands on her, and thereafter Byron found himself paying for her favours.

She'd point out a pair of earrings or a string of pearls in a shop window, and if he bought them for her, he was allowed into her bedroom. He was getting there less and less often as the years passed. Veronica thought once a month quite enough, thank you.

She was five years older than he was. It had seemed nothing thirteen years ago, but she'd aged quickly. Her body was stringy, almost emaciated, and she didn't wear dresses with low necklines any more because her ribs could be counted right up to her collar bone.

Byron was making a point of getting to the office much earlier than he used to. He had his man Perkins wake him very early with tea and toast, then fill the hip bath in his dressing room while he ate it. He'd inherited Perkins from his father too, and wasn't comfortable with being waited on hand and foot, but it meant he could be out of the house in time to catch the first tram down to Chester Street. He walked to the office from there, leaving Samuels and his car to chauffeur the children to school and Veronica to her appointments with her hairdresser.

He told himself he was worried stiff about the possibility of a world war, about keeping the business afloat if war came. He needed to start work early in the day when his head was clear.

It took him months to admit that he was there before seven thirty in order to see Evie Collins. She certainly wasn't the average cleaning lady, despite her big blue apron. He thought her beautiful. She moved quickly and with such grace that she was a delight to watch. He couldn't drag his eyes away from her dark hair and fair skin.

Once he'd established the routine of coming in early, she had his fire drawing up and his office tidy and smelling of furniture polish before he got there.

'Good morning,' she'd say with the slow smile he found so attractive, and she'd go to the kitchen and bring him a cup of steaming tea because he'd once asked her to make one.

She'd busy herself then about his office, sweeping up the hearth, piling more coal on the fire, seeming to make reasons to stay with him while he drank his tea. She was so energetic. She said she had two children but he found it hard to believe because she looked so young.

Talking to Evie made a pleasant start to his day, and though he'd have liked to let his mind linger on her, he couldn't afford to.

'I've got worries, Evie,' he'd told her. 'Thousands of them.'

She'd turned from the hearth and her deep blue eyes had searched his face. 'The war? Everybody's worried it'll come.'

He gulped at the tea and tried to explain about the business. She was frowning, as though trying to understand.

'It's a big business, but it's in poor shape. I couldn't be in a worse position to ride out a war.'

For the last decade, he'd been trying to persuade his father to sell off some of the small ships they ran, while they still could. He'd tried to point out their business had been founded in the eighteenth century and everything had changed now that they were in the twentieth.

It wasn't as if there hadn't been steam vessels sailing regularly to the African Coast since the middle of the last century – and carrying more cargo than he could, quite apart from the mail and the passengers they took. How could Henry Ball and Sons, West Africa Merchants, compete against that?

'We do,' his father had insisted. 'And we make a profit. If we're able to do that, what's the point of selling up? It's an old-fashioned business, of course it is, our family have been running it for two hundred years. You ought to be proud of that, not want to close it down.'

Byron sighed. His father had run the business for forty years and had fought against relinquishing the reins until he was in his mid-eighties. New fleets of steamers were being built up by other firms and proving very profitable. Byron felt that they were being left behind and would soon be unable to compete for business.

He'd persuaded his father to buy the *Boadicea* just after Grace was born. She was a two-masted schooner-rigged vessel of eleven thousand tons, equipped with two engines. He'd hoped it would be the first step to a modern fleet. *Boadicea* had been built in 1890 in Plymouth, one of hundreds of ships of similar size and design being built at that time. She'd been tramping coal from Cardiff to Germany and returning with a cargo of grain.

They'd renamed her the *Grace Ball*. Unfortunately she hadn't proved noticeably more profitable than the small sailing ships.

On her first voyage to the Coast, they'd had trouble with the engines. Only the fact that she had sails too made it possible for her to return to Liverpool, where repairs could be carried out.

On the second voyage they'd loaded an additional cargo of coconuts and bananas in Las Palmas. Somehow rats had got in, and by the time they reached Liverpool they'd drained the milk from the coconuts and spoiled other cargo. A great deal had had to be dumped and the ship fumigated, resulting in a net loss for both voyages.

They'd kept the *Grace Ball* for a few years but she always had problems of one sort or another. His father had insisted on selling her in Athens. He thought her unlucky and there was no persuading him to buy more steamers. He'd closed his eyes to the fact that sailing ships were being used mainly in coastal trading and that the company profits were getting smaller year by year. It had been impossible to tell him that the world was changing and the business would have to change with it or die.

'We do it cheaper under sail,' the old man had insisted. 'The wind is free. Coal costs.'

'But the iron steamships are so much bigger and faster. They carry so much more cargo.'

'And need a larger crew, which also costs. There are still thousands of small vessels like ours. They're all making a profit for their owners or they wouldn't still be in use.'

And it wasn't just the ships. The warehouse had been in use since 1842 and the office had been built a year earlier. This part of town had changed out of all recognition in that time. It had gone downhill. Everything was too small and too old-fashioned.

Byron drained his tea cup and set it back on its saucer. 'But the biggest problem, Evie, is that the whole reason for this trade has gone. What my family shipped out to the Coast was used as currency.

'At one time, everyone who went out there had to buy their trade goods first and barter them for what they needed to survive. Missionaries had to trade glass beads and gin to lease land and buy building materials to erect their churches and schools. The Catholic Church was a good customer for more than a century. Now coins and notes are used there, just as in the civilised world.'

'But aren't you still shipping trade goods out there?' Evie asked.

Byron sighed. 'The natives still like Dane guns, enamel-ware and baubles of every sort. Things like that find a ready market in the ports along the Coast, so yes, I am.'

His father had died a year ago, and since then he'd managed to reduce their fleet of fifteen small sailing ships to twelve. Now, with war on the horizon, Byron wished he'd been less concerned with the prices he'd been offered and sold more of them.

When war was declared on August Bank Holiday Monday, it gave Byron a sinking feeling in his gut. He felt real fear. He said so to Evie.

Her smile was sad. He was watching for her dimple, but it didn't come.

'All the men I know are looking forward to it. They want to get away from their dull workaday lives. They expect war to bring thrills and adventure and fun.'

'And what do the women expect, Evie?'

'Heartbreak, I suppose. They're afraid of the fighting. Afraid they'll lose their loved ones.' He saw her shudder.

'Your husband?'

She nodded. 'He's a seaman, deep-sea. Always saying he hates to leave home, hates to leave me and the children. Yet war's no sooner declared than he's writing about joining the Royal Navy. If they'll have him.'

'You can try to persuade him otherwise. He hasn't signed on yet?'

'No, he's on a tramp due in from New York next week. But he'll not change his mind. He wants to fight for his country.'

Byron sighed. 'He might not be any safer on a cargo vessel. Not in war time.' That was his own worry. He had twelve cargo vessels plying the seas.

Evie's eyes fastened on his. 'I suppose my problems

seem very straightforward?' He could see she was frightened.

'More straightforward than mine, but more important too. People are more important. Perhaps I'm lucky, I don't think war will touch my family.' He had problems with Veronica he couldn't talk about, but plenty more he wanted to get off his chest. 'But it will bring difficulties to this business.' They seemed insurmountable.

'I don't think Germany will allow us to go on trading. Do you know what our ships bring in to Liverpool?'

'Palm oil, I'm told, and sometimes parrots.'

She could always make him smile.

'The crew bring parrots back to make a bit on the side. Parrots bring high prices here. The cargo is mainly palm oil. That's what keeps the great industrial machines of Britain turning, Evie. It's also needed to make soap and margarine. It's a valuable commodity in the war effort.'

He sighed again. 'I don't think my ships will be allowed to bring it in unhindered.'

'You could lose your ships, you mean? They could be sunk by the German navy?'

'Yes, I might lose my fleet as well as my cargoes.'

In the first week of the war, Byron went down to London to find out if compensation would be paid to ship-owners affected by enemy action. No one had been prepared to assure him that it would. He was told the Government had made no decisions as yet.

But he had to make his decisions. He talked them over with Evie the following morning.

'I can't leave my ships tied up in port, earning nothing. They have to trade if I'm to pay my crews.'

Evie sighed. She seemed as troubled by his problems as he was.

'Because they represent a goodly proportion of your company capital?'

That made him smile. 'You understand something of business matters then?'

Her smile widened. 'A little, but a very different business to yours.'

'I hope so. Mine's a dying company, Evie.'

'Surely not! It's big business. An office like this, and ships . . .'

'Dying all the same.'

Byron reflected that being in charge of a dying company was far more complicated than running one that was growing. And a lot less rewarding in personal as well as financial terms. The most important thing was to conserve the wealth the business had built up in its heyday. He was afraid there might not be much more.

The company had used shipping agents in New York and also New Orleans. He'd pondered and pondered, and decided that for the duration of the war, he'd try shipping the palm oil to America. The ships could go back to the Coast loaded with bicycles and Singer sewing machines. There was a ready market for those. He wished he knew how long the war would last.

But if he did that, there would be little for him to do here in Birkenhead. For one wild night, he'd been tempted to sail for the Coast and then on to America. Run his business from there for the duration.

There were several reasons why he couldn't do that. This office was one of them. He employed over thirty people here, most on good wages, a considerable sum each month. He had to find work for his staff or close this office down. The same went for his warehouse. Otherwise the wages would be money down the drain which would eventually bankrupt him.

'There must be something you can use all this for,' Evie said, her forehead creased in thought.

'Yes,' he agreed. A West Africa merchant was very much a general merchant. 'I have trading contacts in many commodities. Salt, for instance. That's always been lucrative.'

For over a hundred years, ships had been sailing from Liverpool to the Coast carrying the weight of their registered tonnage in salt. Henry Ball and Sons had wholesaled salt to other shipping companies.

'Perhaps cloth too.' That wasn't so certain. The African Coast liked such gaudy patterns, that couldn't be sold elsewhere. Plain khaki for the army now, perhaps . . .

'I shouldn't be keeping you, Evie,' he said suddenly. 'You'll want to get home to your children, not listen to my troubles.'

'I didn't realise,' she said, going to the door, 'how difficult things were for you. Your problems make mine seem needless worries.'

When she'd gone, Byron got up from his desk to stare out of the window. He could see over the graveyard of St Mary's and over the dry docks beyond to the river. There was always something of interest going on: tugs fussing about the big ships; smaller vessels scudding up and down the river under full sail. Most of the local coastal traffic was carried under sail. There was still a future for the sort of ships he owned. Not in his business, but others would want them. They had a market price.

He sighed. He'd done no work as yet. He was hungry, having come out without a proper breakfast. He usually made himself wait until he could have an early lunch. Today, he'd go out and have egg and bacon. He couldn't get Evie Collins out of his mind and he needed a full stomach to make his decisions.

* * *

After only a few months, Evie knew that everybody was seeing the full horror that war brought. She found it terrifying. Two of Ned's brothers were killed in the trenches at Ypres with only a fortnight between them. She was spending more time with her mother-in-law, who had barely accepted Willy's death when the news reached her that Ben had died of his wounds.

'What a way for them to go.' Gertie was prostrated with grief. 'Such a struggle to bring them up, and for what? Battle fodder, that's all they were.'

And it wasn't just Ned's relatives. Evie kept hearing of neighbours and acquaintances who were losing their loved ones in the trenches. She was glad Ned had joined the navy. After all, Great Britain ruled the seas, everybody said so. Her navy was twice as strong as Germany's.

Food became scarce and almost unaffordable. Evie found it a struggle to get enough to feed her family and lodger. Now that Queenie was older, she didn't need a rest after her midday meal, so Evie couldn't have one either. She went to bed as early as she could and slept the sleep of the exhausted.

Once she'd settled into the routine of getting up early in the morning, she quite enjoyed it, particularly when the light summer mornings returned. It was a change to get out of her house. She worked alone and saw nobody but Mr Ball, who came in just as she was finishing. He always passed the time of day with her and she enjoyed that. She soon realised he was using her as a sounding board for his business worries.

'There's nothing I can do to help you,' she'd told him more than once.

'You listen, Evie. To talk my problems through makes me see them more clearly. I know then what's the best thing to do about them. So you do help.

'Wasn't I worried stiff at the beginning of the war? I was rerouteing all my ships to America, with an office full of clerks here and nothing for them to do.'

'You needn't have,' she said.

'No, they were all volunteering for the trenches like lemmings and handing in their notice. The staff melted away with the work.'

'It all turned out very well for you, Mr Ball.'

'I was lucky. And you helped. It was your idea that we should rent out some of our office space when we had no further use for it. And at the warehouse. Now we deal only in salt, we've rented storage there to other companies.'

Evie smiled. 'That's common sense. What I'd have done myself.'

'You pointed it out to me.'

'And you made sure I had just as much work by getting your tenants to pay me for their cleaning.'

'It was easy enough to make that part of the renting agreement. Better for me too. I know the whole office is looked after, and you tell me when things go wrong, like that burn on the floor. But once this war's over, they won't want to rent office space like this.'

'There you go, worrying again. You're always thinking so far ahead.'

'I have to. There'll be a lot of new offices built after the war and they'll all have central heating. No need for anyone to be setting fires in them then. I've had the roof botched here so many times.'

'Then you'll be able to rebuild this when it's over.'

'But when will that be? I hoped it would be over before now.'

'Doesn't everybody?'

Evie thought it a curious relationship. Mr Ball treated

her like an equal, going on about his business worries until she knew more about the company than Miss Pringle did, though she'd been promoted to being his personal secretary.

At home, Byron tried to avoid talking about his business to Veronica.

'What the company needs,' she was fond of telling him, 'is more dynamic management. You need to put your shoulder to the wheel and make it pay. If your father could do it, there's no reason why you can't.'

Veronica believed she knew what she was talking about. Her father had been a partner in the firm of accountants that had audited the books of Henry Ball and Sons for many years. She told Byron that it had been her ambition to follow in her father's footsteps and be an auditor too. She'd been articled to a firm of Liverpool accountants but had given up her training in its first months in order to marry him.

'We can't achieve profits like we did thirteen years ago.' Byron had done his best to explain why his business was dying.

The palm oil his father had shipped home had grown wild in the jungle. Nowadays, plantations had been planted and it was farmed. The companies owning the plantations controlled the market. Many used steam-powered vessels. The world had moved on. He couldn't compete, but he couldn't get Veronica to see that.

He'd given up trying now, since the awful suspicion that Veronica had married him for his income had become a virtual certainty. She'd grown impatient with him over the years. Increasingly demanding of money. Increasingly upset at seeing the profits of his business slide away.

He'd got into the habit of trying to head her off when

she started talking about the business, because she wouldn't listen. She argued back, nagging that he should do this or that to make more profit, trying to push him into something he didn't want to do.

That was the attraction of Evie Collins. She listened, and if she didn't have a helpful comment to make, she said nothing.

He now employed only one elderly clerk in the office and one tally clerk in the warehouse. Both were nearing retirement. Alfred, the office boy, was still with them, because he was too young for the forces. Apart from them, there was only Ida Pringle.

At the start of the war he'd employed fifteen accounts clerks. He'd been worried when they'd left practically *en masse*, worried enough to mention it to Veronica.

'I can come to the office and keep the account books for you. It'll save hiring another clerk and I shall be more reliable.'

'There's no need, Veronica,' he'd told her. 'You don't want to spend your time in the office. You've the house and the children to see to.'

'I don't intend to spend all day with you. I won't need to keep office hours like the hired staff. I think it'll be a good thing, I shall be able to put my finger on where you can make savings. It'll be good for me to take more interest in the business. The children don't need me so much now they are older, and the house ticks along. No, I need more to fill my day anyway.'

Byron was appalled. He was unable to stop her. She came when he least expected her, and nagged him to explain all manner of things with which he didn't want her to interfere.

He was relieved when the war took care of that. As the household staff left to take better-paid jobs in industry

142

now that so many men were away fighting, Veronica found she couldn't spend so much time in the office.

She complained bitterly about the amount of work needed to keep the house running. She took the business accounts home with her to do there. Byron thought it the lesser of two evils. He thought she'd soon tire of it. She wasn't the sort to keep at it for long.

It was the first of June but a miserable morning. The rain was coming down in sheets as Evie went to the office at four thirty. She shivered, feeling depressed by the shortages war was bringing. It was 1916 and nobody could see an end to it. Ned had been away since January.

She felt desperately sorry for Gertie, for two more of her sons had been killed. Only Ned remained now. He'd been very shocked to hear about Alfie, and wrote that Evie must not think it would happen to him. The law of averages was against it.

Bobby had started school and loved it. But Evie had to be prompt getting home in order to get him up and ready. She was looking forward to the time when Queenie would go too, then her day would be easier.

She went about her cleaning with her mind on other things. The food she would have to find for her family before tonight. Whether Bobby was going down with a cold. He'd seemed snuffly last night.

She'd cleaned and tidied the whole office. There were no fires to set at this time of the year, but it was such a miserable morning she'd lit one in Byron's room. Now she put on more coal, and the room began to feel warmer.

A copy of *The Times* newspaper was delivered to the office every morning. Evie saw it as one of her duties to pick it up from the doormat by the front door and put it on Byron's desk. She usually gave the headlines a cursory glance, then the following morning, after he'd tossed it aside, she'd take it home and read it carefully. It was the only means she had of following the progress of the war. Some days, Miss Pringle brought it home with her at five o'clock.

This morning, the newspaper was wet when she picked it up. She took it to Byron's office and opened it out in front of the fire.

Her eye caught the headline 'Big Naval Battle in Jutland'. She was instantly transfixed. She dropped the paper when she saw clouds of steam being sucked out of it. Then picked it up and read on. Ned was serving on the *Indefatigable*. As soon as she saw the name of the ship, she could read no more. Couldn't even see the print through the haze of tears. She knew she was shaking.

She went to the kitchen like an automaton to make Byron's cup of tea, because it was that time of the morning. Easier to do what was routine and normal. She couldn't think of Ned being in a battle. She could see him now, suntanned and smiling. There was a lump in her throat. She was filled with an awful dread.

'Evie?' She turned from the kitchen window. 'What's happened?'

She snatched up the teapot and poured tea into the cup she'd set out in readiness. 'Your tea. Shall I take it to your office?'

'What's the matter? You look as though you've seen a ghost.'

She took a deep breath and tried to stop shivering. 'Your paper. There's been a big naval battle. The headlines . . . Ned . . .'

'His ship?'

'It's mentioned.'

Evie watched Byron take another cup and saucer

from the cupboard and pour more tea.

'Drink this. Come and sit down for a minute. You look as though you're going to faint. What does it say about the battle?'

'I don't know. Couldn't read any further.' She was in a blind panic now.

'Shall I read it to you?'

She was surprised to find herself sitting in the visitor's chair in front of his desk, with the cup of tea in front of her.

'Is that what you want?'

She couldn't stop her teeth chattering. 'I want to know what's happened to him. He's dead, isn't he?'

'I don't know,' Byron said, and began to read the article very slowly.

When he came to the name of Ned's ship, HMS *Indefatigable*, Evie drew in a sharp breath.

'I'm sorry,' Byron murmured. When she looked up, his eyes were deep pools of compassion.

'That's it then? Ned's been killed?' She felt numb.

'The ship's reported as being sunk.' His voice was soft. 'But it doesn't say all the crew were lost. There were other ships nearby. The *Invincible* for one, and the *Lion*. The first thing they'd do is pick up survivors. Your husband . . . he might be safe.'

She took a sip of tea but couldn't control the gasp of agony that was choking her.

'Evie?' Byron was on his feet close to her chair. 'I wish there was something I could do . . .'

She stood up and he put his arms round her in a hug. She rested her forehead against the fine worsted of his suit and let her tears flood out. She felt him holding her close against the warmth of his body. Then he made her sit down and finish her tea.

She asked: 'How can I find out? Whether Ned's been killed . . .'

'You'll be notified officially.'

'But when? I need to know now . . .' She felt agonised.

'I'll try and find out for you. I can't promise, but I'll try.'

'Yes.'

'I'll need to know his full name and rank.'

'Able Seaman Edward Albert Collins.'

'Go home, Evie. You'll be better there. I'll let you know if I have any news.'

As she went to the door, she could see he looked very concerned.

He said: 'Shall I take you home?'

'No, I'll be all right, it's only round the corner. Anyway, I have to take Bobby to school.'

Evie wanted to hope but she knew she mustn't. Something had died within her. She knew Ned was no more.

CHAPTER NINE

When Evie had gone, Byron let out a long sigh. How could he not be moved by such obvious grief? He felt drawn to help her, take care of her during her time of trouble.

There must be some way of finding out direct, perhaps phone the Admiralty? But it was easier to ring Charles, his cousin, a Fleet Street reporter. Charles knew exactly how to get any sort of information. Might already know, for the paper published lists of those killed. He'd have to wait for an hour so so. Let Charles get to his desk. He hoped, for Evie's sake, that Edward Albert Collins had been lucky.

When Miss Pringle came to the office she already knew that Ned Collins's ship had gone down. Byron had letters to answer, and he tried to work, but he couldn't keep his mind on what he was doing, and it seemed that Miss Pringle couldn't either.

It was midday when Charles rang back to confirm the worst. Within twenty minutes of sighting the enemy fleet, the battleship *Indefatigable* had received a direct hit which had exploded its magazine and sent its fifty-foot-long picket boat flying hundreds of feet into the air. There had been no survivors from that vessel. Charles told Byron that the list of those who had perished would be published tomorrow morning within a black border. Ned Collins's name would be on it.

Byron sat for a while at his desk, wishing now that he hadn't tried to comfort Evie by telling her there was hope. He'd told her he'd let her know if he had any news; now he wished he hadn't done that either. It would go through him to see hope fade from her face. He thought he might just scribble a note and send Miss Pringle home with it. But in the end, he took his bowler and macintosh off the bentwood stand and went out.

The heavy rain of the morning had eased but it was drizzling and overcast. He'd checked Evie's address from his records. It wasn't far, only a few hundred yards. The house was one of a long row of small, flat-fronted houses. There were white net curtains at the window and the step had been recently holystoned. It looked cleaner and better cared for than its neighbours. Byron thought its smoke-grimed bricks and blue slate roof, wet and shiny in the rain, rather depressing.

Evie opened the door to him with a child in her arms; another was peering round her full skirts. She wore a simple dress of midnight blue. He'd never seen her without an apron before. Her face was white but she seemed more in control. There was the look of a madonna about her. She half smiled a welcome and stood back.

'Thank you for coming. Will you come in?'

His spirits dropped. He was going to dash all her hopes. He shook the raindrops off his bowler and followed her down the narrow hall to the back room.

'I'm afraid, Evie . . .' he began.

'I already know,' she said softly. 'This came mid-morning.' The official yellow envelope was on the table, the buff paper with the message half protruding.

'Excuse me a moment,' she said. 'I didn't take Bobby to school this morning, I think he's getting a cold, and now he's gone to sleep on my shoulder. I'll just put him down on his bed.'

When she'd gone, Byron edged the paper out of its yellow envelope, unfolded it and read: 'We regret to inform you that Able Seaman Edward Albert Collins went down with his ship . . . Please accept our sincere condolences.' He refolded the paper and pushed it back inside.

When he looked up, he saw that Evie's little daughter had been watching him from behind the rocking chair. He felt suddenly guilt-stricken. He'd been caught reading another's private correspondence.

'Hello,' he said, trying to bluff it out. 'What's your name?'

'Queenie.'

She was a beautiful child with big brown eyes that wouldn't leave his face and brown curly hair that hung to her waist. She wore a scarlet dress, covered by a fancy pinafore of broderie anglaise, and looked as well turned out as his own children.

'How old are you, Queenie?'

'Four.'

'I have a little girl, but she's a good bit older than you. Grace is twelve now.'

He felt very close to Grace, but he had to admit she wasn't as pretty as this child. Grace took after him; she'd grow up to be rather short and square.

He asked: 'Do you know who I am?'

She nodded seriously. 'Mr Ball.'

So she was intelligent too. He heard her mother's light footsteps on the stairs. When she came in, she sat down in the rocking chair and pulled the child up on her knee.

'Queenie's a lovely little girl,' he said.

'Her name's Victoria really. Ned started us all calling her Queenie.'

She was speaking more quickly than usual, and he saw now that she wasn't as much in command of herself as he'd first thought.

'And Bobby's name's not really Bobby,' the child told him, cuddling down against her mother. 'It's Robert.'

Byron thought the room surprisingly comfortable, and not unattractive. There was a fire in the kitchen range, making it cosy on this dark day.

He said: 'I'm dreadfully sorry, Evie. I wish I could have brought you better news.'

She was blinking hard. 'Awful to think he's never coming back to us.'

Byron could see love shining from her face as she spoke of her husband.

'All I've ever asked for was that we could be together. I ran away from home to be with him.'

'Did you?' He felt a stirring of interest. He'd known from the beginning that she should never have been a cleaner, that she didn't belong in this neighbourhood.

'My father didn't approve of Ned.'

'Not your class?'

'Not my father's class,' she corrected him. He realised she was using him as he'd often used her, as a sounding board for her worries. 'Class didn't matter, I knew it wouldn't. He loved me.'

'Don't you mind having to clean my office?'

'Not if it meant I could be with Ned. The trouble was, we had very little time together, and I always wanted more. He was always away. I did so want him to stay home with me. He felt he had to provide, you see. For us all.'

Byron saw the tears start to her eyes. She was struggling to control them.

'Whatever am I going to do now? I'll be the only breadwinner.'

He wanted to tell her he'd take care of everything. That he wanted very much to look after her and her family. That nothing would give him more pleasure. But he knew it wasn't the right time to say such things. Not while she was grieving like this.

'Go back to your family, Evie. They'll want to help you now.'

He could see her shaking her head sadly. 'I don't think so.' Queenie was curled up asleep on her lap now. 'At least we'll still have a roof over our heads, and I earn a little from you.'

'Not a lot. You all have to eat, and children cost more as they get older. I know, I've two of my own.'

'I'll manage somehow.'

'Evie, we talked a lot about my decisions. You helped me make them. Now the boot's on the other foot and I'd like to help you.'

'Make the right decisions, you mean?'

'In every way I can. I think your best plan is to go back to your own family. Perhaps they didn't approve of your husband, but you have beautiful children. They'll love them.'

He could see her shaking her head again. 'There's just my father.' Then, slowly, she began to tell him about her early life. 'He doesn't show his emotions, doesn't believe a man should. He didn't forgive my mother.'

Byron could hardly believe what she was telling him about her mother.

'If he couldn't forgive her, he won't forgive me,' she said. 'I can't go back.'

She told him about her Aunt Agatha. 'That's why I dress my children in pretty clothes. I want to see them look their best.' Her hand straightened out the scarlet skirt of Queenie's dress.

She spoke of the happiness Ned had brought her. Byron thought he'd been very lucky to have had her love. She'd brought warmth into his own life too.

For a year or more, he'd told himself she was too young for him, that his affection was that of a friend, but today had shown him how wrong he was. He'd felt sparks of jealousy as she spoke of her love for Ned. Such love as that had never come his way.

Byron couldn't stop himself walking past Joseph Hobson's shop. He'd meant only to look through the window but his curiosity was too much for him, and he had to find out what sort of a man Evie's father was. He went in and closed the door. The strong scent of the shop enveloped him: partly medicinal, partly disinfectant, yet with the scent of herbs and fancy soaps. This then was Evie's background.

He waited his turn amongst the really poor. He'd had a problem with his foot for several days and had put off doing anything about it. It was growing increasingly uncomfortable. He'd ask for some ointment to ease it.

He was watching Joseph Hobson as he worked methodically, slight and narrow-shouldered in his white coat. It was the turn of the woman in front of Byron. She was describing her cat's loss of fur and sore patches on his skin.

'Sounds like the mange,' Hobson said. The patient wasn't produced, but he pulverised herbs with his mortar and pestle to make a powder to dust over the cat.

'Yes?' Eyes of steel switched imperiously to Byron, who started telling him about his foot.

'I'd better see it,' Joseph ordered. He didn't wait for Byron to remove his shoe, but went back behind his counter to do something else. When he reappeared, his glance was cursory.

'Athlete's foot. I'll make up some ointment for you. It will cure it.' He looked a hard and angry man. A selfish man determined not to give an inch to others. Evie wasn't like that. She was all warmth.

Byron searched high and low through the shops to get some fruit and chocolate for Evie's children. He would have liked to buy her flowers but none seemed available. He wanted to give her comfort, but didn't know how. He still thought the best thing would be for her to take her children home and introduce them to her father. Surely he wouldn't refuse to help his only daughter and her children, not now her husband had died a hero's death, fighting for England. Not when Evie was going to need all the help she could get.

Byron deliberated whether he should go round to her house again, or give her the fruit and chocolate when she came to the office the next morning. But perhaps she wouldn't feel like coming in to work. He decided to go to see her. He couldn't get her out of his mind.

She looked surprised to see him again, but pleased with his gifts.

'It's very kind of you, Mr Ball. Thank you.'

'You don't have to come to work for the next day or two,' he said. 'You'll need time to yourself, to rest.'

'I'd rather work. Better if I keep busy. And as I said, I need the money.'

He wanted to say, I'll pay you a little more. Raise your wages. Make good the amount of your husband's allotment. He didn't, for he was afraid of offending her.

Instead, he began persuading her to go and see her father. Nagging her in the way Veronica nagged him. He was sure her father would want to help her. He didn't tell her he'd been anywhere near the pharmacy, and was surprised to find that the ointment had eased his foot already. The problem cleared up within a few days, just as Joseph Hobson had said it would.

Evie felt like a zombie in the first weeks after Ned's death.

Half the time she didn't believe he really was dead. After all, she hadn't actually seen his body, and he was away so much. She hardly knew what she was doing, but found she stuck to her usual routine even if she was in a near-trance.

She began thinking of her mother more often, as though Ned's death had awakened memories of an earlier loss. Her nightmares returned.

It had given Evie the fright of her life to see her mother in such a state.

'Only ninepence in her purse.' Father had laughed cruelly. 'She went hungry all right. I told her she would if she left. Serves her right.'

And he had predicted that Evie would suffer the same fate.

'You'll be on the same downward path. You've heard of the primrose path to hell?' He'd been full of contempt. The phrase had haunted her.

Now, without Ned, it seemed Joseph might be right. She was distraught. It scared her sick. She thought of the four pounds she had in her purse and wondered what she'd do when it was gone. She was thankful she'd made the effort to get Miss Pringle as a sub-tenant. Thankful too for her cleaning job. She knew she couldn't earn more, because she'd already done her best to add to her income. She needed Ned's help and support to bring their children up, and without his earnings, they wouldn't have enough to live on. It would be impossible for her to make ends meet.

'You mustn't worry your head about money,' Gertie Collins had comforted. 'Your dad's got plenty, hasn't he? He's well heeled. He'll not see you starve.'

'He might,' Evie said. She was afraid he would.

'I'd give my last penny to my kids,' Gertie said

indignantly. She remembered then that none of her boys was still alive, and a tear rolled down her cheek. With a little sob she added: 'Or to my grandkids. I couldn't see them starve.'

Evie put her arms round her. 'You're different, Gertie, very different.'

She was spending more time with Ned's mother, and tried to both give and take comfort. She knew Gertie couldn't help her with money. These days, she never had enough herself. When she'd had working sons living at home, there'd been money coming in. Now she had to rely on what she could earn, and Gertie never managed to keep any job very long.

She'd tried taking in washing but found that very hard, particularly when there were so many smuts from the railway yards nearby. She'd been a cleaner at the Argyle Theatre, and had odd nights as a barmaid at the Lighterman's Arms.

'I like that best,' she chuckled. 'More fun, like. But I'll never be more than a stopgap when someone's ill. A young girl behind the bar brings in trade, and I'm past doing that.'

At the moment, she had an early-morning office-cleaning job at the Westminster Bank.

'It's like getting up in the middle of the night,' she said sadly. 'And they're always finding fault with me work. Saying I'm not thorough enough. Cleaning's not my thing.'

Gertie also looked after a baby in the evenings while his mother worked as an usherette at the Queen's Hall. Evie knew she'd look after Queenie if she asked her. Now her sons were gone, Gertie loved to have her grandchildren round her. She often went to New Brighton to see Alfie's three little boys. Evie knew she'd have to pay her, though. Gertie couldn't afford to do it for nothing.

Queenie could be a bit of a handful, and in addition Bobby would need collecting from school at lunchtime and taking back. That meant a good walk from Gertie's house. Evie was afraid she'd be asking her to do too much. Gertie had been in a state before Ned's death; now she reckoned she'd paid the ultimate price for war. Five sons killed in combat. She hardly seemed to be coping now.

Her hair was in need of a wash and cut. Evie trimmed and set it for her, hoping it would make her feel better. She mended one of her dresses and took it home to wash. But it was the tip of the iceberg, and she wouldn't be able to do even that if she found more work. Gertie kept advising her to go back to her father.

'It's the only way, love. Take your pride in your hands and go. That's what I say. That's what our Ned would want you to do now.'

'My father's not the sort to . . .'

'Nonsense, Evie, you don't know what you're saying. Just look at your little Bobby. Doesn't your heart go out to him? Lovely children they are, both of them. His grandchildren. He's got plenty of money, his sort always has. He'll want to help you. Course he will. Who else would he want to give his money to?'

Evie needed a good deal of persuasion.

'Any father would want to help, especially when there are grandchildren,' Byron Ball told her. 'I know I would.'

But she'd seen the reception Joseph had given her mother when she'd come home. She was afraid Byron and Gertie were wrong, but the trouble was, she could think of no alternative. Not in the short term until Queenie went to school.

Evie felt a coward. She didn't want to ask her father for anything. The last time she had, he'd twisted her collar so hard she'd thought she'd choke, and that her end was coming.

She was scared of working close to him again. Of having to stand up to his domineering ways. She tried to tell herself things would be different now. She was older, she had her own home. And the thought of not being able to feed and clothe her children frightened her too. She'd have to go and see Father. She'd be a fool to leave any stone unturned.

Evie made up her mind to go the next Sunday. That gave her three days to bolster her courage.

By two o'clock on Sunday, she had the children ready in newly pressed clothes, with their hair washed and brushed. She'd primed them not to speak unless spoken to, and to be on their best behaviour. She felt proud of them as she walked down Argyle Street with a child swinging on each of her hands. Surely they couldn't fail to make a good impression?

She'd planned her visit for the time Father would be finishing his Sunday dinner, hoping to catch him feeling replete and content. Being Sunday, the shop was closed. For such occasions, there was a bell positioned high on the door frame, though it was rarely used. She reached up to it.

There was no response. She knew this part would have been easier if she'd come when the shop was open, but she couldn't talk to him in front of customers. She rang the bell harder. This time she heard his step on the stairs.

'All right, all right, I'm coming.' He sounded irritable. She heard him pull back the bolts. 'It is Sunday, am I to have no rest?'

The door opened six inches, and his cold grey eyes

stared into hers, astounded. She watched them go slowly from one child to the other.

'Hello, Father.'

'What do you want then?' His wiry eyebrows came down in a frown the way she remembered.

'I've come to see you. Brought my children to see you. This is Bobby and . . .'

'Two of them? Been breeding like rabbits, you and that Collins fellow. I hope he married you?'

'Yes, Father.' She hoped he wasn't going to probe too deeply into how she'd managed that.

'How many years is it now?'

'Six,' she faltered. 'Can we come in?'

'If you have to.' He stood back grudgingly. Evie's heart sank.

'How are you, Father?' He didn't look well. His hawk-nose was red at the tip and there was a bluish tinge to his chin.

'How am I? What do you care? Running away, leaving me in that park without so much as a word. I waited and waited . . . Worried stiff about you.'

'I'm sorry . . .'

'Sorry, is it?' The smell of the shop engulfed her, painfully familiar. But the sight of it was not. There were still two counters but they were back against the walls, along two sides of the square. The middle of the shop had been opened up.

'You've changed . . .'

'Modernised. Have to keep up to date.'

She was glad to see him making for the stairs. It might be easier to talk in the living room.

He asked: 'What's gone wrong, then? Something must have, to bring you back here.'

Evie swallowed hard. Nothing at all had changed

158

upstairs. The scent of Sunday's roast mutton hung heavily in the air. Her past seemed to be closing in on her.

'Ned's been killed.' Evie heard the quiver in her voice. 'He joined up at the beginning of the war, the navy. The Battle of Jutland, you read about that? He went down with his ship. Lost at sea.'

Joseph laughed cruelly. 'Really? I thought it more likely he'd be killed in a pub brawl.'

'He died a hero's death.'

'A hero – that scoundrel? Still, as things turned out, you needn't be ashamed.'

'We're proud of what he did, Father. He died for his country.'

'So that's what brings you back. You've fallen on hard times. The Collinses aren't the sort to take out insurance. Left you with nothing, has he, and two extra mouths to feed? I'm not surprised. I could foresee it happening, even if you couldn't. Though I'd have betted on the pub brawl, or that he'd go off with another lass.'

Evie could feel a ball of anger growing inside her. She swallowed it back. She had to try.

'I was hoping you'd let me come back to work on the front counter. Not a full day, I couldn't do that.'

His eyes were full of suspicion. 'Why? Won't anybody else employ you? Not worth your wages?'

'Bobby's in school, but there's Queenie to think of.' Evie squeezed her daughter's hand. 'She's a good little girl, not a lot of trouble. I thought perhaps Matilda wouldn't mind having her with her for a few hours each day while I was in the shop . . .'

'I mind, Evie,' he thundered. 'Matilda can't manage the work she has now. Look at this place. It's high time she cleaned it out.'

Queenie was twisting away, hiding her face in her

mother's skirts. Evie took a deep breath. If they were to have enough to eat, she had to get him to agree to this.

'It's just that I can't work anywhere else. Not until September. Queenie goes to school then. If you . . .'

'No! You'd be wanting to run off all the time to collect the other one from school anyway. I've been through all this before. Your mother was just the same.'

Evie closed her mind to the jibe about her mother. She felt she had to persist. 'I was hoping you'd help me, Father.'

'Help you? Why should I? You haven't given one thought to me all these years.'

'They are your grandchildren.' Gertie had thought that reason enough. Byron had thought Joseph would offer an allowance and refuse to let her work for it.

'So I'm family now, am I? It's a bit late to think of that. These children are your responsibility, not mine. No, you've made your bed and you can lie on it.'

Evie wished she hadn't come anywhere near him. His eyes were burning with venom.

'You left me, just like your mother did.'

She couldn't look at him. Her gaze went round the room, so achingly familiar.

'Yes, well, you've had your say about that.' Evie felt she'd failed. She turned away and saw Matty watching from the landing.

'Matty!' She rushed to her and kissed her cheek. A cheek that seemed to have aged much more than she would have expected in six years. 'Are you well?' Matty's round face sagged now, tired and careworn, but she was smiling at the children.

Evie introduced them, and Matty made much of them. Joseph ignored them, picking up his newspaper.

'While I'm here, Father, I'd like to collect some of my

things.' She'd left a heavy winter coat and a good pair of boots. She needed them now.

He glowered at her. 'You went. I didn't want any reminders.'

She said: 'Matty, keep an eye on my children for a moment.'

She whisked upstairs and flung open the door of her old bedroom. It pulled her up short to see that everything she'd ever owned had been cleared from the room. Every surface was bare. Every book and ornament gone. She opened her wardrobe. It was empty. The bed was draped in a grey cotton counterpane she'd never seen before. She went down to the living room more slowly. Matty had taken the children to the kitchen. Her father still glowered.

'I didn't know you'd be coming back asking for your old things. Why should I keep them for you? It is six long years.'

'I should have known you'd want everything cleared,' she said stiffly.

'I thought an apprentice might use it. Better room than those in the attic.'

Evie felt like crying. Coming back here had been a mistake. She'd known it would be. Why had she let Byron talk her into it? She turned on her heel and went to the kitchen.

'I shouldn't have come. How do you put up with him, Matty?'

'I have to.'

'You are all right?'

'I suppose so. You know how things are.'

Evie squeezed her hand sympathetically.

'Can we go home, Mummy?' Queenie tugged at her skirt.

'Yes, let's go.' She took them by the hand. The living-room door was still open. She'd been about to say goodbye to her father and tell him she wouldn't trouble him again, but a buff envelope propped up against a vase on the mantelshelf caught her eye.

'Is that a letter for me?' She went closer. It was addressed to Miss Evelina Mary Hobson.

Her father rattled his paper. 'Yes. Been here a week or two now. Didn't know what to do with it. Was thinking of putting it in the fire.'

Evie picked it up and pushed it in her pocket.

'Something to do with your Aunt Agatha, I expect.'

'What do you mean?'

'You haven't heard? She died out in the jungle. Just as I told her she would. Nobody believes what I tell them, but I'm always right.'

Evie was shocked. 'Died? When?'

'Must be a year or more now. She was another who wouldn't listen to sense. I don't know what's the matter with you women. You're all the same. Off with any man who crooks his finger at you.'

The passing years had softened Evie's feelings about Aunt Agatha. Perhaps she'd felt stifled by Father too. Evie wanted to know how she had died but Bobby was pulling on her sleeve. She asked: 'What's the matter, love?'

He whispered: 'Why doesn't he like us?'

Queenie was tugging her towards the door.

Evie said: 'We'd better go, Father.'

'Yes, you go. Everybody goes, then when things go wrong they expect me to welcome them back with open arms. I don't want you back. You'd only be off again the next time some fancy fellow looks twice at you.'

Evie went, wanting to escape as quickly as she could. She was angry. She should have known what to expect.

The children were upset too, asking questions she'd have preferred not to answer.

'How did you get on?' Miss Pringle wanted to know before she'd had time to take her hat off.

'Didn't get on at all. It was a disaster.' Ida's arms went round in her a comforting hug.

'Come and sit down, I'll put the kettle on for a cup of tea. What did he say?'

'He said no, why should he help me. It was my problem, not his.'

'There's still Gertie.'

Although Evie had decided not to ask Gertie, her mother-in-law had come round yesterday and offered to do what she could. That was Gertie's way. She'd said she'd look after Queenie if Evie could find work.

'She'd let Queenie run wild,' Evie said to Ida. Gertie couldn't control the little girl. Matty probably wouldn't be able to either, but at least in the shop Evie would have been close at hand.

The anger wouldn't leave her. Tears were stinging her eyes. She was no nearer finding a way to make ends meet.

'Oh, come on, Evie, you'll find something.'

'Whatever am I going to do without Ned? It's hopeless. I wish I could die too.'

Miss Pringle pursed her thick lips. Her tiny shoe-button eyes were sympathetic. 'Don't say such things. You've still got the children. You love them and they need you.

'You've had more from life than I've had, Evie. You still have your memories.'

Evie had put the children to bed when she remembered the letter. She went to her wardrobe and took it from the pocket of her best coat. It looked like a circular of some sort.

It was from a solicitor with an office in Hamilton Square. He invited her to call and see him, he said she'd hear something to her advantage.

Evie spent an hour speculating with Miss Pringle about what it could mean.

'Your aunt has left you something in her will.' Ida nodded wisely. 'What else can it be? Let's have more tea and I'll read your cup.'

Ida saw many dots, which she said meant that Evie was coming into money. Evie could see only miscellaneous tea leaves. She went to bed unable to think of anything else. Afraid she'd be disappointed. Afraid to hope Ida was right and that her problems might be over. But if so, she couldn't understand why Aunt Agatha hadn't left what she had to her missionary husband.

As soon as she'd put Bobby into school the next morning, she walked down to Hamilton Square with Queenie, full of hope. She found the right office. The clerk on the reception desk ushered her into an inner office to see one of the partners. He was plump and pompous and introduced himself as Mr Fenshaw.

'Ah, the estate of Mrs Agatha Evelyn Appleby. Yes, we have her will here.'

Evie discovered that it was over two years since Aunt Agatha had died, and her husband had died a few days before her in the same epidemic of blackwater fever.

'She's left you a small bequest. It amounts to . . . er, let me see. Yes, two hundred and five pounds. She says, so that you might enjoy some measure of independence.'

Evie felt relief flooding through her like a tide. It was followed by a wave of gratitude. Two hundred pounds was not a small amount to her, it was a small fortune. With that she'd be able to manage until Queenie went to school.

* * *

Evie went home feeling much better. Aunt Agatha was her saviour, the very last person she'd have expected to come to her aid. Perhaps, after all, Agatha had been fond of her but hadn't been able to show it.

The next morning Evie was full of vigour as she cleaned out the offices of Henry Ball and Sons. It gave her pleasure to tell Byron of her bequest and to ask his advice.

'Evie! That's marvellous.' He was pleased for her. She warmed to him. 'And how best to use it?

'If it's enough to buy the house you're renting, I'd do that. Then the rent Miss Pringle pays would be income you could use to live on.'

'I don't know whether it's for sale or how much it would cost. I'll have to ask the agent. Have to think about it too.'

'It would be better than putting the money in the bank and drawing on it to supplement your living expenses.'

'Yes.' That way the money could get used up and she'd have nothing to show for it. If she could buy the house, they'd always have a roof over their heads. And that seemed too good to be true.

CHAPTER TEN

That morning, after Evie had gone home to her children, Byron sat on at his desk, staring into space. He'd made up his mind to help her himself and had been waiting for the right opportunity. Now he felt cheated that she'd received help from elsewhere.

He'd been telling himself he must give her time. Take things slowly. After all, she'd shown only too clearly how much she'd loved her husband.

He couldn't stop thinking of the moment he'd held her in his arms and felt her breasts press against him. It made him tingle now. She looked so young, so vulnerable, how could any man not want to help? He'd found himself watching her closely this morning. The way her dark lashes swept her cheek. He'd never seen her look so beautiful. She had eyes that would melt an iceberg. He couldn't believe her father had refused to help.

Byron couldn't get enough of Evie's company. He couldn't keep her longer in the mornings because she had to go home to get her child off to school. He knew he was coming to the office earlier and earlier. It was the only way he could spend more time with her.

Evie had laughed, and said she was coming to the office earlier too, so that she could get her work finished before he arrived. Now, on his suggestion, she made tea for them both. They sat down together to drink it and talked of their children.

'Best half-hour of my day,' Byron dared to tell her.

'Best of mine too,' she'd responded, and sent his hopes

167

sky high. It was all he could do to stop himself crossing the room and taking her in his arms again. But it would be wrong to do such a thing. It was still too early and might upset her.

That same evening, Byron went home to find himself in the middle of a domestic crisis. He couldn't bring himself to look across the supper table at Veronica's face. He'd never seen her so angry, her grey eyes flashing vitriol in his direction. She'd already unleashed her ire on the children. They were eating silently and keeping their heads down.

'What am I supposed to do now?' she demanded. 'There's a committee meeting tonight. How am I to get to that?'

Samuels, their chauffeur, had given notice last week, and today had been his last working day. He'd been asked to move out of his rooms by this evening.

'It's hard to get staff now,' Byron tried to soothe her. 'I'm sorry. With the war, there's plenty of jobs with shorter hours and better pay.' So far, he'd failed to find a replacement.

'But have you really tried?' Her anger flared up again. 'After all, it doesn't matter to you.'

Byron had tried hard. He always tried to placate Veronica. She'd virtually taken over Samuels and the car. She expected to have them waiting, ready to drive her wherever she wanted to go.

'I suppose I'll have to learn to drive myself.'

'You'd have found that easier last year,' Byron couldn't help pointing out. 'Samuels could have shown you how.'

'Damn Samuels,' she swore, clattering her knife and fork back on her plate.

Byron had offered to drive her down to the Town Hall

tonight, and before supper had gone to check that there was petrol in the car. He found the tank virtually empty. When he looked round for the cans in which the petrol was kept, he found they'd all gone.

There should have been at least half a dozen two-gallon steel cans. He had a ten-gallon drum, and only last month had managed to buy a forty-five-gallon drum and the equipment to siphon the petrol out. It was the only way to have a ready supply, since garages catering for the motorist were few and far between. And these days petrol was scarce, expensive and very hard to come by.

Byron had lost his temper. 'When did I last drive the car? Wednesday night. It was all here then.'

He turned to Veronica. 'Where's it gone? Has Samuels taken it?'

The car was kept in the old stables, and Samuels had occupied the rooms built over them that had once housed the groom.

'He moved his things out on a hand cart,' Veronica said.

'He made several journeys with it,' Grace added.

'Did he take my petrol cans?' Byron was filled with fury. He felt cheated. The car couldn't be used until he found more petrol.

'I don't know. The cart was piled high with his clothes and things.'

'It's not my fault.' Veronica was even more enraged. 'I'd need eyes in the back of my head to see what servants get up to these days.'

Byron sighed. 'I'm not blaming anybody.' He wanted to avoid the subject of servants. Veronica could go on about the lack of them for hours.

She said: 'Perhaps, if we got a pony and trap? Everybody's going back to horses these days. I'm sure I could manage, if it was a quiet animal.'

'Could we, Daddy?' Grace turned to her father excitedly.

Byron sighed again. 'Who's going to put the pony between the shafts for you, Veronica? I don't suppose you'd feel any more capable of that than of driving? Then the beast would need feeding, and his stable mucking out. Are you going to do that?'

'I will, Daddy,' Grace said. 'A pony would be such fun.'

He said dryly: 'It would be easier to walk down for the tram, as I do every morning.'

'So I'm reduced to taking the tram? Waiting at the stop with the servant girls?'

'You can always pick up a hansom or a motor taxi to come home.'

'Surely it's possible to get a cab to come here for me?'

'You can telephone for one,' Grace said. 'I know it can be done.'

'What's the number?'

Byron felt a surge of impatience. 'Lift the phone and ask the operator. She'll know.' He made himself relax. 'Shall I do it for you?'

'And that's how I'm to get the children to school?' Veronica wasn't going to give up easily.

'They can walk. It isn't far, especially for Norman.'

'On wet mornings?' Veronica asked belligerently. 'What then?'

'There's always boarding school,' Byron said. He knew he shouldn't keep arguing with her about boarding school, not in front of Norman. He was worried about his son. Norman was a mummy's boy. Too ready to cling to her. Too ready to sit back and let others do everything for him. He was like his mother to look at, tall and angular; rather gangling at the moment. Byron had told Veronica several times that he'd like Norman to go to boarding school.

'Why?' she'd demanded. 'You said you hated it when you were sent there.'

'I didn't enjoy it,' he admitted. 'But it taught me to look after myself. It'll make Norman more independent. Able to stand on his own feet.'

'He's only ten. I don't want to part with him yet. But Grace is old enough.'

Byron met Grace's uneasy gaze. 'It's different for girls. There's a good day-school here.'

'Daddy's little girl,' Veronica sneered. 'That means you don't want to part with her.'

'I don't,' Byron said, putting his hand on Grace's shoulder to reassure her. Grace was the apple of his eye. Quicker than Norman in every way. He often wondered how his children would cope with the business he'd leave them. He was afraid Norman wouldn't, but war was changing the expectations of women, Grace would manage. One thing was certain, the business he'd hand on would be very different from the business he'd inherited.

The war dragged on; Byron was pleased with the decisions he'd made. He'd wanted to keep his ships well away from any German naval vessels, so he'd been right to direct his fleet to American ports rather than continue bringing them to Liverpool. They were still making a profit for him. It was working out well.

Many small cargo ships were being sunk by the enemy. He didn't doubt that some of his would have been, had they been in European waters. He'd been wrong about compensation, though: substantial sums were being paid by the Government for vessels that were sunk. It didn't bring back the crews, though. Many lives were being lost at sea. Byron was glad his crews were not running that risk. He'd known many of them for years and counted some as friends.

The war was making it difficult to get coal, and therefore small sailing vessels like his were commanding higher prices around the world. Everything was scarce. He still thought it right for his firm to get out of shipping altogether. Once this war was over, he'd be able to charter space on other vessels, but now he could afford to bide his time. Prices of ships would go higher as everything grew scarcer. The only ships being built were fighting ships. Until things returned to normal, he'd still make money with his old-fashioned fleet. Even Veronica conceded that she'd been wrong to insist that he continue trading out of Liverpool.

The house was another matter. The big square building set in an acre of gardens looked imposing, but the roof was leaking badly. He couldn't count the number of times he'd sent men up to fix it. As soon as they stopped the water coming in at one place, it started somewhere else. He was coming round to the opinion that it would cost more to put Parkfield right than it would to build a new house.

'We can't live in it like this,' Veronica complained one night. 'It's a miserable place at the best of times, but now, in the middle of winter, it's colder inside than it is out.' She poked the fire savagely to make it blaze up. 'All these fireplaces and no coal to speak of. What are we coming to?'

'My feet are cold,' Norman complained from the depths of an armchair, where he was reading.

'Bring your chair closer to the fire,' his mother told him.

'Do hush,' Grace said, from the desk under the window where she was trying to do her homework. 'Why don't you put on double socks if you're that cold?'

'There's going to be a hard frost tonight.' Byron was none too warm himself. 'We could close half the place down.' There were four storeys. 'Why don't we shut off the top two floors?' He thought the furniture might be worth more than the building. He'd have to see that it was properly covered and cared for until after the war.

Veronica gave a mirthless laugh. 'What do you mean, shut off the top two floors? Nobody's been up there for months. You say your business is making money, but you quibble when it comes to spending a bit to make the place habitable.'

'It's too old,' Byron said. 'Too big. It needs an army of servants to run it. Just look at the garden. One man can't keep it tidy.'

Much as he loved the house, Byron was thinking seriously of pulling it down. It was no longer practical. He was toying with the idea of building a block of flats on its site. Or perhaps he'd apply for planning permission for four individual houses, and then sell the land for development.

'Surely,' Veronica was exasperated, 'it's more important to consider where we'll live? Business, business, that's all you ever think of.'

The next morning, Byron shivered as he climbed out of bed. It was still dark and the temperature in his bedroom seemed below freezing. He began to think seriously of renting a smaller house, now, right away. Something that was easier to keep warm. The ceiling in his bedroom was fifteen feet high; downstairs the ceilings were even higher, and that made the house almost impossible to heat.

The days when he'd had a manservant to bring him morning tea and run a hot bath had long since gone. These days he made his own tea and toast and took a cup up to Veronica. Down in the kitchen, the windows were opaque with frost patterns. When he crossed the garden to the garage, every branch of every tree was white with frost. It looked beautiful, a winter's fairy tale. The air froze the back of his throat as he breathed in. It came out in visible clouds.

He was glad he'd managed to get more petrol and could drive himself down to the office on mornings like this. He inserted his starting handle and swung it hard. Again and again the engine turned over, but wouldn't fire. He swore under his breath. Unscrewed the radiator cap. He thought the water in the radiator had frozen. Perhaps it would be better to leave the car where it was. The road looked icy.

On the spur of the moment, he went back indoors. He'd bought Grace a bicycle and he wanted to tell her not to go to school on it this morning. He was afraid she might skid on the ice.

When he looked in her bedroom she was still fast asleep and breathing evenly. It seemed a shame to wake her before it was necessary. Instead, he went to Veronica's room and asked her to tell Grace when she woke up.

She scowled at him over her eiderdown. 'I can't stand this weather.' The discontented droop to her mouth had never been more noticeable.

The tram was late that morning. He carried on walking; it was too cold to stand still. He was glad to get to the office and feel the warmth of the fire Evie had built up for him.

Her smile was warm and welcoming. 'Isn't it beautiful outside today?'

Evie felt the war would never end, and she couldn't relax until it was over. It had taken Ned's life along with millions

174

of others, and she didn't want it to take more. She was managing well enough, thanks to Aunt Agatha's legacy. She'd bought her house and knew now she'd always have a home for her children.

All the same, Ned's death had left a great empty hole in her life. There were times when her memory seemed to play tricks on her. She'd wake up in the middle of the night thinking he was still on a ship plying its trade around the Mediterranean and that he'd be home soon. The moment when she realised he was gone for ever always devastated her.

She tried to tell herself she was finding things easier now that both the children were in school, but she longed for Ned. She needed Ida's help and company here in the house, and she also needed Byron and his advice. The half-hour she spent with him every morning seemed to set her up for the day. She was very fond of them both, and between them they kept her going over the first difficult months.

As time went on, she knew that Byron was becoming more important to her. She found herself thinking about him, fantasising about what he was doing when she couldn't be with him. She found herself looking forward to her time with him, saving up the little happenings in her day to tell him. If his hand should touch hers as he took his tea cup from her, it left her tingling.

They talked about everything except how they felt about each other. She worried about that as she worried about most things, and made herself think of what they shared as friendship. After all, he was a married man.

Evie did her housework in the mornings. She had to take the children backwards and forwards to school, and that meant four journeys because they came home for their dinner, but the school was near. In the afternoons, she allowed herself the luxury of an hour's rest on her bed.

She was lying down, waves of sleep washing over her, when she heard the knock on her front door. She longed to ignore it and slide into sleep. The knocking came again. More insistent now.

Still sleep-fuddled, she threw off her eiderdown, pushed her feet into her slippers and ran downstairs, fastening the belt of her frock as she went. She was shocked to find Byron Ball on her doorstep, huddling into his greatcoat, his collar turned up around his pinched face. She'd never seen him look so dejected.

'Evie?' he croaked, his eyes awash with untold misery. She was instantly awake.

'Come in.' She had to take his hand and draw him into the hall in order to close the door and shut out the cold.

'You're frozen. Has something happened?' She knew it had. He'd been quite different when she'd seen him early this morning. 'Come to the fire.'

She took away the nursery guard and poked the fire till it blazed up, then drew up a chair for him. He hadn't moved.

'Byron?' She'd never called him that to his face in all the time she'd known him. She undid the buttons of his coat. Helped him off with it. Took it and his homburg out to the hall.

When she came back, he'd moved nearer the fire and was holding out his hands to the blaze.

'Shall I make you a cup of tea?'

It was what she always did for him. Then, on the hob, she saw the pan of broth she'd made for her children's midday meal because it was such a cold day. There was plenty left.

'Some ham broth? Have you eaten?'

He was shaking his head again.

'No wonder you feel so cold.' She swung the pan over the fire. Set out a bowl on the table and cut a slice of bread. When she turned back to him, his eyes were searching into hers.

'It's Grace,' he said. Evie knew all about Grace; he spoke of her often. 'She was knocked off her bike this morning on her way to school. A cart sliding downhill on the ice. Heavily laden and out of control. Pushing the two horses. One kicked her.'

Evie felt a stab of anguish. 'Is she – badly hurt?'

'She's dead, Evie. She was taken to the children's hospital. She died there an hour or so ago.'

'Oh my God!' She could see the tears welling in his eyes and threw her arms round him, trying to give comfort. With an agonised sob he pulled her closer and put his head down on her shoulder and wept.

'Why did it have to be my Grace? Why?'

Evie shook her head. She knew what it was to lose a loved one. 'I asked myself the same question when Ned died. He had the bad luck to be in the wrong place at the wrong time, and so did your Grace.'

He was shaking his head as he told her how he should have woken her this morning. How he should have insisted that she walk to school and not left a message with Veronica.

'Did she give her your message?' Evie asked.

He took out his handkerchief and wiped his face. 'She said she did, but that Grace went on her bike anyway.'

'You did your best. You delivered a warning,' Evie insisted. 'You couldn't have done more.'

She'd never seen Veronica Ball, and Byron didn't talk about her much. Never criticised her, but said enough to let Evie know that they were not on good terms. She'd asked Ida Pringle about her.

'She used to come to the office quite a lot at one time. Couldn't half throw her weight about. Always finding fault. Nobody liked her.'

Byron blew his nose hard. 'Veronica blames me; in fact, I blame myself.'

'You mustn't . . .' She wished there was some way she could ease his anguish.

'I bought the bike for Grace when Samuels left . . . It was a thirteenth birthday present. Second-hand, it had to be, there aren't any new ones being made, but it hadn't been used much. Almost full-sized, with strings over the back wheel to stop her skirts being caught in it, and a basket on the front to carry her school books. She was over the moon with it.'

'You can't blame yourself for giving it to her.'

'Veronica says I should take the children to school in the car, not let them go alone.'

'But Grace wanted to?'

He nodded miserably. 'She said there was hardly any traffic on the road. Even so, there was so much ice this morning . . .'

'You said you couldn't start your car this morning.'

He brightened. 'That's right, I couldn't.'

'Then you couldn't have taken her to school today. It was an accident. You've got to see it as that. You mustn't feel guilty.'

'Evie, I didn't want to drive her to school. Not any morning, however bad the weather. Do you know why?' His eyes searched into hers, and she shook her head.

'Because I want to get to the office early. If I drove the children to school, I'd be too late to see you.'

Evie felt her heart turn over. She'd seen it in his eyes and wondered. It was eighteen months since Ned had died, and there were times when she longed for a loving

178

companion to share her life. She'd known for some time that she wanted it to be Byron, but she hadn't let herself hope that he would want that too.

His eyes studied her feverishly. 'I love you, Evie. Surely you must have seen . . . ?'

She couldn't speak, it was too momentous a discovery.

'So you see, I am to blame. Veronica's right.'

'No, Byron, it was an accident.' Evie's lips brushed his cheek. 'A terrible accident. Are you to watch your children every minute of the day? Could their mother not do more if she thought it needed? Could . . .'

His lips found hers. He kissed her, but he wasn't giving himself wholly to her. She understood that his mind was on this tragic accident.

He moaned: 'What am I doing? I hardly know. . .'

She made him sit down and eat some broth. The colour came back to his cheeks. She heard more of the terrible details, of how Veronica hadn't got out of bed that morning.

She felt moved by his distress and wished she knew how to comfort him, but she couldn't let him stay long. The moment came when she had to say: 'You'll have to go now, Byron. It's time for me to walk up to the school. I have to fetch my children home.'

'Can I come and see you again?' he asked as she fetched his greatcoat. 'But no, I shouldn't. Forgive me, I'm hardly myself today. It's asking too much, to come to your home.'

'I want you to,' she said gently. 'I want you to come again.' She felt wrung out with his anguish, saddened at another young life abruptly ended.

Evie had never found getting up in the morning so easy. It was a delight to go to the office and get it ready for another day's work. She found herself listening for Byron's step on the stairs when the time drew close.

He'd come running up to kiss her as though it was his greatest pleasure in life. Almost every day, he'd ask if he might come to her house later on, when he knew she'd be alone.

She always put on her best clothes and redid her hair when her housework was finished so that she looked her best for him. Often, from her own little room over the front door, she'd lift her bedroom nets to watch for him coming and feel a shiver of pleasure when she saw him walking down the street.

In his homburg hat and heavy overcoat, Byron looked out of place in Leicester Street. He was not a handsome man in the way Ned had been, but he had an endearing habit of tossing his straight brown hair back from his forehead.

'I shouldn't come.' He smiled guiltily. 'I know it's wrong.'

Evie knew it too, but for once refused to listen to her conscience.

'I look forward to your visits,' she told him. 'I love having you here. All to myself.'

She wondered how she'd come to fall in love with him when he was the very opposite of Ned. He was so much older, more polished and more formal. There were twelve years between them, and he'd seemed too old at first, but now those years were falling away. There was intimacy in his smile and a yearning in his dark eyes that drew her close.

For the first time, Evie had a secret she kept from Gertie Collins and Ida Pringle. She was careful now never to mention Byron's name to either, but occasionally Ida would talk of him. She told Evie he was popular with his staff and had a reputation for treating everybody fairly.

He was a good man to work for, but her colleagues were somewhat in awe of him. It was yes, Mr Ball, and no, Mr Ball. He was the boss and he kept his distance.

That wasn't how Evie saw him at all. What she felt for Byron had crept up on her gradually, and she was very glad it had.

'I count myself lucky,' she told him. 'I thought when Ned died I'd never feel like this again.'

'Evie love, you've transformed my life. I find such peace here with you, but I'm putting you in a terrible position. I'm a married man.'

He'd held her in his arms as he told her about Veronica. How she was the sort of person who took; who thought only of herself. How she wanted money and possessions and status more than she wanted love.

'You're so different. You're the sort that gives, but I'm not sure I should let you.'

'It's what I want.'

'You're an honest widow and I'm going to ruin your reputation. I'll be seen coming here to your house. Your neighbours will count the hours I'm alone with you.'

'My next-door neighbour did ask.' Evie smiled. 'She wanted to know if you were my father.'

He laughed. 'Do I look that much older than you?'

'Not really. You look more sophisticated.'

He sighed. 'You do realise what you're getting into? I'm taking advantage of you.'

'No, you're not doing that. You're urging me to think carefully before I do anything.'

'I've so little to offer you. We met too late.'

Evie knew that the only way she could have his love was to become his mistress. She had plenty of time to think about it. She felt she was learning to be less nerve-racked about the decisions she had to make. She'd flouted the rules of society before. She'd been only eighteen when she'd left home to be with Ned. Society didn't matter to her; what she'd done had been right for her then.

She'd been a widow now for two years and saw this as her second chance. She felt stronger now that she was twenty-six, and she was sure that Byron was right for her.

He took a late lunch break and came regularly to her house now, timing his visit for when she'd return from putting her children in afternoon school. It was another wet day, and she insisted in shaking the rain off his coat before she hung it on her hall stand.

'Even your face is wet.' His white handkerchief was showing in his breast pocket. She pulled it out to mop his face. He laughed and caught her in his arms. 'You take such good care of me.'

'I love you,' she whispered, and felt his arms tighten round her.

'You're sure, Evie? Quite sure?' She looked up into dark eyes that were shining with love. They held her gaze and she saw in them a need as great as her own.

'Certain.' She took a long, quivering breath. 'Absolutely certain.'

After six years of married life she felt well versed in the ways of men. She'd known that this moment would come. This morning, she'd put clean sheets on her bed and made her little room fresh and spotless. Now, as she took him up the narrow stairs, her heart was drumming in anticipation.

At the foot of her little white bed, he caught her to him. 'I feel very honoured,' he whispered before their mouths touched.

When the long years of the war finally came to an end in

November 1918, all England rejoiced. Byron felt he had much to be thankful for. It had played havoc with his business but he'd had time to make careful plans for when it was over. In the early months of peace, he started selling off his fleet of old-fashioned sailing vessels and was delighted with the high prices they achieved.

Trade between Liverpool and West Africa opened up again. Byron started sending out goods of the sort that had traditionally sold well out there: salt and cotton cloth, Dane guns and enamelware. If he hadn't a ship of his own to transport them, he chartered space on the mail boat that sailed every two weeks. Profits would never be what they had been, but it was the only business he knew.

He bought a building plot in the best part of Oxton, and Veronica started planning the new house. He would sell Parkfield when it was ready.

He also planned to put the office on the market. It was too old to keep patching up, and the whole focus of the town had changed. There was heavy industry all round him. It no longer suited his kind of business. Other companies in similar trades had moved elsewhere.

When Byron had heard in the second year of the war, that J. S. Connaught and Company was going into liquidation, he knew it was only through forethought and exceptional luck that his company had avoided the same fate.

The Connaught shipping line had had a much larger fleet of small sailing vessels than he'd had. Like his, they were old-fashioned. They'd also had a very fine office building in South Castle Street, the business centre of Liverpool. He'd had his eye on it for the last few years, waiting for the right time to buy.

He'd secured it a month before the end of the war at a knock-down price. He'd been lucky with his timing. He hoped that now the war was over, the site alone would be worth what he'd paid for it.

He'd talked to Evie many times about moving his office from Knox Street when the war was over. But now, quite suddenly, the moment was here, and he could see she was alarmed.

'The Connaught Building! It's too far for me to come in the mornings. I have to be home again before eight to get the children to school. And there's Ida Pringle to think of . . . She only took rooms with me because it was handy.'

'I'll bear your circumstances in mind, Evie. Of course I will.'

'But if you move . . . I mean, why central Liverpool?'

'I hope to get more business there.'

'Impossible for me. I can't . . .'

He took her hands in his. 'Listen a moment. It's just the place. The Connaught Line was a prestigious business when I was growing up. The building needs refurbishing from top to bottom, but when it's done, I'll be proud to own it.'

'It's big? Too big?'

'I'll only need a fraction of the space. I'm thinking of renting out the rest, floor by floor or even room by room.'

'But what about . . .'

'What about you?' He kissed her cheek. 'Would I forget about you? There's a flat on top. Three bedrooms and a much bigger living room than this. I'll put in a proper bathroom, central heating and electric light. You won't know yourself, everything you could wish for. What do you say?'

'You make it sound so easy . . .'

'It will be, Evie, I promise. There's nothing for you to worry about. I'll put in whatever you want.'

'It's not that. It's a big step. And Liverpool . . .'

'Right in the middle of the business centre.'

'The children will have to move schools.'

'Does that matter?'

'Perhaps not.'

'I'll help you find good ones. They won't lose out, I promise. I know you want to bring them up so they'll be able to earn a good living.'

He could see Evie turning it over in her mind. 'Say you will, love,' he urged.

She smiled. 'If you say it will be all right.'

He swept her into a bear hug. 'I promise. There'll be no outside privies there. Officially you'll be the caretaker, but I'll hire somebody to do the work. I don't want you to . . .'

'I want to work, Byron.' He could see she meant it.

'Then you won't have to do too much.'

'Just fancy – I won't have to leave the building to do it either.'

'I'll be just downstairs all day and can come up any time. You could even come down to see me.'

'What about this house?'

'Rent it out. If it were mine, that's what you'd tell me.'

He loved to see Evie smile like this. It spread across her face, lighting up her eyes and showing her dimple. 'It sounds just the thing.'

CHAPTER ELEVEN

Evie loved to have Byron sit back in the armchair by her fire and hold forth on every subject under the sun. She told him she was afraid she might fall pregnant. For her it happened very easily.

'You're a terrible worrier,' he said, but he was sympathetic. 'It won't happen, I'm taking care of that.' He'd read books by Marie Stopes and thought he understood how to avoid it. He explained it at great length to Evie. She wanted to believe he was right. He was so much wiser in the ways of the world.

Evie was always uneasy if she went beyond her dates. It had happened once or twice. This time it had dragged on until she was several days overdue. She woke up one morning and the signs were unmistakable. She'd had two babies already; she knew she was pregnant again. It was eight months since she'd first led Byron up to her bedroom.

She felt catapulted into another crisis. She'd been through all this before with Ned. The first panic, the difficult decisions she'd have to make. And this time she couldn't run away to marry the father.

She had to dress hastily and rush out to the yard in the darkness of pre-dawn to be sick. She walked slowly to the office and went about her duties, waiting for Byron to come. She told herself he was a truly kind man and she could trust him. He came running upstairs as he always did to take her in his arms.

She whispered straight away: 'Byron, I think I'm having a baby.'

To break it more gently, she'd introduced doubt, though she felt none herself. His lips were against hers. He jerked back to look at her.

'My God! I'm sorry, I'm terribly sorry . . .' The colour had drained from his face. He looked scared, and that frightened her. She'd been trying to tell herself he'd be pleased. Not immediately, perhaps, but when he'd had time to get over the shock.

'I was so sure,' he said through tight lips. 'Those sheaths . . . It's my fault.'

She felt the tears start to her eyes. 'It takes two to do it.'

He smiled, pushed his brown hair back from his forehead. 'I'm sorry, love.'

'Don't be.' She felt a tear roll down her cheek.

'You're not?' His finger wiped it gently away.

Evie took a deep, shuddering breath. 'I'm nerve-racked. Frightened. It's not going to be easy. How do I tell my mother-in-law? And Miss Pringle?'

'Oh God, Miss Pringle.' His fingers stroked her face.

Evie tried to pull herself together. 'I'm a fatalist, I suppose. I half expected it to happen. I've been through this before. I'm trying not to be totally sorry. I like babies.'

'So do I, love, but there's a time and a place. We aren't married.'

'No,' she said quietly. She was assailed by terrible fears. Did he love her enough?'

'What am I thinking of?' Byron's lips came down gently on hers and his arms tightened round her again. 'Forgive me, Evie. I'll look after you. See you're all right. Of course I will.'

'You're pleased? Now you've got used to the idea?'

'I'm not used to it.' He was trying to smile. 'Not yet. I'm still in a state of shock. Give me time.'

* * *

January 1919 was cold and wet. The winter stretched ahead. The war might be over, but the shortages of everything were still with them.

Byron had worked on after the office closed that day, partly because he'd spent three hours with Evie at lunchtime and he had work he needed to finish.

It was dusk when he alighted from the tram and walked the last few yards home. He'd had no petrol for the car this month. He was thinking of his daughter, Grace. There were still days when he mourned for her. Thirteen years was a pitifully short life, and he'd had such high hopes for her.

Against the darkening sky, the black mass of Parkfield looked cold and uninviting. As he let himself in through the front door, he expected Veronica to greet him with more complaints about the house. The new one was like a dream, impossibly distant because there were no building materials available. The hall felt icy. He could see one of the curtains fluttering in the draught.

'There you are, Byron.' Veronica came dancing across the hall to kiss his cheek. It seemed a long time since she'd done that. 'You're late this evening, I was beginning to think something must have happened to you.' She was helping him off with his overcoat.

He tried not to recoil from such unusual behaviour. She smiled and said: 'Come and have a drink before dinner. There's just time.'

He was being led towards his father's old study. For the last few years they'd used that instead of the drawing room, which was over thirty feet square and impossible to heat from one fire. Even here, as well as the fire, Veronica had a paraffin heater, though it was giving out more fumes than warmth. She was still smiling at him, putting a tumbler of whisky and water into his hand, mixed just as he liked it.

'I've been into town today.' Her tone was oddly flirtatious. 'You know I've been looking for a fur coat? I really need it, and goodness knows how much longer this weather will last. There's nothing in the shops, of course. Well, they had a few cheap ones in coney. Nothing I liked.'

Byron knew what was coming now. Veronica wanted more money from him to buy a fur coat. He sat down, tried to switch off from her. She came and sat on the arm of his chair.

'I saw this chinchilla coat at Broads. Not new, but they said they could remodel it to fit me. It seems to be the only way to get decent furs now, don't you think?'

Byron sipped his whisky. 'I'd take the coney. It'll keep you warm and at least it'll be new.'

'Oh, but they said the chinchilla belonged to minor royalty. Supreme quality, there's a beautiful shine on the fur. It would be completely relined and nobody would know it wasn't new.'

'You do what you want.' Byron knew she would anyway.

'I want the chinchilla. I've made up my mind, but it will be quite expensive.'

'Anything you want is bound to be.'

'I was wondering if you'd help me buy it? I need another fifty.'

Byron sighed. It had taken Veronica a little longer than usual to get round to it. He opened his mouth to say no, that he gave her a very generous allowance and she must learn to manage on it. She didn't give him the chance.

'I'll just refill your glass.' She snatched it from his fingers. 'Then we must go and eat.'

They'd given up eating meals in the dining room except

in high summer. Nowadays they ate in the kitchen where
the Aga was kept burning day and night. It was the only
really warm room in the house. They had supper at seven
o'clock sharp, so that Mrs Tilley, who came in daily, could
get it on the table before going home. She was putting on
her hat and coat in readiness now.

Byron felt the light and warmth envelop him. The
savoury scent of steak and kidney pie cheered him. Mrs
Tilley had a light hand with pastry. Norman was playing
with his train set in the corner.

'Wash your hands and come and sit at the table, dear.'
Veronica was pretending to be an entirely different person,
light-hearted, loving even. Byron knew that if he gave her
the money she wanted, he'd be offered a rare visit to her
bedroom. Veronica was building up to it. Then, as soon as
she had what she wanted, she'd be back to carping
normality.

He couldn't help but watch her eating on the other
side of the table, comparing her to Evie. Evie was the sort
who gave freely; all she wanted was his love. From time to
time he took her little gifts that Veronica would despise. A
dozen eggs, a joint of beef. Some pears from the garden
here. His reward was to see her face light up and her blue
eyes sparkle as she thanked him.

He thought Evie truly beautiful, and he loved to sit
beside her fire in her cosy little house. He felt heavy with
guilt. It made matters worse because she'd said:

'I love you. Of course I want your child. Don't worry.
It's not all bad. At least Bobby and Queenie are too young.
I mean, they won't realise it's a half-brother or sister.'

He did worry. A child was a responsibility. Evie was a
responsibility now. He had to do his best for them.

When they'd finished their meal, Norman filled the sink
with water and dumped all the dirty dishes in it to await

Mrs Tilley's return in the morning. Veronica put away the food that remained.

Byron went back to his father's study to sit by the smoking fire, while Veronica oversaw Norman's homework and preparations for bed. She'd come to him, he knew, probably wearing what she considered to be her most glamorous négligé. She'd perch on the arm of his chair and eventually lead him up to her bedroom where, for once, she'd have lit the fire to take the chill off the room.

He poured himself another drink and made up his mind that this time he would not go along with Veronica's plans.

Two hours later, Norman came to say good night to him. He was a thin child, underweight for his age. Veronica devoted a good deal of time and energy to his homework but he didn't get good reports from school. Byron longed for Grace . . .

He'd got up to get himself another whisky when he heard Veronica's step in the hall. As he'd guessed, she was wearing a pink satin housecoat over a matching nightdress of pink lace.

'There you are, Byron,' she said, and ran her hand up his arm. 'Now then, would you like another whisky?'

'I'm helping myself as I usually do,' he said.

'I'm only trying to please you.' She gave a self-deprecating little laugh. 'You know that.'

'Too true,' he sighed.

'What would please you, Byron?' She was smiling, inviting him to suggest sex. How many times had he done that on cue? She teased, 'What can I give you?'

He took a deep breath. 'What I really want is a divorce.'

'Don't be silly . . .' Her smile was uneasy. It slid away, leaving a look of sour disbelief.

'I mean it.'

'No!' She was shocked. Her face was twisted and ugly.

192

'I'm a practising Catholic. I don't believe in divorce. You don't either.'

Byron tried to keep calm. 'I've changed my mind. You don't love me, Veronica. I doubt you ever did. You married me because you thought I'd be a good meal ticket. And you're disappointed even in that.'

Her eyes shone with horror. 'You married me for better or for worse. In the sight of God you promised to . . .'

'I know that . . . Haven't I been paying for it ever since?'

Byron knew that money had always been important to him. He'd spent years struggling to keep his business afloat; years working hard to stop the fortune his family had built up from leaking away. Now, suddenly, he was prepared to give it away. Evie was more important to him than money.

'I'll play fair with you,' he said slowly. 'I'll make over to you half of everything I have. You'll have your meal ticket and be able to buy as many fur coats as you want.' No use pretending it didn't hurt; he'd balked at doing this for a long time.

'No! A divorced woman! Are you going to turn me into that? Ruin my reputation? I won't be accepted anywhere. What sort of a life would I have then?'

'What sort of a life do we have now? Either of us? You can be the innocent party and divorce me. I'll arrange it. I'll give you grounds.'

Veronica straightened up. There was disgust in every line of her face.

'You've got another woman, haven't you? A fancy woman. A mistress.'

Byron winced but said evenly: 'There's somebody else, yes. Somebody I love.'

'Oh, don't tell me! You've got her pregnant. You want to make an honest woman of her.'

Byron swallowed. He didn't have to admit that that was the truth. His face told her everything.

'You want to make your bastard legitimate! Well, I'm not going to let you.'

She turned on him even more fiercely. 'I deserve better than this. I've borne two children for you, kept a good home for you, given you the best years of my life . . . I won't let you toss me aside.' She took another rasping breath. 'And what about Norman?'

'He'll want to stay with you. You're closer to him than I am. You shall have full custody.'

'But what about the business? You want to split everything in two. You'll leave your share to your fancy woman and her children. Norman will be the one to lose out. I'll not have that.'

'I'll treat him fairly.'

'You inherited it from your father. It's only fair Norman should have it in his turn.'

'Yes, well, if he's interested when he grows up.'

'It sounds as though you want to cut him out! You're going to . . .'

'No, Veronica. Norman can start working in the business just as I did, when he leaves school . . . If that's what he wants. If there's any sort of business left. It's difficult to see what the future holds there.'

'You want to throw us both over. Do us both down.'

'I won't do either of you down. Norman is still my son, I have no quarrel with him. What I want is my freedom. A divorce. I want to call an end to all this pretence.'

'Never! I'll never agree to it. Not on any terms. In the eyes of God I'm your wife and always will be. Your bastard will stay a bastard in my lifetime.'

Byron felt full of frustrations. He consulted a solicitor

about getting a divorce, but was told Veronica had given him no grounds for it. He was the guilty party, the one who'd committed adultery. If she was condoning that and didn't want a divorce, then there was nothing he could do about it.

He knew he had to change the direction of his business to meet present-day conditions, and was eager to make a start.

It was no longer necessary to be a ship-owner to trade with West Africa. Goods could be sent out quite cheaply on the mail boat, and it seemed to Byron that many small manufacturers were trying to gain a foothold in the market. He thought that with his experience and knowledge of import and export regulations, he could meet a growing need by acting for those who wished to sell abroad. He wanted to develop this if he could.

He now had plenty of capital, because he'd sold all his old-fashioned fleet. The last four had gone to a firm in Haiti and would carry cargo round the Caribbean.

He felt he'd done very well from them. Throughout the war, his sailing ships, mostly of less than a thousand tons, had sailed from Lagos to New York with cargoes of palm oil, rubber, parrots and monkeys and returned to the Coast with sewing machines, rum, tobacco and patent medicines. The round trip had taken six months and they'd been very much in demand when the war made steamers scarce. He'd lost none from enemy action. Several were now registered in Monrovia. All had made high prices, even the barque *Elma*, nearly forty years old.

With the capital, he'd bought shares in the businesses of others. It meant less work and worry, and provided him with income. He hoped business would boom for everybody as the country recovered from the effects of the war.

His plans for the new office were making only slow progress. He knew exactly what he wanted done to bring the building he'd bought in Liverpool up to date, but there were constant delays: getting the materials to do it was difficult. He wanted it finished so that Evie could move in.

He knew he'd put Evie in a vulnerable position and that it was in her nature to be nervous.

She said: 'I'm all right, Byron. I'm not going to worry about money or anything. I'm taking each day as it comes.'

'Are you worried about money?'

Byron could see she was, and it filled him with guilt and remorse. He eased his conscience by consulting his stockbroker and asking him to work out a balanced investment portfolio. Then he invested a good slice of his capital in Evie's name and gave her the share certificates. When she saw them, her blue eyes were wide with astonishment.

'Byron! It's a fortune! You've made all this over to me?'

'I don't want you to worry about money. It isn't important.'

'It is if you haven't enough for your needs. It was just the thought of another mouth to feed . . . In the years ahead, I mean. I wouldn't know what to do with money like this.'

'There's nothing you need to do. Leave it where it is,' he told her. 'I've opened a bank account for you. The income the capital earns will be paid in there. Enough for you to live on.'

'You don't have to . . .'

'I do. You're having my child. You must have financial security. Enough money to take care of yourself and your children.'

'But it's more than I'll ever need.'

'No, I want you to feel secure whatever happens. I don't want you to have to work.'

'If I hadn't been cleaning your office, we'd never have met. I don't think I want to stop just yet.'

'I do love you, Evie.'

She smiled and he saw her dimple come and go. 'I didn't think I'd ever have money like this. I don't know how to thank you . . .'

'You don't have to.'

'It's very generous . . .'

He smiled. 'I want you to think I'm generous, and I want to keep it away from Veronica.'

He felt a little guilty about that, but he made atonement by allowing Veronica to choose exactly the sort of house she wanted built on the site he'd bought. It wasn't going to be over-large. It had every modern convenience, so she'd be able to run it with just a cook-general and some daily help with the heavy cleaning. It was taking a long time to complete and it wasn't going to be to his taste, but he didn't mind that. He wasn't intending to live in it. Not now.

He sold the old house for its site and was sorry to see it being pulled down. It was the end to an era. It didn't please him at all when Veronica wanted to call the new house Parkfield too.

Evie had been filled with relief when he'd seen her in the office this morning.

'I made myself tell Gertie Collins yesterday. Time's going on and I didn't want her to notice. Not without my saying something first.' She was smiling, showing the dimples in her cheeks.

'Do you know what she said? I can hardly believe it. "I went through three husbands, Evie, but our Ned wasn't fathered by any of them. That's why he was different. His father was a lovely man and Ned took after him. Married to someone else just like your fellow, he was. I'm not going to say it's wrong. I know things would have been different if our Ned was still alive." '

Evie had gulped. 'I was too full to say anything to her. I don't think Ned knew that about his father.'

This was one of the things Byron enjoyed about Evie. She was so happy when things worked out well for her. She never blamed him for making the problem in the first place.

He said: 'Are you going to tell Ida Pringle?'

'She keeps wanting to read my tea cup. She'll see it there sooner or later. Shall I tell her?'

'That's up to you, love.'

'It just that she knows both of us. It makes it that much harder.'

'I've told her I'm moving the office to Liverpool, but not that you'll have a flat in the building.'

'I'm going to have to say something soon. I don't want to upset her. She's upset enough about the new office. About having to travel further to work.'

He sipped at the tea she'd made for him. 'I'd rather you didn't offer her lodgings, Evie. We'd have no privacy if she lived with you. After all, if the flat was her home, she could pop up any time too.'

'She's been a good friend . . . We get on well.'

'With the new baby, you'll need all three of the bedrooms there. Bobby needs his own room now he's getting older. It'll mean big changes for us all.'

'Ida doesn't like changes. She's only got another year before she retires and she'd prefer things to stay as they are.'

'That's an idea!' Byron grinned at her. 'I could make it

worth her while to retire when we move. Wouldn't that be the best thing? What do you say?'

Evie had laughed up at him. 'She's looking forward to it. I don't think you'll have to twist her arm.'

'But you agree? It'll be safer for us. Nobody need notice me coming and going to your flat. You'll be happy with that?'

'Of course I'll be happy. If you talk to her about retirement, I'll tell her about us.'

Ida watched Evie frying the cod. It was filling the little kitchen with such heavenly scents. Evie was moving with quick, neat movements between the table and the stove. She was full of bounce and energy. It was impossible to believe she'd been up at half past four this morning.

'Are we ready?' Evie turned from the stove to check that they had what they needed on the table.

'Yes.' There were times when Ida couldn't take her eyes from Evie's face. Her fair skin had a slight sprinkling of freckles that gave her face a glow. Once, seeing such stunning looks would have given Ida a twinge of jealousy. Fate was so unfair. She was podgy and plain while Evie was really beautiful. But now she knew better. Evie's looks brought her the wrong sort of attention. Ida was afraid that men wouldn't leave her alone.

'Is the fish all right?' Evie was asking, and her blue eyes seemed to see what Ida was thinking.

'It's lovely. You're a good cook, Evie.'

Ida wondered for the umpteenth time whether she'd done the right thing by arranging for Evie to work at Henry Ball and Sons. There'd been rumours going round the office for some time. She'd ignored them. It could be sour grapes. Evie's looks could make other women jealous enough to say things that weren't true.

But it was whispered again that Evie Collins had caught
the eye of the boss. That Byron Ball came in to the office
every morning to see her. To be alone with her for half an
hour.

At first, Ida had found that hard to believe. Mr Ball
was a married man and a gentleman. He'd know he had
no right to be looking at Evie Collins.

But on the way home from the office this evening, Ida
had fallen in step with their next-door neighbour, a frail,
elderly spinster, and offered to carry some of her shopping.
The woman happened to say how close Evie and her father
seemed, and how nice it was to see families like that. He
was coming to the house to see Evie almost every day.

'Such a nice man. Don't see many as well dressed as
him any more. Always wears a hamburg.'

Ida was truly shocked. Evie had told her all about her
father, so she knew it couldn't be him.

Her mouth was suddenly dry. 'And a dark overcoat?'

'Yes, always says good morning if he sees me.'

It sounded like Mr Ball. For the first time Ida believed
the rumours she'd heard. The truth must be worse if he
was coming to the house nearly every day. Of course, he'd
know she was safely in the office; he'd see her typing away
at her desk before he set off.

And he was going out more than he used to. It was
every day! And never at lunchtime, when Ida would be
free to go home. At one time he used to tell her where he
was going, but not any more. Ida felt quite shaky with the
shock.

What was Evie thinking of? Getting embroiled with
another man, even a gentleman like Mr Ball. Men were
all the same. Only one thing they ever thought of.

But Evie could land herself in the most desperate
trouble this way. Ida ought to warn her, but how? Evie

hadn't confided in her. She wasn't supposed to know about this, and Mr Ball was her boss!

Ida made a pot of tea while Evie cleared the table, and afterwards suggested that she read her cup. When she looked at the scattering of tea leaves adhering to the sides, Ida wasn't sure what she was seeing, but she laid it on thick.

'I see crossed knives,' she said ominously. 'That means trouble.'

'What sort of trouble?' Evie wanted to know, not one whit worried. Ida wanted to say 'man trouble', but the words stuck in her gullet. She didn't want to fall out with Evie over this. She might be in need of her friends.

'There's another knife here at the very tip, blade upwards, that indicates scandal.'

Evie had been poking up the fire, but that brought her face jerking round.

'It won't be long coming,' Ida went on. 'It's near the brim, that means it's immediate. It's on the handle side too, which represents home.'

Evie was somewhat taken aback. Ida knew that that had registered. For good measure, she threw in another warning.

'There are leaves at the bottom of the cup and they generally mean ill fortune. Not a future to look forward to, I'm afraid.'

She could see the colour draining from Evie's cheeks. 'Thank goodness it's only the tea leaves saying these things,' she said in a strangled voice.

'I believe them. You said you did too. Didn't I tell you Queenie was on the way before you knew it yourself?'

Evie spent the next three days wondering just how much Miss Pringle knew. Byron said there was no way she could know anything. But the dire prophecies she'd made under the guise of reading Evie's cup had seemed like a warning. Evie wanted to tell her, to get it off her chest. It was going round in her mind, making her anxious. She felt she'd lost an opportunity not to have done it then. The prophecies had taken her by surprise. She hadn't been able to think fast enough.

A couple of days later, a Saturday, Ida came home from the office at lunchtime positively beaming.

'Such a weight off my mind, Evie, I can tell you. I was dreading that journey into Liverpool every day.' Her podgy face shone with relief.

'You're a bit later than usual.'

'Mr Ball wanted a word. I stayed talking.'

'I've made us some ham sandwiches. The children have gone to Gertie's.'

Ida sat down by Evie's fire as usual. 'Mr Ball's very generous. He's offered me the same pension I'd get if I worked for another year. He said I was the best secretary he'd ever had and he'd be sorry to lose my services, but he quite understood. All these changes, it was asking too much of me.'

Evie knew this was her chance. She was casting about for the words to tell her, but Ida went on.

'I'm afraid it's the end for you too, Evie. Liverpool's much too far away. Goodness knows why he has to change everything, but perhaps it's all for the best.' Evie didn't doubt Ida was pleased about that too. 'We'll both have much quieter lives.'

Evie poured them each a cup of tea. She had to get it out now. 'Mr Ball's been explaining his plans for me too. Guess what? He's asked me to be the caretaker of his new building.'

Miss Pringle gasped audibly. Evie rushed to tell her

more. 'It's much bigger than the old one and he's going to rent off most of the space.'

'But how can you get back in time to get the children to school?' Miss Pringle's eyes were mere slits above her plump cheeks.

'There's going to be a flat on top. I'm to have it rent-free. There's electric light and a proper bathroom . . .'

'You'll be living there?' There was no mistaking the horror in Ida's voice. 'Evie, I don't think you . . .'

'This is private information, Ida.' Evie swallowed hard. 'You mustn't say anything in the office. Mr Ball wouldn't want that. You see, he and I have an understanding.'

Miss Pringle's puffy eyelids lifted higher than Evie had ever seen them before. Her black button-like eyes were round with shock.

'You were right when you saw the horse and the parasol in my cup. Two . . . admirers. Ned and Byron Ball.'

Miss Pringle's Adam's apple was lost in folds of flesh, but Evie saw it move. Then Ida reached across the table and took both her hands in hers.

'Don't do it, Evie. You can't trust a man like that! There's only one thing they're after. Living there with just the children, you'd have no protection. He could do what he likes once the offices empty, and who's to know? Don't do it.'

'I've said I will . . .' Evie would have liked to chicken out. Leave the rest of her confession until later, but there was no stopping Ida.

'He'll use you, ruin you. Tell him you've changed your mind,' she urged earnestly. 'Before it's too late.'

Evie took a deep breath. 'It's already too late,' she said slowly. 'I'm expecting his baby.'

CHAPTER TWELVE

Evie was unhappy about the way Ida had taken her news. Her manner cooled. She was prickly with ill humour.

'Byron Ball of all people! Having a child by him! Going to live under a roof that he owns. You'll be a kept woman! I'd be terrified. I don't know how you dare.'

Evie didn't want to admit to Ida that she had any misgivings.

'I did dare.' Now with a baby coming there could be no drawing back. Her only comfort was that this had happened before, with Ned, and had turned out fine. 'I have to trust Byron.'

'Trust him? You've sold your body. You might as well trust the devil.'

Ida's frostiness upset Evie and brought back all her old anxieties. She wasn't sleeping well; she had a nightmare, and felt her father's strangling fingers on her throat. She woke up choking. It revived all the unsettling memories of her mother. She wondered for the umpteenth time what had happened to Helen after she'd left the shop.

Evie poured all this out to Byron early on Monday morning.

He said rather sadly: 'I seem to be bringing you nothing but trouble. You can trust me, Evie, I promise. I shall try very hard to make you happy.'

She nodded and tried to smile. Ned had said much the same thing, in similar circumstances.

'I wish I wasn't such a bag of nerves.'

He took her hand between his. 'You aren't usually.

Bringing a baby into the world is a big responsibility. I'm just the same. When I have a new problem all my old ones return to overwhelm me.'

'Really? Gertie calls me a worry-guts.'

'We all worry. You'll feel better when things are more settled,' he said. 'Come out with me this morning. We'll go over to Liverpool. I want you to see my building, and especially the flat. I need to know if there's anything else you want done.'

Evie felt cheered. 'That would be a nice change.'

'Perhaps lunch?'

She shook her head. 'I can't. The children . . . Unless we leave it until tomorrow. I could ask Gertie if she'd mind seeing to them at dinnertime.'

'Tomorrow it is, then.'

Evie dressed carefully the next morning. She wanted to be as smart as possible. At ten o'clock Byron had his car outside her door. Evie hadn't had a day out for years and was determined to enjoy herself. She felt excited at the prospect.

Byron had talked endlessly about the building, but to actually see it, to go from floor to floor, looking in the rooms, and then to stand in the flat that would be her home, seemed to make everything much more certain.

Evie loved the flat. It was much bigger and smarter than her old house. The rooms would be heated with hot-water pipes and bulbous radiators. It had a proper bathroom, and hot water would come from the taps.

Lunch was long and extravagant. Evie had never been to such a smart hotel. In the afternoon, they looked at furniture and tried to decide what they'd need. Evie was going to rent her house out and intended to leave the furniture there.

'How about this?' Byron stopped at a double bed.

Evie felt the heat run up her cheeks. At the moment she was sleeping in a single bed because her room was so small. The double bed she'd shared with Ned was now used by the children. If it hadn't been for the fact that Byron came to her house, she'd have moved in with Queenie and put Bobby in the single room.

'Will you be able to stay with me? Every night?' It was something she had to ask.

'If you'll let me.'

'It's what I want.' Evie told herself she was silly to be anxious. A new life was opening up for her. She should be optimistic about it. But she couldn't be optimistic about Ida Pringle, for she was afraid she'd ruined their friendship for good.

Ida still felt shocked when she went to work on Monday morning.

'Good morning, Miss Pringle.' Byron's head had come up from his work and gone straight back down again. His pen scratched on the paper. It was what always happened.

Ida had spent the weekend angrily rehearsing what she was going to say to him. That she was disgusted with his behaviour. That he'd lured Evie away from her, ruined her life as well as Evie's.

'Good morning, Mr Ball,' was all she managed.

She flounced back to her desk. She couldn't get on with her work. Her mind was boiling with resentment. She'd given him respect up till now. She'd worked here for thirty years, for him and for his father before him. She'd liked Byron Ball. He came from a class above her. But that made it easier for him to get his way with someone like Evie. He'd taken advantage of her, a widow with two children to support.

Ida didn't understand how Byron had managed to do

it. To her his manner was always formal. He distanced himself from everybody. Never encouraged anybody to get close. Ida had believed she was the closest. She sat outside his door all day. She took his dictation and typed his letters, but never once had he ever mentioned any personal concerns to her. He never mentioned his wife and family, but like everybody else, she knew they existed.

The only time he'd ever mentioned Evie's name was when Ned's ship had been sunk. Then he'd told Ida how it was he knew, so she could go home and comfort Evie. It was what she'd expect a boss to do. He'd always seemed so honest and above board, yet he'd gone behind her back. Evie had gone behind her back too. That was what she didn't like. It left a nasty taste in her mouth.

Yes, she'd welcomed the chance to retire early, but that was when she'd thought her home life was happily settled and secure.

To find that Evie meant to leave her was very hurtful. She felt her whole life was collapsing. Things were moving too fast. Evie had explained that she could remain in the house, but she wasn't sure she wanted to be there all alone.

Evie had suggested she ask her sister to come and live with her, but the house wasn't in a good area and the whole reason for living there would be gone. She couldn't help this spiral of jealousy and resentment that the two people she spent her life with were abandoning her.

When the time came to move to the new flat, Evie asked Gertie to look after her children for the weekend. With all the packing and unpacking, she thought it better if she could give that her full attention. Byron was doing all he could to help.

'I'm afraid you're going to exhaust yourself,' he said.

Her baby was due in six weeks, and if she were truthful, she didn't have her usual energy.

Although Evie was officially going to be caretaker of the building, she found that Byron had hired a Mrs O'Casey to come in at five every morning to do the work. He'd asked her to clean through the flat in readiness, and she was waiting to help Evie unpack and get the place straight.

'There's Alice too,' he said, taking Evie into the kitchen, where a brisk thirty-year-old was unpacking boxes of food. 'She will come in daily to help you.'

'Help me?'

'With the housework.' Alice smiled.

'She cooks too,' Byron said.

'Plain cooking,' Alice said.

'What am I going to do?' Evie smiled. 'I thought I was coming here to do a job, not to be waited on hand and foot.'

'Not just yet. Not until after the baby's born. That's soon enough to decide how much you want to do.' The furniture she and Byron had chosen had already been delivered. They had two matching sofas covered in mustard-yellow fabric for the living room. Evie positioned one in front of the window to take advantage of the view over the rooftops to the docks and the river beyond. But she found that once she sat down, all she could see was the skyline opposite.

Outside, the trams clanked along the middle of the street. Motorcars, buses and horse-drawn vehicles of every description followed one another continuously in both directions. At the junction with Lord Street, traffic swirled round the statue of Queen Victoria.

It was never truly dark here. A yellow glow shone up from the streetlights and blue flashes sparked from the tram wires as the vehicles rattled past. Evie was never tired of peering down into the cavernous street below.

Although they were busy, and the flat seemed full of people and hardly private, Evie loved having Byron with her all the time. It seemed a luxury to have him to herself all night. A luxury to see him in slacks and pullover instead of his formal chalk-striped suits. She thought she could be truly happy here.

Gertie brought the children back in time for supper on Sunday evening. Alice had worked through the weekend, and had set out a cold meal on the table for them. She was on the point of going home.

'Is this where we're going to live?' Queenie stood in the middle of the living room, looking round with wide eyes. She had grimy knees and had spilled milk down the front of her dress. Bobby was none too clean either. He had his nose glued to the window, peering down into the street.

'Isn't it lovely?' Gertie's hoarse, throaty chuckle sounded round the flat. 'I'm dying to see it all.'

Evie showed them round. Gertie wanted to know all about the central heating, and was delighted to use the new bathroom before sitting down for a bite to eat. The children were tired and somewhat fractious, and they ate little.

Gertie got up to leave. She kissed Evie and the children and said: 'You've done her proud, Mr Ball. Evie's a lucky girl.'

When the door closed behind her, Evie said brightly to her children: 'Bathtime now. You can try out the new bath before going to bed. Come along.'

'Isn't Mr Ball going home?' Bobby asked, loudly enough for him to hear.

'No, dear.' Evie tried to keep her voice steady. She was

worried about how her children were going to take this. 'He's going to live with us now.'

'Instead of Miss Pringle? He's got rooms with us?' Evie started running the bath.

'Course not, silly,' Queenie said, sounding superior. 'He's the boss, isn't he? Mummy's boss. Have we got rooms with him?'

Evie knew she was floundering. 'It's not like that at all. He's your new daddy.'

'We don't want a new one.' Queenie stared at her defiantly. 'Do we, Bobby?'

'Take your shoes and socks off.'

'Not Mr Ball,' Bobby said. 'Not him. We love the daddy we've got.'

Evie went back to Byron with a heavy heart. The pleasure she'd found in her new home had evaporated.

'They'll accept me in time.' Byron pulled her down beside him on the new sofa. 'It can't be easy for them, this is a big change.'

'They remember Ned. Perhaps I've talked about him too much.' She'd kept the three photographs she had of him displayed in frames about their old home so they'd know what he looked like. She'd brought them here and put them in their rooms. She hadn't wanted them to forget Ned, but perhaps it was making it harder for them to accept Byron.

'Mum?' At the sound of Bobby's childish treble, Evie pulled free of Byron's arms and straightened up. He'd come to the living-room door in his striped pyjamas and was staring at them. His curly hair was rumpled, and he looked the image of Ned.

'Bobby! It's past your bedtime. You must go to sleep.'

'You forgot to read us a story.'

'Bobby, your mother's tired tonight. Go back to bed, there's a good boy.'

'We always have a story.' Queenie had come behind her brother. 'You know we always have a story.'

Evie tried to get up. She felt heavy and ungainly. Byron helped her to her feet.

'I'll read you a story,' he said. 'Have you got your books?'

'We want Mummy,' Queenie told him. 'We want Mummy to read to us, not you.'

Evie loved the feeling of having people all round her. The building buzzed with life during office hours. Byron was to run his business from two rooms on the ground floor. He planned to rent out the rest of the building. It took a little time, but gradually other businesses took up tenancies.

The Bulwark Insurance Company took the whole of the second floor, and a firm of solicitors the third. A notice by the front door offered separate rooms for rent at five shillings a week. All of the tenants wanted the caretaker to clean for them. Another cleaner had to be taken on to help Mrs O'Casey, and Evie found she had little to do except order the cleaning materials and see to the laundry.

She felt she'd gone up in the world. That she had money for everything she wanted now. One thing she did feel strongly about was that Bobby and Queenie should have the education and training to earn a decent living when they were grown up. Ned had never had that. It meant a great deal that his children should have a better start in life.

Byron had entered them in fee-paying schools. The best in the neighbourhood. Both had settled down well and their first reports were good.

They seemed to enjoy their new home. They both loved

riding in the lift. Eight-year-old Bobby raced it as it sped up to the ninth floor with Queenie inside. Evie had to ban them from playing in it. They found a new game. There were two flights of stairs, one up each side of the building. They started together in the front lobby, racing up to the flat each using a different staircase. Evie had to stop that too during office hours. She was afraid they'd disturb the workers.

On weekdays, Byron spent a good deal of his time with her in the flat. She could reach him in his office when she wanted to. She knew he was pleased with the arrangement.

'Fewer prying eyes here,' he said. 'And Veronica doesn't come so often now she has to cross the river.'

Evie felt safer. She was further from Father's shop. Nobody knew her here and she liked that. The only thing that bothered her was that the children didn't seem to be taking to Byron. She'd been at pains to keep them apart back in Birkenhead. Perhaps it was too much to expect that they would instantly meld into a family.

'We must give them time,' Byron said. 'Not rush things. It might be better if I'm not always here when they are. They need time alone with you. We can arrange that for them, can't we?'

They did. Evie got the children up in the mornings and saw them off to school, while Byron stayed out of their way. And again, when the children came home from school in the afternoon, he made himself scarce. He did most of his work in the evenings, so that Evie and the children could have time to themselves.

Gertie Collins was coming over on the ferry on Saturday mornings to take the children home with her. She loved having them to herself.

This meant that Byron and Evie could spend the afternoon alone in the flat. They went out to a theatre or to dinner in the evening, and had a lovely lazy Sunday.

'We can't ask Gertie to go on doing this for ever,' Evie said guiltily.

When Gertie brought the children home, Byron would go downstairs and work for an hour or two until they were in bed.

Bobby loved going over on the ferry with Grannie and staying in her house. There were no rules at Grannie's like having to wash your hands before meals. No set mealtimes either. When he was hungry he was told to help himself to whatever food he could find in the kitchen. Or Gran would give him a few pennies to get chips for them all from the chip shop.

'I love it when she takes us shopping,' Queenie sighed blissfully.

'Specially to that cake shop.'

'Darty's. They're friends of Grannie's.'

Bobby loved peering into the window where the cakes were all set out.

'Go on,' Gran would urge. 'Which one do you want then?' And he'd be torn between a cream bun and a jam tart, or possibly an Eccles cake. Queenie always knew what she wanted.

'Such a pretty little girl.' Mrs Darty would look at her with admiring eyes. 'She's beautiful. Takes after your Ned more than Evie. Going to turn a few heads when she's older.'

Then her quick dark eyes would dart to Bobby. 'Handsome little fellow you are too.'

It was just the same this Saturday. Gran and Mrs Darty talked for ages, punctuated by Gran's hoarse, throaty chuckle. Other customers came in and were served, and still they chatted on.

'How's Evie liking it over there?'

'Is he good to her?'

'Poor girl, getting caught like that with another little one.'

Bobby liked to sniff the lovely smell of baking and to pick out the ten cakes he'd choose if he was invited to take that many. Today, Queenie nudged him, pointing out the fly-catcher hanging over the sticky buns.

'Count the dead flies there. I make it a hundred.'

'You can't count to a hundred yet,' Gran had laughed. 'Isn't she a card?'

Bobby wrinkled his nose at the flies sticking to the tape.

'There's an awful lot. Is there room for any more? They look horrible, all those dead flies together.'

'Come on, you two.' Mrs Darty was taking a halfpenny from the till. 'Go and buy me a new one. Next door but one that way, the grocer.' She pointed. 'He sells them.'

Queenie grabbed the halfpenny first and was out giggling on the pavement in seconds.

'This way,' she said, pulling Bobby towards the chemist's shop next door. 'Let's go in here.'

Bobby clung to her. 'Gran'll be cross,' he whispered, peeping back round the cake-shop door. He could see her and Mrs Darty were talking again.

'You know what she's like about this place.' Queenie was at the chemist's door. 'Always craning her neck. Staring at him inside.'

'What are you looking at?' Bobby had asked her once. Gran had been quite strange about it and hadn't wanted to say. Queenie had kept on at her until she'd told them the man who owned it was their grandfather.

'Don't tell your mother I've told you,' she'd said, looking all round as though afraid of being seen on the doorstep. 'It's a secret.'

'It isn't,' Bobby had said. 'We know that. Mam took us inside once. We went upstairs. He wasn't nice to us, was he, Queenie?'

'Can't remember,' she'd said then.

Now she pulled at his coat. 'They sell fly-catchers in here. Let's go in. Why shouldn't we know what he's like if he's our grandfather?'

'Funny to think Mam lived here once.'

'And worked here. There's only ladies serving.'

'There's a man on the other counter.'

'That's not him.'

The door pinged loudly as a customer came out. Another was behind them waiting to go in. Bobby took his sister's hand and a moment later they were inside. It smelled very strange, and the man who'd come in behind them was urging him forward faster than Bobby wanted to go. Queenie felt like an anchor on his arm.

'Come on,' he urged, his heart pounding.

The next instant she shot forward until she could see inside the strange little room with all the shelves. She came back giggling. 'He's in there.'

Bobby saw a swirl of white, and an angry voice barked: 'What are you children up to? This is not a playground.'

He jumped as a large hand clamped on his arm, and looked up to find a ferocious face glowering down at him.

His voice quivered: 'We've been sent to buy a fly-catcher, sir.'

'The other counter for that.' The man's eyes burned with irritation. Bobby felt the grip on his arm slacken as he was turned round and given a little push.

'Remember, next time you come in, no horseplay. Miss Lister? Serve this lad with a fly-catcher. Let's get them out of here.'

Bobby had to nudge Queenie twice to get her to put

the halfpenny on the counter. She looked terrified. They were both glad to get outside and had to take deep breaths in front of the cake-shop window to make themselves feel normal again.

'I'm not having him as a grandfather,' Queenie hissed. 'He's nasty.'

'Didn't I tell you he would be?'

Back in the cake shop, Bobby's heart slowed its thumping. He closed his eyes and sniffed the heavenly smell of newly baked bread. Mrs Darty changed her fly-catcher and Gran went on talking.

When they were finally ready to depart, Polly Darty gave them each a custard tart to eat on the way home. The creamy egg custard in crisp pastry was delicious.

As soon as she'd finished hers, Queenie asked: 'Are we going to have a new brother or sister? Is that what you were telling Mrs Darty?'

'Oh, my! No, I said no such thing. Talking about somebody else, I was. Somebody we know and you don't.'

But later, when they were sitting on the mat in front of the fire and Gran had gone next door to try and borrow some tea, Queenie turned her big brown eyes on her brother.

'Bobby, we are going to have a new brother or sister. I know it.'

'Gran said no, you'd got it wrong.'

'I don't care what she said. It wasn't what she said to Mrs Darty.'

'But when will this happen?'

'I don't know that, do I?'

'I don't think you know anything.'

Queenie tossed her long brown curls over her shoulder. 'Didn't you hear Mrs Darty say: "Good Lord! What is the poor girl thinking of?" '

Bobby shook his head, he hadn't. He'd felt sort of shaken up. He hadn't been listening.

'You'd know more if you didn't day-dream so much.'

Byron went down to his office and let his eyes linger on the gilt wording printed on the half-glass in his door:

Henry Ball and Sons
Importers and Exporters to All Four Corners of the World.

Actually, most of his business was still with West Africa, but he had built up a little trade to America and hoped to expand to other regions.

He was very pleased with his decision to buy this building. There was a demand for rented office space, and it was now fully let. He'd kept only this one large, prestigious office on the ground floor for his own business. Once it had been used by a director of the Connaught Line. He'd partitioned off one end to make a private cubbyhole for himself. The larger part had been furnished with five desks.

One was occupied by Myrtle Parker, his new secretary. He'd chosen a middle-aged woman again, who was rather frumpish in appearance. She had a large mole on her chin with three long hairs curling from it. Byron found it took a conscious effort not to look at it.

He'd brought the three clerks with him from his Birkenhead office. Two had worked for him for years and were now nearing retirement. The other, Harry Penn, the junior accounts clerk, was aged nineteen and had finger-nails bitten down to the quick. Byron could see him gnawing away at them as he worked.

He said good morning to them as he went through to

unlock his desk. He took out a file and tried to get down to work. He'd been feeling on edge these last weeks as Evie's time drew closer.

She'd tried to reassure him, told him the baby wouldn't be early, she always went her full time. But now the waiting time was over, and her baby was due this very day. She was not overly large or ungainly, her cheeks were rosy and her eyes bright. He thought she looked the picture of health and more beautiful than ever. He'd asked her half a dozen times how she felt before he'd finished breakfast.

He was trying to keep his mind on other things, but today it was hard. He heard the outer door burst open, and looked up to see Veronica coming in. She'd come before when he'd first moved in, but he hadn't seen her for weeks. He could have done without a visit from her today of all days. His spirits sank further when he saw she had Norman in tow. She threw open the glass door of his cubbyhole without bothering to knock.

'Hello, Byron. I'm glad to see you're still in the land of the living.' Her big bulging eyes flashed resentment.

Frowning, he got slowly to his feet. 'What d'you mean?'

'You haven't been near for weeks. Why don't you come home?'

'I thought I'd made it clear that I wouldn't.'

Norman was crowding in. Byron went to close the door behind him but wasn't quite fast enough.

'You made it clear you had a fancy woman.'

Byron saw Harry Penn stir with interest at that. He lowered his voice.

'Do you have to let the whole office know our business? I said I wanted a divorce . . .'

'And I said you wouldn't get it. You're still a husband and father. You still have responsibilities to me and Norman, and I'm not going to let you forget it.'

'I haven't forgotten.' The whole point of keeping this business alive, of trying to tailor it to present-day needs and build it up was to provide for Norman.

He turned to his son. 'There's a job waiting for you here, when you need it. I'll teach you how to run this business, and when you've mastered it, I'll retire.'

Byron felt that was only fair. After all, he'd received a business from his own father. He could meet the needs of his new family from the rents of the Connaught Building and his investments. He didn't want to go on working until he was eighty, like his father had done.

'I can't say fairer than that, can I?'

'No, Dad, thank . . .'

'What you say and what you do when the time comes could be very different,' Veronica interrupted. 'I don't trust you. I don't like the way you've cut yourself off. You've shown no interest in the new house. You never come home now.'

'I didn't think you'd want me . . .'

'Surely you want to see Norman?'

'Yes, of course.' Byron looked uneasily at his son. He should show more concern for him. 'I've been busy these last few weeks, with the move and things. It's further away . . .'

'You can come for regular weekends. You need to, to keep in touch with Norman. And the new neighbours are asking about you. I want you to show your face, show some interest.'

'Not next weekend,' Byron said hurriedly, thinking of Evie. 'But I will come soon.'

'Right. Now the new house is finished, I'll have more time to come here.'

'There's no need,' Byron protested. 'I'm managing very well on my own.'

Veronica went to a file cabinet and pulled on a locked drawer.

'Where are the keys? I've always helped with your business accounts. I'd like to go on doing it, to keep an eye on Norman's inheritance.'

'Not in there.'

Veronica moved to another cabinet, that opened to her touch. 'What do you keep in that one?'

'Nothing that concerns you or Norman. I have interests other than this business.'

He watched the sour lines on her face deepen. 'You're splitting up your business. Hiding your assets. Keeping things away from me and Norman.'

Byron flushed with indignation. He was doing exactly that, but how could she expect otherwise?

'I've treated you fairly, Veronica. I've made the new house over to you and I'm paying you a generous allowance to live on. I've said I'm making provision for Norman. How I provide for myself as well has nothing to do with you.'

'It has! You've saddled yourself with two families to support. If you can't afford it, Norman and I will be the ones to go short. How can I have any confidence . . .'

Byron was on his feet. 'Veronica! I've told you what my intentions are. I don't care whether you have confidence or not. It would be better if you went home and let me get on with my work.'

'I've done a lot for the business in the past. I want to go on helping with your accounts.'

'In other words, you want a reason to see the books on a regular basis. Make sure the business will still be worth inheriting.'

There was suspicion on Veronica's face. 'How can I trust you?'

'You'll have to.'

Veronica had come to his old office for much the same reason. He'd expected to see her here. That was why he'd provided a spare desk in the front office. He led her out to it now. He didn't think she'd come often; she wasn't the sort to persevere.

'Here?' She looked sourly at Harry Penn, who was chewing his nails again. Then round at the other clerks, who were pretending to be too engrossed in their work to listen to this exchange.

'You won't want me working on company figures here. They need to be kept confidential. I need somewhere more private.'

'There isn't anywhere.'

'Perhaps if you moved this desk to your office?'

'There isn't room, surely you can see that?' He'd arranged it this way. He wanted to discourage her visits.

'I'm glad I've come.' She was showing anger now. 'I need to keep a closer eye on things.' Two chairs were pulled up to the desk. Files were being opened on it.

Their presence riled Byron. He was unable to work himself and unwilling to leave his office to them. Veronica was back and forth to him with questions, mostly about things that needn't concern her. He wished she hadn't chosen today to make such a nuisance of herself.

Book Three

1919–1930

CHAPTER THIRTEEN

It was a beautiful Friday in early September. Evie felt heavy and lethargic from the time she got up. At mid-morning she went out and walked down to the Pier Head. She stood against the railings in the spring sunshine and watched the seagulls swooping behind a small freighter as it chugged downriver.

She thought about her mother and wondered if she'd ever had another child. Perhaps, somewhere, she had a half-brother or sister? But her mother was a ghost she couldn't lay. She knew very little about her. All this was in her own mind.

Evie told herself she had financial security, she needn't fear that she was still treading in her mother's footsteps. She'd never be poor, nor would her children want for anything, thanks to Byron's generosity. She walked slowly back to the Connaught Building and peeped through the glass door into Byron's office on her way upstairs.

'I don't want you to come in,' he'd explained. 'Well, not often.'

'Not in my present condition?'

'More discreet if not at all, Evie. We don't want talk. Won't do either of us any good. I have to think of your reputation. Use the telephone to contact me.'

Evie saw several heads bent over their desks. But there were more people here than usual. Her attention was suddenly riveted on one in particular.

A woman with greying hair that showed the cut of a good hairdresser. She wore an expensive-looking costume in dignified black wool. Evie knew who she was although she hadn't seen her before. Mrs Ball was said to come to the office occasionally. Not every week, sometimes not for months at a time, but she came when she felt like it. Byron said she thought of herself as the company accountant. Ida Pringle had told her she had a high opinion of herself.

Evie shivered as she studied her through the glass of the door. This was the woman who was keeping her and Byron apart. Making what should be open and acknowledged a hole-in-the-corner affair.

She was taller and heavier than Byron, older too. Evie saw her look across the office and call for something. She had bulging, exopthalmic eyes and a deep, manly voice. Evie thought she looked sour, a bitter woman with deep lines of discontent marring her face.

She had to put her hand against the wall to steady herself. If she thought of Veronica Ball in those terms, how would the other woman see her? The woman who had stolen her husband. Ruined her life. A woman, much younger and more attractive, who had lured Byron away. A wicked, amoral woman, brazen and shameless, on the point of giving birth to his child. The room seemed to spin on a wave of guilt. Evie was afraid many would think she was all of those things.

She didn't notice him until he moved, a young lad of fourteen or so. Evie's heart turned over. She knew he must be Norman, Byron's son. She searched his face, looking for a likeness. It wasn't there. He wasn't as handsome as Bobby, not even as confident, though he was six years older. He was kicking the toe of his shoe against the desk, and she could tell he was bored. Hadn't she seen Queenie do that many times? A mother's boy, Byron had called him. She watched him pluck at Veronica's sleeve for attention.

Evie knew Veronica had brought Norman to his father's office to claim what she thought of as his rightful inheritance. How could she blame her? She felt a sudden dragging in her abdomen. She went up in the lift feeling light-headed and shaken.

She found that Gertie had called in to see her. 'I came over to get myself some new shoes and thought I'd pop in to see if the baby had come. Not on the way yet?'

'I've got the feeling it won't be long.' Evie collapsed on the sofa. 'Stay and have something to eat with us.'

Alice had boiled a joint of ham for lunch and made parsley sauce. Evie lifted the very latest in-house telephone to tell Byron it was ready.

'I can't come up.' His voice sounded taut with stress. 'Veronica's come. Better if I stay away from you while she's here. Are you all right?'

She told him she was, but she couldn't eat much and she felt the first pains as the meal was finishing. She drank tea with Gertie and admired her new shoes. By two o'clock she was sure labour had begun, and rang down to let Byron know. He came rushing up to see her and rang for the midwife.

'Veronica's still here. I feel I need to keep an eye on what she's doing.' He seemed on edge, couldn't stand still.

'I'll stay with Evie for a while,' Gertie said. 'Nothing's going to happen just yet.' She'd already filled several kettles and pans to get the boiling water that would be needed.

Byron came up again an hour later. 'I told Veronica she must go,' he told them. 'That she must have seen all she wanted to by now. I had to get rid of her.'

Evie watched him change out of his suit, put on a comfortable pullover. His face was set and anxious. There was no formality about him now.

When it was time for Bobby and Queenie to come home

from school, Gertie went to meet them. Byron gave her money and asked her to give them tea at the Kardomah café and then take them to the pictures.

For Evie, the pains seemed never-ending, though the midwife kept telling her she was making good progress. She was conscious of Byron's support, of his whispered endearments, of his hand holding hers, though the midwife had made him pull his chair to the head of the bed, out of her way.

When she said it was time for Byron to leave them, that the birth was imminent, Evie hung on to his hand and protested.

'I want him here,' she panted, feeling another pain building. 'I want him to stay.'

The gas and air mask went over her face again. The rubbery smell was horrible.

'Come on now, another big push,' she was told briskly. The pain was filling her mind and body, until she could think of nothing else. 'Keep pushing. We'll do it this time.' The room seemed to spin round her.

'A little girl.' She heard Byron's voice, thick with relief. 'She's lovely.'

She knew her baby was born at eight thirty that night, because the midwife timed it. 'She weighs in at seven pounds two ounces.'

A few minutes later a bundle was put into Evie's arms, and she found her new daughter gazing up at her with round blue eyes. They were locked together in minute examination of each other. Then Byron was there with tears in his eyes, trying to put his arms round both her and the new infant. Evie saw it as a moment of happiness and triumph.

When Gertie brought Bobby and Queenie in to see her in their nightclothes, Byron was still with her.

'Thank goodness that's safely over.' He was smiling. 'What shall we call the baby?'

Evie's older children were staring at him resentfully.

'What about Daisy?' Byron suggested. 'It's sweet and flowery. Do you like the name?'

Bobby said nothing.

'I like Poppy better,' Queenie said. 'Can I hold it?'

'Hold her,' Byron corrected gently. He made Queenie sit down and laid the child momentarily in her arms.

Byron felt sky-high on an emotional roller-coaster. He hadn't intended to stay and see his daughter born, but it was an experience he wouldn't have missed for worlds. He hadn't expected to feel like this. Evie had been wonderful, making so little fuss.

He'd held his newly born daughter in his arms, feeling absolutely thrilled. She looked as he remembered Grace looking at birth. He felt he was being given a second chance. He was ready to burst with love for mother and child.

When the midwife had made Evie comfortable for the night, he stayed with her, holding her hand.

'She's gorgeous. We'll be all right now, Evie. We're a family, an ordinary family.'

Evie was tired but trying to smile. 'I wish we were more ordinary.'

'We'll have a good life. You'll see.'

Gertie was staying the night in Queenie's room. At the midwife's suggestion, she'd made a temporary bed for Byron alongside Bobby's. When they'd all gone to bed and settled down, Byron crept into Evie's bed and snuggled down beside her, holding her close. He felt far too excited to sleep.

* * *

Now that the baby was born, Byron knew it would bring big changes, a new routine for them all. He hardly left Evie during the weeks of her lying-in. He wanted to be with her and the baby.

Evie said she wasn't concerned about their not being married, but he knew she was. It was her love for him that made her say otherwise. She worried about the effect the situation would have on Bobby and Queenie.

'I'm a bad example to them,' she said sadly.

'Of course you're not!'

Evie shook her head. 'Perhaps it's my own conscience. Perhaps I'm being silly.'

'They're too young to understand, love.'

'Perhaps. I keep telling myself I'm not going to be embarrassed, but I am.' She patted his hand. 'It's all right, I know it's something you can't change.'

Byron's arms went round her. 'I'm sorry, love. I take too much for granted.'

'Sometimes I feel like a loose woman.'

'You're not! Don't think like that. I love you, Evie. I wish things could be different for us.'

Once Evie was up and about again, Byron felt he should start spending a few hours in the flat when Bobby and Queenie were there. He wanted them to get used to seeing him with their mother.

Tonight was the first time he'd tried it, and he was well pleased up to now. They'd all eaten early in the evening and the children had cleared the dishes away to the kitchen so that they could use the table for their homework.

Evie had fed the baby. He'd pretended an interest in his newspaper, but he loved to watch her do that. Now she was nursing Daisy with a look of utter contentment on her face.

Bobby was poring over his geography books. 'Mam, I don't understand what it says here. What it's asking me to do.'

Evie got to her feet and put the baby in Byron's arms. 'Go to your daddy for a moment,' she said.

He tightened his hold on the infant. Daisy's eyes were wide open, staring up into his. Seeming to search his face. He felt such a wave of adoration. Bobby's voice cut across it.

'Is he Daisy's daddy?'

Byron knew that his head jerked up. Bobby's innocent gaze seemed somehow accusing.

'Yes,' Evie answered. Byron saw her tense up, afraid of what was coming.

'But not mine and Queenie's?'

She recovered and said: 'He is, Bobby, I keep telling you. Your first daddy was killed in the war and can't be with you any more. He'd want Byron to look after us all. He'd want you to have a new daddy.'

Byron beamed at her. Trying to tell her she'd said exactly the right thing. He felt it was all out in the open now. That he'd officially joined the family.

Byron went with Evie to register Daisy's birth. He wanted her to have his surname.

Evie had hesitated. 'If you feel strongly about it . . .'

He knew from her manner that she'd have preferred Daisy to be Collins like the other two.

'It'll split the family,' she tried to explain. 'Make Bobby and Queenie feel different. Make them pull in a different direction. They are already.'

But Daisy was Byron's daughter. He wanted her to have his name. He did feel strongly about it.

'You're besotted with Daisy,' she'd smiled.

231

'Aren't we all?'

'I certainly am. I'm enjoying her, she's lovely.'

That brought him some comfort. Bobby and Queenie were making it quite clear that they were not of like mind. It was troubling Evie.

'You mustn't worry,' he'd said. 'Time should sort that out.'

Evie was frowning. 'I wish I'd stopped to think about Bobby and Queenie. About what effect this would have on them.'

Byron felt full of love for her. He couldn't take his eyes from her troubled face. This was wrenching him in two. They were sitting on the yellow sofa, staring out into the night sky and the glow of lights reflecting up.

She said: 'Did you know that in the old days, women who committed adultery were forced to wear a red letter A on their breast so that everybody would know?'

'Evie, you haven't committed adultery. You're a widow.' He knew it was on her mind that he definitely had.

'I've had a child out of wedlock, and that's a sin. But I don't regret it. How could I regret having Daisy?'

She was trying to smile at him. 'History isn't clear about the fate of adulterous men, but poor Daisy would have been branded in that way.'

Byron could see a pulse beating in her throat. She looked at him squarely for a moment and her eyes were wet with tears. Then her dark lashes swept down against her cheeks and nothing he said would make her look up again.

He took her in his arms. 'Oh, Evie love. The war changed everybody's thinking. People don't worry so much about things like that now.'

As the New Year brought the start of a new decade, Evie

tried to put such thoughts out of her mind and get on with her new life.

She didn't like Byron leaving her at the weekends to see Norman. He seemed to sense that and didn't go more than once a month. She'd found out the hard way that a flat like this wasn't the best place for growing children. Having Daisy pegged her to it, yet the other two were wanting to get out and do things. They didn't like being confined and were always trying to escape to play elsewhere in the building. She hated to think what they could be getting up to. She forbade them to go out into the street. Queenie wasn't seven yet; Evie didn't really trust her out of her sight.

She didn't find Byron's absence easy to cope with. He worked Saturday morning and went over to see Norman after lunch. The first time, he didn't return until Sunday night, after she'd put the children in bed. She missed him. Now that she'd got used to having Alice do most of the cooking and cleaning, she missed her too. She had a day off on Sunday.

The building emptied in minutes at lunchtime on Saturday. There was less traffic in the streets. As it was in the business centre of Liverpool, the place seemed to die. Evie felt as if she and her children were the only people left in the world. When she said something of this to Byron, he stayed with her until Sunday morning and then went over to see his son just for the day.

That was better, but she much preferred the Sundays when Byron stayed with her and the children. Usually then he took them all for a run in his car in the afternoon. The children loved going to the beach at Formby. Even Bobby was pleased to go on trips like that.

The next Sunday Byron was away turned out to be a fine

summer's day. The flat was hot, with the sun flooding in. Bobby lay back on the yellow sofa and half closed his eyes. The sun dazzled and sparked off the new silver tea service on the sideboard.

He asked: 'Where did that come from?'

'It was a present,' Mam said, looking up from the baby.

'From Mr Ball?'

'Yes.' She smiled at him in the sad way that she had. 'Bobby, dear, couldn't you call him Dad?'

'He isn't my dad.' Bobby flushed with resentment. 'It's silly to call him that if he isn't.'

'He'd like it if you did. So would I.'

He said nothing.

Evie broke the silence: 'Queenie does.'

'Queenie only does it because . . .'

Queenie had been sitting in the opposite corner of the sofa. Now she dived across his legs, fixing him with her big brown eyes, stopping him from saying any more. Queenie called him Dad to get round him. She was after a new doll she'd seen in Lewis's window.

'If you really can't, Bobby . . .'

'Well, he isn't my dad.'

'Perhaps you could call him Uncle then? Uncle Byron. To call him Mr Ball is . . .'

Bobby slid lower on the sofa, putting his hands over his ears. He didn't want to call him anything. Mr Ball was always here. Pushing in where he wasn't wanted.

Outside the sun hardly reached into the deep canyon of South Castle Street.

'I wish something would happen,' Queenie said. 'It's awful quiet.'

'Like the grave,' Bobby agreed. They were so used to hearing the banging of doors and the whirr of the lifts and the sounds of lots of people below.

'Why couldn't we go to Gran's?' Queenie let her book slide to the floor. Bobby knew she was bored.

'You can't go every weekend,' Mam said. 'It makes a lot of work for her.'

'She likes having us.' Queenie pouted. 'She says we're no trouble. We want to go, don't we, Bobby? There's lots to do there.'

'Well, this week you can't.' Mam sounded a little short as she lifted the baby from one breast and turned it so it could feed from the other.

'You never have time for us any more,' Queenie complained. 'You're always busy with that baby. Feeding it or bathing it or playing with it or trying to get it to sleep.'

'You must call her Daisy, darling. "Her", not "it".' Bobby heard Mam say that about fifteen times a day.

'I wish it had never come,' Queenie had said to him when they were on their own. 'It never stops crying. It's a pain.'

'Mam likes it.'

'Yes, better than she does you and me.' Queenie had been angry. 'I wouldn't mind, but it's ugly.'

Bobby had to agree. The new baby had a shock of straight brown hair that stuck upwards. He'd even heard Gran say it would never be as pretty as Queenie.

'We'll go and see Miss Pringle this afternoon.' Mam looked up and gave them a wan smile. 'She's asked us to go for tea. You'll like that just as much, won't you?'

'No,' Queenie said mutinously. 'We like Gran's.'

Bobby met his mother's gaze. He knew she was upset. He tried to explain: 'Gran lets us stay up late and play out . . .' Queenie's foot jammed painfully into his tummy, making him gasp, but Mam didn't seem to notice.

It seemed an age before they were ready to go. Bobby

changed his shirt and washed his face without being told. Queenie got cross and impatient because it took Mam such a long time to get herself and the baby ready to go anywhere.

The perambulator, a new one, had to be packed with napkins and the baby dressed up in a woolly jacket and bonnet. It cried all the way down to the Pier Head, although there was a lovely breeze smelling of rope and tar and the sun sparkled on the water.

Queenie skipped along, happy now they were out. From the boat the Birkenhead bank looked leafy and green. It was an uphill walk to their old home. Soon they were walking through streets that were familiar.

Miss Pringle was smiling when she let them in. She seemed in a good mood. She kissed Queenie. Bobby remembered her being very cross before they'd moved to the flat. Quite tetchy with him. She'd kept complaining he was making a noise though he'd crept around like a mouse. Mam said Miss Pringle didn't want them to go. There was another old lady with her today, who was shaking Mam's hand.

'My sister, who's come to live with me,' Miss Pringle told them. The sister was fat too, with the same sort of rubbery face that Miss Pringle had, and the beginnings of a moustache. Miss Pringle pulled Queenie up on her knee, just as she used to in the old days. Like everybody else, she was very fond of Queenie.

Bobby thought it strange to be here in the front room again. The glass-fronted china cabinet was tightly packed with cups and saucers and glasses, but Miss Pringle had always kept a few more interesting things there. He liked the little clown made of deep red and blue glass with a white walking stick and black boots. There was a Buddha too, but Queenie liked the corn dolly best. Miss Pringle sometimes took them out so they could play with them.

Ida told her sister to open the cupboard now, and Bobby felt the cold glass of the clown against his hand. Once, Miss Pringle had kept a sugar pig in her cupboard too. They'd been allowed to play with that as well. Both he and Queenie were very fond of sugar pigs. They always had them in their stockings at Christmas. Sometimes they were white and sometimes pink. Miss Pringle's was rather grey.

'Why don't you eat it?' Queenie had asked her one day when she had it on her palm. 'They are for eating.'

'When you get to my age, you won't like all that sugar.'

'Can I have it then?' Queenie had asked eagerly. 'I love them.'

'I don't think you'd better have this one,' Miss Pringle had laughed. 'I've kept it for the last twenty years. A keepsake. My little niece gave it to me for my birthday. It wouldn't be nice to eat now.'

'I think I'd still like it. So would Bobby. I'd give him a bite.'

'No, it might make you sick. It won't be fit to eat after all this time.' She'd whipped it off Queenie's palm and put it back in her cupboard. 'We'll keep it as an ornament, shall we?'

It took weeks for Miss Pringle to notice it was gone. Then, one day, she came rushing to the back room where Bobby had been curled up in the rocking chair. Queenie had been playing on the rug at his feet. She jumped up straight away.

'Look at my farmyard,' she invited. 'I've got two new cows.'

'You didn't take my pig to play with, did you, Queenie?'

'Oh no, Miss Pringle,' she'd said, tossing her curls.

Ida had turned on Bobby then, catching both his hands

in hers and making him stand up. She'd asked sternly: 'Did you take my sugar pig, Bobby?'

He'd shaken his head while his cheeks had run with heat.

'You must own up if you did.' Her button eyes had held his in a long-drawn-out stare. He could see she believed he had.

He'd shaken his head again, feeling weak with guilt. Not because he had taken it, but because he'd eaten part of it. It had been so hard, Queenie had been unable to bite through it. He'd tried too but had failed to do more than put teeth marks on it. They'd had to take the coal hammer to it. There'd been trouble from Mam because they'd wrapped the pig in a clean tea towel and that ended up covered with dirty marks and coal dust.

Miss Pringle had been wrong about it making them sick. It hadn't, and the lumps had lasted longer in their mouths. Queenie reckoned that pig had tasted better than any other. Once the dusty taste had gone.

When all they had left was the string tail, she'd said: 'Mustn't get caught with this.'

Bobby had thrown it over the nursery guard on to the fire and shaken the towel there too. The sugar and coal dust had caused the flames to gust up the chimney. That had frightened them both. Bobby knew it was more than his life was worth to tell tales on Queenie.

Today the table was set for tea in the back room which used to be their living room. Miss Pringle often made pink blancmange and raspberry jelly for Sunday tea when they lived here.

'For the children,' she used to say. She'd made it for them again today. Afterwards, she started reading the tea cups.

'Lots of dots and dashes in your cup now,' she told Evie.

'That's the rent you pay me,' Evie laughed.

'Read my cup for me,' Queenie pleaded. 'Please.'

Miss Pringle made her go through the ritual of swilling the dregs round her cup and emptying them into her saucer.

'You're going to have a very happy life,' she told her. 'You'll be rich like your mother and marry young.'

'What about me?' Bobby offered his own tea cup. 'Will I be rich?'

'I don't see the dots and dashes for riches, not for you, Bobby.'

'I'll be a soldier though, won't I?' That was his ambition. To wear the red jacket and golden helmet of a guardsman.

'I don't see that for you either,' Miss Pringle said.

Bobby couldn't help pulling a face. He thought she was refusing to tell him what he wanted to hear. She didn't like him as much as she did Queenie.

Bobby liked living on top of the Connaught Building. He only had to mention the name at school and everybody knew the place. Most of the boys lived out in the suburbs, and came in on the trams. They thought the town centre rather a rough place to live until he mentioned the Connaught.

'You can see why,' Queenie told him when they were heading out to school one morning. 'Just look.'

There were three boys just ahead of them, wearing jerseys with their elbows out. Two had neither shoes nor socks.

'The pavement must feel icy to bare feet.' Bobby shivered and snuggled into his uniform gabardine.

Mam didn't like them playing out in the street here. She said the traffic and the horses were dangerous. Queenie said she wouldn't want to play out with those slummies and there was plenty to do inside.

The Connaught Building had white marble steps leading up to a massive front door. This led into a rather grand foyer with lots of polished mahogany. There were noticeboards on every floor giving the names of the companies who rented offices there.

All the offices were locked at night but that didn't deter Bobby and Queenie. There was a master key so the cleaners could get in. They soon discovered there was a kitchen on each floor, and most had a biscuit tin. Queenie was not above raiding them.

There was a commercial school on the third floor. It rented three rooms; one had a typewriter on every desk. They both had a go on them and then had to secrete the paper they'd used in the basement.

'I shall come here to learn properly when I'm old enough,' Queenie said.

On the teacher's desk was a gramophone with just one record. Queenie wound it up and set it to play. It was 'Alexander's Ragtime Band'. She sang with it. 'Come on and hear. Come on and hear.'

Often if they crept past the door during school hours they could hear the music belting out and the ten typewriters clattering in unison. Queenie hung round there quite a lot, chatting to the pupils.

Bobby was fascinated by a private detective who rented a single room on the fifth floor. 'Specialist in Matrimonial Cases', it said on his door. Sometimes he'd ask Bobby to go out to buy cigarettes for him. When he came back he'd reward him with a striped humbug.

CHAPTER FOURTEEN

Bobby had bought a stamp album with his pocket money and was keen to build up a collection. He was down in the basement, looking through a waste-paper bin for discarded stamps, when another boy came in. He was about three years older, tall and skinny, with a home haircut.

'You're wasting your time. I've taken all the good ones.'

'Who are you?' Bobby wanted to know.

'Wilf Hutchins. I'm the office boy at Bulwark Insurance.' The second-hand suit he wore had been made for a man with wider shoulders. 'It's my job to open the post, and stamps are one of my perks.'

'You can't want them all?'

'Course I do. All the good ones, anyway. I can swap them or sell them.'

'Well, that's only Bulwark's. I live here, it's one of my perks to have them from the other offices.'

'Lots of people collect stamps and they get their hands on them before you can. I've asked round already, see. Those they don't want, they keep for me. The high-cost ones.'

Bobby felt piqued. 'Well, I should be able to have the stamps from Henry Ball and Company. My mother works for them.'

'Oh yes.' Wilf had canny brown eyes. 'She's Mr Ball's fancy woman, isn't she?'

'What d'you mean?' Bobby knew from his tone that fancy woman was a derogatory term.

'You know. His bit on the side. His lover.'

'How d'you know?' Bobby was indignant.

'Everybody knows here. You should hear the old spinsters in our office rattling on; sounding holier than thou about it.'

Bobby had been made aware, by Mam's obvious tension, that she was ashamed of something, but he couldn't have said what it was until Wilf spelt it out. He leapt to her defence.

'Well, they're all wrong and so are you. Mr Ball is her boss. She's the head caretaker here.'

'All right, all right.' Wilf held up a hand. He had a grin that stretched from ear to ear, showing perfect teeth. 'Don't get worked up about it. I'll bring you some stamps tomorrow, all right?'

Bobby went up in the lift fulminating about what Wilf had told him. He'd known something was wrong for Mam. He'd sensed it.

The flat seemed quiet, then he heard his mother's voice from her bedroom. The baby's cot was in there. He went to the door. She was changing the baby's napkin.

Bobby gulped and said furiously: 'They're saying things about you and Mr Ball downstairs. Nasty things. I told them it was all lies.'

That Bobby was upset was like a knife through Evie's heart. She could see him blinking hard, trying to hide his tears.

'What are they saying?'

'Calling you a fancy woman. A bit on the side. Why do you let that man come here? I hate him. I'm never going to call him Dad, nor Uncle Byron or anything.'

In a rush of guilt she put an arm round his shoulders. Pulled him down to sit beside her on the bed. What sort of an example was she setting her children?

It was all very well for Byron to say that everything was fine and they were just like an ordinary family. How could they be ordinary when this sort of thing happened?

'Oh, Bobby love,' she said. 'Don't worry about what you hear.'

'It's you I worry about, Mam. It's you they're talking about.'

Evie knew there was gossip about her and Byron. She'd been heading for the lift one day after taking Daisy for a walk when she saw Alice laughing with a clerk further down the corridor. She distinctly heard her say Byron's name. They were both so mortally embarrassed to see Evie that she was left in no doubt that some of the gossip was about her.

When she'd mentioned it to Byron, he'd said: 'Alice is well placed to know what's going on. She sees me here with you most of the day. People are bound to be curious. They know I own this building.'

'I don't like her talking about us,' Evie said. 'She'll have to go.'

'She knows the job isn't permanent, I told her it was only for a few weeks. It'll mean more work for you.'

'But more privacy. Anyway, I need more to do. I'll be happy to do the cooking.'

'The office cleaners can do the heavy cleaning. They can come up early in the morning while I'm opening up the office. And the laundry can be sent out.'

But by then their circumstances were common knowledge. Evie felt full of remorse. When she'd agreed to come here she hadn't foreseen this. She'd known before coming that she'd lost Ida Pringle's friendship. They still met and talked of their concerns, but there was a rift between them now. Ida had stepped back; she hadn't wanted their close companionship to continue.

Evie knew she'd been prepared to lose Ida. What she hadn't been prepared for was the pain the situation was causing Bobby. Or the enmity he felt for Byron.

The following day, Wilf Hutchins caught Bobby in the lobby. Bobby hadn't wanted to talk to him.

'I've brought my stamp collection to show you.'

Bobby was tempted, he wanted to see that.

'Come up to the office. It's all right, the boss is out.'

Bobby went. He liked going into the offices. A type-writer clacked away. From a drawer in the table on which he opened the post, Wilf brought out two full albums of stamps. Bobby looked through them, fascinated. Wilf brought out a fat envelope stuffed with swaps.

'For you,' he said. 'To get your collection started.'

Bobby couldn't resist Wilf's wide, cheerful grin and friendly overtures. He asked him countless questions about stamps and about his duties as office boy. He learned that Wilf's ambition was to be an insurance collector, because then he'd be given the use of a bicycle with the company name on it. He'd be able to get out of the office and go round the policy holders, collecting their premiums in weekly instalments.

After that, Bobby made a habit of calling in to the offices of the Bulwark Insurance Company to see Wilf. When he'd read his weekly copy of the *Magnet*, he gave it to Wilf in exchange for more stamps. It wasn't long before he was inviting Wilf up to the flat.

Byron pondered the sad mess he was making of everything. The years were passing. Daisy was four years old and he felt no closer to Bobby. If anything, things were getting worse.

Byron did little during normal working hours, choosing to spend that time upstairs with Evie and Daisy while the older children were at school. And here he was still at his desk long after the office had emptied. He worked late into the evening to give Evie time to get Bobby and Queenie to bed. As they grew older, of necessity, they went to bed later and he put off going up to the flat while they were still up. It rankled, and he was finding it harder not to bear malice.

It seemed a charade after all this time, but he knew Evie loved them all and it tore her in two to see them failing to get on.

Byron felt he'd done everything he could to get on better terms with Bobby. He'd tried taking him on outings, just the two of them, so they'd be on a one-to-one basis. He tried a football match, horse racing, dinghy racing on the river, cricket, men's things. He had no more success with Bobby than he had with his own son, Norman. After a few outings, Bobby had said he preferred to stay at home. Things seemed to go from bad to worse. It was making Evie unhappy. Casting a damper over them all.

He'd very much wanted Daisy to call him Daddy, but it had added to their difficulties. Made Bobby more determined not to accept him into the family. He knew Bobby resented him living in the flat. His silences and sidelong glances told him that. Byron felt that things would have been different if he and Evie were married. Bobby thought, although he couldn't put it into words, that Byron was compromising his mother. Well, he was. He was taking advantage of her generous nature.

Evie thought Queenie resented him too, but he wasn't sure. She was friendlier towards him. If only there were just Evie and little Daisy, all would be fine. The sad fact was, Byron told himself, he didn't feel comfortable anywhere these days.

On his visits to Norman, Veronica glowered at him with bitter intensity. He was left in no doubt that she hated him. He was going less often. It seemed pointless going at all, but if he let too many months go by without a visit, she complained. She wanted Norman to grow up knowing his father. She made him feel guilty.

Byron and Evie had had to work things out as best they could. At the flat he tried to keep out of Bobby's way as much as possible. One or two weekends each month, Gertie still took the older children home with her. He and Evie looked forward to that. It was the only time they seemed to have a normal life. Evie and Daisy were his family.

Then they'd get a baby-sitter and go out on a Saturday night. He felt guilty again because Evie seemed to have so little entertainment in her life.

The intercom rang at last. Evie's voice said: 'The children are in bed, Byron. Supper's almost ready.'

Bobby often dropped into the Bulwark Insurance office to see Wilf Hutchins. He asked him up to the flat but Wilf rarely came. He thought of Wilf as a grown man because he earned a wage. He'd discovered he was three years older than himself.

'How old were you when you started work then?'

'Thirteen.' Wilf was fifteen now.

'That's awfully young.' Nobody left Bobby's school until they were sixteen, and many went on to eighteen.

'I was sick of school anyway.' Wilf shrugged.

He kept a packet of Woodbines and a box of matches in his pocket and seemed to be lighting up whenever Bobby saw him. He'd have a few puffs and put it out, pushing what was left back into the packet for later. Even when only the butt remained, Wilf didn't throw it away.

'Why not?' Bobby wanted to know.

'I collect fag ends. Go round the desks I do, before we close. Empty all the ashtrays.'

'What for?'

He showed Bobby how to break them down and roll the tobacco bits in a fresh cigarette paper. 'I make new ones. It's cheaper this way. Want to try one?'

Bobby felt much older than his twelve years as he lit up, but he wasn't sure that he liked the acrid taste in his mouth.

'It's good to get them from the office. They're all nice and clean like. Lots of men walk the gutters looking for fag ends to reroll.'

Bobby wasn't sure he believed that. Mr Ball smoked cigarettes in their flat every day. The butts were often to be seen in the fancy ashtrays, proof that he was there while Bobby and Queenie were at school. Bobby had seen Mam dispose of them in the waste bin.

Wilf's fist prodded into his stomach in a friendly fashion. 'If you're asked what sort you smoke, you can say "Other People's".'

After four puffs, Bobby thought he'd had as much as he could take. Wilf showed him how to nip off the end before pushing it into the top pocket of his school blazer.

'It'll do you again, see.'

Bobby thought that with practice, he'd soon get the hang of it.

One Saturday morning, Bobby was on his way out of the building when he met Wilf on the stairs.

'You've got to come and see my bike.' Wilf was now sixteen and had been promoted to collector. 'It's kept in the basement.' Bobby watched him pedal off on the bike he'd been allocated and was very envious. Especially as he was allowed to ride it home and use it at weekends.

Soon, by special arrangement, he met Wilf in a quiet back street nearby and learned to ride the bike himself. Bobby could think of nothing more wonderful than having a bike of his own.

When his thirteenth birthday was due, Mam asked him what he'd like as a present. He didn't hesitate, although Mr Ball was having tea with them. Queenie said it was Mr Ball who provided most of the expensive things for them, and if only he played his cards right, he'd be given more. Bobby preferred to do without rather than be beholden to Mr Ball. But a bike was a different matter.

'I'd love a bike.' He couldn't stop that coming out.

Mr Ball looked very earnest. 'Your mother and I have talked about a bicycle . . .'

'I could go to school on it, Mam.'

'Your mother would like you to wait until you're older.'

'Thirteen's quite old. Wilf Hutchins started work . . .'

'The roads are busy round here.' Mam was frowning. 'Many more cars about since the war ended. More lorries too. It's not safe, Bobby.'

He hadn't expected that. Hope died within him. 'I'd be very careful.'

'Perhaps when you're older.'

'There must be something else you'd like,' Mr Ball was asking.

There were a thousand things he'd like, but not nearly so much as a bike.

Mr Ball's eyes were questioning. 'A train set?'

He nodded.

'Perhaps next year, Bobby, we could think of a bike.'

★ ★ ★

248

When the train set came, Bobby had to admit it was magnificent, a Hornby Double O. He set it up in his bedroom and brought Wilf Hutchins up to see it. Wilf said he was very impressed, he'd never had a hope of anything so fine. Never seen one as good, except in a shop.

All the same, Bobby envied Wilf his Bulwark bike. On Friday afternoons, Wilf had to work in the office getting his weekly accounts up to date. He told Bobby that if he wanted to, he could take the bike out and ride it. Just so long as he had it back by five o'clock, which was going-home time.

Bobby rushed home from school that Friday, because he wanted to make the most of the three-quarters of an hour he'd have to ride the bike. He was looking forward to the school holidays, when he'd be able to have it all Friday afternoon.

The bike was propped up in the basement passage. He slung his school satchel and his cap in the cupboard where the buckets and mops were kept and wheeled the bike out through a side door.

It was a very heavy bike, and rather too big for him. He had first learned to ride it by putting one leg through under the cross bar, but now he could get his leg over and sit on the seat, if first he adjusted it to its lowest point.

It felt good to be astride the bike with the wind blowing through his hair. It was all downhill to the Pier Head and he could get up a decent speed. In front of him, he could see a horse-drawn beer waggon heading towards some dock road pub. He pulled out to overtake it, whizzing along now.

Traffic was fairly heavy, but Bobby was sure it was perfectly safe. Down on the Pier Head, which was usually thronged with passengers changing from the ferries to the buses and trams, was a lock-up kiosk selling sweets and newspapers. He had a halfpenny and wanted to get some treacle toffee. He waited for a break in the oncoming traffic and then sent the bike swooping across the great open expanse of cobbles. He did it properly, first looking behind him then putting out an arm to signal his intention.

The sudden jolt came without warning. There was a screech and a smell of burning rubber. His bike seemed to stop dead and he felt himself catapulting over the handlebars. Wilf had warned him to watch out for the tram lines: 'Be sure to cross them at right angles.'

Bobby knew what he'd done. He'd been riding in the same direction as the lines. His front wheel had locked in one of them. The crash knocked the breath out of his body. From the corner of his eye he saw the massive motor wheel come within inches. He heard the bike crumple under it like silver paper, then a searing pain shot through his left ankle and everything seemed to swim round him and go black.

When Evie heard the ring of her front doorbell she ran to answer it, half expecting to find that Gertie had come over to see her. She knew the man who stood there by sight. He looked anxious.

'Dixon,' he said awkwardly. 'Manager of the Bulwark Insurance Company, second floor.'

'Of course. Yes?'

'I'm sorry to have to tell you, Mrs Collins, but your son's been involved in an accident.'

'What?' She felt for the door post. She'd always had this fear; the roads were so busy here. 'What's happened?'

'He was riding one of our bicycles.'

'Is he . . . badly hurt?'

'I don't know. He's been taken to the children's hospital in Myrtle Street.'

Evie felt panic tighten her throat. She gasped: 'But how did he come to have one of your bikes?'

'I'm sending Wilfred Hutchins up to explain that. It's against company rules to lend it to anyone.'

Evie felt half paralysed with shock. As soon as Mr Dixon went, she rang down to Byron. Her mind was filled with the memory of Grace being killed in a bicycle accident.

'Please come up,' she said, and collapsed back on the sofa, hugging Daisy to her for comfort. It was after five o'clock and she'd been wondering where Bobby had got to. He was never this late. Queenie had been home from school this last half-hour.

By the time Byron arrived, Wilf Hutchins was standing awkwardly just inside the door, explaining how the situation had come about.

'He wanted to borrow the bike. I told him he could.'

'You shouldn't have . . .' Evie was all on edge. She kept glancing at Byron, knowing how he'd feel because of Grace. 'It was dangerous.'

Byron had gone white, and his voice was devoid of expression. He said to Wilf: 'What's done is done. Nothing can change it now. You'd better go home.'

'Sir, Mr Dixon says I'll get the sack for this.' Wilf's face screwed up with worry. 'Please . . .'

'Not now.' Byron's tone was not unkind. 'We've other things to think about.'

Evie blamed herself. She expected Byron to blame her too. In spite of Grace's accident he'd recommended that Bobby should have a bike for his birthday and be taught to ride it safely. He'd said: 'Grace was safe enough in normal conditions. It was just the ice.'

'I'll ring for a taxi, Evie,' he said now. 'You'll want to go and see Bobby.'

Evie wanted Byron to come with her. She wanted his

arm to hold on to, but she couldn't ask for it. He was somebody else's husband. Perhaps he wouldn't want to be seen supporting her in public.

It was Byron who rang the hospital and found out that Bobby was being admitted. That he had multiple fractures of his left ankle and would need surgery. It was he who steered Evie to Bobby's room and suggested she take his pyjamas and dressing gown.

'I don't suppose Bobby will want to see me.' He smiled sympathetically. 'I'll stay here and look after the children. Get them a meal.'

Queenie was glaring at him defiantly. 'I want to go with Mam.'

Byron paused. 'All right then, but you must be a good girl. Try and help her. I'll stay here with Daisy.'

Evie went up to the ward with Queenie's hand in hers. They found Bobby asleep.

'We had to give him something for the pain,' Sister explained.

He looked worse than Evie had expected. His hands and face were grazed and his cheeks were the colour of paste. She stood staring down at him, hating to think that her son's perfect body had been mutilated like this.

'His ankle is the serious injury,' Sister told her. 'An open wound with compound fractures, I'm afraid. He'll be put on the list to go down to theatre tomorrow.'

By the time they got home, Byron had given Daisy her supper and put her to bed. He'd set the table and had a meal prepared for them.

Queenie was subdued. She ate swiftly and seemed glad to go to bed. When Evie came back from tucking her in, Byron put a glass of brandy in her hand and pulled her down beside him on the sofa. She sipped the drink then put her head down on his shoulder and wept for Bobby.

His arm went round her shoulder in a comforting hug. 'He'll get better, love. The sister said he'd walk on it again, didn't she?'

'Yes, but he may be left with a limp.'

Evie couldn't stop her tears. Now they were as much for herself and Byron as they were for Bobby. She very much wanted to have this kind man as her husband.

Bobby was in hospital for three weeks and came home with his leg in plaster. Byron discounted the rent on the Bulwark Insurance Company's office by the amount required to replace the bicycle, on the understanding that that would be the end of the matter.

Wilf Hutchins came up to the flat to see Bobby the day he came out of hospital. The younger boy was lying on the sofa, looking out over the rooftops.

'Sorry about the bike,' he said. 'A car squashed it. Did you get into trouble?'

'Nearly got the sack for lending it to you.' Wilf's cheerful grin lit up his face. He dropped his voice because Evie could be heard clattering dishes in the kitchen.

'He's not a bad sort, is Mr Ball. He put in a good word for me. Made everything all right with the boss. He's all right.'

Bobby didn't agree. He felt full of resentment. Mr Ball wasn't treating his mother properly.

Daisy had started at Queenie's school three weeks ago and Evie feared that she hadn't yet settled in. She'd taken Daisy there for the first few days and the little girl had cried when the time came to leave her. The teacher had suggested that perhaps Queenie should bring her instead. Since then, Queenie had said there'd been no problem.

This morning, Daisy hadn't wanted to get up. 'Don't want to go to school, Mam,' she'd moaned.

'You have to go, darling,' Evie had insisted, and helped her dress.

At breakfast, the child had said again: 'Don't feel well, Mam.'

'In what way, love?' She'd put a hand on Daisy's forehead. It felt normal.

'Don't know.'

'A headache? Tummy ache?'

Daisy shook her head in misery. 'Don't want to go to school.'

Evie was afraid that this was because she didn't like her teacher. Daisy had already told her several times that she didn't.

'I think you should go.' Evie felt she had to be firm. 'You can't stay at home unless you're really sick.'

There was no comfort from Queenie. 'Hurry up and eat your breakfast or we'll miss the tram.'

Daisy pushed her half-finished plate away from her.

'Don't you want that bacon?' Bobby's fork was poised above it.

Daisy shook her head, and he whisked her bacon to his own plate. Evie felt a niggle of doubt then, and wondered if she'd made a mistake.

Queenie felt she was towing Daisy to the tram stop. 'Come on,' she urged. 'Let's get a move on.'

Once upstairs on the tram, amongst her own friends, Queenie pushed her sister against the window and ignored her, until Daisy dug her in the ribs and said: 'I feel funny. Sort of queer.'

'Sick, you mean? Queasy?'

Daisy nodded miserably.

'If you'd said that before, Mam would've let you stay home.'

'I feel worse now.'

'You ate too much banana custard last night.' Queenie wasn't sympathetic. 'More than your fair share. You'll be all right. Think of something else.'

Once she'd delivered her sister to her classroom, Queenie's mind was on her own affairs. She was not too pleased to be fetched from her art lesson in the middle of painting a cat. She thought it would be the best cat in the class. Instead, she was told that her sister had been sick and must be seen safely home.

'Fancy throwing up on the floor like that,' she told Daisy as they crossed the school yard. 'In front of everybody.'

'I couldn't help it.' Daisy was close to tears. 'I put up my hand to tell Miss Murgatroyd, but she took no notice. She was telling us about China.'

Queenie giggled. 'Bet that brought the lesson to a halt. You're all right now?'

'No, I've got pains in my tummy. I feel awful.'

Queenie took her hand and helped her on to the tram. 'I won't speak to you if you throw up again here. You'll make the conductor mad and he'll put us off.'

She saw Daisy close her eyes and sink back on the seat. As the tram jolted forward, she sat up straight again.

'It churns me up. My inside's all wobbly. It's swaying too much,' she moaned.

'I'll be glad to get you home,' Queenie said as they went up in the lift. She had to use her own front-door key to let them into their flat.

'Mam?' Daisy called, as they went into the living room.

'She won't be here.' Queenie was impatient. 'She'd have answered the bell if she was. She's gone out shopping or something. You'll be all right now you're home. I'll go back.'

'Will she be long?'

'How should I know?'

'Don't leave me, I still feel awful.'

Queenie watched Daisy climb on to the sofa and curl up at one end.

'Shall I get you the rug?' It was something Mam always did when they didn't feel well. She'd cover them with a tartan rug and tell them to go to sleep. Queenie did that, and decided that if Daisy nodded off, she'd go back to school. She plumped up a cushion and settled in the opposite corner to wait. The sky was dark over the rooftops opposite. It looked like rain.

She heard the lift whirr several times. Each time she thought it might be bringing her mother up, but each time it remained on a lower floor. Then, suddenly, she heard her outside on the landing, talking to somebody. A key turned in the lock and two people came in, laughing.

Queenie knew immediately that it was Mr Ball who was with her. She peeped over the back of the sofa. He had his back to her, Queenie could see that he was kissing Mam on the lips, as heartily as if he hadn't seen her for months. And Mother was opening her arms to him, welcoming his attentions. Queenie felt unable to move and was only half aware of Daisy pulling herself up to see over the top of the sofa too.

Mr Ball was helping Mam off with her coat. He tossed it over the back of their sofa without so much as a following glance. Queenie felt the fur collar tickle her cheek.

'Evie, love.' He was starting to undo the buttons on Mam's crimson wool dress, and she was letting him do it. Queenie could see her fingers fondling the hair at the nape of his neck, and she was pressing herself tightly against him. It was Daisy who broke the spell. She made a choking noise and pulled herself higher.

'Mamma, I'm sick. I've been sent home from school.'

Queenie sat up too, and saw her mother and Mr Ball shoot apart and spin round to stare at them. She thought they looked numb with shock.

'What's the matter, pet?' Mam's voice sounded strange. Her fair skin had flushed scarlet, right up her neck and into her cheeks.

'She threw up on the classroom floor.'

'Couldn't help it, Mam.'

'They made me bring her home,' Queenie told them. 'The other girls were holding their noses and pretending to puke too.'

Daisy wasn't far from tears again. 'Not after Miss Murgatroyd got some sawdust to cover it.'

Mam was holding out her arms to Daisy then. 'How d'you feel now?' She felt the little girl's head to see if she was hot. 'Are you better?'

'No, my tummy hurts.'

Mr Ball hovered, looking embarrassed. 'I'd better go. Shall I send for the doctor?'

'I don't know . . .' Mam was worried now.

'Better had, to be on the safe side.'

Mam was still shaking her head.

'I'll be downstairs, Evie. Let me know if you want one.'

He went then, shutting their front door quietly behind him.

Feeling tense, Evie fumbled to do up the buttons on her dress. She could scarcely breathe. Queenie was thirteen now, growing up, understanding more of the ways of the world. It must have been clear to her what her mother and Byron felt for each other. He'd had his hands inside her dress. Even married couples would keep that sort of love from their children's eyes. She braced herself for the awkward questions she was afraid would come.

Daisy mumbled: 'What was Daddy doing to you?'

That took Evie's breath away.

'Making love,' Queenie answered for her, her voice cold with condemnation.

Evie felt her cheeks burning. Oh God! How much had they seen?

Queenie went on: 'You make such a show of yourselves. Everybody talks about you. How do you think I feel? You're my mother! Why can't you get married like everybody else?'

Daisy piped up: 'Aren't you married to Daddy?'

Evie felt the word was being squeezed out of her: 'No.'

Queenie added: 'They're living in sin.'

'They ask me at school why Queenie's name is Collins and mine is Ball when we're sisters. Is Daddy going to marry you?'

'No!' Evie was aghast at the questions but felt powerless to deflect them.

'But he likes you. He kisses you a lot. I'm sure he wants to.'

'Wouldn't that be great?' Queenie mocked. 'He's rich and he's the boss here.'

'Don't say such things!'

Evie could see that Daisy still didn't understand. 'Don't you want to be married?'

'We can't always have what we want. It's not always possible.' Evie knew she was floundering.

'But he's Daisy's father. You want him to be our father too, you said so. I know you want to marry him.'

'Yes, well . . .'

'Bobby says you're already married.'

'Bobby? Is he here too?'

'No, he's been saying that for a long time. But I've told him he's wrong.'

Oh God! Her children talking like this! She'd had her head in the sand. It didn't bear thinking about. She couldn't leave it at that.

'Why has Bobby been saying that?'

'Because he wants it. Goes round telling everybody.'

Evie straightened up in consternation.

'I told him he's a fool. But he said, if you're not already married you soon will be.'

'Well, we won't.'

'Why not?'

'You know why not, Queenie! If you've heard so much talk, you must know. Byron's already married to someone else.' It sounded like a cry from her heart.

'It's supposed to be a secret, then, that you aren't married? I said to Bobby that that must be it.'

Daisy made a choking sound. 'I think I'm going to be sick again.'

Evie was glad to rush her to the bathroom and bring the conversation to an end. She should have explained the situation to her children. To have Queenie work it out for herself and then wring such an admission out of her!

And Bobby, poor Bobby, trying to make out that she and Byron were married. He'd been trying to shield her, and that pulled at her heart.

She wished she'd been more open with them. But she hadn't been able to because the whole world looked down on women who lived in sin, and it wasn't the way she wanted her children to think of her. And it debased what she and Byron felt for each other. Their relationship had been going on now for more than six years. That was as long as she'd been married to Ned. Byron had been unfailingly kind and generous. She owed him a lot, but she hadn't been able to explain that to her children.

Queenie passed the door as Evie was washing Daisy's face. 'I'm going back to school.'

Evie heard the front door slam behind her.

When she told Byron that Daisy had been sick again, he sent for the doctor. When he arrived, a couple of hours later, Daisy had fallen asleep.

Later, when Byron came up to see how she was getting on, he said: 'Evie, you look exhausted! Is Daisy . . . ?'

She shook her head. 'The doctor thinks it's just a bilious attack. Something she's eaten. He thinks she'll be all right tomorrow. It's Queenie I'm worried about.'

'I was mightily embarrassed that she caught us like that.'

'She said some hurtful things.' Evie shuddered. 'That everybody in this building knows about us; knows about Veronica too; that they gossip about us because we're living in sin.'

He put his arms round her. 'We've known that for a long time,' he said softly. 'You're not still upset about it?'

'I'm upset at the way it's affecting Queenie. She knows exactly what we are to each other. So does Bobby. They don't like us living like this.'

'Queenie can be a little minx.' Evie knew he'd always had a soft spot for her. 'We should have expected this, tried to explain to her.'

'And Bobby.' She told him what Queenie had said about Bobby. She felt his arms tighten round her.

'I'm sorry, Evie. I haven't been thinking either. I'm causing a lot of trouble for you.'

'I'm not setting a good example to my daughters, am I?'

Byron pulled her even closer. 'I'm taking advantage of you.'

260

'I always knew it had to be this way,' Evie said sadly. He loved her and not Veronica, and that had to be enough.

He lifted her chin and smiled down at her. 'Now they both know, Evie, there need be no further embarrassments.'

Byron went down to his office and shut himself away from everybody. He knew he wouldn't be able to work while his mind was swimming with self-reproach like this.

He hated to see Evie upset. He blamed himself. He'd let her down. He told himself he was a weak-kneed fool. He'd pandered to Veronica's wishes and Evie had suffered.

He tossed a file on to his desk, opened it and lifted a pen. His staff were close by. He'd had a glass door fitted to his cubbyhole so he could watch them, but it also allowed them to look in. He didn't want them to see him in this state.

He'd always thought of himself as a person who gave, but he'd taken too much from Evie. He should have taken a stronger line with her children. Let them know he was to be regarded as their father, that he had a position in their family. Instead he'd stood back and left everything to do with their care and discipline to Evie. He hadn't done enough to help her. He asked himself angrily what he could do about it now. He needed to calm down and make plans. He was good at planning ahead.

From now on he was going to look upon Evie's family as his own. He wasn't going to make himself scarce when Queenie and Bobby were about. That had been a mistake. He would throw his weight about more.

He would go once more to Parkfield. His visits were not improving his relationship with Norman. He'd pack what clothes and possessions he kept there and tell Veronica he wouldn't set foot over the doorstep again. He should have done that years ago.

In future, he would think more of Evie's needs. She was the one he loved.

CHAPTER FIFTEEN

Evie felt that things improved after that. Byron was always about the flat and making an effort to be part of the family. He was determined that they would all enjoy life more. At weekends he took them on outings, and they had a holiday in London that pleased the older two.

The mid-1920s were bringing many changes. Women were given the vote. Byron said that class barriers were coming down and Edwardian propriety was gone. Evie felt a fashionable new woman when she shortened her skirts and had her hair bobbed.

Bobby was keen to build one of the new crystal sets. He and Wilf Hutchins started, but progress was much faster when Byron started to help. The three of them spent hours poring over instructions and catalogues of parts, and the whole family was thrilled when they could share earphones and hear 2LO calling from Savoy Hill. Byron enjoyed it so much, he bought more parts so they could do it over again, and Bobby could have a set in his bedroom.

Byron was opening a bottle of wine to go with the ham sandwiches Evie had made earlier. 'We're happy now, aren't we?'

'It's been a very happy day,' she agreed, flopping down on the sofa. She'd been to Daisy's bedroom to kiss her good night. The child was already asleep.

Today had been her seventh birthday, and to celebrate, Byron had taken all the family to the Royal Court Theatre to see *Peter Pan*. Evie thought fondly of her younger daughter. She was never going to be beautiful like Queenie. She had Byron's rather square figure and straight dark hair, but she had his gentle, easy-going manner too.

'Not just this evening.' Byron smiled. 'I mean generally. You are happy, Evie?'

She nodded. 'Contented.'

'Let's drink to our contentment then,' and he put a glass in her hand.

Evie dropped her voice. 'Things have been better since you built the crystal sets. You and Bobby . . .'

'We're on better terms? On the surface, perhaps, but deep down nothing's changed.'

'Not with Queenie either.'

'It's understandable,' he said gently. 'I came between you and them. It'll be all right when they're grown up. The teenage years are hard for all parents.'

'Where are the years going to? Teenagers already!'

Bobby and Queenie came noisily from the kitchen with the steaming mugs of cocoa they'd made for themselves. Evie thought they were all on a high after the excitement of the theatre.

Byron started to talk of something else. 'I told you I was taking Norman into the business? He's written to me. He wants to start in September.'

Evie said: 'I was beginning to think he'd changed his mind.'

'So was I. He decided to train as an accountant first. That'll be his mother's influence. She'd want him to do that.'

'A good idea, surely?' Evie said. 'For a career in business.'

'I'm glad, because he's old enough now to manage on his own when he's had a bit of experience.'

Evie smiled. 'And if he can't, it'll give him something

to fall back on.' She knew that business confidence was falling in the country. 'Your firm's all right?'

'Still expanding. Bucking the trend. I shall be handing it over to Norman in good shape.'

'That must please him.'

'He doesn't know. I haven't said a word about handing it over. Not to him or to Veronica. They think he's coming to work for me and I'll leave it to him in my will.'

'That's mean,' Queenie told him, biting into a sandwich. 'Why keep it to yourself?'

Evie jumped to his defence. 'Byron's never mean. He wants to see how Norman will turn out before he commits himself.'

Byron laughed. 'Kind of you to say that, Evie, but Queenie's probably right. His mother's always demanding her rights and Norman's. I didn't want to give her the satisfaction of knowing he'll get the company sooner than she expected.'

'But you have made up your mind?' Queenie wanted to know. 'You are going to give it to him?'

'Yes, within a couple of years at the most. I don't need to spend every day at that desk down there. I'm getting tired of it. I want more time to myself. I've plans . . . But I also have this obligation to do for Norman what my father did for me.'

'In other words, you'll make Norman rich?' Queenie took another sandwich.

'No, I'll make the business over to him. He might manage to make himself richer than he'd otherwise be. If he learns to run it properly.'

Queenie didn't take her beautiful eyes from him. 'And you're rich enough not to have to work any more?'

'Not rich.' Byron smiled as he refilled Evie's wine glass. 'But a wise man knows when he has enough.'

'I don't know why you're expected to give him anything,' Bobby said hotly. 'If he's an accountant, he can earn a good living for himself. He mightn't want your help. What if he wants to stand on his own feet?'

'He won't,' Byron said. 'Who in their right mind would turn it down?'

Evie was finding her children's teenage years hard to cope with. She no longer knew how to handle Queenie. She'd always been a beautiful child and she was blossoming as she grew older. She looked older than she was; by the age of fifteen she looked adult, and Evie was afraid she was embracing the pleasures of the adult world wholeheartedly. She had Ned's large brown eyes and lustrous curly hair, but Evie feared she didn't have his generous, loving nature.

Queenie seemed to have a will of iron. She was determined to have her way with everything. Evie was afraid she wanted to control what others did in the way that Joseph Hobson, her grandfather, had.

Evie had thought herself daring when she was young, but Queenie's daring left her breathless. All young people seemed to smoke these days. Queenie even smoked in public. She and Bobby talked of larks and japes.

'They're the bright young things of today,' Byron told Evie.

Evie was half sorry she'd bought the wind-up gramophone for Christmas. Queenie had it blaring out endlessly in the living room, practising the steps of the Charleston and the Black Bottom. Evie had also heard it playing in the basement during the school holidays and found Queenie attracting office boys and junior clerks down there. She'd had to put a stop to that.

Almost simultaneously, Queenie and Bobby seemed to

get fed up with school. There was vague talk about leaving. It wasn't what Evie had planned for them and it upset her. It was Bobby who made up his mind first.

'I'm seventeen,' he said. 'It's time I went to work.'

'There's no hurry. Better if you learn all you can first.'

'There's no end to learning, Mam. Wilf started work at thirteen.'

'You're not Wilf,' Evie told him. 'I want you to have every chance.'

'Mam!'

Ned hadn't had a decent chance. She felt so strongly that his son must. Bobby was becoming more and more like his father as he grew up. He still walked with a slight limp after that accident on the bike. It was more marked when he was tired.

'All right, we'll see if Byron can find a good opening for you.'

'No!' Bobby's ferocity shocked her. His brown eyes, usually so gentle, were angry. She found it hurtful that Bobby couldn't get on with Byron. She loved them both very much.

She had to protest. 'I didn't mean in his business, love. He knows every company in the Connaught Building, he's got a lot of pull. He's already said he'll be willing to help.'

'No, Mother.' Bobby's chin was determined. 'I'll find my own job.'

'But darling, you don't understand. If Byron puts in a word for you, your prospects will be better. I want you to have a reasonable start in life.'

'I don't want him to do anything for me.'

'He'll want to . . .'

'I don't want to be beholden to him. I'll do it myself.'

That took Evie's breath away. She'd known Bobby's antagonism for Byron ran deep, but she hadn't realised he'd turn down help from him. She'd thought things were improving now.

She took a deep breath: 'What are you going to do?'

'I'm going to apply to the banks. Wilf thinks a bank clerk would be the thing to be. It can be a career. In time, if I'm good enough and pass exams and things, I could rise to be manager.'

'It could be worse,' Byron said, when she told him. 'At least he isn't going to run away to join a circus. It might work out all right.'

Evie had to be content with that. Bobby found an opening he thought would suit him. He left school in July and started the following week at the Liverpool Savings Bank in Bold Street.

'You're a fool,' Queenie railed at him. 'Why don't you let Dad help you? A hand up now and you'd earn much more.'

Evie had wanted to say that too but had kept silent. Not that it made any difference. Bobby wouldn't listen to anybody.

'I want to leave school too,' Queenie announced the day after she had broken up for the summer holidays. She and Bobby had been mulling over the possibility of leaving for months. She'd persuaded him to come out with it first; after all, he was the elder. He'd taken the brunt of Mam's displeasure and got his own way. She felt it had cleared the way for her.

Now it was her turn. She had it all planned. They all got up late for breakfast. Byron had already gone down to his office.

Mam looked taken aback. 'But you've chosen the subjects for your higher . . . It's all arranged. You said you'd go on.'

'You said I should. You knew I wasn't keen.'

'Only two more years.'

'I'm sixteen,' Queenie said defiantly. 'I've had enough of school. Girls get married at my age.'

She saw her mother flinch. Any mention of marriage was guaranteed to do that.

'I was hoping you'd have a career. Teaching, I thought . . .'

'Mother, I've been telling you for years. I want to learn typewriting. Isn't that enough of a career?'

She could see that Mam was at a loss. 'Well – it has to be something you want to do.'

'Exactly.'

There was no mistaking Mam's reluctant sigh. 'Then we'll have to look for a commercial college for you.'

'Don't you ever listen to what I say?'

Queenie didn't know what drove her on to be so hateful to her mother. Across the table, Bobby had stopped eating. He'd told her he didn't know how she dared, and if he was Mam, he'd slap her face.

'No need to look far. I want to go to the Boardroom Commercial College. Down on the third floor. What could be easier?'

Mam's lips were pursing. 'We'll have to see, dear.'

Queenie knew that that meant she wanted to discuss it with Byron first. Queenie knew how to make him say yes. She'd bring it up at suppertime, before Mam got her oar in. She'd tell him what she wanted, flutter her eyelashes at him and smile. Byron wasn't the sort to refuse her anything.

Later that night, in bed, Byron said to Evie: 'Queenie's a determined little miss. If she's set her mind on leaving school we'd have a hard time changing it.

'I don't think the training at the Boardroom College is the best, but it's not the worst either. Why don't you go in tomorrow? See if they'll take her next term?'

Queenie was delighted when September came round and she found herself one of the Boardroom girls.

Long ago, she'd told the two middle-aged sisters who ran the school that one day she'd be one of their students. The Misses Ermintrude and Edith Worstenholm rented what had once been the boardroom of J. S. Connaught and Company and used it as their main classroom. They also rented two smaller adjoining rooms. One was their office and the other was the room with a typewriter set out on every desk where Bobby and Queenie had played as children.

The sisters called it the Boardroom Commercial College and charged higher-than-average fees. The prospectus claimed to train secretaries in the Boardroom, for the Boardroom; and to give them the extra polish and sophistication needed to handle management affairs.

For Queenie it was familiar ground. She'd been hanging round the place and the girls who attended it for years, in the way Bobby had hung around the Bulwark Insurance Company. She'd learned a lot from past pupils. They'd moulded her thinking on men, on working for a living, on clothes and hairstyles, on the need to colour her lips and her nails. She'd held them up as experts to her friends at school.

As she looked round the class on her first day, the present crop of pupils seemed younger and more callow than in previous years. Some were only fourteen, though most were at least sixteen. Queenie had been looking forward to the extra polish promised in the prospectus. She had only to look in a mirror to know she was very good-looking, but even a good-looking girl could look cheap and trashy, or intelligent, or cool and classy, depending on her clothes and make-up.

Queenie wanted to look fashionable and attractive to men – the sort who had money. She wanted to make sure she was always perfectly turned out. The 'extra polish' was provided by a Miss Dauber, who came on Thursday afternoons to teach grooming and deportment.

Queenie was disappointed to find that deportment consisted of walking in a line round the boardroom with a book on her head, and of sitting up straight at her typewriter. The grooming was keeping her fingernails clean and her skirts pressed. The girls thought Miss Dauber a bit of a laugh and said nobody needed grooming lessons more than she did. She wore skirts that were shapeless tweed tubes.

Queenie had also looked forward to learning to type. But every typewriter had its keys covered so that they couldn't see what letter it would type. She was given a chart of the keyboard.

'So you don't develop bad habits, girls,' Miss Ermintrude's voice brayed. 'No point in looking at your fingers. Keep your eyes on what you are copying.'

Within a day or two, the gramophone was being wound up and playing 'Alexander's Ragtime Band'.

'Listen to the beat, girls. Press one key to each beat. Return the carriage to one beat. Nothing like it for getting your speed up,' she told them heartily.

Queenie felt all thumbs, and the tune raced along far too fast. Miss Ermintrude seemed always to be behind her, shouting above the clatter.

'Keep in time to the music, Miss Collins. Strive for accuracy. Speed is no use without accuracy.'

And she kept winding up the gramophone and playing the tune over and over until Queenie was heartily sick of it.

She found it harder to master the skills of Pitman's shorthand than she'd expected, and Miss Edith's voice dictated at faster and faster speeds. It was just like being back at school and none of it was as much fun as she'd expected.

Both the Misses Worstenholm told them they must behave like ladies. It was very unladylike to ogle at the clerks employed in the Connaught Building, and it was absolutely forbidden to hang about the lifts and stairways in the hope of talking to them.

Years ago, Queenie had heard Wilf Hutchins laughing with Bobby, telling him that the lads in the buildings called the school the Passion Pick-up Point, and that they hung around the stairs and the corridors hoping to get themselves a girlfriend.

The girls thought that an even greater laugh. Each whispered to the other that they considered the clerks beneath their notice. They were seeking husbands who would be able to keep them in comfort. A clerk wouldn't do at all.

But as men of the right calibre were not competing for their attention at the moment, most girls thought they might as well meet the clerks halfway, just for practice and a bit of fun, so it went on all the time.

Queenie was having a late Sunday breakfast in the living room with Bobby when she heard Byron talking to her mother in the kitchen.

'Norman's going to start tomorrow.'

'You'll be pleased to have him. He'll be able to take some of the work off your shoulders.'

'I suppose so.'

'Of course it's so, Byron.' Queenie thought she heard her mother kiss him. 'It's what you planned. If you're ever

272

to give up the office desk, he has to come.'

'Veronica will probably come with him and I'm not looking forward to that. She'll be trying to negotiate privileges. She'll call them his rights, but privileges are what they'll be.

'She'll want him to have a fat salary for a start. She'll expect the business to pay his fares and his lunches. It's nit-picking and it annoys me.'

'Perhaps accountants are all like that,' Mam laughed. 'Why don't you tell him he can have the whole business just as soon as he can manage it?'

'And give her the satisfaction?'

'This has more to do with fighting Veronica than anything else.'

'It's all she ever thinks about, making sure I don't do Norman down.'

'As if you would.'

'No, but I'll let her sweat on it a bit longer.'

When Queenie finished her morning class the next day, instead of going straight up to the flat for lunch, she took the lift down to the ground floor and peeped inside the office of Henry Ball and Sons. She'd never seen Norman and was curious about him. Besides, she wanted to give a full report to the girls in her class. Particularly Louisa Fanshaw, who boasted that she had a boyfriend who came from a wealthy family. Queenie was disappointed. He wasn't there and there were no signs that the spare desk had been taken over.

'Veronica rang,' she heard Byron telling Mam over the meal. 'She had to go to the dentist this morning and she wants to bring Norman in herself. She thinks nobody else could introduce him to our accounts. Talk about mother's boy!'

Mam asked: 'When will they come?'

'They'll be in this afternoon.' Byron was hacking irritably at the pot roast Mam had spent all morning cooking.

Queenie ate silently, thinking about wives and kept women. Byron's wife had upset him by delaying Norman's start. Mam's efforts to please had not soothed his irritation. It was easy to see which women held power in this world. Queenie had already decided she would become a wife as soon as she possibly could.

When she went again to peep into Byron's office late that afternoon, Norman was there with his mother. Both were seated at the spare desk, with documents spread out before them.

Queenie thought Norman looked a cut above the average clerk in the Connaught Building. At twenty-two, his shoulders had broadened out; he was already a man. He wore a good suit that had been made for him, not a hand-me-down. There was no look of the mother's boy about him.

He wasn't handsome like Bobby, but he wasn't bad either. Lots of straight brown hair that he kept tossing off his forehead. Nice clear skin, past the acne age, unlike many of the young clerks here. Queenie was sure the girls would vote him a winner. And he wasn't just a clerk. Soon he'd own that business. He'd be able to keep a wife in comfort.

His mother looked formidable and really sour. Her nose and mouth twisted as though she had smelled a bad smell. She was tall and angular, with eyes like organ stops, and grey waves set with mathematical precision.

Queenie could see why Byron preferred Mam. Anybody else in the world would too. Yet Veronica was dressed with more style, in a velvet dress of soft green, and she'd thrown back a handsome coat with a fox-fur collar.

* * *

Byron was in a worse temper when he came up at teatime.

'You'd think it was Veronica who was teaching him to run the business. She said she'd come every day for a month. So she could explain our accounting system.'

'He is a qualified accountant,' Evie murmured.

'I'm afraid I was rather rude. I said learning to make a profit was more important than counting every last penny.

'It's my business but she treats it as though it's hers. And then you wonder why I don't just say take it.'

'Could she run it?' Queenie wanted to know, her mouth full of sponge cake.

'No. He won't be able to either, unless I show him.' Byron crashed his cup down on his saucer.

'Veronica wasn't satisfied until she found out exactly what it earns now. She hasn't been near for eighteen months and just as I expected, she wanted to jump his salary up. And a car, she wanted me to buy him a car. To come to work in, she said.

'I told her he'd do the journey in half the time if he used the boat or the train. No one in their right mind is going to drive a car on and off the luggage boat just to cover half a mile or so on this side. And it's not so easy to park these days, not round here. Veronica had the neck to say he deserved one. Not from me he doesn't.'

Evie cut a slice of the sponge cake she'd made for him. He was too angry even to try it, though the whole flat smelled wonderful from its baking.

'Norman hasn't been near me in years. Even now, he wouldn't come without her. He'll have to learn to leave go of her hand or he'll never be able to run anything.'

'Don't let Veronica upset you,' Evie was saying.

'She put me in such a bad mood I refused to budge on anything. I said he's here to learn the business and that means others have to give time to him. I said he'd be more of a hindrance than a help for the first six months. I told him I'd think about a rise then, if he proved to be useful.'

Queenie lay back on the settee and let her gaze linger on the darkening skyline. The crystal set was on a stool beside her, but she held the headset an inch from her ear so she could hardly hear Henry Hall's orchestra. That was the way she wanted it. She was doing some serious thinking.

Norman Ball interested her. Mam's embarrassing position had made her decide long ago that she wouldn't get caught that way. She was going to be married. A legal wife, and she wasn't going to marry a poor man and have to work either.

It occurred to her now that Norman Ball was a likely candidate. Anyway, she knew of no other, so she might as well find out if she liked him enough. Mam wouldn't like her taking up with him, but she'd never known which way her bread was buttered, and besides, there was no need to tell her just yet.

Norman Ball chewed the end of his pen and looked round his father's office. He didn't feel at ease here. The only sound was the clack of Miss Parker's typewriter. The three clerks scribbled away in files and ledgers on their desks.

For as long as he could remember, his mother had been going on about his birthright. About how she'd fought to get him this chance to claim it. About how his father had reneged on all his other obligations, but he mustn't be allowed to renege on this. She was absolutely determined that Father shouldn't cheat him out of his share of this business.

'You'll have to go and work with him,' Veronica had

said. 'Learn all about it. I'm afraid he's built up other family commitments. He may want to keep the business for them. It'll be up to you to make sure he doesn't.'

Norman felt he hardly knew his father. He hadn't seen very much of him since he was eleven years old, and nothing at all in recent years. His mother spoke of Byron often, but never with affection. She told Norman that his father was a hard man, selfish, cruel and particularly mean with his money.

Norman had put off coming here for as long as he could. He thought now that it was a mistake, even though the profit generated by this small office was much greater than he'd expected. Greater than Mother had expected too. He'd seen her glow of interest when she finally got at the books.

'It's worth having,' she'd told him. 'You must stand up for yourself. Not let your father browbeat you.'

Then yesterday, on his first day, the staff here had spoken warmly of Father. They seemed to think he was a fair man. 'Generous and easy-going,' his secretary had said.

'I hope you'll settle down and enjoy doing the work, Norman.' Byron had shaken his hand when they'd met. 'The men of our family have been doing something like this for over two hundred years. I hope you'll want to carry on the tradition.'

Then Byron had taken them to his little office for privacy, and Mother had put forward her demands on Norman's behalf. She hadn't told him what she intended doing, or what her demands were. If she had, he'd have said she was expecting too much. Norman had been embarrassed to hear them arguing over what he should or should not be given. What he remembered most about the time when Father had lived with them was the way his parents were always at each other's throats.

Father had dug his heels in and both had ended up angry and frustrated. Mother had come with Norman again this morning. There had been more of the same argument. He'd tried to keep out of it this time. Then she'd opened the accounts for Henry Ball and Sons but was too angry to concentrate. He'd have learned more about them if he'd been left to examine them in peace. He was glad when she'd given up and gone.

All this made him wonder whether he'd done the right thing by coming at all. He hadn't been convinced it was what he'd wanted in the first place.

Accountancy hadn't been his thing either. He'd completed his articles and passed his exams because Mother was forever telling him it was a means to an end, and that he'd manage to run this business more efficiently if he had a background in accountancy.

He hadn't yet found his niche, and he didn't think he would here. At the back of his mind was the thought that he'd like to work with dogs. He had a Labrador and his mother kept a Pekinese. Yes, something to do with dogs would be more his sort of thing.

Norman pulled himself to his feet with a heavy sigh. First days in a first job could never be easy. He hadn't expected they would be. His father had disappeared, no doubt to his flat at the top of the building. Norman wished it was time for him to go home. He'd go along to the gents to get away for a few minutes, stretch his legs.

He was no sooner in the corridor when he saw a girl coming towards him with a swinging stride. An absolutely stunning girl. She was looking him confidently in the eye and smiling. He felt bowled over in those first few seconds.

'Hello, Norman.' She planted herself squarely in front of him. 'I'm Queenie Collins. Have you heard of me?'

His first thought was that she must be some star of stage or screen. She was wearing lipstick and nail varnish, but it was discreet and enhanced her beauty. Her dress was eye-catching too. Was this some publicity stunt?

He felt at a loss. 'No, should I have done?'

'I just wondered.' There was something almost intimate in her manner. 'I live in the flat on top of this building – with Byron.'

That took his breath away. Was she telling him . . . ? No, she must be too young . . .

'My mother and him.' Her smile was dazzling. 'I belong to the other half of the family.'

CHAPTER SIXTEEN

Queenie smiled seductively. 'How about having a cup of tea with me?'

Norman's face lit up. She had him outside in South Castle Street in moments.

'I don't know whether I should be leaving the building now,' he protested half-heartedly. 'Got to keep my slate clean, new job and all that.'

Queenie laughed and steered him towards Macey's Café. 'You'll be safe for half an hour. Your dad's having his tea. He always takes his time.'

Macey's was only a hundred yards away and was much patronised by the Boardroom girls at lunchtime. It was open all day and specialised in light savoury snacks and cakes. The décor and the crockery were designed to appeal to office workers, of which there were many in the district. At four thirty in the afternoon, it was almost deserted. Queenie settled at a table near the window. Service was swift.

'I thought we should know each other. We're sort of related.'

'We are not,' Norman said firmly. 'Not related at all. I don't think my mother would approve of this.'

Queenie giggled. 'Your father won't mind. It's sort of bringing both sides of his family together.'

Norman's eyes were searching her face. 'I don't see it as a bad thing. We're adults, aren't we? Tell me about your family.'

He was listening avidly to all she told him about Mam

and Bobby. She found he knew nothing about them. He was even more interested to hear about Daisy.

'She's your half-sister,' Queenie assured him. 'Fancy you not knowing about her.'

He looked quite shocked. 'I didn't know she existed. My father has an illegitimate child! Mother will be shocked!'

Queenie laughed. 'She knows. She just isn't telling you.'

'Really?'

'I'm sure.'

Norman said slowly: 'Perhaps you're right. Once she did say something like: "He has other commitments. He may want to leave his business to . . ." '

'She feels Byron's rejected her. She doesn't want to talk about that and she doesn't like us,' Queenie said, never taking her eyes from Norman's face. 'No wonder she's got it in for him.'

'Has she?'

'Very definitely.'

Norman would have been willing to linger, now that Queenie had primed his curiosity. He wanted to know more about Evie, more about Queenie herself. When the bill came for their tea and scones, she made a show of picking it up, but he insisted on paying.

'When can I see you again?' he wanted to know as they were crossing the dignified foyer of the Connaught Building.

'Tomorrow?' Queenie turned her eyes full of eager anticipation on him.

'Lunch? The same place? We won't have to waste time getting there.'

'Lovely.' Queenie gave a little squeal of delight and surreptitiously planted a kiss on his cheek. That was to tell him they could be more than friends.

* * *

Queenie's first impressions of Norman were favourable. She liked the way his gaze explored her face; she liked the smile that played about his lips and the masterful way he'd taken that bill from her.

She spent most of the evening trying to work out the best way to manage this affair. All her instincts were to play it fast; she wasn't one to drag her feet anyway. A whirlwind romance might be the best way, not allowing him time to catch his breath.

The lunch was a great success. Norman seemed as eager as she was. He invited her to the theatre that evening.

'Shall I try to get tickets for the Playhouse? I've heard the new play there is very good.'

'Yes, please,' Queenie breathed. 'I'd love that.'

'What if there aren't any seats?' He couldn't get in touch with her once she was in class again.

'We'll go to the pictures instead, and you can try for tickets on another night.'

Some of the girls from her class had been eating in Macey's too. They wanted to know all about Norman. Even Louisa Fanshaw seemed impressed when Queenie mentioned that he was Byron's only son.

To meet Norman, Queenie had to miss family meals. She'd had to say: 'I won't come up for lunch today, Mam.' Now she had to add: 'I'll be missing supper tonight. I want to go out.'

'Where are you going?' Mam wanted to know.

'Lots of the girls eat at Macey's. It's fun, all of us together.'

'But tonight as well?'

'They're all going to the theatre. The Playhouse. I'd like to go with them.'

'All right.' Mam seemed reluctant.

'Let her go,' Byron had urged. 'Let her have her fling with her new friends.'

He'd taken out his wallet and given her a pound. 'To ease the financial strain,' he'd said.

Queenie had kissed him; Byron could be very generous.

In the following days Queenie flaunted Norman in front of the Boardroom girls like a prize she'd won.

Louisa Fanshaw tried to belittle him. 'He's not all that handsome,' she said.

'But he's going to be rich one day.' Queenie rushed to point out his advantages. She almost told them more than she should.

'And he knows how to treat a girl,' she added instead. 'Dinner at the Adelphi last night. Always the best theatre seats. Taxis to the door. He's fun to be with.'

It wouldn't do to start any gossip. Not about Byron's intention of handing over his business to his son. Byron wouldn't be pleased if it got to Norman's ears before he told him himself. He'd know it had come from Queenie.

Norman was showing an increasing interest in her company even though she'd told him every fact she could think of about her family. He asked a lot of questions about Byron; he said his father was going out of his way to be kind to him. That he thought after all that the job might suit him. He'd met Queenie through it after all.

Norman spent the first hour of every day with his father in his little office. He found these sessions very helpful. He was picking up the knowledge he needed to work here. He tried to be as attentive as possible and show enthusiasm for the job. He wanted Byron's approval.

Now, as he went back to his own desk, he wished he could get to know his father better. Byron never spoke of his new family, nor invited Norman upstairs to meet them.

He was affable, even friendly during working hours, but he kept his distance. Norman was careful not to mention that he was getting to know Queenie very well.

Last night, he'd taken her to dinner at a new nightclub that had just opened in Lord Street. He'd had a wonderful time, holding Queenie in his arms as they shuffled round the tiny dance floor. She felt soft and yielding and had put her head down on his shoulder. He hadn't meant to stay more than a few hours, but time had flown.

Norman stifled a yawn. He'd managed to get a taxi to bring Queenie back here. He'd seen her in, then climbed back in the taxi and asked to be taken to the underground station in James Street.

'Last train goes at half eleven, gaffer.'

Of course it did. Norman had sat back on the seat for a moment, trying to collect his wits.

'The Pier Head? You might just catch the midnight ferry if I put me foot down.'

He knew the boats only ran every hour during the night, and he'd have to find a taxi on the other side. It hardly seemed worth the trouble when he had to be back here by nine in the morning.

'The Stork Hotel,' he said. He'd stay overnight. No doubt his mother was waiting up for him. He'd have to ring her when he got there.

Norman sat at his desk, expecting his mother to come through the door at any moment. She was usually here by mid-morning. She'd agreed with Byron that she'd come in daily for a month until Norman had got the hang of the accounting system. After being articled for all those years to Lampton and Fiske, there had never been a need for her to come. He'd worked it out for himself within the first few days. He wished she'd give up coming.

The trouble was, if she hadn't gone by lunchtime, it made it difficult to meet Queenie. His mother would hate the very idea of his being friendly with her. Queenie was Byron's mistress's daughter. One day, he'd had to scribble a note at the last moment, and ask Miss Parker to run up to the Boardroom College with it when Queenie's class was being dismissed. He'd had a boring heavy lunch with Mother instead, and longed for Queenie's company.

Last night, on the telephone, Veronica had asked if he had a girlfriend who was keeping him out late. He'd had to say yes. What else would keep him out so many evenings on the run? At least, at that moment, he didn't have to introduce Queenie, and he hadn't explained who she was. Mother was none too pleased as it was.

Lunchtime came, and he was thankful there'd been no sign of his mother.

Queenie was all giggles. 'Wonderful night last night, wasn't it? The girls are green with jealousy. Not many have been to a nightclub.'

'A quiet night tonight, eh?' Norman wasn't used to so many late nights.

Queenie beamed at him. 'What about the pictures then? I'm dying to see *Sadie Thompson*, and it's showing at the City Picture House. Gloria Swanson's in it.'

Norman had been about to suggest that they have a night in to recover, but he didn't want to disappoint her. She was always brimming with energy and enthusiasm. At the back of his mind was the fear that if he didn't take her, she'd find somebody else who would. He'd seen the clerks ogling her and knew she'd have no difficulty. Queenie was a prize. He felt incredibly lucky that she seemed to like him.

There was also the problem that he was running out of money. The hotel bed had taken the last of what he'd had.

If his mother had come in this morning, he'd have been able to ask her for more. She was always generous if she had it. That was one thing he could say for her. A free spender herself, she expected it of him.

Since his father had left them, his mother had found her pleasure spending the money he allowed her. Everything she bought was of the very best. She liked getting out and about. Every few months, she went down to London for a week. She liked theatres and restaurants and expensive hotels. If she was going out, she telephoned for a car to come to her door.

Norman had always thought her attitude to money at odds with her training in accountancy. He'd told her so.

She'd laughed: 'It's fun spending it, but work adding it up.'

He thought she might still turn up this afternoon. When she'd missed the odd morning previously, she'd always come in later. He watched the clock, but by four he'd decided she wasn't coming. It was hardly worth her while.

Norman wondered if he dared ask his father for money. There was no other way he could take Queenie to the cinema, and she'd want something to eat afterwards. He quailed at the thought, but Queenie had said Byron was easy-going.

He made up his mind to do it before he disappeared upstairs for his tea. He had to get money from somewhere. He tapped on the glass door of his father's office. Byron was frowning when he lifted his head.

'Father,' he said slowly. 'Could I have a sub against my salary?' He was conscious of the searching look Byron was giving him, and tried to explain. 'Working for a whole month before I'm paid. It isn't easy to manage.'

'You weren't paid by Lampton and Fiske?'

'A small honorarium. Mother gave me an allowance.'

'And that's no longer forthcoming?' Byron opened his wallet and gave him five pounds. 'This once only,' he said.

Norman pocketed it quickly. Byron's eyes locked on to his.

'To be successful, a businessman must have a firm control on his spending. Whether his own or that of his business.'

'Yes, Father.'

Norman's cheeks were burning when he returned to his desk. It seemed that Byron's attitude to money was different to his mother's. He mustn't do that again, if he wanted Byron's approval.

Queenie sat beside Norman in the warm semi-darkness of the Palais de Luxe in Lime Street. His hand came over the plush armrest to hold hers. He squeezed it gently now. She turned to smile at him and he leaned across to kiss her. His arm went round her shoulders, pulling her closer.

'I'm falling in love with you, Queenie,' he murmured against her cheek. 'You're very beautiful.' She felt a spurt of triumph as she nuzzled against him.

It was a shame he wouldn't let her concentrate on Janet Gaynor. Queenie had been enjoying *Seventh Heaven*, but it was more important to bring Norman to the point of proposing, and this was a big step forward. She'd definitely made up her mind to marry him. Where would she find anyone more suitable?

She'd had to fight a battle with Mam at breakfast-time this morning to keep pursuing him.

'You're overdoing things, Queenie,' Evie had told her. 'Burning the candle at both ends. I don't mind you having the odd late night if you're out with the girls, but this is too much.'

'I'm sorry, Mam.'

'You'll stay in tonight?'

'I've said I'll go to the pictures.'

'Well, I think you should stay home.'

'Just this once, Mam. Please,' she wheedled.

'And you're missing too many meals. You aren't eating properly.'

'I'm too fat anyway.'

'Nonsense,' Mam said. 'You'll make yourself ill.'

'No, Mam, I won't.' Queenie had a healthy appetite and Norman was tempting her with wonderful food.

'You haven't got the money to pay for decent meals out.'

'I have a boyfriend now. He buys some meals for me.'

Queenie thought Norman paranoid about wanting to keep from his mother the fact that they were going out. She knew he was also worried about how his father would take the news. For her own part, Queenie couldn't see any special reason why Byron and Mam should object. But she didn't want to tell anybody of her plan. It wouldn't do at all for people to know about that. She'd thought it better to keep silent about Norman for the time being. Until she knew whether it was going to work out.

Telling Mam she had a boyfriend brought ten thousand questions about him, and a demand to bring him up to the flat. Mam wanted to meet him.

Choosing a moment when her mother had gone to the kitchen, Queenie had walked out at five o'clock to meet Norman. She knew there'd be more trouble when she got home. But it was worth it because she was having some success with her plans. Really, it hadn't taken all that long, not quite a month. Norman hadn't taken the final step and asked her to marry him, but she was fairly confident now that he would. He was like putty in her hands.

It was a fine evening, and for once they walked back to the Connaught Building.

Norman sighed. 'I do love you, Queenie, but it would be so much easier if you had no connection with Father.'

'It does make things difficult.'

'I'm worried that my mother won't like this.' Norman had an arm round her waist. 'I'm afraid she'll be upset. Because of your mother. I mean, living with . . .'

'It'll probably upset my mother too,' Queenie said. 'She'll blame herself, she's that sort. But I love you too much to let that put me off. We won't let them come between us, will we?'

When Norman reached home late that night, he found a note from his mother, telling him she'd gone to London for a few days and would be staying at the Savoy.

His first feeling was one of relief, but then he knew he'd have to be careful with his cash. It had to cover daily fares over to Liverpool, and lunches, and he'd already made a good hole in the five pounds Father had advanced. There was another week to go to pay day. Somehow he'd have to make it last out.

Queenie was in his thoughts as he snuggled down in his bed. He could see her smiling face before him, feel her lips against his and the touch of her fingers on the back of his neck when he took her into his arms. He wanted her beside him in the flesh, for always.

Towards the end of the following week, Norman felt he'd made a big step forward in his career. His father empowered him to sign cheques on behalf of Henry Ball and Sons. Only up to a limit of twenty pounds, but he felt he was taking on some responsibility.

Byron said: 'Veronica hasn't been in these last few days.'

'She's down in London.'

'Oh! I hoped she was backing off. Is there anything else she can teach you about the accounting system?'

'No, it's all straightforward. Easier for me to cope with than your import licences.'

'Discourage her from coming in again, Norman.'

That alarmed him. 'She'll probably want to. It makes her feel useful.'

His father said more forcefully: 'I don't like her sitting around my office, poking her nose into my affairs. She's come in from time to time over the years to make sure I didn't forget about you. You're here now, so there's no further need for her to come.'

'I'll tell her,' he said.

It wasn't something he felt he needed to worry about for the moment. Mother was away. Lack of cash was more pressing. His five pounds was dwindling fast. Queenie wanted to go out and about, and he was keen to take her.

Over lunch with her at Macey's, he'd admitted that he was a bit strapped for cash. 'Just until pay day on Friday. With Mother away, I can't borrow any.'

Queenie sighed. 'We'll still be able to go out tomorrow night? You said something about taking me to the Empire.'

Norman was tempted, but he knew he should say no.

'I can pay for myself, Norman. I want to go.'

He sighed. He was broke.

Queenie said brightly, 'I know what I'll do, I'll ask Byron. He'll give me at least a pound. I'll be able to treat you for once.'

That made Norman nervous. 'Won't he ask who you're going with?'

Queenie smiled. 'I won't tell him.'

Queenie was disconcerted. She hadn't expected Norman to say he was short of money. He always seemed to spend freely and have plenty. He'd never let her pay for anything, and pressed frequent gifts of chocolates and perfume on her. She thought of him as being rich. That was the whole point: she wanted to share his life of plenty.

She reminded herself it was only temporary because his mother had gone away. He'd be paid on Friday. He'd be wealthy in his own right once Byron had made over the business to him. Everything would be fine then.

Queenie knew that she and Byron would be eating lunch alone today. Bobby took sandwiches to the Liverpool Savings Bank, Daisy stayed at school, and Mam was going over to Birkenhead to see Gertie and collect her rent from Ida Pringle. She'd left a casserole and baked potatoes in the oven for them. The table was set for two.

It gave her just the chance she needed to talk to Byron on her own. She wasn't on good terms with Mam at the moment and she didn't want to ask him for money in front of her. Mam might tell him not to give her any.

Queenie had the meal on the table and had rehearsed her request for extra pocket money when Byron came through the door.

'Ah, Queenie.' He was rubbing his hands. 'It seems we're lunching alone for once.'

'Yes.'

'I'm glad, it gives me a chance to talk to you. Haven't seen much of you recently.'

'I'm here now.' She started dishing up the casserole.

'Yes, I want you to tell your mother what you're up to.'

Queenie let the ladle crash back in the dish. 'What?'

'You tell her you're going out with the girls from the school, but you're not, are you?'

He took over from her, heaping their plates. 'All these lies . . .'

She said defensively: 'I've told her I have a boyfriend.'

'But you haven't told her who it is.'

She knew her mouth had dropped open. She was shocked. He seemed to know . . . This wasn't going to be the right moment to ask him for money.

'Norman sits a few yards in front of my desk. I can hardly miss what's going on.'

Queenie heard her fork clatter down on to her plate. She'd been careful to stay well away from Byron's office. With those glass doors, she'd known he could see what was going on.

'I heard you laugh, Queenie, out in the corridor. Then Norman came in. I've even heard your voice. And then there's the gossip. It's difficult to keep secrets in this building. Anyway, what's the point?'

Queenie felt disconcerted. 'I didn't want to upset Mam.'

Byron hooted in derision. 'That's exactly what you are doing. You're a manipulative little minx. You're up to something and you don't want to tell us what it is.'

Queenie drew herself up to her full five foot five. 'Why should I tell you? You're not my father . . .'

'I feel as though I am. Do you know that? I feel as though I am.'

Queenie couldn't look at him. He looked hurt.

'Anyway, that's no reason to tell your mother lies. She's worried stiff about you. You're staying out late at night, missing meals, and you're rude and rebellious to us both.'

He was sitting back in his chair, glaring at her. She could see he was angry.

'It's got to stop, Queenie. I'm not putting up with any more. And you'll tell your mother that Norman is your boyfriend.'

Queenie managed to choke out: 'All right. I will.'

'I could tell her myself but it would be better coming

from you. If you don't want to drive an even wider rift between you.'

What was there she could say to that? Queenie moistened her lips.

'She loves you very much, Queenie. She's always thinking of your welfare. Yours and Bobby's. She's always put your needs above her own. Did you know that? Above mine too. It's time you started thinking of her.'

Norman was having a difficult day. His father seemed in an unusually abrupt mood, not only with him but with everybody in the office. He thought Queenie would be lucky to get anything out of him.

At lunchtime, he stayed at his desk, eating the sandwiches he'd brought and longing for Queenie's company. Harry Penn was eating at the next desk.

'Not going to Macey's today? he asked.

'Can't. I'm broke.'

'Never mind. Pay day tomorrow.'

Norman found himself thinking of Queenie all the time. He could see her face smiling up at him from every file he opened. He was desperate to know if he'd be able to see her tonight.

With his mother away, he'd toyed with the idea of taking Queenie home with him. He'd love to do that, and it wouldn't take much cash. He'd even told the maid to take the night off, but she lived in. She was middle-aged and not one for the pictures, and he was afraid she'd stay in and see Queenie. If she told his mother there'd be an inquisition. Mother might even come home herself. She rarely stayed away more than six or seven days.

She'd been very put out to hear he had a girlfriend. There'd been just the two of them for so long, it wasn't surprising she wanted to keep him close. She wanted him to spend time with her, not be out on the town with a girl, and definitely not married. And if she found out who Queenie was . . .

Norman sighed. It was too dangerous to take Queenie home with him. He'd have to think of some other way to see her.

Byron came back after lunch angrier than ever. He disappeared again without staying long. It was mid-afternoon when something of a crisis developed. Miss Parker, Byron's secretary, discovered she didn't have enough stamps to put on the day's heavier than usual output of mail. Then Harry Penn, who kept the petty cash, found he didn't have enough to buy more, and the banks were due to close in fifteen minutes.

'I can make out cheques on the firm's account,' Norman told them, and felt his credibility rise. He knew from the records that the usual amount withdrawn for petty cash was five pounds. His pen was poised over the chequebook when the idea came to him. Immediately his heart began to pound. Did he dare?

There was no time to think it through. He made out the cheque on the spur of the moment, tore it out and handed it to Harry. His writing looked shakier than usual.

Harry stared down at it. 'Eight pounds, eh?'

'It seems five isn't enough,' Norman said. Even his voice sounded shaky. 'Off you go, or the bank will be closed.'

Norman couldn't concentrate on work for the rest of the day. He was shocked at what he was doing, but he had found a way to have his night out with Queenie.

He spent the rest of the afternoon dreading that Byron would return. It would be so much more difficult if he were sitting the other side of that glass door. He had to wait until everybody else went home. When he was the only person left, he took the extra three pounds from the petty cash box and put them in his pocket.

He kept telling himself it was perfectly safe. Tomorrow was pay day and he'd put the money straight back. There'd be no paperwork to show what he'd done. He'd tell Byron later that he'd increased the amount, and it would never be missed overnight.

Queenie felt really churned up after Byron's ticking-off and had been too upset to keep her mind on shorthand dictation. Miss Edith picked on her and asked her to read it back. She made a hopeless mess of it in front of the whole class, and that made her feel an inadequate fool.

When school was over for the day, she went out and window-shopped up Lord Street. Norman had to work on until five o'clock and she didn't want to come face to face with Byron again just yet. When she got back to the Connaught Building, Norman was waiting for her in the foyer. She was delighted when he took her arm and said there was no longer any problem about money.

He took her to have a drink first. She always asked for a dry martini, although she didn't like the taste. It sounded sophisticated and very grown-up, and she didn't want to appear too young to Norman. She asked him twice where he'd managed to get the money, but he wouldn't tell her.

Then they went to the first house at the Empire to see a very slick variety show. The sand dancers cheered them both up. It did her good to hear Norman laugh out loud. Queenie began to feel better too.

When they came out, Norman suggested supper in a little place in Church Street that they'd tried before and liked.

'You've really solved your cash problem then?' Queenie was hungry. She'd hardly eaten anything at lunchtime.

'No. Haven't really,' Norman sighed, and then began

to open up and tell her what was on his mind.

'I wish I'd come to work for Father straight from school. I kept putting it off and I've wasted four years. I didn't need to train as an accountant to run his business. I'd be settled and earning a decent salary if I'd come straight away.'

Queenie was glad he hadn't. She'd have been only twelve when he was leaving school.

'It's so hard to think of the future without thinking of money. It makes such a difference to what one can do.'

'Norman, you've managed to get money from somewhere. Don't worry, we're having a nice time.'

'I don't just mean for a night out.' He was frowning.

'You'll be paid tomorrow.'

'A month's salary won't go far. It's real financial security I'm hankering for.'

Queenie felt hope spiral through her. If he was thinking of the future, and of money, could he be thinking of marriage?

'Why?'

'Oh, Queenie! I love you. I want to marry you, but how can I ask a girl like you when I've no money?'

Queenie was bursting with triumph. Her troubles were over. She was smiling. 'I love you.'

'I shouldn't really have mentioned it yet. We'd need a house and a hundred other things. Then living expenses . . . It'll be years before I can afford it.'

'It won't,' Queenie said. 'No, it won't. Your father's planning to give you his business.'

'Yes, I'm hoping to inherit . . .'

'No, you won't have to wait for him to die. He means to give it to you soon. Within a year or two. I know he does. I've heard him tell Mam he's had enough of working nine till five. He's rich, Norman. He owns the Connaught Building – and other things.'

Norman was staring at her, wide-eyed.

'I shouldn't have told you. I mean, it's something he wants to do himself. Don't let on I have.'

'Of course not! But are you sure?'

'Certain. He talks to Mam about it all the time. Perhaps he'll give it as a wedding present, if you marry me. We'll have a wonderful life, Norman.'

'If you're right,' he said cautiously.

'I know I'm right.' Queenie leaned across the table to kiss him. 'I know I'm right.'

CHAPTER SEVENTEEN

Norman knew before he reached the gate that his mother had returned home. The lights were on all over the house. He let himself in the front door and locked it behind him. Veronica was on the stairs, wearing a white satin dressing gown trimmed with angora, and matching high-heeled satin mules.

'Hello, Mum.'

'Where've you been? I've been worried about you.'

A heavy pink sleep-net protected her permanent wave and cut across her forehead, at odds with the elegance of her clothes.

'There's no need to worry.'

'Darling.' She came and hugged him against her hard, angular body. 'I've been home since four o'clock. Waiting for you.'

'If only you'd let me know.'

He kissed her cheek. It had received its quota of night cream and felt sticky to his lips. Her face was grim and haggard. Norman knew he'd disappointed her again.

'I expected you to be here. Where've you been?'

'To see a show at the Empire. It was good.'

'But who did you go with, darling? Not the new girlfriend again?'

Norman was tired and wanted to get to bed. He'd been dreading a cross-examination about this since he'd admitted on the phone that he had a girlfriend.

'Yes.' He took a deep breath. 'What have you been doing in London?'

His mother wasn't easily deflected. 'You must tell me all about her. What's her name?'

He hated to upset her, and this was going to. He didn't feel up to it tonight. He knew he was everything to Veronica. She made all his decisions and fought all his battles. She provided him with everything he needed: a home, meals, holidays and entertainment. She chose and paid for his clothes. All she asked in return was his devotion.

He knew that without him, her life would be empty. She'd always resented his friends, even his schoolfriends. She'd managed to see off two girlfriends already. Veronica wanted to be all in all to him. Until now, he'd relied on her and basked in the close relationship. His only ambition had been to have an easy life.

Veronica had pushed him to train as an accountant and selected the firm to which he'd been articled. She'd always been paranoid about the need for him to work for Henry Ball and Sons. She was going to see that he inherited it as his father had done before him. She was going to make sure Byron didn't do him down.

Norman had gone along with it because his mother wanted it. He wanted to please her, though recently he'd begun to resent her very heavy hand. Now there was something else he wanted. He wanted Queenie Collins, and his mother was not going to let him have her without a fight.

'Queenie,' he said, though he knew it was going to change everything. 'Queenie Collins. She's Evie Collins's daughter. She lives with Father in the Connaught Building.'

'Queenie Collins? Don't be silly, darling. She won't do at all.' The colour was draining from her face.

'Your father introduced you?' Suddenly she was stiff with rage. 'He's done it to spite me. It's all a plot. You must have nothing more to do with that girl.'

'Mother, I'm very fond of her . . .'

'No! This was why he agreed to let you start. He wanted to get at me through you.'

'You're wrong. We didn't tell anybody.'

'Norman, they're using you. You just don't realise it. What's Byron been saying about me?'

Norman felt ready to collapse. But there was something he had to tell her and he might as well get it over with now.

'He doesn't want you to come to the office again. He says I know all I need to about the accounts.'

She clutched at his arm, her fingers biting into his flesh.

'I knew it. He wants me out of the way. He knows he can twist you round his fingers.'

'No, I'm sure it's all right.'

Well, he was almost sure. Perhaps he should tell her that Byron meant to give him the whole business. But Queenie had sworn him to secrecy on that. Norman found it hard to believe Byron would be so generous in the face of Mum's suspicion and hate, and it wouldn't do for Mum to go blasting off about it to Father's face.

'Ohhhhhh!' Veronica screamed with frustration. 'Silly boy, it's not all right. Ohhhhh!'

'Let's talk about this some other time,' he said. 'I'm very tired. I want to go to bed.'

'I'll never sleep. Not after this.' Norman could feel her shaking as he helped her upstairs. 'What am I going to do?'

He said: 'Don't do anything, Mum. Please don't do anything.'

It was close on midday. Norman felt agitated as he stretched his legs under his desk. His mother sat beside him. The day-to-day account books which catalogued the business of Henry Ball and Sons were spread between them.

He'd spent the first hour of the morning in his father's office. They'd read the mail. Father had been discussing the orders, and explaining how he'd handle them, when Norman heard the office door slam and saw Veronica come in. It made him catch his breath. He thought he'd said enough to stop her coming.

Beside him, Byron growled, 'Didn't you tell her not to come?'

They were both watching her. She slipped off her coat and sat down at Norman's desk.

Norman dropped his head in his hands. 'I did.'

'Tell her again,' he'd ordered brusquely. 'I don't want her in my office.'

Norman had been working himself up to that for the last two hours. He wished Byron would do his own dirty work. Veronica's eyes were red this morning, and Norman felt sorry for her. He didn't want to hurt her any more, and he didn't want her to start screaming as she had done last night.

But her presence was embarrassing all round. Harry Penn had nothing to do because Veronica had taken over his work. She was sorting small bills due for payment. Entering the cheques that came in in the mail.

Although Harry was twiddling his fingers at the next desk, she didn't say a word to him. Norman was afraid this would infuriate Byron. She was making no pretence of instructing him. Instead, she'd taken over the day-to-day book keeping.

Norman swallowed hard. This was interfering with the running of the office. It wasn't even his work she was doing.

'It's kind of you to take all this trouble for me, Mum, but I can manage now. Really I can. Father doesn't want you here any more.'

'So you said last night. But he agreed that I should.'

'For a month. To make me conversant with the accounting system. The month is almost up and you've done that very well. I can manage now.'

Harry Penn was picking his teeth. He got up noisily from his desk and stamped out of the office.

Mother's head came closer to his, and she whispered: 'I know you can, Norman. I have my own reasons for being here. I'm seeing to things now.'

'There's nothing that needs seeing to. I'm afraid Father will be rude to you. Order you out.'

Norman had his own reasons for wanting her gone. It was almost lunchtime and he wanted to meet Queenie. He was afraid Veronica would want to join them. That she'd be rude to Queenie, create a scene.

But his mother was getting to her feet and pushing her arms into her coat. Her face was like thunder but she was going. He felt awash with relief.

Queenie had been asking for a sewing machine for a long time. Evie had bought her one for her sixteenth birthday and thought it a very sensible thing for her to have.

'I'll be able to make all my own clothes now, Mam.' Queenie had been delighted. 'Magazines are giving away lovely patterns. The very latest fashions, and they say they're easy to make up. Just think of the saving.'

The living room had been awash with tissue paper and pink satin since then. The pink satin had become underwear of a sort Evie had never seen before. Queenie had even made French knickers.

'Artificial silk,' Evie had said. 'There's no warmth in that.'

'You're old-fashioned,' Queenie had laughed at her. 'Nobody wears flannelette underskirts any more.'

'Even I don't,' Evie had retorted indignantly.

Daisy had been painting. Colouring pictures in a book. Her eyes were going from one to the other.

'But I do,' she piped up. 'Why can't I have silk ones?'

'I expect you will when you're older,' Evie had told her. 'Children need warm underclothes.'

Black taffeta had covered the living-room table every day during Queenie's half-term holiday. Evie didn't think that very suitable either.

'You're too young to wear black,' she'd said several times, and suggested that Queenie add collar and cuffs in pale pink or blue to relieve the drab colour.

'Oh, Mam, it won't need it,' Queenie had said irritably. It was Saturday, and the machine had whirred all morning. Evie hadn't foreseen that the sewing machine could lead to further trouble between them.

She'd set the table for lunch, and was picking up off-cuts and bits of thread from the floor, when Queenie came back from her bedroom. She was wearing the dress she'd made.

'Do you like it?'

It was sleeveless and cut low round the neck. The long, straight bodice skimmed her hips, and it had a skirt of three narrow frills. She gave a theatrical twirl on the living-room lino.

Daisy stood up, clapping her hands. 'It's wonderful. Will you make one for me?'

Evie felt shocked. 'It's too short,' she protested. 'You can't be seen in public like that.'

'It's the latest fashion, Mam. Everyone's been wearing their dresses this length for years.'

'I haven't!'

'But you're old. The young and fashionable have.'

Evie gasped. She was thirty-seven; that wasn't old. She was wearing her dresses shorter, just covering her knees. She'd thought herself fashionably dressed. Byron had said she was.

'Come on, Mam, you must have seen them.'

Evie was afraid she wasn't coping with the roaring twenties. Or coping quite so well with her children, now they were grown-up. Queenie considered herself to be of the new generation that called themselves flappers, or Bright Young Things.

'That skirt's really very short. It shows all of your knees. And really, your hair too. It was a shame to cut off all those lovely curls.'

'Mam!' Queenie swung round on her mother, making her frills flare out. 'You can turn off your Edwardian propriety. Fancy you thinking short hair and exposed knees such terrible sins!'

Evie took a deep breath. The innuendo was there but she wasn't sure whether it was intended or accidental.

Queenie was twisting her face, making it ugly. 'You've got some very funny ideas, Mam. You're a kept woman, the mistress of a married man, yet you go on at me about short skirts.'

Evie felt the strength drain from her knees. It was the same problem over and over. Her children couldn't forgive her for that.

Queenie was angry. 'I'd be ashamed to do what you're doing.'

'You don't understand, love,' Evie said softly. 'Things were hard when your father died. Byron has always been very kind. I couldn't have managed without him.'

'Daisy's his illegitimate child. How could you bring such shame on us?'

'What's illeg . . .' Daisy's head came over the back of the sofa. 'What's that?'

Queenie gave a mirthless laugh. 'Everybody knows about you and Byron, and you just turn a blind eye. The girls in the college call you a scarlet woman. It makes me curl up.'

Evie felt cut in two. 'A husband and father couldn't have done more for us, Queenie. I owe him more than anyone else in the world. You've never gone hungry.'

'I'm hardly likely to have gone hungry.'

'Without him, you . . .'

'Well, I shall have more sense than to be caught like you. I won't spend my life living in sin. I shall be a wife and be taken out to dances and theatres, not kept on top of an office building and be called a caretaker.'

Evie felt tears sting her eyes. Byron had tried very hard. She loved him.

'I can't bring my friends here. I'd be ashamed to.'

Evie felt a spurt of anger. 'You've had too much of your own way. You're growing up half wild. What you need is a stronger hand.'

'Don't worry, Mam, I'm getting all that. Byron's been throwing his weight around on your behalf. He's ordered me to tell you . . .' Queenie paused and started backing out of the room.

'What?'

'That I'm going out with Norman. We're in love. He wants to marry me. There, so now you know.'

Evie felt transfixed. She could only stare at her angry daughter.

'I'm shocked at what you dare to do. You needn't worry about Norman or my bare knees. You've done much worse yourself.'

* * *

Evie went back to the kitchen, feeling numb. She was making boiled beef and carrots for lunch. Bobby and Byron would be here at any moment now. A white-faced Daisy came in and slid an arm round her waist.

Evie pulled her closer, Daisy laid her head against her apron. 'I've put Queenie's machine away. What else can I do to help?'

That upset Evie more. This was the effect a row with one daughter had on the other. She gave Daisy the mustard to put on the table.

Byron came in, looking tired. 'A busy morning?' she asked.

'Veronica,' he murmured over Daisy's head. Then he smiled. 'What shall we do this afternoon, Evie? It's such a sunny day, a shame to stay in.'

She gave him the joint to carve.

The front door slammed behind Bobby. He came straight to the kitchen door, grinning all over his face, his coat on his arm. Evie made an effort to appear normal.

'Guess what, Mam?'

'Hello, Bobby.'

'Bob, I'm not a little boy any more.'

'Robert, then?'

'Bob will do. Guess what? I've been offered a transfer to the Birkenhead branch.' His eyes danced with satisfaction. 'I'm to be a fully fledged cashier from now on. Got a rise too.'

'Congratulations.' Byron thumped him on the back. 'That didn't take you long.'

Evie kissed him. 'I am pleased for you. Really pleased.'

'Is that good?' Daisy was pulling at his sleeve. 'Will you be rich too, Bobby?'

'Rich enough. I've brought you some chocolate.' He pulled it from his pocket.

'Not until after your lunch.' It was Evie's habitual caution. She was delighted for Bobby, and it went some way to make up for her brush with Queenie.

'We'd better eat. It's all ready. Get Queenie, love,' she said to Daisy.

Evie could feel Queenie's reluctance to come to the table. She looked white and drained, and took no part in the general chatter about Bobby's promotion.

'I'm proud of you, Bobby.'

'You've done well.'

Evie said: 'You'll have to get up a bit earlier in the mornings. Where exactly is the Birkenhead branch?'

Bobby didn't answer for a moment. He put down his knife and fork.

'I thought I might get lodgings, Mam. Over the water.'

Evie felt as though she'd been doused in cold water. This was Bobby's way. He didn't want anything to do with Byron. No help of any sort. But she hadn't expected him to move out of the family home so soon. She felt he was deserting her. It was hurtful.

'Easier,' he said, 'than travelling back and forth all the time.'

'It isn't difficult,' Byron told him. 'Harry Penn does it. Lots of people working here do. We're convenient for James Street station.'

'I know.' Bobby was looking down at his plate. Evie had to stop herself screaming out at him to stay. It would be the end of an era if he left home.

Byron went on evenly: 'It would be cheaper for you to live here and travel over daily. More comfortable too. It's only a few minutes on the train to Hamilton Square.'

'Birkenhead Central would be nearer,' Bobby started to eat again, 'and it's a fair walk up to Grange Road West from there. But it's not just that . . .'

'Stay with us a bit longer, Bobby. Your mother would like you to, wouldn't you, Evie? Seventeen is very young to go it alone.'

Evie felt sufficiently in control to add: 'Please stay. Lodgings can be lonely, you know.'

'You're a fool,' Queenie burst out. 'You don't know which side your bread is buttered.'

Bobby's face was pink with discomfort. He said quietly but firmly: 'I'd rather go, Mam. You know how I feel about things.'

'Don't go,' Daisy pleaded. 'I don't know why you want to.'

Bobby turned to her. 'It's like this, Daisy. I'm out of step with your father. I'm pulling in the opposite direction and it isn't good for Mam. Better if I go and leave you all in peace.'

Evie had to get out her handkerchief and blow her nose. She was proud of Bobby. He'd always done things his own way. There'd be no changing his mind. He felt Byron wasn't treating her properly, but he was wrong. There were tears in her eyes, her throat and her voice.

'You can always come back. You know we'll always be glad to have you.'

He nodded, pushing his hair off his face with an embarrassed gesture.

'Yes,' Byron added. 'Come back if you don't like it. You know we'd both want that. Welcome you back.'

Evie got to her feet hurriedly, glad of the excuse to fetch the treacle pudding from the kitchen. She wiped her eyes on the tea towel before going back. She hated to think Bobby would be leaving.

She lifted the pudding and the plates and opened the door with her foot.

'What a day this is for news,' she said, knowing she

sounded falsely bright. 'Queenie's been telling me about her boyfriend.'

'You mean Norman?' Bobby put in. Evie could see him watching Byron. 'That's last month's news.'

'They're talking of marriage,' Evie said in Byron's direction. 'Did you know?'

'Heard it on the grapevine.' Bobby was tucking into his pudding.

'It's serious then, is it?' Byron asked Queenie.

Evie's family started to clear away the meal and wash up. She had to leave them to it. She went to her bedroom and collapsed on the bed, letting her tears come. Byron found her there a few minutes later.

'I knew you'd be upset.' The bedsprings sank under his weight. He pulled her up to sit beside him, and put an arm round her shoulders.

'I used to find my children so rewarding. How could they have turned into such difficult creatures?'

'They've grown up, Evie. They're going to go their own way now. You'll have to let them.'

'Only sixteen and seventeen.'

'Bobby will be all right. He knows what he wants and he's got his feet on the ground. And Queenie . . .'

'I'm worried about her.'

'She told you she was going to marry Norman? I didn't realise it had gone that far.'

'Yes.' Evie sniffed into her handkerchief.

'Then nothing we say will change her mind.'

'Doesn't it bother you, Norman and her?'

'It doesn't make life any easier. I'd rather they'd both picked on total strangers. But we have to accept it, Evie, if that's what they want. Veronica won't. She's going to be furious.'

Evie was thinking of her own father. The fact that he hadn't accepted Ned had made her run away. She didn't want Queenie to do that.

Byron was going on: 'I don't know what Norman's planning to live on. He won't keep Queenie on the two fifty a year I pay him.'

Evie sighed. 'But you're going to give him the business. Queenie's heard you say that, even if he hasn't.'

He groaned. 'I should have been more careful, shouldn't I? I might have brought this on us.'

'You'll still make it over to him?'

'Yes, it's time I thought of you. I want to take you right away from this place. It's the only way we'll get away from the gossip. From now on, we're going to think of ourselves. Daisy too, of course.'

'Daisy's easy.'

'At the moment.'

'She always will be.'

'Because she belongs to us both? She doesn't have divided loyalties?'

'Because she's like you, Byron, easy-going. Takes everything in her stride.'

He smiled. 'I know what we're going to do this afternoon. We're going to start looking for a house. When I give the business to Norman, he won't want me here, breathing down his neck. Better all round if we get right away.'

Evie felt warmed by the thought of a new house. 'Something to suit just the three of us.'

'In a place where nobody knows us. We'll move in as a family. You, me and Daisy. We won't have the blessing of Church and state, but we'll be a family in every other way. Come on, wash your face while I get Daisy organised. We'll start looking today. Over the water, I thought.'

Evie was comforted. She liked going over the water, and was glad he wanted to live that side too. They took the car across on the luggage boat.

'Not Oxton,' Byron said. 'We don't want to be anywhere near Veronica. And it's got to be what you want. A comfortable house. Not too big.'

'A garden?' Daisy wanted to know. 'Can we have a garden?'

'Yes.'

Evie enjoyed the afternoon out. They came back with particulars of several very nice houses, but not exactly what they wanted. They hadn't even decided which district they wanted to move to. It was enough that the plan was under way.

Norman was not happy. His mother was becoming more difficult. She was on at him all the time about Queenie.

'Drop her, Norman. You've got to drop her before it's too late.'

Veronica's prominent eyes seemed to burn with a terrible intensity. 'Can't you see that Byron's tying you up with his mistress? You're going over to her side. Where do you think that leaves me? Out on my own. Have you no shame?'

Norman tried to explain that it wasn't like that, she'd got it all wrong. He'd been bowled over by Queenie the moment he set eyes on her. She was beautiful, outgoing and enthusiastic about his job with Byron. He thought about her constantly. He'd never felt like this about a girl before.

'Byron's getting his revenge on me. He wanted a divorce, wanted to throw me on the scrapheap. Now he's taking you from me. He's coming between us.'

'No, Mother!

'Stuffing this girl down my throat.'

For Norman, the only good times were those he spent in Queenie's company. She was so wonderfully loving towards him. Queenie's warmth went some way to make up for the terrible change in his mother.

Norman had never wanted anything more than a comfortable life. Suddenly nothing was easy any more, and he never had enough money to last the month.

'I'm not giving you money to spend on that girl,' Veronica stormed when he asked her. 'Come to your senses. Promise not to see her again and I might.'

He knew now how to sub himself, but it was dangerous. He couldn't hide the fact from Harry Penn, and now Nosy Parker had found out too.

His mother waited up for him every night. As soon as she heard his key turn in the lock she was out on the stairs. He oiled the lock but she still heard him and came down to nag about Queenie. She started getting up early in the morning to have another go at him while he ate the egg and bacon her housekeeper cooked for him. Norman always felt rushed at breakfast, but her presence guaranteed that he'd be out in good time for his tram.

She was still coming over to the office, though he told her repeatedly he didn't want it; that Byron didn't like it. She didn't travel over with him, but while he was in with his father, he'd suddenly see her sitting at his desk, pushing documents about. Not every day, but two or three times a week.

'What's the point of it?' he'd asked her. 'What are you doing?'

'Looking after your interests,' she'd hissed.

It was Harry Penn who told him that she was removing cheques. Taking them away. That he'd seen them come in the morning mail but then they disappeared.

Norman went cold inside. 'You must be making a mistake,' he'd told Harry.

One morning, Byron suddenly broke off in the middle of explaining something to Norman. He leapt to his feet and went bounding out. Veronica was shrugging off her coat. He pulled it back on her shoulders and tried to steer her towards the door.

'I don't want you to stay, Veronica,' he told her. 'I don't want you to come here again.'

She turned on him with the ferocity of a big cat. Norman crawled with embarrassment as he heard her say things to his father that she'd previously said only to him, while Harry Penn sniggered into his handkerchief. She called Daisy his bastard, and that transfixed Miss Parker and the older clerks. Soon the Connaught Building was buzzing with the latest turn of events.

Even that didn't stop her. She came again the following day, and Byron immediately walked her outside. Nobody heard what he said to her, but later he told Norman that he thought she'd taken leave of her senses.

CHAPTER EIGHTEEN

Looking at houses became a regular weekend outing. Evie liked Byron to take his car across the river. One of the main routes through town took them past the pharmacy in Argyle Street.

'Surely your father should have retired by now?' Byron said as he drove past. 'He's still got his name over the shop.'

'Gertie says he's still working.'

'But how old is he?'

'Sixty-seven, I think.'

'Good Lord! Why doesn't he give up? I can't wait to retire. Just as soon as we can find somewhere to live.'

'You're not old enough, Dad,' Daisy said from the back seat.

'I am, I'll be fifty this year, and that's old enough for me.'

'Fifty's nothing.'

'Your dad's tired of spending every day in the office, and it brings nothing but problems.'

'What's the point of me working on? If Norman is going to have the business, he can do the work. I can afford to retire, Daisy, and I'm going to.'

It didn't take them long to decide that they'd prefer to live outside the town of Birkenhead. Evie thought that the Wirral countryside was very beautiful, and that West Kirby or Heswall would suit them. Byron had very definite ideas about the sort of house he wanted.

'It'll be our home for many years, perhaps for the rest

of our lives. I want you to be pleased with it, Evie.'

Evie thought she was more easily pleased than he was. The houses they looked at were at the top end of the market. She would have been delighted with many of them, but not one pleased Byron. Too close to its neighbours, or on a main road, or the rooms were too small. He toyed with the idea of buying a plot and building exactly what he wanted, but really he preferred houses of the older type.

Evie was disappointed that they weren't making better progress, and she missed having Bobby about the flat.

'I won't lose touch, Mam,' he'd told her when he was packing his belongings.

He came over to see her and have a meal at least once a week. He said he was pleased with his lodgings.

'Come and see them,' he invited. 'If you're over there motoring around looking at houses, come and see where I live.'

They did so the following weekend, and Evie felt that her worst fears were justified. It was in a terrace of small houses behind the gasworks.

'Very central,' Bobby had said. She'd known before seeing it that the neighbourhood was run-down. It looked terrible now that her eyes were used to the wide leafy roads of Heswall. The house itself was in need of a good scrub and a coat of paint. Bobby rented one room and shared the kitchen. The furniture provided for his use was battered and broken. There was no bathroom.

Daisy looked round and screwed up her nose. 'This isn't very nice,' she told him. 'Not like your room at home.'

Evie knew Byron would pass no comment. He'd already offered to pay for rooms in a better part of town. She said:

'Why not look for an unfurnished place? Then you can do it up. Make it more homely.'

'This is all right for me.' Bobby smiled. 'And it's near

Gran's. I go round there quite a bit.'

Evie thought Bobby was looking more like Ned as he grew older. She was glad Gertie had taken him under her wing, that he had somewhere to go to get away from these depressing rooms.

The following Saturday, after a trip to West Kirby, Evie wanted to call on Gertie while they were over. They found Bobby there, about to have tea with her. He seemed very much at home. Gertie was pleased to see them.

'Come and sit down. Bobby's brought cakes from Darty's for me. We haven't started on them yet, you're just in time. He's a real chip off the old block, always brings plenty.'

It brought the past flooding back to Evie. 'I suppose you still see Polly Darty?'

'All the time.'

'Does she ever say anything about my father?'

'Just that he's grumpier than ever.'

Bobby said: 'I went in to buy some aspirin the other night when my ankle was paining me. I told him who I was.'

Evie felt uneasy. 'What did he say?'

Bobby laughed. 'He said: "You needn't think you'll get them any cheaper by claiming to be related." '

She sighed. It was what she'd have expected from Father. It niggled that Bobby didn't have a higher standard of living. He had a better job than Ned, but his lifestyle seemed very similar.

'Cut off his nose to spite his face,' Byron said as he drove to Woodside that evening.

When Miss Parker brought his mid-morning cup of tea to his desk on the following Saturday, Byron said: 'What about a biscuit?'

'Sorry, they've all gone.'

'You've run out?' That surprised him. It had never happened before. Not since he'd told her to provide tea and biscuits twice a day for all his staff, and to buy what was needed with petty cash.

'Send Harry out,' he said. 'Ginger nuts.'

He sat back and sipped his tea. Through the glass he saw her go to Harry Penn's desk. Harry didn't leap up immediately to do what he was told. Instead he was protesting, waving his hands about. Byron watched him take out the petty cash box and show her what was inside.

They both appealed to Norman. It was the way his son turned round to look at him that first told Byron that something was wrong. Norman's face was running with guilt as he put his hand in his pocket. Harry went then.

Byron asked himself why there wasn't at least sixpence in the petty cash box. Usually it was replenished when it was getting low. All sorts of queer things were happening. Everybody seemed to spend more and more time looking for things.

A little while later, Miss Parker came in holding a tea plate with three ginger biscuits sliding about on it.

'Bring me the petty cash book and box,' he told her. 'I'd like to check them.'

He'd never, ever done that before. The whiskers in her mole twitched with alarm as she bustled out.

When the petty cash ran down, Harry Penn used to bring the book and cash box to him and ask for more, but once Norman had started, he'd told him to take care of it. Byron could see without moving from his desk that his request was causing consternation. When Miss Parker came back, he could see why.

The book showed a credit balance of four pounds two

shillings and threepence, but the cash box contained only three pennies.

Byron was angry. He bounded to the door, snatched it open and bellowed: 'Norman, come in here.'

There was no mistaking his son's guilt. His cheeks were scarlet, his step reluctant, his shoulders bowed. Byron threw himself back on his chair. For once he didn't invite Norman to sit.

'Explain this to me.' He spat the words out, jabbing his finger at the box.

'I borrowed it. I'm sorry, Father. But I always pay it back.'

'You mean you've done it before?' Byron was outraged.

'Yes, I'm sorry. I was short . . .'

'I don't care how short you are, Norman. Company money and private income are two different things. Never must they become mixed.'

'No, sir.' Norman wouldn't look at him.

'You are here as an employee. Helping yourself to the petty cash is dishonest. Akin to stealing. And you're a rotten example to everyone else. You wouldn't dare do it if you weren't my son. I ought to throw you out. I'm disappointed . . .'

'I'm sorry . . .'

'Disappointed that you'd stoop to this, and disappointed in what it shows. You've no grip on money, Norman. And that's vital in business if you are to succeed.'

Byron took a long, shuddering breath. 'I won't ask why you took it.' He guessed it had gone on entertaining Queenie. 'I'll give you until tomorrow morning to put it back, and don't you ever dare help yourself to company cash again. Now get out and let me forget about it.'

But Byron couldn't forget. The thought rankled. He was afraid that Norman took after his mother. Money ran through her fingers like water. Up to now, he'd not been displeased with his son's progress. Norman had been here just over three months now, and was managing to cope with the documents needed to move goods from one country to another. He'd assumed he would have no trouble with the accounts; after all, he was a qualified accountant.

Byron couldn't settle back to work. He felt uneasy. On the spur of the moment, he went to the door again and shouted for all the other account books to be brought to him.

He didn't really expect to find anything wrong. He just wanted to reassure himself that all was well. He'd trusted Norman; for the first time he wondered if that had been wise.

One o'clock came and the office emptied. Byron sat over the account books, his shoulders hunched in shock. He tried to tell himself he wasn't really suspicious, just upset and disappointed. The petty cash shortage had soured him.

The figures showed a big drop over the last few weeks. He hadn't expected that. In fact, he'd had the impression that turn-over was continuing to rise. He'd thought there were more orders than ever coming in, yet they didn't seem to be down in the book.

He was afraid Norman was taking more than just the petty cash. Up until three months ago the business had been thriving. The dates tied in. He compared this year's takings with the same period last year, and they were well down. Byron had a sinking feeling in his gut and was glad Norman had gone. He was angry and knew he'd have called him in and raved at him if he'd been here. He had to be quite sure before he accused him of fraud.

Some of the business they'd handled hadn't been entered in the books. He shivered when he pinpointed one item. John Robinson was one of their best customers. They regularly arranged for raw cotton to be shipped from Alabama to Liverpool on his behalf. Byron had handled last month's order himself. Demonstrated to Norman what exactly it entailed and how it must be shown in the books. Yet it wasn't here. No order, no sign of a bill being sent and no payment. Robinson's settled on the last day of the month. Always.

He looked through the freight book. Henry Ball had paid for shipping space for Robinson's. Byron felt sick. Could it be anything other than fraud? Norman had taken over the accounts, but Harry Penn dealt largely with routine bills, and old Simms kept the order book. Byron couldn't see how he could hide what he was doing from them. They'd always been very reliable. It couldn't be incompetence.

Until today, Byron had prided himself that he would be handing a growing business over to Norman. He wanted him to have a good living from it.

He himself had inherited a dying business. Nurturing it back to profitability had been the hardest thing he'd ever had to do. For him, the early years had been a fight for survival. He'd had to feel his way and change the nature of the business. He didn't think Norman would be capable of that.

Byron felt agitated, put upon. He knew that Norman went out with Queenie almost every night and must be spending more than he could afford.

He slammed the ledgers shut and made up his mind that if Norman was stealing, he'd sack him for theft as he would any other employee. There'd be no question of making the firm over to him. He'd put in a manager and cope with it himself. Norman could please himself how he made a living and Byron would do his best to see that Queenie didn't marry him. What chance of happiness would she have, married to a thief?

When he went upstairs, he found that Queenie had gone out with Norman again. After he'd had lunch and Daisy had gone to her dancing lesson, he sat on the yellow sofa with Evie and held forth at great length about Norman's failings.

At five o'clock he went down to his office to get the ledgers. He wanted to go through them again. He couldn't believe the mess they were in. Evie tried to help him tie bank statements to the entries in the book. It was impossible.

'He's a qualified accountant! What's he playing at? He must know he can't get away with this.'

'Are you sure it's his fault?' Evie asked.

'I gave him the responsibility of seeing to the books. I thought it would be in his line.'

'What can he hope to gain by this?'

'He's more likely to lose,' Byron thundered. 'Wait till I see him on Monday morning.'

'That's what I mean.'

Norman enjoyed his Sundays. It was a rare delight to turn over in bed and have another hour or so to snooze. He had a leisurely bath in the late morning and pottered about the house until it was time for a Sunday lunch of roast beef.

Today, the Yorkshire pudding was crisp and perfect, and there was his favourite apple pie to follow. He tried to close his ears to his mother's nagging voice. She was trying to persuade him to go out with her, but only because she knew he intended to go over to Liverpool to see Queenie.

'I'll ring for a car to take us to Parkgate,' she said with a great show of enthusiasm. 'A lovely run. We'll walk along the front to give ourselves an appetite, and then have tea and cakes at the Boathouse Café. You used to love doing that.'

Perhaps he had done once, Norman mused, but it didn't compare with what was on offer from Queenie. On Sunday afternoons they had the flat to themselves, because Byron took her mother and Daisy house-hunting. Norman would be spending it lying on the yellow sofa with Queenie in his arms. She was free with her kisses and didn't stop him going further. Last week, he'd fondled her breasts and thought himself very daring. This week he was hoping she'd allow more. The fact that he was doing it in his father's house made it all the more exciting.

He was in his bedroom, getting ready to go out, when his mother came running upstairs, her cheeks red with temper.

'Darling, I'd like you to light the boiler before you go. Bessie hasn't lit it today, would you believe? And now she's gone out on her half-day.'

'It's quite warm.' Norman looked out of the window. The sun was shining. 'You won't need central heating today.' He'd just put on one of the new sleeveless pullovers in Prince of Wales check. Queenie had chosen it for him and he didn't want to take it anywhere near the boiler.

'I can't stay in all evening without it,' his mother complained.

'The fire's set in the sitting room, you could just put a match to that.' It was May, for heaven's sake.

'It's still chilly in the evenings. Do light it for me, there's a dear.'

Norman was afraid it was a ruse to delay his going.

'You just can't rely on servants these days.'

Reluctantly he took his new pullover off. He didn't want to dirty his shirt either. In a bad temper himself now, he pulled that off too and rushed down to the kitchen to do the job as quickly as possible.

He didn't think the boiler had been lit for days. He found some paper and sticks and opened it up. On a bed of cold ash were a lot of documents that were browned and charred. He put in the poker and started to rake out the ash. A half-burned cheque fell out at his feet.

Norman straightened up in horror. It was a moment before he could bring himself to pick it up. The cheque was for three hundred and twenty pounds, and it was made out to Henry Ball and Sons.

He carefully lifted out the other papers. There were orders and letters and more cheques. Charred bits of paper disintegrated and showered down on the floor. He couldn't get his breath. His heart was thumping madly.

Norman was very late going over to see Queenie. He'd wrapped up the half-charred documents in a clean piece of newspaper and hidden them in his wardrobe. His head was reeling.

He knew his mother must have taken them from the office. He knew she must have stuffed them in the boiler and the fire must have been almost out when she did it.

He was still crawling with the horror of it. He couldn't bring himself to face her with what she'd done. He was too shocked. It must have had a terrible effect on his father's business. And perhaps she'd done it before. Perhaps several times.

He wished he knew why. For years she'd spoken of the business as a prize that one day he'd inherit. She'd worked hard on Byron to give Norman this chance of learning to run it. To get him involved in it. Now she was trying to ruin it. How could anybody keep track of what was happening if letters were being destroyed wholesale? And cheques weren't being paid into the bank?

Norman felt sick. It must be Mother's way of getting revenge. But revenge on Byron or revenge on Norman because he preferred Queenie's company to hers? He hadn't thought his mother capable of revenge like this.

He felt desperate. He was hoping for a lot from his father. Byron had treated him well so far, but what would he say when he found out about this? It would bring the business to its knees, ruin it.

He was also worried about how Queenie would take it. He couldn't tell her what his mother had done. She'd be distraught because it was going to upset her plans. How could they get married without the business to support them? This could ruin their future, and he didn't know what to do about it. For her sake, he had to think this out carefully.

By Monday morning, Byron felt even more bitter. He'd had two bad nights. He was down in his office waiting for Norman to come in.

'In here,' he said, the moment he saw him. He closed the door carefully, so the other staff wouldn't hear.

Norman was sweating and very pale. Byron could see a slight tremor in his fingers. He looked the picture of guilt. He hadn't meant to jump on his son; he just couldn't stop his own anxiety spilling out.

'You've got the books in a terrible mess. I trusted you to oversee them. What have you been doing?'

'Not my doing,' Norman stuttered, his chin quivering. 'Not at all.'

'What about this?' Byron's finger stabbed at an entry on the bank statement. A twenty-pound cheque had been cashed. He'd given Norman the power to sign cheques up to that amount. That had convinced him that Norman was at the bottom of it.

'No,' he wailed in agony. 'No.'

'I haven't signed it, Norman, so you must have.'

'Well . . . Yes, I've signed cheques. But . . . you think I've drawn money out for my own use, and I haven't. No, I haven't.'

'It wasn't so long ago that you helped yourself to the petty cash.'

'Yes, but not since. Honestly, not since. And never a cheque, not for me.'

'This cheque was made out for cash and it isn't shown in the accounts. There's another for petty cash on the same day, so it wasn't that. You can't have forgotten, it's only three weeks ago.'

'I don't know, I feel terrible about this.'

Byron sighed. 'I'll get the cheque back from the bank, it might tell us something.'

'I think I might have signed it. Probably did. I've been worried stiff. Out of my mind.'

Byron thought the lad was going to burst into tears. 'If it isn't you, it must be your mother. Did you sign that cheque for her?'

The tale came out then of how Norman had discovered cheques and letters stuffed in the boiler at home. Byron covered his face with his hands. That explained a good deal. He should have known Veronica would be up to something. She'd come so regularly; it wasn't like her to stick at things.

'Have you asked her about these burned cheques? Why she took them?'

Norman was shaking his head in misery.

'Why not?'

'Well, it couldn't have been anyone else.'

'Where are they? Have you brought them back?'

Again he shook his head. 'I didn't know what to do.'

Byron lost his temper. 'Didn't you think I'd want them? You can't run a business without records. Isn't that the first thing you learned as an accountant? You could have made a start at straightening things out. I put you in charge of the books. Surely you noticed that things were missing?'

'Harry Penn did. He said Mother was taking cheques.'

'For God's sake! When was this?'

'A couple of weeks ago.'

'Why didn't you say so then? You let your mother go on? Goodness knows what's missing, we're in a right mess. We've lost orders, we've shipped freight on behalf of unknown clients and cheques have gone missing before they've been paid in. And you do nothing!'

'I'm sorry, Father.'

'This was a profitable business. You'd have earned a good living from it. You've got to speak up, for goodness' sake! Why didn't you tell me?'

'She's my mother . . .'

'She's out of her mind. She knows this firm is going to be yours. She's always been on at me to hand it on to you. Why would she want to destroy it? It doesn't make sense.'

Norman gulped. 'She thinks you deliberately set me up with Queenie. That I'm going to turn my back on her and come over to your new family. That having me work here is part of some plan of yours to get even with her. That you're twisting both of us round your finger.'

'And that's what you believe too?'

'No,' he groaned.

Byron tried to think. 'No, you wouldn't. You're close to Queenie. She knew what I intended to do.' He paused.

'Queenie told you, didn't she? That I meant to make

the business over to you quite soon? And you told your mother?'

Norman nodded, too full of emotion to speak. Byron wondered how he'd managed to father someone so lacking in drive and common sense. 'And she didn't believe you?'

'No, she said it was all a trick. That you'd never part with it while you lived. You were too mean.'

Byron was appalled. 'She was bent on destroying me. Bent on destroying a profitable business. What a senseless waste.'

Norman blew his nose hard and then pushed his hair off his forehead. Byron recognised that gesture. It was the only thing Norman had inherited from him.

'Go home and get those papers you found. Don't let your mother take them from you. I've got to have them.' He sighed and asked himself if Norman were capable of that. 'Shall I come with you?'

'I'll get them,' he gulped. 'I'll see to it.'

'Make sure you bring them here.'

Byron closed his eyes and lay back in his chair. Norman was never going to run any business. He needed help even to wipe his nose.

When he could summon the strength, he got up and went to speak to Miss Parker. He made sure the rest of the staff heard him.

'Mrs Ball is not to be allowed into this office again. She's not to have access to any of our ledgers or records. If she comes when I'm not here and you can't get her to leave, ring security for help.'

Then he went upstairs to Evie and poured out his problems.

Byron felt he'd been sitting on the yellow sofa for hours, staring out over the rooftops of Liverpool. Evie had listened to his diatribe, made tea for him and held his hand. He wasn't feeling any better.

'What a mess I've made of everything,' he said sadly.

'Not you,' Evie said.

'I should have been more careful. I certainly will be in future. I said too much in front of Queenie. She stirred things up.'

'It was Veronica.'

Byron sighed. 'Yes.' It didn't stop him blaming himself. He remembered the vindictive hate he'd seen on Veronica's face. 'I made her hate me.'

'You've been very fair to her.' Evie was indignant.

That made him feel worse. Evie was trying to support him but her quick retort and indignation showed only too clearly that she felt he'd been too generous to Veronica. Perhaps he had. Evie's life would have been easier if he'd made a clean break in the first place. Not only Evie, her children and he himself would have been much better off. But the law saw Veronica as the innocent party and held Byron responsible for her and Norman.

He sighed. 'It'll be a miracle if Norman ever learns to manage anything. He hasn't got it in him.'

'You had to trust him.'

'He knew his mother was trying to ruin the business. He said he was worried sick about what he should do. I believe him. He was torn in two, Evie. Divided loyalties. He's a ditherer and he did nothing. Can't stand on his own feet. I've always known that. I hoped he'd grown out of it.

'I knew myself that Norman was borrowing from petty cash, I'd even searched the files for documents and failed to find them. That should have made me check through everything sooner.'

'Will you be able to sort it out?'

'I hope so. I hope they're working now on what Norman

brought back. They'll all have to work their fingers to the bone. I'll go down and see soon.

'I'll ring round our main clients, they should be able to give me details of our transactions. Certainly Robinson's will. Bedwell's too, and the salt manufacturers. We'll have to piece together the records for the last few months.'

'You'll have to tell them you've had your own records stolen.'

'Yes. This changes everything, Evie. I won't be able to give this business to Norman, not in the foreseeable future. He couldn't cope with it. After all the effort I've put into building it up, I can't just walk out. It would be like pouring money down the drain.'

He could see the disappointment on Evie's face. 'Does that mean no house for us? We stay here?'

'No.' He had to get Evie away from the Connaught Building and the gossip. She'd gone through enough, and so had he.

'I'll put a manager in. Travel over myself once or twice a week to keep an eye on it.'

'I was looking forward to having you at home with me.' Evie's smile was resigned. 'I suppose it's as well you found out about Norman now.'

Byron felt low all week. He'd been looking forward to having more leisure but instead he was working overtime trying to piece his records together. And worse, he'd have to go on working. By the weekend he had copies of most of the orders that had been given to his firm. He'd chased up many of the cheques that hadn't been paid in, and his main clients were going to issue replacements.

On Sunday, Byron suggested they go house-hunting again. It was a fine day and they all needed to get away from the Connaught Building for a while.

A LIVERPOOL LULLABY

An estate agent had sent them details of a house in
Heswall that looked interesting. This had happened before,
but when they saw the house they'd been disappointed.

The moment Byron saw this one, he felt his spirits
rise. It was square and sturdy under a blue slate roof. Ivy
grew in profusion up walls of old brick. The sun gleamed
on the small panes in its windows. It was built in the
Georgian style, with a portico porch. It surprised him to
find it was only forty years old.

'The garden's beautiful.' Evie's eyes sparkled with
interest as she looked round. 'And the views . . .'

Byron turned to look. The house faced south over the
River Dee. They could see the hills of Wales beyond.

'It's got a tennis court.' Daisy was pulling at his sleeve.

Once inside, Byron was sure. The whole ambience
seemed inviting. Lots of space downstairs, and panelling
in the drawing room.

'I love it,' Evie said, when they were out in their car
again. 'But it's big for just us three. Four bedrooms on
the first floor and three more in the attic.'

'Do let's have it,' Daisy pleaded. 'I'd love to learn to
play tennis.'

'Shall I put an offer in?' Byron asked Evie. 'You do like
it?'

'Living there would be fabulous,' she breathed.

'Let's go back to the estate agent and do it now.' It was
just what he'd been searching for all these months. Sod's
law that he should find it the week he discovered Norman
wasn't capable of running the company. But at least he'd
found the house he wanted for Evie.

CHAPTER NINETEEN

Queenie had thought that everything she'd planned was falling into place. Norman had proposed and she'd told her family. She'd had to keep talking about him to Mam and Byron. To let them know that her mind was made up and there'd be no changing it.

'It's a bit sudden, isn't it?' Mam had said over dinner a few days after she'd told her. 'You've only known each other a few weeks.'

'I knew the moment I saw him. We want to get married, Mam. Soon.'

'All right, but you must finish your commercial course first.'

She'd flared up. 'What's the point in waiting until we're old?'

Byron had put down his knife and picked up his drumstick to nibble. 'You'll be finishing that next July and you'll only be seventeen. That's not asking you to wait too long. You won't be over the hill by then, Queenie.'

She'd had to agree. She had to keep on the right side of Byron because she wanted him to give his business to Norman. That was an important part of her plan.

'Anyway,' Byron went on, 'you were keen to do the course only a few weeks ago. You wanted an office career. You'll have to finish before anyone will employ you.'

'I'm not expecting to have to work, not when I'm married.'

Mam had pursed her lips at that. 'You never know what'll happen, Queenie. I'd have been very glad to have the sort of training you're getting. It might have made all the difference.'

Queenie had sniffed, but she knew there was no point in arguing; it wouldn't get her what she wanted.

She'd known Norman was apprehensive about how his mother would take it.

'We aren't going to worry about what our families think,' she'd said to him. 'The problems are of their making, not ours.'

Mam and Byron were expecting trouble from Veronica, but not trouble like this. Everything had been going so well until she'd wreaked havoc on the business. Queenie felt a hot flush of anger every time she thought about it. What on earth did Veronica think she was doing? Deliberately ruining the business so that Norman wouldn't be able to marry her. She'd never heard of anything more selfish.

Poor Norman had been very upset. He'd wanted to walk out and find himself a job somewhere else, where he wasn't related to the boss. It had taken a lot of persuasion to make him see that his prospects were better where he was. She'd spent all her time kissing him and trying to rebuild his confidence.

'After all,' she told him, 'it's not as though you've done anything wrong. It was your mother. You've had to work very hard to piece the records together again. Byron will appreciate all the help you're giving him.'

Byron had been in a foul temper. Mam said it was because he was worried and was working too hard. He kept going into a huddle with Mam, telling her all about it, but he was keeping the details from Queenie. He had never been like this before. Queenie knew he was watching his tongue.

But she'd got enough out of him. He said he was sorting

things out, that the business would survive. She heard him telling Mam that he'd still make a profit this year, though perhaps not as much as he'd hoped. She was glad then that Norman had seen sense and stayed with his father. Everything could still work out as she wanted, provided the business survived in a profitable state.

The girls in the college heard all about it and laughed at Norman's mother. Louisa Fanshaw crowed with delight: 'Who'd want to be saddled with a mother-in-law like that?'

That needled Queenie, but she thought she'd be able to sort Veronica out. She still thought Norman would make a good husband. He couldn't take his eyes off her; they were full of devotion. Couldn't keep his hands off her either. It gave her a lovely warm feeling to know he adored her; that as far as he was concerned she was the centre of the universe.

She could get him to do anything she wanted, and it made her feel strong and powerful. He was keen to marry her but thought he couldn't afford it. She kept telling him that Byron meant to give him the business.

'It'll happen, I know it will. I've heard him talking to Mam. All we have to do is to go ahead with our plans.'

Norman didn't seem convinced, but she was.

The house-hunting had dragged on so long, Queenie had thought they'd never make up their minds, but now suddenly they had, and the offer Byron had put in had been accepted. Mam said they mustn't count their chickens until the contract was signed, and anyway it would take about three months to complete.

Queenie counted up the months. She'd been pressing for an August wedding, and finally it was agreed. She wanted to go to Torquay for her honeymoon, and Mam's gift was to be two weeks at the Palace Hotel there. She was really looking forward to that. By the time they came back it would be September. The family would move to their new house and Byron would give the business to Norman. Everything she wanted was falling into place.

Evie was worried about Queenie. She was afraid that the way she lived with Byron had influenced Queenie in all the wrong ways and that she was determined to be a wife at any cost.

She wasn't acting like a girl in love. She was very determined and seemed to be ruled by her head rather than her heart. Evie tried to warn her.

'If you don't love him, you mustn't marry him. You won't be happy.'

'I'll be happy, Mam. Don't you worry about me. I can look after myself. I certainly won't end up like you. I'm going to get myself a husband who'll look after me. Keep me in comfort for the rest of my life.'

'What makes you think Norman will be able to do that?'

'He's got a job, hasn't he?'

Evie knew that Queenie expected the business to be made over to Norman. She'd heard her questioning Byron about what had transpired in the office, and knew he regretted letting her know so much. Nobody had told Queenie he'd had a change of heart.

Evie said very carefully: 'If that was all he had, would it be enough?'

Queenie's lovely eyes looked innocently into her mother's. 'Of course.'

Evie knew that she herself had married with less security than that. Perhaps, after all, she was wrong and Queenie did care for Norman. Perhaps she was worrying unnecessarily. She'd asked Byron to be careful not to belittle Norman in Queenie's hearing, not to let her hear how disappointed he was with him.

'A gutless, lily-livered fool,' he'd called him. 'He'll be putty in Queenie's hands, I'm sure. She might be good for him.'

'But will he be good for her?' Evie asked.

'I don't know, love. But we'll have to accept that the marriage is going ahead. They're both set on it.'

'But what are they going to live on?'

'Did you ask that when you ran off with Ned?'

'No.'

'Don't worry, I'll see they don't starve.'

Now that they were no longer house-hunting, Evie wasn't over in Birkenhead so often. They used to call in to see Ida Pringle and Gertie Collins from time to time before returning home. Now, Ida owed her rent. On Monday, Evie decided to go over while Byron was working. She meant to call in and see Gertie too, to tell her about the house.

Gertie's place looked more untidy than ever, but Gertie had had her hair cut and permed.

'D'you like it, love?' Gertie stood in front of her cracked mirror, fluffing it out with her fingers.

'All those waves, it's the very latest style. I've never seen you looking better.'

'Much less trouble, having it short. Bought myself a new frock too. I'll put the kettle on for tea, then you can tell me about your new house.'

But Gertie came back from the kitchen saying: 'Did you know your Bobby's got a girlfriend?'

It was only then that Evie realised she hadn't seen him for two weeks. He'd hadn't been over for his weekly meal. It made her feel empty inside. Somehow a gulf seemed to be opening up between them. She'd been afraid of this since he'd left home.

'Got better ways of spending his time now.' Gertie gave a hoarse, throaty chuckle. 'I met them. He was taking her to the pictures. *All Quiet on the Western Front*. Have you seen it? No? Don't miss it, it's wonderful, all about . . .'

'Tell me about the girlfriend,' Evie interrupted. Everything seemed to be happening at once.

'Her name's Sylvia,' Gertie reported. 'She works in the bank with him. A typist, I think he said. Lovely girl.'

'Is it serious, do you think?'

Gertie guffawed. 'How would I know? You'll have to ask him.'

Before she went home, Evie went round to Bobby's room, though she knew he'd be at work. She pushed a note under his door asking him to come over for his dinner the next evening.

She knew he'd ring if he wasn't coming. She made dumplings because he always liked them. Bobby came but seemed prickly about his girlfriend. He didn't want to talk about her.

'When are we going to meet her?' Evie wanted to know. Bobby wouldn't be like this if the girl wasn't important to him, and she was curious about her. 'What about next Sunday? Either lunch or tea.'

He asked: 'Will you be here, Queenie?'

'If you want me.'

'Of course I want you. Sylvia might as well meet the whole family if she's coming.'

'Ask Norman too,' Evie suggested. 'We'll make it a big family meal.'

'I told you, Norman doesn't like coming here,' Queenie said irritably. 'It embarrasses him, and his mother doesn't like it.'

'Queenie, you don't care whether his mother likes it or not.'

Bobby asked: 'Will Byron be here?'

Evie thought that Bobby was almost as embarrassed as Queenie about bringing his friends to the flat, but for a different reason.

She said gently: 'Yes, he's part of the family, isn't he?'

'I suppose.'

She kissed his cheek. 'You know he is.'

Evie had made up her mind that even if she didn't take to Sylvia, she'd do her best to hide the fact. This was up to Bobby. He was the sort who knew his own mind. She'd never forget her own father's attitude to Ned, nor that he'd been wrong about him. Ned had been a wonderful husband and father.

As soon as Sylvia came through the door, Evie felt reassured. She felt she could grow fond of this shy girl, with her big anxious brown eyes and fluffy brown hair.

It turned out to be a rather stiff lunch party. The young people had little to say and left as soon as they decently could. Bobby rang up and invited himself over to the flat the following week.

Evie was alone with him for the first half-hour. He said: 'I hear Queenie wants me dressed up like a dog's dinner for her wedding.'

'You men are all to be in morning suits.'

'I'll hire it. I won't be wanting a show like that when I get married.'

'You're thinking of it too? Already?'

'Must be catching, Mam. Yes, I'm thinking of it, but it won't be for a long time, we'll need to save up.'

'Byron and I . . . We've always tried to treat you and Queenie the same. If you don't want a big wedding . . .'

'Definitely not.'

'A honeymoon in a good hotel?'

'No.'

'Perhaps Sylvia would like that.'

'We'd rather spend the money on setting up house. More important to us.'

'Then I shall give you something towards that.'

'No, Mum, I'll do it on my own. I don't want Byron's money.'

'My money, not his.'

'Where does yours come from, Mam? Only from him.' He bent to kiss her cheek.

'You're too proud.'

'Yes – well.'

'He's a good man, Bobby. A generous man. We'd all have had a much harder time if it hadn't been for him.'

'I know, Mum. But I don't want to be beholden to him. This is the way I want it.'

Evie told herself she ought to feel proud of Bobby. He had strong ideals and wouldn't have them compromised. He was even more handsome than his father had been, and strong and wiry. A pity about his ankle, it had left him with a slight limp which became more marked when he was tired.

Evie was making a cottage pie for their Saturday dinner and felt rushed because she was late with her preparations.

Queenie came in, slid a hat box on to the kitchen table and flopped on to a chair. She'd been out all morning, going round the big shops with her friends.

'I've bought a lovely hat, Mam. The very latest. Just the thing for my going-away outfit. What d'you think?'

Evie turned to look. 'Very nice.' It was one of the new small caps covered with veiling. 'It suits you, dear. I thought you were going to look for a costume?'

'I didn't see anything I liked.'

Evie mashed the potatoes. They were a little hard and could have done with more cooking.

'Nothing smart enough. I want a stylish wedding.'

'Yes, dear.'

'It's my big day, Mam, surely I'm entitled to a bit of a splash? I know so many people, all the girls from the college. I can't invite some and not the others.'

'Why not? Surely you'll just invite your friends?'

'I don't want to make it a hole-in-the-corner affair. I want everybody to know I'm married.'

Not tarred with the same brush as her mother, Evie thought as she spread mashed potato on top of the savoury mince. 'How many guests do you think you'll want to ask?'

'More than a hundred. Norman's got a lot of friends.'

'But that's far too many for this flat,' Evie said, aghast. She'd thought of clearing out Bobby's bedroom and moving the dining table in there for a buffet.

'Mother! I'm not having my wedding reception in this place. I want it to be a smart affair.'

'We won't have moved to the new house. If you put it off for a month or two, let us get in and sort . . .'

'We were thinking of a hotel. Norman likes the Adelphi.'

'Good Lord! The Adelphi? That's the most expensive . . .'

Evie thought of her own wedding all those years ago. There had been no possibility of a hotel reception for her.

'Byron will be happy to pay. He's a rich man.'

'You can't expect him to foot endless bills for you, Queenie.'

'Why not? He'll be doubly connected soon. Father-in-law and acting father.' Queenie's smile was dazzling. 'I'm going to look in the shops up Bold Street to see if I can get a really elegant wedding dress. Norman will be in morning dress, of course.

'As the bride's mother, you'll have to get yourself something smart too.'

Evie was intent on putting her pie in the oven.

'You will, won't you?' Queenie asked anxiously.

'Of course.'

'Thanks, Mam. You're good with clothes. Always did dress nicely. Dressed me nicely too.'

Evie sighed. She knew Queenie would expect them to pay for her wedding finery. Queenie had inherited something of her grandfather's personality. Like Joseph Hobson, she was a person who took rather than gave.

'I made most of your clothes, Queenie.'

'Yes, but not this time.' Again the dazzling smile. 'Not for my wedding.'

Two weeks later, when Evie saw the wedding dress Queenie had chosen, she didn't like it. Not for Queenie.

It came in a huge box, packed in layers of tissue paper. Queenie lifted it out and held it against herself.

'Isn't it unbelievably gorgeous? What do you think?'

It was of stiff white silk, cut straight to skim the hips, with an uneven hem. There was a fringe which dipped from above the knee on the left side to mid-calf on the right.

'It's the height of fashion,' Queenie boasted. 'The very latest twenties design.'

Evie fingered it and thought it would be very easy to make. 'I could have run something like this up for you. There's nothing to it.'

'It wouldn't look like this. You'd never get the cut right.'

'It's not formal. The men are to be in morning suits. I would have thought a traditional floor-length gown . . .'

'That's all out now. Old hat.'

Evie found the price unbelievable too.

'Perhaps you could make a bridesmaid's dress for Daisy?'

Byron said: 'If it pleases her, Evie, why worry?'

'I've indulged her too much. She expects everything now.'

'Norman needs somebody like Queenie. Somebody who knows what she wants. She always looks beautiful, she'll make a splendid bride.'

'You've got a soft spot for Queenie.'

Byron smiled. 'Since she was four years old, and I saw her in a red wool dress with a lace apron over it. I thought she was absolutely charming, just like her mother.'

Queenie was feeling very pleased with herself. Her college course had finished and she'd come top of the class in the final exams.

'I'm proud of you.' Mam had been as excited as she was. She kissed her. 'Clever girl.'

'I'm delighted you've done so well,' Byron told her. 'We must have a special celebration supper. What about it, Evie? Tomorrow?'

'Bobby doesn't like me ringing him at work, and tomorrow doesn't allow much time to write.'

'We won't ask Bobby this time,' Byron said, giving Queenie a wink. 'Ask Norman up. There are things we need to discuss and get sorted.'

'The wedding,' Queenie said, because she didn't want to appear pushy, but it wasn't the first thing she thought of. She'd asked Norman several times if his father had said anything about giving him the business. It was high time Byron showed his hand on that. He'd signed the contract for his new house. They were to move early in

September so Daisy could start her new school at the beginning of the term. He would have made plans for his business. Byron always planned everything to the nth degree.

'The wedding, yes,' Byron said. 'Amongst other things.'

Queenie felt even more pleased with herself. She was certain he meant to hand over his business to Norman. He wouldn't want Bobby here while he was doing that.

Queenie visualised Byron opening a bottle of wine. The five of them sitting round the table, raising their glasses to her exam results. Then Byron would say he was moving out and was handing over the business. It made sense, that if he'd planned to give it to Norman, he'd be even more keen now they were getting married. He'd want to be generous to her too. Then they'd toast the future.

There was a ball of excitement in Queenie's stomach as she set the table with their best tablecloth and silver cutlery. Byron came up half an hour earlier than she'd expected. He went straight to the kitchen and opened a bottle of wine.

'Come and sit down, Queenie. I want a word with you before Norman gets here.'

Her heart leapt with pleasure as he put a glass of wine in her hand. This was working out just as she'd have wished. She wanted to know his exact plan and he was going to tell her now, before Norman came.

She went to the yellow sofa in front of the window and found Daisy curled up in the corner.

'Why don't you go somewhere else?' she suggested. 'Your father and I need this for a serious talk.'

'I will if you let me taste your wine.'

Queenie held out her glass for her to take a sip.

'Yuck.' Daisy pulled a face. 'Don't like it.'

'You will when you're older. Go away now.'

Queenie started talking about their wedding to give Byron a lead-in.

'You've been very generous. I should start by thanking you for that. I'm very grateful.'

Byron had agreed that they could have the reception at the Adelphi but insisted they must keep the number of guests below a hundred.

Fortunately, she had foreseen that. She'd kept mentioning a vastly inflated number of guests. Now she and Norman had sent invitations to everybody they could think of and the list totalled eighty-four. She was able to tell Byron that she'd kept his wishes in mind and had thought of his purse.

Byron began: 'We're all facing a lot of big changes in our lives, and there are many things to consider.'

Queenie felt a swirl of triumph. It was all going to happen just as she'd meant it to.

'Your mother and I need to know more about your plans.' Mam was leaning against the window, sipping her wine. 'Are you going to work, find yourself a job?'

Queenie was stunned. Everybody knew she wasn't. She'd made no secret of that. This wasn't what she'd expected at all.

They were all watching her, even Daisy, who was snuggling against Mam. Byron said slowly, 'You don't expect to be carried for the rest of your life?'

That infuriated her. 'Of course not! I shall have the house to take care of. My own duties.'

'But you've done very well on your commercial course. The whole point of that was to fit you for work. Wouldn't you prefer to come and work for Henry Ball and Sons? Help to run it?'

It was the last thing Queenie wanted. The whole point of marriage was to avoid that.

'One of my clerks is due to retire. Why don't you come down and see what he does? Come and use the training you've had.'

'Help Miss Parker, you mean?'

'No, not exactly. I think you could manage more than she does.'

'I thought Norman was going to manage the business.'

'He's going to need help, Queenie. He won't be able to do it by himself.'

'Can't you hire somebody to help him?'

'Yes, that's the other alternative. I've considered putting a manager in. To run it for me from now on.'

This wasn't what she'd been led to believe. It sounded as though Byron had changed his mind about parting with the business.

'But then I thought, Queenie's the bossy sort. She's got her wits about her. It wouldn't take her too long to learn what's what. I'll come in every day to teach you, until you do.'

Queenie put her glass down. There was a cold feeling in the pit of her stomach. 'But why can't Norman run it? I don't understand.'

'Not everybody is capable, Queenie. Norman is not a leader. I don't think he wants to be left in charge.'

'But he does, he tells me he does.' Tears of disappointment were stinging her eyes.

'I think Norman knows it's beyond him, he just isn't admitting it.'

'How d'you know I'd be any better at it?'

'You're very good at getting what you want from others. You're stronger, a more demanding personality. I hope you'll prove to have more money sense. A better grip on finances.'

Queenie didn't doubt that. 'You said you were going to

give him your business; that you were tired of coping with it; that you were going to retire.' It was a wail of distress.

This was death to her plan. Everything had hinged on that. Queenie was fuming. Norman was hardly earning anything – a clerk's wage. The wedding was almost on her, and it wouldn't give her the life of luxury she'd expected.

Byron sighed. 'I had hoped to do that, but I shall have to carry on.'

Mam refilled Byron's glass. Queenie had hardly touched hers.

'It's like this, Queenie. I've spent years of my life struggling to keep this firm afloat. It was touch and go whether it would survive at one time, but it has and it's thriving again. I don't want to see my work wasted.'

She took a deep breath. 'Norman will be very careful to . . .'

'What I'm trying to tell you is that giving it to Norman is no longer an option. It's going to be one of two things.

'Either I put a manager in now to run it for me. I would then leave it to Norman in my will.

'Or you can come and see if you can do it. I'll make it over to you both jointly if you prove you can.'

'That seems very fair,' Mam told her. 'There's no easy ride in this life, Queenie. You'll have to pull your weight.'

'Probably pull more than your weight, when you're married to Norman.' Byron was smiling at her as he refilled his glass again.

'You'll probably enjoy it.' Mam was trying to reassure her. 'Better to be in the thick of the things than just keeping house.'

Queenie couldn't help herself. 'How would you know?' she demanded. 'That's all you do.'

'It hasn't always been like this for your mother,' Byron

was saying gently as the doorbell rang.

Daisy was letting Norman in. Queenie felt numb. She had an unexpected disaster on her hands but she was too proud to let them see she'd made a mistake. She stood up and kissed Norman in front of them all, just to show that she did love him. Perhaps she'd been in too much of a hurry to tie herself down. Particularly since Byron seemed to think Norman was stupid. What was she going to do?

But Norman did look nice in the pearl-grey suit she'd persuaded him to buy. He'd brought flowers for Mam, just as she'd suggested, though he looked a bit self-conscious now as he presented them.

Queenie listened to Byron telling Norman what they'd been talking about. He cut out much of what he'd said about Norman being incapable, but Norman got the message. Queenie could see the colour running up his cheeks. His eyes wouldn't meet hers. She wanted to scream.

Once the roast chicken had been carved and they were all eating, Byron was off again. Queenie wished he'd give it a rest.

'We've all been so busy these last few weeks, we've left some important decisions to the last moment. You two will need a home of your own once you're married.'

Queenie tried to pull herself together. She'd already thought about that and taken Norman to see several houses. She'd have settled for one in Aigburth, which they'd both loved, but Norman had said: 'We'd better leave if for the time being. Until Father offers me the business. Can't think of buying until . . .'

She'd agreed they might have to rent for a while. They'd had a look at several for rent too.

Byron went on: 'As you know, this flat will shortly be empty. It seems a good place for you two to start married life. If you both come and work in the business, you can have it rent-free.'

Norman beamed round the table. 'Thank you, that's very kind. Very kind, isn't it, Queenie?'

Queenie almost choked on a roast potato. 'I'd like to get away from this place. We're looking for a small house.'

Byron turned his gaze on her. 'How are you going to pay for that? Then there'll be the fares backwards and forwards. You'll find it very convenient to live over the job.'

'This flat's very nice, Queenie.' Norman was diffident.

'It is not.' She could feel her temper rising. Byron knew she didn't like this place. Mam knew she hated bringing anybody here. It was a caretaker's flat.

'Don't be silly, Queenie,' Mam was telling her. 'It's a generous offer and you can't afford to turn it down.'

'Her business sense will tell her that.' Byron was leering at her. He knew he had her over a barrel.

'It's nice here,' Daisy said. 'Looking out over the roofs. Being on top of everything.'

Queenie didn't agree. They expected her to work for a living and live here in this awful flat?

'Think about it, Queenie, there's a good girl. I'll need to know very soon. If you don't want the job and you don't want the flat, I'll need time to find a manager.'

'And a proper caretaker,' Mam added.

Queenie was in a state of agitation for the next three days. She spent a lot of time alone in her bedroom. Evie could hear her jazz records being played very loudly on the gramophone. If she came to the living room she rarely spoke. She'd lean up against the window, staring down at the traffic in the street. As they waited for her decision, Evie felt worried.

'You've put her under pressure,' she said to Byron as they were getting ready for bed.

'She was trying to take us all for a ride.' They were keeping their voices low so that Queenie wouldn't hear them in the next room.

'Is she going to call off the wedding?'

'Norman asked me if she was ill. She hasn't been out with him since.'

'If she does, it's for the best.'

'You think she doesn't love him?'

'I think she was aiming to share his rosy future, and that wouldn't have worked out.'

'That's how Veronica saw me, and I wouldn't want the same thing to happen to Norman. I had to make Queenie take a more realistic look at him. Little minx! Seventeen and looking for a meal ticket for the rest of her life.'

Evie climbed into bed. 'Queenie's one who takes.'

'There's a limit to what she can expect others to give. Why shouldn't she work for a living like the rest of us?'

'She knows now she'll have to, whether she marries Norman or not.'

'She can run rings round him. She's more capable than he is anyway.' Byron opened his book and began to read.

Queenie announced on the fourth day that she'd take both the job and the flat.

'We won't be living here for ever, though, just until we see what we can afford.'

'That's fair enough. When you want to move out, you can offer it to a caretaker.' Byron took her down to the office before she changed her mind.

For him the next few weeks flew past. He'd never been so busy. He had to sort out the mess Veronica had made. As he'd expected, Queenie was picking up the work more quickly than Norman had. He told her so.

Her big brown eyes looked into his. 'I'm going to do my best. If I have to work, I want to learn to run the company, get the best out of it. I don't want to spend my time just typing letters.'

That pleased him. There was a quiet confidence about Queenie. Once he'd moved house, he'd travel over two or three days a week. He'd keep his eye on things for a year or so, but he'd make the business over to them once he was sure they could manage it. It wasn't fair to keep them waiting indefinitely when he didn't need the income from it. He had more than enough for his and Evie's needs, and to ensure Daisy's future. He was looking forward to having a more restful life.

The day of the wedding dawned. Veronica had been invited, of course, and he was a little nervous that she might make a scene and spoil the day. But she stood aloof and alone, staring at Byron but saying little to anyone except Norman.

Byron enjoyed himself. He looked fondly at Evie, who was wearing a very smart blue costume and little hat. She was beautiful still, a little tense on this very special day, but everything was going without a hitch. Evie meant everything to him.

He felt full of love for the rest of his family, particularly Daisy. She was Queenie's only bridesmaid, in a dress of mauve taffeta that Evie had made for her. He recognised himself in Daisy. She had his square figure and the russet-brown hair he used to have. Her eyes reminded him of Grace.

Daisy would never have Queenie's striking good looks, but she had her mother's dimple and wide, gentle smile. She had a quick mind too, and the same level-headedness that he had. As a daughter she was a delight, and he knew Evie found her so too.

'So much easier than Queenie,' Evie had said only that morning. 'She never pits her wits against mine. She goes out of her way to please me. Just like you do.'

Today, Queenie was dazzlingly beautiful beneath her white veiling. She'd made her choices and Byron hoped she'd be happy with them.

Her handsome brother was acting as best man. He'd have been proud to accept Bobby as a son, if only he would unbend and cease looking on him as the enemy.

Norman stood up straight and made his vows in a strong voice. Byron hoped fervently that Queenie would love him and be kind to him.

Book Four

1930–1942

CHAPTER TWENTY

Evie thought the move to the new house was near to being chaotic. They had to move in before it was redecorated so that Queenie and Norman could have the flat to themselves at the start of their married life, and so Daisy could start her new school at the beginning of the term.

'It'll seem funny, just the three of us. Without Queenie and Bobby,' Daisy had said when they sat down to a makeshift supper on the first night.

Evie knew Byron wouldn't be sorry. He said that it would make life a lot easier. She knew she'd miss her children, but they'd grown up and this was their choice.

'I want everything to be easier,' Byron had said when Daisy went to bed. He wanted Evie to be known as Mrs Ball.

'We'll change your name by deed poll to make it legal,' he said. 'Here in Heswall, where nobody knows us, it's the obvious thing to do. There won't be any more gossip. We'll seem too ordinary. After all, we have a daughter of eleven. It'll be a fresh start for the three of us.'

The painters and decorators came in. Evie's mind reeled with colour schemes. She was busy choosing furniture and carpets. She thought it a very grand house and knew it would take time to get it straight.

'It's too big for you to manage without help,' Byron said firmly. 'We'll have a cook and a maid. We don't have to worry about them gossiping about us now. We'll start as we mean to go on. We'll have a bit of comfort.'

Byron helped Evie hire Mrs Minto, a lady of mature

age who'd worked as a cook-general for the last twenty years. She would live in. She was plump and cheerful and came with excellent references. Evie picked out Kitty Hunt as their maid, chiefly because she liked her shy smile. She'd just got married and chose to live out. Her home was in the village.

They'd been in the new house a matter of ten days. It was beginning to smell of fresh paint and new carpet, and Evie was beginning to feel at home in it.

It was a Monday and a stormy autumn night. The wind was howling up the estuary and there were frequent heavy showers. She'd drawn the new heavy velvet curtains to shut the storm out, and Byron had asked Kitty to build up the fires.

'Come and sit down.' He put a glass of sherry in Evie's hand and drew her to the fire. She couldn't get used to waiting for Mrs Minto to serve meals. The habits of a lifetime made her feel she should be in the kitchen doing it herself.

Evie sipped her sherry and let her eyes linger on the handsome furnishings in her new sitting room. She was pleased with the way it had come together. Daisy had just started piano lessons and was practising at the other end of the room. Evie tried to ignore the occasional discord. She could see across the hall and through the open door to the dining table set for supper. The dining room hadn't yet been papered, but there was a bright fire in there too. Cook was just carrying in a steaming casserole dish when the front doorbell rang.

'Who can that be?' Byron frowned. Kitty went to see. They all listened. Even Daisy stilled her fingers on the keyboard.

There was a gasp of nervous astonishment. 'Oh, I'm looking for Evie . . . Is this where she lives?'

'This is the residence of Mr and Mrs Ball.'

Evie had recognised the voice. She sprang up and went to the door. The maid was eyeing Gertie Collins doubtfully.

'Come on in, Gertie,' Evie said. She was surprised to see her. She'd invited her to lunch and to see over the new house in two days' time, when Byron would be at the office and Daisy at school.

'Evie, I'm sorry to disturb you. I couldn't wait till Wednesday.'

Gertie looked old and anxious. Her nose was red and her face wet. Against the new and luxurious furnishings, she looked very shabby.

'Come to the fire,' Evie said. 'You're frozen.'

Byron pulled himself to his feet and put out his hand.

'I couldn't find the place and it's a terrible night. Been walking round for ages.'

'Let me take your coat,' Byron said, helping her with it. 'It's very wet. I'll get Kitty to shake it well and try to dry it off.'

'Sorry to come when you're just about to eat.' They could all see more dishes being taken to the dining room.

'As good a time as any,' Byron assured her. 'I'm hungry. Come and have something with us. There'll be enough, Mrs Minto, will there? Come along, Daisy.'

Gertie paused to look round. 'How posh,' she said, as Kitty, newly kitted out in full maid's uniform, set another place at the table for her.

'My, Evie, you've landed on your feet. You wouldn't have had anything like this with our Ned.'

'What brings you out on a night like this?' Evie wanted to know. 'Is something wrong?'

'It's your dad. Polly Darty says he hasn't opened the shop today. Miss Lister couldn't get in. She couldn't rouse him. Nobody's seen sight nor sound of him since he closed the shop on Saturday night.'

Evie felt a wave of guilt wash through her. She hadn't given her father a thought for ages. She'd turned her back on him. It was the only way she could deal with his vindictiveness.

'Polly reckons he's ill. He's an old man now, hasn't looked well for ages. Getting slow too. Anybody else would have given the shop up years ago.'

Byron's sympathetic eyes met Evie's. 'If he's not looking after the shop, Evie, you'd better do something.'

'That's what me and Polly thought.' Gertie nodded.

Evie was worried. 'What about Matilda?'

'No sign. Polly hasn't seen her for ages. The shop girls call round for the bread, but not today, of course.'

'But Matilda's still there?'

'Polly thinks so. Nobody's said otherwise. He doesn't let the shop girls upstairs and he hasn't taken apprentices for a long time.'

Evie shivered. Byron said: 'We'd better go and see if they're all right.'

'I had to come and tell you right away. I was scared to let it wait, in case something's happened.'

Evie's neck crawled with dread.

'We've got the telephone in,' Byron said, helping himself to mashed potato. 'Evie should have given you the number.'

'She did, but I don't know how to use them new-fangled things. I thought it would be easier to come.'

'I'll run you down in the car, Evie, as soon as we've eaten. You'll be anxious.'

'Can I come?' Daisy wanted to know.

'No,' her father said. 'Better if you go to bed, young lady. You've got school tomorrow.'

Gertie was tucking in. 'I'd be glad of a lift back.'

'Of course, Gertie. It was kind of you to come.'

'I don't know how we'll get inside,' Evie worried. 'Father was always security-conscious. He used to bolt the shop doors on the inside every night, top and bottom, and lock them as well.'

They set out as soon as they'd eaten. Byron drove to Gertie Collins's home first.

'I wish it was broad daylight,' she told him. 'So that the whole street could see me getting out of this posh car.'

'We'll have to do it again,' he said cheerfully.

As he pulled up outside the pharmacy, Evie said: 'The lights are on in the shop. He's got electricity now.'

'They have all along this parade.' The shop windows were all lit up. 'Had it for years now. But there's no light upstairs in the flat.'

'Father's bedroom is at the back. Matilda's too.'

'It's only half past eight.'

'But if they're ill . . .'

Evie tried the shop door. It was firmly locked, as she'd expected. She rang the bell but there was no response. 'I'll go next door to Darty's.'

The years had made Polly Darty rounder and heavier, but her pudding face shone with welcome.

'Evie, I'm right glad you've come. Your dad's been depressed for a long time and getting worse, everybody says so. Miss Lister says his temper's terrible. Can't help worrying about him, even if he is awful to everybody.'

'The lights . . .'

'They've been on all day, though there's been no sign of him. I think he switched them on when he closed up on Saturday and hasn't touched them since.'

Evie sighed. 'How am I going to get in?'

'We've been thinking about that. Our Herbie thinks he

could get in through the bathroom window. It's open a little at the top. We didn't like to do it off our own bat. You know what your dad's like. Herbie was afraid he'd bawl him out. We thought we'd wait until you came.'

'We'd be very grateful if he would,' Byron answered for her. 'We were thinking we might have to break in.'

'No, no, I'll shout for Herbie.'

'Does Herbie work in the business with you?' Evie put her mind back to the little roly-poly toddler she used to take for walks.

'No, we told him he'd have to find work elsewhere. He's got a job with a builder, so he's well used to climbing ladders.'

Evie wouldn't have recognised Herbie. He was now a young man in his prime, tall and slim and looking very fit.

'What do you want me to do when I get in?' he asked.

'Just let Evie in,' Byron said.

She said: 'There's a keyboard on the first landing at the top of the stairs. The keys are all labelled. You'll find the ones for the back door and the yard door there. They'll all be bolted too, top and bottom.'

She and Byron were ushered through the cake shop to the back yard. The first thing she did was to look up at the windows over the pharmacy. In Matilda's bedroom, the curtains were drawn, but she could see the glow of light shining through them. Her father's room was in darkness. She could see the others looking up too, but nobody made the obvious comment. It seemed an ominous sign.

They watched Herbie get out an extending ladder and climb up the dividing wall with lithe ease. Then Byron helped him lift the ladder over into the pharmacy's yard, and a few moments later he had it up against the building.

'Good job it's stopped raining,' Byron said. Evie shivered in the cold night air. Herbie was reduced to a darker shadow against the black building. She pulled her macintosh more tightly round her and wished the gale would blow itself out.

'There,' Polly said proudly as Herbie edged the bathroom window down and disappeared inside. The light went on inside, and then on the stairs. Moments later they could hear him struggling with the bolts on the yard door and went to the other side.

'If there's anything else we can do to help . . .' Polly was hanging back.

'We'll let you know what's happened,' Evie said. 'Thank you for what you've done so far.'

The strong medicinal aroma in the shop caught at her throat. It seemed stronger than she remembered. The shop seemed no different from other pharmacies now that it had been modernised. There was a new door at the bottom of the stairs. She went up feeling stiff and tense. Here, the atmosphere seemed to close round her, heavy and threatening and redolent with her adolescent misery. She was glad of Byron's supporting footfall behind her. She passed the living room, found the light switch and headed up the next flight.

'Father?' she called. The only sound was the creak of the stairs as they took their weight. All was in darkness on this landing. She knocked on her father's bedroom door and opened it.

'Father?' She felt for the light and put it on. She didn't know what she was expecting to find. She hadn't dared think about it. Gertie had said he could be dead in his bed.

For two awful seconds she thought Gertie was right. He was just a hump under the bedclothes. Then he turned over with a speed she wouldn't have thought possible, and his dark, malevolent eyes peered up at her.

'Oh, it's you! What do you want?' He was struggling to pull himself up the bed, but hardly seemed to have the strength. She went to help him.

'Walking in here in the middle of the night! You frightened me.' His hand brushed her away.

'I'm sorry. I came to see if you were all right.'

His face was grey and drawn. He looked ill and disorientated.

'I don't want you here. You left me.'

'I'm back now,' Evie tried to soothe.

'It's too late, I'm done for.' He was wearing a flannel nightshirt that badly needed a wash.

'Father, you need somebody to look after you.' Evie looked round the room. There was a thick layer of dust on his bedside table.

'I was fast asleep,' he complained. 'It's the middle of the night, isn't it?'

'It's evening, not nine yet. How are you?'

'What do you care?' His dark eyes glared up belligerently from the pillow. His chin was covered with half an inch of black stubble.

'You didn't open the shop. Everybody's worried.'

'Of course I opened the shop.' With a burst of irritable energy he sat up. 'What are you talking about? I wouldn't not open it.'

'Father, Mrs Darty says you didn't open today. Miss Lister knocked and knocked this morning and couldn't make you hear. That's why I've come.'

He stared at her as though he didn't believe her. Then dropped back against his grubby pillows with a long sigh.

'I'm sick. Flu or something. You could make me a cup of tea now you're here.'

'Where's Matilda? Is she all right?'

'Yes.'

'Is she making meals for you?'

'I don't feel like meals, damn you. I want a cup of tea.'

'I'll put the kettle on,' she said, and turned on her heel.

Byron shifted his weight to the other foot and marvelled at Evie's patience. He met Joseph's hostile gaze.

'I haven't seen you before. Married again, has she?'

'Yes,' he said shortly. This wasn't the time to go into that. 'I'm Byron. You'd better come to our house until you're better. Evie will look after you. I've got my car outside. The best thing is to take you now. We'll get a doctor out to see you in the morning.'

'Doctors,' Joseph snorted. 'They won't do anything for me. Don't know as much about prescribing as I do.'

Byron went over to a large cupboard and opened the door.

'What do you think you're doing?' Joseph was heaving himself higher in the bed.

'Looking for a suitcase. Evie will put a few things together for you.'

'I don't want to go anywhere. A cup of tea is what I want.'

'Yes, well . . . What do you want Evie to do about the shop?'

'Do about the shop? What can she do about the shop?'

'Get somebody in to run it for you. Another chemist.'

'I hired another chemist, and do you know what he did? He called me a miserable old sod and walked out without so much as a day's notice.'

Byron wasn't surprised. 'We could try and find somebody else.'

'Impossible to get decent staff these days.'

'You don't want the pharmacy to close, do you? You'll lose the trade.'

'What do I care?' Joseph asked with another spurt of antagonism. 'I've no further use for it. It'll have to be closed. I'm finished. Everybody's left me. Deserted me. I've nothing to live for.'

'The pharmacy could be sold.' Byron was determined not to lose his temper. 'Much the best thing.'

'Who are you to tell me what's the best thing?'

'You aren't well, and it's too much for you now. It's time you relaxed a little. Everybody's entitled to a year or two of retirement. We could find you a more comfortable place near to us.'

'I'm not going anywhere.'

'Well, come to our house for a week or two, until you feel better. Then we'll see.'

'Don't you understand what I'm saying?' Joseph's voice cracked with anger. 'I'm not leaving here. This is my home and here is where I'm going to stay.'

Byron looked round the unkempt clutter of the room and shuddered. This old man and his room were giving him the creeps. Joseph was so unlike Evie it was impossible to imagine them being father and daughter. He went in search of her.

Evie climbed the stairs to the attic, where Matilda had her bedroom. She could hear the rasp of Matty's breathing before she was halfway up. Her bedroom door stood ajar. Evie pushed it open. The sight shocked her.

Matty's eyes were closed and her mouth was wide open, showing a furred tongue. Her cheeks were sucking in and out as she breathed. Her false teeth were on her bedside table, one set on top of the other, with a thin layer of dust collected on top. Long grey hair, matted and wispy, was spread across her pillows.

Evie took the withered hand on the soiled counterpane

between her own. It felt deathly cold. It was going through her to see Matilda like this: a sick and wizened old woman who looked as though she hadn't washed or combed her hair in days. She'd been the one person Evie had been able to turn to for comfort as a child.

'Matty? How are you?'

She thought for one moment that the old woman was beyond hearing her. 'Matty?'

The breathing stopped, then after a second started again more softly. Matty closed her mouth and tried to open her eyes. They were sticky with exudate.

Evie ran down to the bathroom for a bowl of water to wipe them. There was no hot water to be had. No fire had been lit in this house for several days. She used the water from the kettle and put more on to boil for tea. She was shocked when she tried to wash Matty. The old woman was very weak and in a pitiful state.

'Evie?' she croaked, and the rheumy eyes searched her face. 'Little Evie?'

'Not so little now. How long has it been?' she wanted to know. 'How long since you were up and about?' Matty wasn't sure.

Evie looked for a clean nightdress in her drawers but failed to find one. She'd have to lend her one of her own. She eased Matilda's arms into a dressing gown she found hanging behind the door, which she recognised as once belonging to Aunt Agatha. Found a pair of bed socks to put on her poor deformed and swollen feet, and then put her feet into the men's carpet slippers that she usually wore. It was cold, so she tucked a coat round her too, then put her to sit in an old basket chair.

'I'm taking you home with me. I'll see you're looked after better than this. You're poorly, Matty.'

'It's my chest,' she wheezed.

There'd be plenty of room in the new house. 'I'll get you a cup of tea first.'

She went down to the kitchen and tried to stop the cold tap dripping over a sink full of dirty pots. It proved impossible. Byron came in and was more successful.

She said: 'I should have done something long before now.'

'Nonsense, Evie. He wouldn't have let you.' Byron came and put his arms round her. 'Still won't. He refuses point blank to come to our place. You'll never get him out of here. Goodness only knows why he wants to stay.'

'He's been working all these years. Why did I never stop to think? He's getting too old. He can't even look after himself.'

'He didn't exactly invite your concern. Doesn't invite anybody's.'

'Who else does he have?'

'Nobody would expect you to watch over him, not when he's treated you the way he has. Not many would want to help now.'

'I thought when we left the flat I was getting rid of my problems. Suddenly I've got a whole new set.' It scared her.

'We'll have to re-open the pharmacy as soon as possible. It'll need to be sold as a going concern.'

Evie liked the way he said 'we' to show he meant to help her. She half smiled. 'Trust you to think of the business first.'

'After all, it will come to you eventually.'

'Perhaps.'

'Who else does he have to leave it to?'

'He's the sort who'd leave it to the dogs' home.'

'Is he interested in dogs?'

'He used to treat all animals. Sometimes he was called

out to sick horses. Yes, he likes dogs well enough. He might want to do that to make sure I don't benefit.'

'I told him the best thing to do was to sell the business straight away. That it was too much for him.'

'I'll bet he told you it was none of your business?'

'Yes, we'll just have to do the best we can for him. Do you know any other chemists, Evie?'

'Once I did. I was quite friendly with Bertie Pugh. He was apprenticed to Father years ago. He's got a pharmacy of his own now in Conway Street.'

'Telephone him, Evie. He may know of somebody willing to come here at a moment's notice. I saw a phone down in the shop. I'll look his number up for you.'

Just like Father, Evie thought, to put a phone in the shop but not one up here. She found it in what used to be the dentist's room. It seemed he was doing his prescribing in there these days. She dialled the number Byron gave her.

'Bertie?' She recognised his voice the moment he spoke. 'It's Evie. Evie Hobson that was. Remember me?'

'Ye-es. Yes, of course. It's a long time.'

'About twenty years.' She explained about her father, and that she needed a trained chemist to run his pharmacy.

'Thought old Joseph would go on for ever,' he said. 'I'll find somebody for you, Evie. Maybe not for tomorrow morning, but as soon as I can.' They chatted briefly, and she learnt that he was married with three children now, then she gave him her home phone number and rang off.

Back upstairs in the kitchen, Evie found that Byron had already made the tea. She opened the cupboard where they kept their food. There was a small square of cheese covered with green mould, and a jar of jam crystallising into sugar. In the bread bin she found a heel of mildewed bread.

'There's nothing to eat in the house, and Matty's really ill.'

'They're both too old to cope, Evie. And that's not your fault. It happens to everybody.'

'I'll have to get some milk. I'll see if I can borrow some from Polly Darty.'

She ran next door and told Polly what she intended to do about the two invalids. As well as a pint of milk, Polly found two teacakes that hadn't sold and buttered them for her father.

'They'll do him for tonight, since he refuses to come to our house. I need somebody to clean the place up for him and make his meals. Can you think of somebody? You know everybody round here.'

'I'll have a think. There's always women looking for work.'

Evie took the tea and cake to her father on a tray.

'You've taken long enough,' he complained, reaching for the cup.

'Polly sent you the teacake.'

'Is there any jam to go with it?'

Evie called down to Byron to bring up the jar they'd seen. Then she said:

'Father, I need a bag to pack some things for Matilda. We're taking her home with us.'

'Sooner her than me.' He took a noisy sip of tea.

'A bag? Do you have one?'

'No.'

Evie knew he had. She opened his walk-in cupboard. His suits hung on one side, and there were shelves crowded with hats, shoes and bric-à-brac on the other.

'There's one here. Can I borrow it?'

She was pulling it out from below the bottom shelf when she saw some books bundled together and tied with string. One had a lockable gilt catch across its pages. Another had the name Helen Bryant inked across its closed leaves. She knew immediately that they must be her mother's diaries.

Feeling on fire, she glanced surreptitiously behind her. Byron had brought the jam and was standing between her and her father. She eased the bundle of books into the open carpet bag.

'What are you doing in there, Evie? I don't want you messing with my private things.'

She heard the tremor of fear in his voice. Was it just the diaries he didn't want her to see, or was there something else here?

'Just getting this bag out, it's exactly what I need.'

She stood back for a moment and looked more carefully. Under the carpet bag was another much smaller one. It looked vaguely familiar, and yet . . . She pulled it out. It came to her then and made her go weak at the knees. It was the bag her mother had been carrying when she'd come back to the shop the day she'd died.

'Leave my things alone. I don't want you touching anything.'

Father was more nervous, no doubt about that. Evie rammed the smaller bag into the carpet bag too. Joseph was throwing back his bedclothes as though bent on stopping her, but Byron was tucking them back like a mother hen.

She said: 'I'll bring this bag back tomorrow,' and made a breathless exit, flushed with excitement.

She ran upstairs to Matilda's room and surveyed her prize, unable to believe she'd had the luck to find her mother's things. Perhaps now the questions that had puzzled her for so long would be answered.

When she'd calmed down a little, she started putting

together a few things that Matilda would need, packing them round the books. She found less than she'd expected. Matilda seemed to have no clean clothes left. Getting her down to the car was no easy matter and took all Byron's strength as well as her own.

'Perhaps it's as well your father's refused to budge,' Byron panted as he half lifted Matilda on to the back seat.

Evie could think of nothing but locking up this oppressive house, getting back home and settling down to look through her trophies. But she knocked next door first and left a spare key with Polly Darty.

'So Miss Lister can get in in the morning.'

The sales of proprietary medicines and cosmetics provided an important part of her father's turnover.

CHAPTER TWENTY-ONE

Back home in Heswall, Kitty had long since gone home. Mrs Minto had gone to bed, but she heard them and came in her dressing gown to help Evie make up a bed for Matilda.

'In the room next to mine,' she suggested. 'Then she can call in the night if she wants anything.'

Then she went down to the kitchen and warmed up some soup. Evie stayed with Matilda until she'd eaten and was settled for the night, but her mind was on her mother's diaries. She was thrilled to have found them.

When she went to her own room she found that Byron was reading in bed. She showed him her mother's grey canvas bag and the diaries. Explained what they were.

'Your father was all on edge when you opened that cupboard. He was worried you might find them. There's something he doesn't want you to know.'

Evie looked in the bag. 'He'd be furious if he knew I'd taken this. He wouldn't tell me anything about Mother. Wouldn't even talk about her.'

Evie undressed quickly, poured herself a cup of tea from the tray Byron had brought up for her and climbed in beside him. At last it seemed she might find out what had happened all those years ago.

She looked through the diaries and put them in date order, feeling a niggle of guilt. 'Was it wrong for me to take them, do you think?'

'Evie! You need to know and understand what happened.'

'Need? I'm certainly curious.'

Byron's dark eyes were full of affection. 'It *is* a need. Losing your mother suddenly like that when you were small; being brought up by your father, a despot; finding out your mother was still alive when you'd believed her to be dead: it's left you with a permanent wound.'

He moved across the bed and put his arms round her. 'That sort of upbringing is bound to have an effect. It would on anybody. You had a childhood deprived of love, and ended up full of insecurities.' He kissed her cheek.

'You haven't been able to grow out of them, Evie. You're full of worries and can't shake them off. You're too sensitive to other people's worries and take them on board as your own. You're tormented by ghosts of the past and you need to lay them if you are to be truly happy. You need the answers, love.'

'Yes.' Evie knew he was right. He understood more about her than she did herself. 'I'm going to start reading.'

'And I'm going to sleep.' He kissed her again and put out his bedside light, leaving the room in semi-darkness.

Filled with nervous anticipation, Evie opened the first diary, which was for 1887. The frontispiece was inscribed: 'The Diary of Helen Kathleen Bryant, Bryant's Pharmacy, Argyle Street, Birkenhead.'

Her mother would have been only eighteen when she started writing her diaries. It seemed another age. There had been no cars or aeroplanes then. Evie started to read.

January 2nd, 1887 Today, my father Harold Bryant took on a new apprentice, who is much more to my liking than Joseph Hobson. He's called Bill Smith and he has a belly laugh that echoes through the whole building. I can hear him from upstairs when he's down in the shop. He seems very jolly.

Dadda isn't well again. Mama says he needs more help in the shop and this is the best way to get it. Bill Smith will be able to make himself useful after a few months' training.

Evie skimmed a few pages until her eye was caught again.

May 2nd, 1887 Today, Joseph Hobson proposed to me and I giggled when I turned him down. That led to a lot of embarrassment. I apologised for showing amusement but it made things worse. It was so unexpected. He'd never given any indication that he even liked me and he's always so stiff and pompous.

Dadda was cross with me. He was expecting it because Mr Hobson had already asked his permission. Furthermore, he'd received it. Dadda said it was a great honour that Mr Hobson wanted me to share his life with him, and that he'd soon be in a position to support a wife.

He went on and on about him being a serious young man who'd make a good husband. I told Dad he was *too* serious for me. I don't like him. He looks so aloof, his hawk-nose is always in the air. Bill doesn't like him either, he thinks he's a cold fish.

I think Joseph might have been wiser to pay me a little attention first. I could have told him then, quietly and without fuss, not to bother proposing. He went to a lot of unnecessary trouble. The embarrassment is of his making. Anyway, Bill Smith is more my sort.

May 3rd, 1887 Dadda came into the dining room and caught me and Bill laughing together. He accused us of laughing about Joseph Hobson, which we were. I'd just told Bill that yesterday Joseph had proposed and I'd turned him down. If Dad had come a moment or two sooner he'd have caught us kissing, and goodness knows what he'd have said then. He told us both off, and later that night, when Dad and I were alone by the living-room fire, he urged me to reconsider Mr Hobson's offer. He said he was much to be preferred to Bill Smith.

'Not by me he isn't,' I told him. 'Bill's the one I really want to marry.'

'He's not in a position to think of it,' Dadda snorted. It made him cross with me again. 'He's apprenticed to me for five years.'

As if we didn't already know that. It was the first thing me and Bill worked out. We can't marry all the time he's an apprentice and he's still got more than four and a half years to go.

He says he loves me and he'll never change his mind. He asked me to wait for him. I told him I couldn't even think of marrying anyone else. Bill makes me feel wonderful. Lifts me away from all that is humdrum, away from all the soft soap and worming powders I have to sell. Just hearing his voice from the drug run gives me a warm feeling. I'd wait for ever for him. Dadda doesn't like him half so much as he does Joseph, who he says will make much the better apothecary.

July 8th, 1887 Bill very upset tonight. He confessed that he doesn't care much for the life of a chemist after all. He's thinking of giving up his apprenticeship. He hasn't completed one year of the five yet, and feels that after all it isn't the calling for him. His father and grandfather were in the army and he has a mind to follow in their footsteps. He says we could be married so much sooner. If that's the case, I'm all for it.

Bill has spent days working himself up to tell Dadda. Usually he and Joseph go to their rooms after supper to study, but tonight he came back down. He said he wanted me there when he did it, to lend support. Dadda flared up at Bill.

'What a waste of my time! A waste of your own too. A young man like you, not knowing your own mind for ten minutes at a time.'

Father is in an exceedingly bad temper as a result. Bill is packing his bags to leave and I don't like this a bit. It will be horrible not to have him here in the house with me. He kissed me and tried to cheer me up, but really it didn't.

August 13th, 1887 The furore hasn't died down yet. Dadda is upset too. He told me he always knew Bill was a wastrel, and what a good job we found out sooner rather than later.

The days drag now. I'm lost without Bill. He writes every day to tell me his news. He's hoping for a commission. His father isn't pleased because he paid to have him apprenticed to my father, but his grandfather is willing to pay for a commission for him. It's just that it all takes time and I can't be with him.

August 21st, 1887 Bill came to take me out today (Sunday). It was heaven to see him again and take his arm when we walked in the park. Dadda wasn't pleased. I thought he was going to forbid it. He only allowed it because Mother came too. Well, she walked ten yards behind us, so we could talk together. I know he'd have kissed me if she hadn't been there. I do love Bill. My tummy turns right over just to look at him.

October 1st, 1887 Bill is now officially in the army and seems mightily pleased to have it so. He reckons it will be a good life. I'm just dying to see him in his uniform, I'm sure he looks exceedingly handsome. Dadda said it would be wiser if I put him out of my mind. He thinks he's not a man who will stick at anything. I'd find it easier to fly than do that. I think of nothing else.

October 19th, 1887 Bill came today, looking even more handsome than I'd expected. Second Lieutenant William Smith. He asked my father if he could marry me. I pleaded and pleaded to have it so. Dadda rather unbending on this. He says he's given me too much of my own way in the past. I told him if I could have just this one thing more, I'd be forever grateful.

Mamma is not against Bill. She says she likes him, but she won't take my part against Dadda. He is trying to talk me out of it, but nothing will make me change my mind. I keep telling him that I love Bill and always will and nobody else will suit me so well. He said I must be exceedingly popular to have two proposals in so many months.

Bill came again to plead with Father. He gave his consent at last and insists it's to be a long engagement to give me time to change my mind, but I never will. I'm so happy, over the moon. Joseph Hobson is looking very dour at the news.

November 10th, 1887 Bill has given me an engagement ring. An opal with a tiny diamond each side. Mother doesn't approve, she says opals are unlucky, but I love it and wear it all the time. I've started collecting for my bottom drawer. I have a pair of pillowcases and I'm embroidering them with hearts and flowers. To think of them side by side on our bed with our heads making dents in them makes me ready to swoon with happiness. Mother is tatting some cushion covers for me.

December 1st, 1887 Such a crisis! I don't know whether to be pleased or horrified. Bill's regiment is going out to India, where they will serve for seven years. Probably before the new year. He came to tell us the news and asked as a great favour that we might be married before he goes.

He has thrown my whole family into a great tizz. Father stamped downstairs to the shop and refused to listen to any more.

Bill implored Mama to stay. She sat down again while he explained that if I am his wife, the army will provide me with a passage to India when he's served there for six months. He'll be allotted a married quarter and I will be able to share his life.

I am almost overcome with the anxiety and excitement of it all. If Father refuses to give his consent then we must wait until Bill returns, as he thinks it will be too difficult for me to go out as a single girl and marry him there. I would perhaps need to pay my own passage out too.

Mother sent Bill home but we talked late into the night. I pleaded and wept. I've never wanted anything so badly. Mama told Dad I'll be impossible to live with if I don't have my way with this. I told them I didn't think I would live at all. There can be no more wait-and-see, Father has to say one way or the other straight out.

He said he'd sleep on it, but I could hear them still arguing it out long after we'd all gone to bed. Mama has taken my part at last, thank goodness.

Father has said yes! I can't believe my good fortune and could hardly get the words out to thank him. Bill was over the moon when I told him. His belly laugh was ringing through our house every five minutes. The thing now is to fix up the wedding as soon as possible. Bill will sail on January the fourth.

Everything is such a flurry and an excitement and a joy. Christmas coming in the middle of it too, it's almost too much to bear. It has been decided and fixed, we are to be married on Boxing Day. The vicar has agreed, and after the service we'll all walk home for the wedding breakfast. Mama complains now about the lack of time to get things ready, but she is as thrilled and excited as I am.

Mrs Jackson, our dressmaker, is making me a dress of white satin. Mama suggested white velvet but the cost was very high and Bill says I will be able to wear satin for regimental occasions in India. I'll not want the warmth of velvet there.

Dadda is still shaking his head and hoping he's done the right thing, though I keep telling him he has. Boxing Day is very convenient because the shop would be closed anyway. For most of our guests too, because they will not be at work. Then Bill and I will go to Chester for a honeymoon. It will last until the day his leave finishes which is the day before he sails.

The last few pages of the diary were left blank. Her mother had been having too exciting a time to write in it. Evie hurriedly turned to the one for the following year. It was bound in Moroccan leather.

January 6th, 1888 Our wedding and our honeymoon were absolutely wonderful. I've never been so blissfully happy in all my life as I was with Bill. Now he has gone everything seems very flat.

I've come back home. I'm working in the shop again. My wedding seems like a distant dream. I need my lovely, lovely dress hanging in my clothes cupboard and my wedding band on my finger to remind me that it all really did happen.

The thought of a new life in India fills me with anticipation. I have that to look forward to. I'm crossing the days off my calendar but only two have gone so far. Bill has given me a book on Indian history and its people. I shall read it from cover to cover and I shall keep myself busy helping Father in the shop.

He says he needs all the help he can get. He isn't feeling too well and has dropsy in his legs. I've started making myself a trousseau for India, and have bought ten yards of fine white cambric and some lace for this. I'm also still collecting for my bottom drawer and have a tablecloth to embroider.

I am not to bear his child just yet, though might so easily have found I was. I'm relieved, because it might have delayed my departure for India and Bill. There will be plenty of time for that when we are together. He says he wants a family.

A lovely, lovely letter came from Bill today, reams

long and written on the boat. He says he's eating huge meals and sitting in the sun, but that he misses me most awfully. I wrote back immediately. I told him it's a thousand times worse to be left at home trying to imagine all the delights he describes.

April 4th, 1888 Another letter from Bill today, letting me know he's reached Bombay. He tells me he saw a line of thirty elephants roped together walking through the main streets of that teeming city with their young behind, the last of which was just a baby. He's horrified by the poverty and the beggars and I am not to be upset to see such things when I get there.

Evie paused and looked in the grey canvas bag. The letters her mother had received from Bill Smith were all here, neatly tied up in bundles and dated. Each was in its envelope, addressed to Mrs Helen Smith. Each had been read many times, as evidenced by the well-thumbed paper. It brought a lump to Evie's throat to see them so carefully preserved. She went back to the diary.

June 6th, 1888 I have finished embroidering a fine cambric nightdress, which I stitched all myself. Mama says my needlework is improving fast. I need bodices now, and shall make them of fine cotton for the heat.

Father is much worse and has taken to his bed. The shop is very busy without him. Joseph Hobson is doing all the prescribing. Mama is worried about that, as he has three more months of his apprenticeship still to run and isn't qualified. Father says he's good enough but we should find another chemist.

There is too much work for one person. Mama advertised the vacancy today.

She sent for the doctor again today too. Dadda said it was a waste of money because his prescription is for foxglove tea, which he started taking last year without much effect. Poor Dadda has no energy and can hardly dress himself. There is no question of him working in the shop.

Mama is very worried. She wanted me and Hobson with her when she chose the chemist from the three who applied. It was Joseph who picked out Albert Vance. He's quite old. Joseph says that gives the customers confidence.

Poor Dadda hardly seems to care. Today he asked me to take care of Mama if anything should happen to him. He says he's sorry I shall soon be going to India, as he's afraid Mama will need me here.

July 8th, 1888 Two letters came from Bill this morning. He and his battalion have taken up duty in a fort at Razmak on the North-West Frontier, and that is where he expects I'll join him. He tells me to bring warm clothes with me. He thought all India was hot, but finds it's freezing cold up there.

He has to go out on expeditions for a week or ten days at a time. It's meant to show the British strength and frighten the warring local tribes into submission. They march in a column through narrow gorges between huge high peaks very bare and raw. He hopes I won't be afraid of being left but there are other wives there, and always two battalions are left to guard the fort. I don't think I would be.

The post from India takes so long he won't yet know how poorly Dadda is. I sit with him in the evenings and write my letters or embroider my trousseau, but he hardly notices I'm there. I worry whether I could leave if permission came now.

Poor Mama is worried to distraction. Dadda doesn't rally at all. The dropsy is filling his limbs. Joseph recommended a purge. We try it, of course, but not with much hope.

There was another gap of several weeks, then, with another, larger lump in her throat, Evie read:

August 2nd, 1888 Father died last night. He was only forty-three. His funeral is on Wednesday. Mama is prostrated with grief.

Poor Mama, she's found it very hard over the last few months. We gave up expecting him to recover some time ago.

September 7th, 1888 Joseph Hobson is a great comfort to Mama. He brings up camomile tea and lavender oil to soothe her. Mama took to her bed last week. All the worry she's had with Father and trying to manage the business on her own has made her ill now.

Another letter from Bill, who says there have been more attacks recently by marauding Pathan tribesmen. The Pathans live high in the mountains and attack the villages of the lowland tribes on both sides of the mountain range. Bill says they have to because there isn't enough for them to survive on in the bare uplands. The army tries to keep order but last week the Pathan tribesmen attacked a column out on expedition.

He urges me not to worry and promises to take

good care of himself. He fears that the army won't want to bring out another wife to the fort until things settle down again.

He hasn't yet had my letter telling him that poor Dadda has passed away and the other troubles I have here. I don't think Mama wants to get better. She says she can't live without him. I've told her she must. I couldn't bear it if I were to lose her too. I couldn't possibly leave her just now, even if my boat tickets were to come.

The shop continues busy. Joseph is very helpful.

There were more blank pages in the diary. Evie turned them over with a heavy heart. Reliving the troubles her mother had gone through and expecting to read that her grandmother had passed away too was agonising.

To gain a moment's respite, she turned to her mother's grey canvas bag again, and noticed an official-looking envelope addressed to Mrs Helen Smith. Long ago, it had been torn open in a great hurry. Now she carefully slid out the single sheet of paper.

Evie's head reeled with the horror of it. She couldn't believe the run of trouble her mother had had at that time. The letter was from the War Office, and it reminded her of the one she'd received when Ned had been lost at sea. It offered condolences on the death of Second Lieutenant William Smith in a native skirmish on the North-West Frontier. It told Helen that her husband had died bravely, together with all the senior officers of his regiment.

This was a loss Evie understood only too well. Hadn't she gone through it too? She wiped away a tear and took up the diary again.

November 15th, 1888 I haven't been able to do anything for the past month, not even write in my diary, which has always been a comfort to me.

I feel numb with grief. First Father and now Bill, all in the same year. The only good thing is that Mama is a little better.

Evie slid that book on to the floor beside her bed and reached for the next. She had to turn to June before she found anything written in it.

June 15th, 1889 I ought to feel better about things. Mama is better and now gets up every afternoon. She says that next week she'll get dressed straight after breakfast. The shop is functioning well and is profitable, which is a great relief to us.

Joseph has taken on a Miss Lister to run the front counter. He's had to because I've needed to spend so much time upstairs with Mother. But even upstairs we are better organised than we were.

He heard of Matilda Best, who was working for some church acquaintance being sent abroad to do missionary work and has thus been released from service. Matilda is certainly a find. I virtually leave all the housekeeping to her.

If only Bill were still alive. I feel half dead without him. I'm desperately disappointed that I won't after all see India with him. I feel I was given a glimpse of Utopia only to have it snatched from me. What remains seems empty. If only I had been having his child, it would be something left of him.

I'm down helping in the shop again and feel better for it. Mama continues frail. She says she can't get over losing Dadda, that she feels useless without him.

I told her I feel the same about losing Bill. I don't even have a grave on which to put flowers each Sunday. It would be some solace to do that for him as well as for Father. It haunts me that Bill lies in such alien soil, and that I can never see the place. I can't really imagine what it's like either.

The other pages in that diary were all blank. Clearly her mother hadn't had the heart to write more during that year.

Evie knew that Byron was asleep. His breathing was deep and even. The house was silent, but for her, sleep was a thousand miles away. Her mind raced with the agonies her mother had suffered all those years ago.

Once she'd feared that it would be her lot to follow her mother's downward path. Joseph had predicted it, and the thought had given her nightmares. But she'd been fortunate. Her life had been good and would continue to be so. Byron was a kind and understanding man. Evie reached down for the next volume and went on reading.

January 1st, 1890 Mama thinks that now that more than a year has passed I should be getting over Bill, though she puts it more delicately than that. She thinks it's easier for me because I was married for so short a time. I lived as a wife for a mere eight days; what could be more cruel than that?

She says that I'm young enough to marry again if only I would cheer up and smile a little. She said today that she'd like to see me settled before she goes. I told her she wasn't going anywhere, but it frightens me to hear her talk of death like this. She's very down. A ghost of herself really. She's lost so much weight. She praises Joseph Hobson. Father liked him and thought him most suitable for me. She says that he offered for me once and she's sure he would again. With the business being in her gift, what could be more suitable for me than a husband who could run it?

Joseph has been very good to us since our troubles, I have to admit that, and I know from the way he looks at me that Mama is right. But he falls so short of Bill.

I don't know if I'll ever get over him and the thought of another does not please.

There followed a good deal about working in the shop, but it wasn't answering the questions that thronged Evie's mind. She began to flick over the pages, and then turned to the next volume.

January 1st, 1891 It's now over two years since I heard of Bill's death. Mother is no better. She eats little and does little. I fear she'll never pick up. Matilda waits on her hand and foot.

Today, Joseph Hobson proposed again. He said he has always loved me and has wanted to tell me for a long time but he saw that I grieved for Bill. This morning he heard me laugh with Miss Lister over the antics of a dog that was brought into the shop. He said I sounded as though I was over Bill, and would perhaps be able to consider him now.

He runs the shop, does all the ordering and prescribing, keeps the accounts and presents me with the results at the end of each month.

I asked for time to think about it, but I know of no other. Perhaps I'd be happier as Joseph's wife than as an old maid. I'd be more sure about that if he'd show more affection.

He's made no attempt to kiss me, though he did hold my hand. I don't feel for him one whit of what I felt for Bill. There's no warmth about Joseph, he's such a stiff, strait-laced sort of person. So earnest and wrapped up in his work, but he is a good apothecary. Everybody reports his medicines as effective, and he is kind to us.

Mama has hardly been to church since Dadda died. She hasn't been well enough. So every Sunday, Joseph and I walk there together. He talks of the weather on the way there and the sermon on the way back. Despite living under the same roof all these years, I don't feel I know him well.

February 2nd, 1891 Mama is not at all well and has taken to her bed again. She pleads with me to accept Joseph. She thinks he'll make an excellent husband.

Mama doesn't come to the table for meals any more. Matilda eats with us but gets up quickly to clear away. After dinner, Joseph put his hand across the table to touch mine and asked me gently if I'd had enough time to make up my mind. He looked so hopeful and there was love in his eyes.

I said that yes, I would marry him. It made him lean across and kiss my cheek and take both my hands in his. He said I'd made him very happy and promised to do his best to make me happy too.

Mama was overjoyed when we went together to her bedroom to tell her. I haven't seen her so animated in years. She insisted I fetch the Sunday sherry bottle and some glasses. It's a Sunday ritual that we all take a glass of sherry before dinner.

'To warm us up when we come in from church,' Dadda used to say, though we did it even on hot Sundays in summer.

Joseph fetched Matilda from the kitchen and she raised her glass to us too. I feel better now I've made up my mind. Joseph seems quite different, all smiles. I don't suppose it's been much fun for him living here with Mama and me. Things will be different now.

Joseph wants us to be married soon and so does Mama. She says I already have a wedding dress. I took it out of my wardrobe for the first time in years and tried it on. It still fits. I went in to show myself to Mam and she said excellent, silly to think of getting another. I went back to my own bedroom and cried for Bill and for what might have been. It reminds me too much.

I haven't exactly told Joseph he'll be second best, but I said I still think of Bill, so I'm not marrying him under false pretences. He says love will come and he'll be happy with what I can give him. He really is very patient with me and very kind to Mama. Perhaps I could do worse.

March 1st, 1891 The deed is done, I am now Mrs Hobson. I wore the same white dress and felt as cold as ice in it. I couldn't stop shivering all through the ceremony. Joseph hired two separate carriages, so that Mama could ride to church and not get tired out. Mr Vance, the assistant, gave me away in lieu of Father. I helped Matilda make a special lunch. It was a very quiet wedding this time. Only the shop staff and the Harveys from the butcher's.

Joseph is certainly kind and thoughtful but there

is no passion in him. He is not such a good lover as Bill and doesn't show much affection. He's very self-contained. He says he would like children and I pray for them to come. I would like that very much myself.

Mama seems to be fading away. She says she's happy to know I'm settled and I've done the right thing. I can see her getting weaker, and though Joseph continues to prescribe for her and she says his medicines do her good, I fear they won't keep her in this world.

June 3rd, 1891 Today I discovered I'm with child. Joseph is thrilled and even Mama whispered that she was delighted, though she hardly had the strength.

She said: 'I can go now with an easy mind. You're settled and will be content with your children.'

June 4th, 1891 I sat up with poor Mama most of the night. Joseph persuaded me to bed at two in the morning. When Matilda went to her at six with a cup of tea, she'd gone.

I wept because I wasn't there at the end, but Joseph said it was his fault, that I must have my rest. Matilda said she'd gone peacefully in her sleep and that she'd been ill for so long I must look on it as a release.

Everybody is being kind. I'm hanging on to the thought of the baby and that keeps me going. I feel quite fatalistic. I'm afraid those I love are doomed to die young. Mother is only forty-three. Exactly the same age as Father was at his death.

CHAPTER TWENTY-TWO

Evie looked at the diaries that remained. From this point on, Helen was not making regular entries. One book seemed to cover several years. She had a lump in her throat as she started reading again.

February 2nd, 1892 My baby is born, a lovely little girl. Joseph wanted a boy but he says he's not unhappy as this is the first. He wants to call her Evelina and I think that's pretty. She has a dimple in her cheek and such dark, silky hair, not like Joseph's. We are both besotted with her.

I feel content at last. At peace with my circumstances. Joseph says there is no need for me to work on the front counter now I have the baby to look after, but I like to go down for an hour when Evie takes her rest. After all, Matilda is here in the house with her all the time and she likes to play with her too.

Working in the shop keeps me in touch with everything. I really enjoy the change. The customers seem to like Joseph and are prepared to wait for him rather than talk to Mr Vance.

He says he would like to start taking apprentices now that he's had some experience. He thinks the business would be more profitable because apprentices would pay us for the privilege of learning and we can utilise their labour and thus avoid paying Mr Vance, who is a trained pharmacist and expects a due wage.

Joseph is very wrapped up in all aspects of the business and I count myself lucky he's prepared to do so much. We had the old accounts out last night and find we have increased our turnover and are making more profit than did my parents. That pleased Joseph very much.

May 8th, 1892 Evie has cut her first tooth. She is a delightful baby, always gurgling and smiling up at us all. Joseph brought up a little rattle from the shop and tied it over her cot. She tries to knock it, first with her hands, and then with her feet. She laughs and giggles when it makes a noise.

The rattle was by way of being a peace offering from Joseph. I realised I had not seen any figures for the shop for over two months. I asked him if he'd made up the books, and of course he had. He said he didn't want to bother me with figures but he didn't even mention them, and it is my business. My father started it, he willed it to my mother and she willed it to me. He was cold and cross all day, but tonight he brought up the rattle and Evie loves it. I'm glad we can melt his bad moods between us.

June 9th, 1892 Something has upset Joseph and I don't know what it is. I've asked him several times but he says he's perfectly all right. The business is still thriving. I had to see the figures to settle my mind, I thought it must be that.

We have Monty Baines, an apprentice, living with us now. He seems to please Joseph. Miss Lister says there's been no trouble downstairs while I've not been there. Matilda says he's not found any fault with her. But Joseph seems so changed, everybody agrees with me about that.

I can't make up my mind whether he's frightened or angry. Perhaps it's both. He's very short with everybody, and cold even with little Evie. He's bottling something inside him and it's making him very intense. I do wish he'd confide in me. I can't think what's troubling him. If it isn't the business, or the family, or the staff, I don't know what else there is to upset him.

We all tiptoe round trying not to give Joseph any aggravation, but he gets no better. He blows up at us all without warning. He can be boiling with anger when five minutes earlier he'd seemed in a mild mood.

I chose my moment, and asked when he came to the tea table if he were ill, as it seemed the only possible explanation. He erupted like Mount Vesuvius. I'm sure they could hear him shouting in the shop. I fear his temper will never be what it was, he's been like this for so long now.

He's changing in other ways too. He doesn't like me to work on the front counter any more. Doesn't like me to be in the shop at all. It's useless telling him I enjoy it, that I want to help. He says nowadays for a man in his position it isn't seemly to have a wife working as a counter assistant.

I had to remind him that I was the owner, and he said I should act more like it then. In order to keep him calm I don't go down any more.

Old Mrs Cartwright, at the newsagent's, says she wishes her husband was more that way inclined. She'd like less to do in the shop. She's exhausted by the time bedtime comes. She thinks I'm making a fuss about nothing.

Sometimes I think Joseph's mind has turned. He says it's nothing I've done. He even said he loves me, but he does nothing to show it.

February 3rd, 1894 I asked Joseph, now that Evie's two years old, if we should be trying for another baby. He said yes, he'd like a son, but he gets into bed and turns away from me. There's no possibility of having another child this way.

I don't understand him at all. Despite what he says, he seems to have gone off me. Sometimes I wonder if he married me for my business. Truly he takes more interest in that than he does in me.

Since the Married Woman's Property Act he cannot take it from me, but I fear he would like to. He doesn't consult me at all now. He runs it without any reference to my wishes, nor does he show me the accounts unless I ask.

When I faced him about this, he says he wishes to shield me from business worries as any good husband would, but I am so horribly suspicious of his motives. I feel so distanced from him. The profits are being banked in an account which is in our joint names. He doesn't question what I draw from it and since he works so hard I do not question what he takes out either. In truth, it seems little. I wish I did not have this suspicious streak.

September 10th, 1896 Evie is very sweet. She started school today. I'm pleased because it gets both of us out of the house. Joseph doesn't like me leaving it, but I have a good excuse now, I have to take Evie backwards and forwards to school and once I'm out, I can go round the shops or the market before returning. I feel much better for the freedom.

April 7th, 1897 Joseph was in one of his better moods at breakfast today. He sprinkled extra sugar on Evie's porridge for her and started telling her the story of the three bears. We had to rush all the way to school after that, but I was pleased that he seemed to be improving.

When I got back he was raving at Miss Lister because she'd gone to get more shaving soap from the store and left the front counter unattended for a few moments. We've always done that, sometimes several times each day, and he's been happy to have it so until now. In future, he said she must check the stock each evening and replace what's been sold before she goes home.

The apprentice whispered that it was something Joseph received in the morning post that put him in such a black mood. The mail was still on the back counter and Joseph caught me looking through it when he turned round. He blew up again at me, demanding to know what I was looking for.

I'd seen nothing but a few bills. It was just routine business mail. I thought the apprentice must be mistaken, but he said Joseph put one letter in the pocket of his white coat.

I'd swear Joseph is frightened. He had a nightmare last night and was talking in his sleep.

The apprentice tells me Joseph is often at the door when the post is due. That he seems uneasy and that he's told the postman to bring the mail to the drug run and not toss it on the front counter as he used to.

We have easier times that last sometimes a few

weeks and sometimes a few months, but according to the apprentice, it's always the post that sends him into one of his rages.

June 6th, 1897 I'm the one who caused the trouble today. I came home from seeing Evie to school and found the sign-writers changing the name above the shop windows from Arthur Bryant to Joseph Hobson. I screamed at them to stop and caused a commotion in the shop that brought business to a standstill.

Joseph took my arm and led me upstairs away from them all. In our bedroom, he insisted I swallow some pills and lie on the bed. He said I was hysterical. He sat with me then and explained that it was bad for business to keep Father's name over the shop. Everybody knew Joseph now as the pharmacist practising here and it was only right his name should be outside. He said I was being unreasonable and that after a little sleep I'd see it his way.

I told him it was equally unreasonable not to give me some inkling that he was about to do it. Why could he not have discussed it first?

Whatever he gave me made me sleep all day. Matilda went to collect Evie from school in my stead, and next time I went outside it was Joseph's name that was up. I wept because all my suspicions seem confirmed by this.

I'll go to see Myerscough and Rudge and get them to draw up a will leaving the business to Evie. They know me there, they handled Father's will and know the business is mine. I want to guarantee Evie's future. Perhaps after all I am being silly about this. Joseph loves her too, she's the only one who can make him smile. He'd want to ensure a good future for her too, I'm sure.

If anything Joseph's temper is getting worse. He took on a new apprentice who left after two weeks saying he couldn't cope with such moods. Unfortunately, the rest of us have to.

Evie fell back against her pillows in a rush of anger. Her mother's suspicions had been well founded. Father had taken over the pharmacy as his own though he knew he had no legal right. He'd wrested it from his own wife. Deprived his own child of her legal right.

Evie let out a long, juddering sigh. If only she'd known this when she was eighteen! She could have had so much more of Ned's company. They could have lived together in comfort. There would have been no need for him to go away to sea; no need for the long, lonely months without him.

She felt hot tears roll down her cheek. She'd have given anything to have kept Ned at home with her. He could have worked on the front counter and helped where he could. The business would have paid him more than his seafaring wage. They could have made the most of the few years they'd had.

But even after Ned's death, when she'd been afraid they'd all go hungry, a job on the front counter and care for Queenie was all she'd dared ask him for. Even then, he hadn't told her that the pharmacy was legally hers. He'd refused any help, keeping all it earned for himself.

True, he'd given her the letter about Aunt Agatha's legacy, and that had cushioned her. He must have known what that was. No doubt it had salved his conscience.

Evie had read late into the night, totally absorbed in her mother's life, growing more and more astounded at her revelations. She flicked through the remaining pages for further entries, but there were none. The last date was 15 June 1898, the date her mother had disappeared. The date Father had said she'd been killed in an accident.

There was a lot more she hadn't yet looked at in her mother's bag, but her eyes were so tired she could hardly focus.

Evie had learned a lot about her mother and about her own early life. She was shocked at Father's deceit and the lengths he'd gone to to get his own ends, but there was still something she didn't understand. What had made her mother leave home without her? She mustn't think about it now. She yawned and switched off her light.

Byron was sleeping deeply beside her, but for Evie sleep was far away, even though she ached for it. She tossed and turned while her mind swirled with questions. She couldn't see to read any more tonight but she still craved the answers.

It came to her then that Matilda had been living with her mother through all those times. She must know what had happened. Once it was in her mind, she had to get up and see if Matilda was awake.

As Evie went quietly up to the top storey, she heard a little cough. She pushed open the bedroom door and said softly: 'Matty?'

The figure on the bed turned. 'Is that you, Helen?'

That made her shiver. 'It's Evie.'

She'd left the landing light on and the door open. In the half-light she pulled a chair close to the bed and sat down.

'Evie, yes.' Matilda's eyes shone feverishly. 'I'm thirsty.'

'A drink of water?' Evie raised her a little and held the glass to her lips.

'Matty,' she said. 'I want you to tell me about my mother. What happened to make her run away? You know, don't you? She must have confided in you. She had no one else.'

Matty's anxious eyes were searching her face. 'There's nothing to worry about now,' Evie soothed. 'Father forbade you to tell me, didn't he? He used to get angry if he saw us talking together, but this is my house. He isn't here. He has no power over either of us now.'

Evie was desperate to know what had happened to her mother. 'I want you to think back, Matilda. To the time Helen left home.'

'Yes.'

'Helen would want you to tell me. Why was my father so angry with everybody?'

Evie felt work-worn fingers close tightly on her own. 'Afraid,' the dry lips croaked.

'No need to be afraid. You're safe here with me.'

'Your father – was afraid.'

'What of?'

'Helen's first husband.'

'But he was dead long before this.'

'No, no, he wasn't,' she whispered.

Evie was afraid Matilda's mind was wandering. 'He was killed. In India.'

'All a mistake,' she wheezed. 'A terrible mistake.'

Evie had seen the War Office telegram and the letter of condolence that followed it. A further letter from an officer serving in India, telling Helen about the Pathan ambush in which so many had died.

At the back of her mind, doubt niggled. Years ago, somebody had whispered the word 'bigamy'. She thought it had been Bertie Pugh.

Matilda's eyes were flashing fear so tangible that Evie

felt the skin crawl at the back of her neck.

'What happened, Matty? Why did Helen go away? Try to think back. It was June 1898. I was six.'

Evie had to wait. She could see Matty's face creasing with concentration. When she started to speak, her voice was a hoarse whisper.

'There was always trouble. Joseph was always finding fault. The house was being turned upside-down. Painters and decorators were in.'

She coughed and cleared her throat.

'That morning there was more trouble at breakfast. Joseph said his bacon was overcooked but it wasn't my fault. He was late coming down.

'Helen tried to cut up your bacon for you. It was so crisp it snapped and shot right across the table. You laughed, and that upset him more. When Helen was getting ready to take you to school, Joseph was out on the landing, arguing with her.

' "That child's old enough to go on her own now. It's time she learned to stand on her own feet."

' "She's only six," Helen protested.

'He hated to see her leave the house. Hated to see her walk through the shop. He wanted her safely upstairs in the house all the time.

'Your mother felt like a prisoner. She wanted to go out. She told me she was going round the market to buy some cloth to make another dress for you, instead of coming directly home.'

Matilda's knotted fingers twitched at the sheet. 'It was an ordinary day, sunny and bright. I cleared the breakfast pots and washed up in my new sink.'

'And then?'

There was no hurrying Matilda. She'd been forbidden to speak of these facts for so long that now she wanted to tell her everything. Her voice was stronger now. Evie told herself she must be patient.

'There was a commotion in the shop. So loud I crept down the stairs to see what it was all about.

'A soldier was shouting at Mr Hobson: "Helen stopped writing to me. I was left out there in limbo, not knowing what had gone wrong. I thought at first it was the post, but others were getting mail."

'He was an officer in full uniform with a polished Sam Browne belt. A captain now, with three pips on his shoulders.

' "Where's Helen? I've written countless letters to her. I wrote to her mother, I wrote to you pleading for news, but nobody answered."

' "We thought you were dead," Joseph said. He was in a real state, all worked up. Absolutely terrified. "Killed in action. That's why." '

Evie felt the soles of her feet crawl with horror. Matilda was more animated now. She went on:

'Everything had stopped in the shop. All the customers were watching them. It came to me then, and fair took my breath away. I couldn't believe my eyes. It was Bill Smith all right. Knew him right away, though he'd filled out and held himself more upright. More of a man. My legs went weak, I can tell you. I had to hold on to the stair rail.

' "You knew I wasn't dead. You returned some of my letters marked 'Not known at this address'."

'Bill was sort of menacing him, moving closer.

' "Get out of my shop," Joseph shouted, staggering back. "I don't want you here." His face was the colour of putty.

'Bill moved even closer. They were in the drug run by now. I went up a couple of stairs, so that I could see over the ointment jars.

' "I know it was you, I know your writing, no one else writes so small and neat.

' "Didn't you understand what you were doing to me? You knew I was serving out on the North-West Frontier. I couldn't just come home to sort things out. I asked for leave on compassionate grounds but it wasn't granted. I'd volunteered to serve out there, and I was made to do it."

'It did me good to see Joseph so scared for once.' Matty's rheumy eyes smiled into Evie's in the half-light.

'Bill kept shouting at him: "I was given permission to bring Helen out, but she didn't reply to official letters either. I was out of my mind with worry. I asked my friend Walter Caine to call on you. To find out what had happened to her. He wrote that you now owned this business and you didn't know Helen's whereabouts. You told him you thought she was with another man. I couldn't believe it. Helen would never do such a thing. I asked my uncle to come down from Glasgow to see you, but he wrote much the same thing. He asked you to write to me direct but you never did.

' "I only found out this year that I'd been wrongly listed as killed in action. Then I understood why Helen had stopped writing to me. I could guess what you'd been up to then. You intercepted my letters to her, didn't you? You didn't want her to know it was all a terrible mistake".'

Evie felt overwhelmed. 'I don't understand,' she said slowly. 'How was it possible for him to be wrongly listed as killed?'

'I asked Helen about that later. There were two Lieutenant William Smiths in the same battalion. It was the other who lost his life, along with the senior officers who knew him.'

'In some sort of native uprising?' Evie had read of them in the diaries.

'Helen did tell me . . .' Matilda was frowning, trying to remember. The facts as she told them were disjointed. Evie had to piece them together in her mind. It was horrible, far worse than she'd supposed.

'The death roll had to be sorted out at headquarters, hundreds of miles away. It was a terrible mix-up.'

Evie understood now. Helen had married Joseph bigamously because the War Office had wrongly reported Bill as dead.

She said: 'Joseph knew Bill was still alive. He was intercepting his letters. He wanted to keep my mother in ignorance . . . I think that's horrible.'

'He was afraid she'd leave him. Bill was her rightful husband, not him.'

'What happened after that?'

Matilda went on: 'A punch-up. Bill had Joseph by the collar. The apprentice was trying to pull him off. We all thought he was going to kill him.

'I didn't notice your mother come into the shop until she dropped her shopping with a thud and the oranges she'd bought rolled all over the floor.

' "Bill?" Her voice was all squeaky.

'I thought she'd faint, she went so white, then the next minute they were clinging together, sounding hysterical. Laughing and crying at the same time. Everyone was excited and pleased to see Bill, and clapping him on the back.

' "What's this then?" they were saying. "A ghost back from the dead?" The news spread up the shopping parade and old Mrs Cartwright from the paper shop came in, and Florrie from the barber's.

'Everybody was pleased except Joseph. He had a face blacker than Satan. If anybody looked as though he'd seen a ghost, it was him.

'He was shouting at the apprentice: "Get everybody out who isn't buying. This isn't a peep show. We're going upstairs where we can talk."

'I went back up to the kitchen but Mr Hobson came to the door. "Away with you, Matilda," he said. "This is family business and not for your ears." He tried to shoo me up to my bedroom but I ran out to Gladys at the bakery with the excuse that I needed to get bread.

'Gladys could talk of nothing else. All along the parade they couldn't. They were all out on the pavement.

' "The child," they were saying. "She'll be the stumbling block. Little Evie." There was more talking than selling done that morning.

'Joseph was in the wrong, you see, Evie. He'd known for a long time that Bill Smith was alive. That's what turned his mind. He knew his marriage was bigamous and that Helen, if she knew, would leave him.

'He hid it from her and he tried to keep her out of sight in case Bill sent somebody else round and they saw her. The trouble was, both of them loved Helen. They both wanted her.'

Evie let out a long, agonised sigh. 'And that was it? She went off with her first husband and left me?'

'No! I went back after an hour, but nothing had been settled one way or the other. Helen's face was wet with tears. Bill Smith kept shouting that the law was on his side and that Helen was his wife.

'She had the letters out to show him. Those she'd received telling her he'd been killed. I made some tea. Helen asked me to. Then I went upstairs to make the beds and thought what a terrible mess it was.

' "If you go, you go without the child," Joseph was shouting. "She's my daughter and I'll not allow it." I could see Helen was torn in two.'

'But she left me.'

'She asked me to pack her clothes, and yours too. She was pleading with Joseph to allow her to take you. Helen planned to meet you from school and not come back.

'But Joseph foresaw that might happen and went to meet you too. There was no thought for the shop that day. The apprentice had to manage on his own.'

Evie felt wrung out. 'My father kept me against her will?'

'She tried to escape with you again the next day, but Joseph caught you on the stairs and sent you to your room. He sent her away without you. That was when she gave me that photograph to give you when you were old enough to understand. She guessed Joseph would get rid of everything that reminded him of her. Sort of banish her from memory.

'At suppertime the following night, Bill Smith came back to plead for you. He said Helen was heartbroken without you. He threatened to go to court to get custody.'

'But he didn't, did he?'

'Joseph remembered I was there and I was sent off to bed before I'd cleared the dishes. So was the apprentice. I don't know what happened after that. Joseph never let anyone know his business if he could help it. He liked to play his cards close to his chest.

'But there was a lot of noise and argument. Always about you. It went on for hours, well into the night. I don't think Bill Smith meant to give up. I was expecting to be called down to get you out of bed and dressed.'

'But you weren't?'

'No, I know there was a fight in the living room that night because one of the chairs was broken. He hid it in the attic. I heard him bring it up. Yes, definitely a fight.'

'Father won, you mean?'

'It wasn't what I'd have expected. Bill Smith seemed the stronger man, but you stayed where Joseph wanted you, so he must have won.'

Evie sighed again. 'Remember the photos on the landing. Father was a boxer. He had the greater skill.'

'I felt so sorry for Helen. Such a pretty, kind-hearted girl. She tried to stand between me and Joseph when his ire turned on me, which was more often than I liked. She deserved better of life than she got, poor girl. My heart goes out to her still.

'If it weren't for you, your mother would have gone away with Bill and that would have been the end of it. Having you gave Joseph the means to prevent her going. Poor Helen, there was no easy way out for her. She was in a cleft stick.'

Evie tiptoed downstairs to make a cup of tea for them both. It was almost five o'clock. She ached with fatigue but she'd never felt more awake. Her mind was on fire. She knew now how difficult her mother had found it to leave her. And years later, she'd come back to make her peace.

When she went back with the tea, she asked:

'What was my mother like, Matilda?'

'To look at? Smaller and daintier than you. Her hair was not so dark as yours, but there was the same look about the eyes, and the same dimple. She was more inclined to do what Joseph told her than you ever were.'

'Why didn't you leave, Matty? You knew what he'd done. How cruel he was.'

'You were still here and only six years old. I promised Helen I'd stay and keep an eye on you. She was afraid he'd turn on you once she'd gone. But you were his own flesh and blood, and in his way, he loved you.'

'He has a strange way of showing it,' Evie said.

'Then when you went I was too old to start afresh in another house. Soon too old to work at all. No one else would have wanted me. I decided it was better to stay where I was than go to the workhouse.'

'Poor Matty. You can stay here with me. This will be your home from now on.'

'Not for very long.'

'Yes, for always. You'll be no trouble to us.'

'Thank you.' Matilda's voice was low and lacking in energy. Evie could hardly hear her. 'I don't think I'll be troubling you for long. I'll be for the next world soon.'

Evie understood then. 'Not too soon, I hope.'

CHAPTER TWENTY-THREE

The night was virtually over when Evie eventually went back to bed. Even then sleep wouldn't come. Her mind raced with the thought that some people gave and some people took, and those who took never knew when to stop. They could bleed others dry.

Those who gave often did so when they could ill afford to do it. And often to those less in need. Byron was one who gave. Bobby gave, and Gertie.

The takers, even when so much was given to them, never did seem happy. Father never had been. She didn't think there was a more unhappy man in the whole world. He'd trampled on others to gain personal possessions and money, and he'd antagonised everybody.

Evie slept at last, but it seemed no time at all before she heard Kitty come in with their morning tea. Byron was asking the maid in a low voice not to draw the curtains as she usually did.

Evie yawned and turned over.

'I didn't want to disturb you.'

'I was awake.'

Byron was solicitous. 'Have your tea, then try and go back to sleep. You were reading half the night.'

'More than half.' Already she could feel her indignation stirring again at what Father had done.

Byron said: 'I'll call out doctors for the invalids and then go down to make sure your father's all right. Mrs Minto can put some food together for him. Something that can be easily warmed up.'

'You're far too concerned about his welfare.'

Evie had hardened her heart. She told him what she'd found out from her mother's diaries and from Matilda. It brought another rush of anger.

'I'm getting up. I'll come down with you, I'm going to let him know what I think of him.'

'He's an old man and he's sick.'

'You're too soft. He had no thought for anybody else. What he did to my mother was despicable. He walked all over me when I was young. I'm going to let him know I've got his measure now.'

Evie climbed out of bed. 'But I'm not going to rush. We'll have breakfast as we usually do, and I'll see to Matilda.'

Matilda was drowsy. She drank the tea but took little interest in the porridge. Evie tried to feed her, but couldn't get her to take much. She ordered a fire to be lit in the old woman's bedroom and asked Mrs Minto to make her some soup for lunch.

When she went downstairs, Byron was on the phone, asking the local doctor to call and see Matilda. Then he rang Dr McDonald, whose surgery was round the corner from the pharmacy, and asked him to call on Joseph Hobson.

Evie collected the carpet bag she'd promised to return and the basket of food Mrs Minto had packed. Byron drove into town. When he pulled up outside the pharmacy, everything seemed as it should be. It was open for business, and Miss Lister and her assistant were behind the counter that sold toiletries. There were plenty of customers.

Evie was inside the shop before she heard the coughing and realised that her father was in what had once been the dentist's room. The door had been removed and dispensing was now done in there.

'He had the shop open before I got here,' Miss Lister whispered.

Evie was astounded. There was a customer waiting to consult him.

She went to his counter. 'Father, you aren't well enough to work.'

'So you're qualified to decide that?' He looked and sounded sour. He'd cut himself shaving, his face was grey and his chin had a bluish tinge.

'You were ill last night.' Byron was beside her. 'So ill you didn't open the shop yesterday.'

'All the more reason for me to work today. I've got customers to attend to.'

'I've asked the doctor to call and see you.'

'You've no business to do any such thing! I'm seeing no doctor. Don't believe in them. I've got all the medicines here and I know more about them than they do.' He lifted his mortar and pestle and started to pound. 'You can tell him not to bother coming here.'

'Come upstairs, Father,' Evie said firmly. 'I want to talk to you.'

'I've a shop to run. Say what you've got to say and get out. I can't be doing with you in here now.'

She said in a deliberately loud and clear voice:

'I came to tell you that I read my mother's diaries last night. The diaries you hid from me. I know now what you did . . .'

He abandoned any pretence of work and clutched at her arm. 'Be quiet!'

His fingers were biting into her flesh as he led her towards the stairs. Evie climbed up so quickly she left him behind. He didn't have much strength. She was glad to see Byron following. Once in the living room, he closed the door.

'I know what a cheat and a liar you are. I took her diaries . . .'

'I knew you were taking more than that bag from my cupboard,' Joseph blustered. 'You've no business to take anything. That's theft.'

'Don't accuse me of theft. I took what I believed I had a right to. My mother's diaries and the bag she tried to give me the day she died. You didn't want me to read those diaries, did you? They explained too much. Much more than you wanted me to know.'

'Of my personal concerns, not yours. I didn't want you involved. I didn't want you to worry about your mother's madness or be afraid that you might go mad too.'

Evie swallowed hard. That almost deflected her. She didn't know anything about any madness.

She said: 'The pharmacy belonged to my mother, not to you. You stole it from her. But she willed it to me. It's my inheritance.'

Byron put in: 'When she died, the will was never produced. Probate was never applied for. That's how you've managed to keep it.'

'She was not in sound mind when she had that will drawn up,' Joseph retorted. 'It was null and void.'

At that moment there was a tap on the door. Miss Lister called:

'Dr McDonald's here to see you, Mr Hobson.'

He snatched open the door. 'Get rid of him. I don't want the likes of him here.'

'I asked him to come,' Byron said. 'I'm going to bring him up. You aren't well enough to work yet.'

Evie went to the window, her heart pounding. She was afraid this wasn't going to settle anything. Her father was as hard as nails.

Byron brought the doctor in.

'Good morning, Mr Hobson.' He put his bag on a chair and opened it. 'How are you?'

'Get out,' Joseph said. 'I didn't ask you to come. I don't need a doctor.'

'Do be reasonable,' Byron put in. 'He's here now, you might as well let him check you over. You know you were ill over the weekend.'

'I noticed you didn't open your shop yesterday.'

'Then it would have been more appropriate to call then. I'm better now.'

'I'm glad to hear you're feeling better, but you don't look well. Was it flu? There's a lot of it about just now. Perhaps if I could listen to your chest . . .'

'No! Go, can't you?'

Dr McDonald was closing his bag. 'I'm sorry you don't think I can help. I'd advise rest in bed for another day or two. You might find your temperature goes up again tonight . . .'

'Get out.' Joseph's face was going purple. Evie saw the doctor turn without another word. Byron followed him downstairs to see him out.

'I don't think that was very wise,' Evie said. 'We won't be able to get him to come back, not after that.'

Joseph had sunk on to a chair. He looked depressed and ill.

She went on quietly: 'I'm not surprised you're a lonely old man. You rave and kick at everybody. You cheated my mother, but I'm not going to let you cheat me. Not any longer. I'm going to apply for probate on my mother's will.'

Byron came back.

'Did that scoundrel ask for his fee?' Joseph turned on him. 'I bet he did.'

'I thought he was entitled to it,' Byron said stiffly.

'Let's go.' Evie was impatient.

'This is getting us nowhere,' she told him grimly as she headed for Polly Darty's shop. They had to wait for Polly to finish serving a customer, then she turned to them with a smile.

'I hear your father's down in the shop this morning. From what you said, I thought he was at death's door last night.'

'So did we,' Byron said. 'Wouldn't let the doctor near him. But he thought he'd probably had flu and was now on the mend.'

'And Matilda?'

'Not on the mend yet,' Evie said sadly. 'She won't be coming back to work.'

'Well, she must be eighty, poor old thing.' Polly was wrapping up a cream cake for Evie to take to her. Evie hadn't the heart to tell her she didn't think Matty would eat it.

'I think I've found someone to take her place. I told you I'd have a think, didn't I? Do you know Eliza Cryer from Parkfield Avenue? About fifty? She kept house for John Martin, the tripe dealer in Lowe Street. He died last month.'

Evie shook her head: she didn't.

'I haven't spoken to her yet, but her husband was in for bread earlier on. He said she was looking for another job, and he'd tell her to come round.

'Speak of the devil, here she is. Good, you can talk to her now.'

Evie thought the woman looked very capable. Grey-haired and angular, she hoped she'd be strong enough to stand up to her father. She'd brought excellent references with her. Evie studied them in the cake shop.

'Just the person,' Byron said. 'Let's take her next door and settle this.'

Joseph was still sitting in the living room when they

went back. Even he had to accept that he needed help in the house. He agreed to Mrs Cryer and seemed pleased that she didn't intend to live in.

Satisfied that they'd done all they could, Evie and Byron went home after that. As the car turned into the drive, the doctor Byron had called for Matilda was just going up the front steps.

Evie showed him up to her bedroom and told him her symptoms. Matilda was hot and feverish and still drowsy. He looked down her throat.

'Another case of influenza,' he said. 'There's a lot of it about. It can be nasty.'

He listened to her chest. 'She's very chesty, I'm afraid. I fear for the very old. There's not a lot that can be done to stop it running its course.

'Keep her warm and give her plenty to drink. Light meals if she'll take them. She'll need an expectorant for her chest and aspirin for the aching limbs.'

Evie went to lie down on her bed after lunch. Her eyes were heavy and she was sure she'd sleep in the chair if she stayed downstairs, but once upstairs she was overcome with curiosity. Her mother's bag was by her bed where she'd left it. It looked shabby and smelled faintly of mildew. Her heart went out to Helen. She couldn't stop herself delving into the bag. She had to know more.

She drew out several envelopes. Her fingers shook as she untucked the flap of the largest and took out her mother's will. It cut her to the quick, took her back to that awful day when Helen had come to the shop. Making her relive all she'd felt then.

'I bequeath to my daughter Evelina . . .'

Tears clouded her eyes so she could read no more. If only she'd known. If only she'd received this when her mother had first brought it. She might have had a very different life.

She drew out another envelope. She saw it was addressed to Miss Evelina Hobson, and her heart seemed to turn over. It had been ripped open already. That could only mean that Father had read it. And, having read it, decided he didn't want her to do so. With a lump in her throat, she started to read.

My darling daughter,

I'm sure you must think I turned my back on you; that I went away without a second thought, abandoning you when you were a tot of six. Nothing could be further from the truth. Please don't think ill of me. I loved you dearly.

The truth is, I tried hard to take you with me. I pleaded with your father to allow it over several days. I stated the case for it over and over.

Bill wanted me to go away with him. I loved him and wanted that too, but I didn't want to go without you. Bill knew I wouldn't be happy without you, that I was being torn in two. We both pleaded for custody of you. Where is the sense in separating mother and child?

I was in a terrible state by this time, and hardly knew what I was doing. Twice I tried to escape with you but both times your father caught me and eventually he threw me out of the house.

I was in an overemotional state by this time, unable to get the words out or stop my tears. The next night Bill went alone to plead on my behalf. I was waiting outside because I couldn't face your father again. I was so sure Bill would do it better that I let him go in alone.

Evie, he never did come out again! Of that I am certain now. I waited outside, growing more and more desperate. I did hear voices raised in anger at one stage but only for a few moments. Mostly it was quiet.

I never saw Bill Smith again after that. I had been so uplifted, so overjoyed to have him return to me that to have him gone again so quickly seemed viciously cruel.

I knocked and rang the bell to get in then. Joseph ignored me for a long time but eventually came down and told me to make less noise. He accused me of being hysterical and said I'd disturb the neighbours.

He swore, first of all, that Bill had never gone in. I told him I'd seen him enter with my own eyes. Then he said he must have made off the back way in order to avoid me. I knew he wouldn't do that.

I've always been a little afraid of your father, but at that moment I was terrified. Of what he'd done to Bill and what he might do to you.

I ran to the police station in Brandon Street. I needed help and thought that the best place to seek it. I was hysterical with terror.

When I started to tell my story, they were sympathetic, but I couldn't tell it clearly. I told them about Bill, my first husband, being wrongly reported as killed in action. Of how he'd come back to look for me and found I had a child from a subsequent marriage. I told them how strangely your father had behaved. That he'd kept me a virtual prisoner for years and that I feared for the child he refused to give up.

I told them of how I'd been pleading for your custody until I could stand it no more. That Bill had gone in alone to plead one last time and had not come out.

I told them I thought Joseph had killed him. I think that stretched their credence too far. They didn't believe me then. I heard one mutter something about it being a far-fetched story. But I made such a fuss, demanding that a policeman should return with me to face Joseph and search the premises, that one eventually came.

The living room had been newly cleaned and tidied. Joseph was well in command of himself and put on a good performance. He told them I had strange obsessions that had upset our family life for years. He'd had to keep me at home for my own safety. He was always worried when I went out alone. He told them I wasn't capable of caring for my child. He'd had to employ help for some time. He said that I had delusions and was touched with madness.

At that moment perhaps I was. I raved at him that it was all untrue. With hindsight I don't know how I expected anyone to believe me. Joseph's story sounded so much nearer the truth.

A doctor was sent for and Joseph went through his version again. I heard him say so many times that he'd let Bill out the back way because he'd specially asked him to that I came to believe it must have happened. Joseph tied me up in knots. I was confused and didn't know what to believe.

The doctor gave me some pills and told me he'd arrange for me to have a good rest in hospital. That it would do me good and I'd soon feel better. The next day, Joseph gave me more pills and ordered a fly to take us to the station. My memory is blurred about what happened next, but I know we went by train. When we arrived, they put me to bed and gave me something to help me sleep.

I don't know how long they kept me asleep. I know, as soon as I stirred, that I was given something to eat and drink and then more pills. It was a long time before I discovered I'd been admitted to the Frensham Lunatic Asylum. They told me it was for my own safety and for that of my child. Once there, I found it impossible to convince anybody I was sane. I spent ten years there.

It was only when I needed treatment for physical illness that I was transferred to another hospital. They told me I had consumption, and I was sent then to a sanatorium, where they tried to restore me to health. I now know I cannot live much longer. I have no strength left.

I don't think I was ever mentally ill. I spent some of the years in that institution helping those who were, and I don't believe I was like them. Do not fear that it could be your inheritance from me. I think it suited Joseph to pay them to keep me there. I think he knew I would never live with him again from choice.

I have grieved endlessly for Bill. I've had many years to think about what happened on that dreadful night. He would not have walked out on me after waiting for ten years to be reunited. Had he been still alive, I'm sure he'd have found me in that asylum and rescued me. The only logical explanation I can give is that Joseph killed him and hid his body somewhere on the premises.

Evie dropped the letter and felt an icy shiver go down her spine. This was terrible, worse than anything she could have imagined, but she'd reached the stage when she could believe any ill of her father. She now knew he was an evil man. She picked up the letter to read the last page.

Dearest Evie, for me, the worst effect of all this is that it deprived me of seeing you grow up. You will be a young woman now and I long to see you again before I die, even though I will have to brave seeing Joseph too. I want you to understand how things were for me and to make my peace with you.

I want you to know that not one day has passed that I haven't thought of you and longed to be near you.

Your loving mother,
Helen Kathleen Hobson.

When she'd finished reading, Evie felt as though her heart would break. She curled up on her bed and cried for her mother. She understood now the agonies she must have suffered.

She was so tired, she fell into an uneasy doze, and the next thing she knew was that Byron was sitting beside her on the bed.

'It's four thirty and Daisy's home,' he told her. 'I didn't want you to sleep too long, or you won't sleep tonight.' He put a cup of tea in her hand.

Evie's mind was still on her mother. She poured out the awful details she'd read and saw the horror on Byron's face. Then she pressed the letter on Byron so he could read it for himself.

'I know the full story now,' Evie said slowly.

'Not quite.' Byron had a perplexed frown on his face. 'Even Helen didn't know what had happened to Bill Smith.'

Evie shivered. 'I can't bear the thought . . . Do you think my father killed him?'

'Perhaps Helen was mistaken about that,' Byron said. 'Don't worry about it.'

Later that night, Byron and Evie were getting ready for bed. Byron had found time to read Helen's story. He was shocked.

'What she must have gone through. Locked away from the world, unable to get out, parted from her child. It shows your father in a terrible light.'

'He's evil.' Evie shuddered. 'I'm not going to help him, not now I know what he did.'

'You've already done all that's needed. He's up and working again.'

'Bertie Pugh's even found a newly trained chemist to help him in the shop. A Mr Almond. He's going to start on Monday. I don't know how long he'll stay. He was told he'd be in sole charge.'

'You've done your best. Your father's going to do things his way. The best thing is to forget him.'

'I can't forget what he did to my mother. He isn't going to get away with that.'

'Don't fight him, love. I don't want you to be bitter. He's not worth it.'

Evie had already made up her mind. 'He took the pharmacy from my mother. She wanted me to have it. I'm going to take it from him.'

Byron said, 'Of course do that. Why shouldn't you? I've looked at the will. She owned the property as well as the business. She left everything to you. There was a note with it that she had a savings account at the bank in her own name. She also had a joint current account with Joseph. I expect he'll not give up anything from that without a fight.'

He took the will from the envelope again and spread it out. Her eyes caught the words:

'I Helen Kathleen Hobson, being of sound mind . . .'

'Was she of sound mind? Father says she wasn't.'

'At the time it was drawn up, yes. The solicitor – what what was his name?'

'Myerscough.'

'He must have believed she was. She appointed her bank as executors. Joseph didn't tell them she'd died, so they didn't apply for probate.'

'So I can do that now?'

'I don't see why not. It'll take a little longer than it would have done at the time.'

Evie smiled. 'I'm looking forward to telling Father that the pharmacy is mine. He won't like that. He must have wanted it very badly to do what he did.'

'What will you do with it?'

'Sell it.'

'He's refusing to move out. He was very determined about that.'

'If he wants to go on running it and living there, he'll have to pay me rent. Can I claim for all those years he's had it, when it was legally mine?'

'You'll have to ask the solicitor about that.'

Matilda didn't improve. The doctor came to see her again. He said her chest was worse. Evie had already noticed that she was having difficulty in breathing. That night she looked in on the old woman when she was going to bed at eleven o'clock. Matty seemed a little better, more animated. She thanked Evie for taking her in.

The next morning, Kitty came bursting into their bedroom. She'd found Matilda dead when she'd taken in her morning tea.

* * *

It took the best part of two years to prove the will and for the solicitor to negotiate a settlement with Joseph Hobson. Evie didn't go near him in all that time, but she knew from Gertie Collins that Mrs Cryer was still keeping house for him and Mr Almond was still helping in the pharmacy.

When it came to the settlement, Joseph agreed, rather than moving out, to pay rent to Evie and to hand over a substantial sum to compensate her for loss of rent for the years since her mother had died.

'It's ridiculous,' she fumed to Byron. 'He's sixty-nine, well over retirement age. How much longer does he think he can go on?'

'You won't change him. Let him be,' Byron advised. 'You've got what you wanted.'

Evie found that less rewarding than she'd expected.

'It's come too late for me, hasn't it? It would have meant the world at the time of Mother's death, but now . . . I don't need more money.'

'There must be something you want to do with it.'

'Yes.' She'd been thinking it over for the past two years and had already made up her mind.

Bobby still came every week to have a meal with them. Often now it was Sunday lunch, and usually he brought Sylvia with him. They were engaged and still saving to get married.

This Sunday, when the meal was over and Byron suggested a walk down to the river, Evie asked Bobby to stay behind.

She took him into the room they used as a study and laid out all the documents she'd received from Mr Myerscough about the pharmacy.

'What's all this, Mam?'

'You know all about my mother leaving me the

423

pharmacy in her will, and how Joseph hung on to it. Well, this is the money he's finally had to pay to compensate me.'

Bobby whistled through his teeth. 'As much as that?'

'Do you know what I'm going to do with it?' She could see him trying to puzzle that out. 'I want you to have it and to take over ownership of the pharmacy.'

'Me?' His eyes opened in wonderment. 'Why?'

'Byron and I are very comfortable. We can afford to give Daisy a good start. Queenie and Norman are making a success of that business, but you're still struggling.'

'You offered . . .'

'And you were proud and you refused. You didn't want money that had come from Byron. Well, this hasn't. It's come from my side of the family, so there's no reason why it should offend you. I want you to have it.'

She could see he was tempted, but he was still cogitating.

'I don't know anything about running a pharmacy. I'm not trained to do it.'

'Your grandfather's going to carry on doing that.'

'But he won't be able to for much longer.'

'Then it can be sold.' Evie paused. 'I could look for a buyer now, but I can't just put him out. I want you to take this money, and have the rent in the meantime. I know what it's like to be poor. To want things you can't afford. There's no need for you to do that, Bobby.'

He grinned at her then. 'I'm daft, aren't I? Queenie thinks I am.'

'Byron and I . . . we admire people who stick to their principles, but this doesn't go against them. There's no reason to refuse.'

'No,' he said. 'Thanks, Mam.'

She hesitated. 'What will you do with it?'

'You know already. I want to get married. Set up home.'

* * *

Evie took Bobby to her solicitor and had the pharmacy legally made over to him. On Byron's advice, Bobby appointed an agent to act as an intermediary between him and his grandfather. He saw the business accounts regularly. Byron checked them through for him and confirmed that Joseph was managing well.

When Evie knew her father had turned seventy, she began to worry.

'I can't let him stay there for ever,' she said to Byron. 'He's too old to be working. I'm going to tell him so.'

'It won't get you anywhere,' Byron told her. 'Leave him be.'

'Surely he'll want to retire? Take things easier?'

'He's determined not to move out of that place.'

'I can't sell it until he does. I'll put it to him. Get him to move, if I can. Better all round.'

'I'll come with you,' Byron said. 'I don't want you going there alone.'

'You're not afraid I'll disappear like Bill Smith?'

He smiled, but said: 'I'm not going to risk it.'

They went when the shop was open. Now it had been modernised, there wasn't much to remind Evie of her early days there. Only the medicinal smell, and the four onion-shaped glass carboys filled with coloured water that remained in the side window.

Her father looked older than his years, bent and wizened. When he saw her, he said straight away:

'You'd better come upstairs. No point in letting everybody know our business.' He was much slower getting up than he'd once been.

Nothing had changed upstairs. The living room hadn't even been given a coat of paint. It was neat and clean, and there was a fire in the grate.

Father hadn't changed either. The first thing he did was to send Mrs Cryer out to do some shopping. Then he invited them to sit at the dining table covered with the shabby chenille cloth she remembered so well.

'Now then, what d'you want?' he said to Evie. She told him that Bobby was now his landlord, that she had handed over the business and property to him some time ago.

Joseph's lips tightened. She knew he'd hated having to relinquish that. 'I know. Agent told me.'

'You look tired, Father.' He looked pathetic. She felt a stirring of sympathy, though she'd told Byron she didn't mean to be kind.

'Yes, I'm tired. The shop's busier than ever and it's a long day for one of my years.'

'That's what I've come to talk about.' Evie was grateful Joseph had brought it up himself. 'Bobby would like to sell this place. Wouldn't you like to retire? It's really too much for you now. We'd help you move to a small cottage. You could take things easier.'

'No.' She watched him feel for a chair and lower himself on to it. 'This has been my home and my business all my life. I'm not moving now.'

'But why not? You say you're tired . . .'

'I'm not moving and that's the end of the matter. He's getting his rent. He's nothing to complain about. I'm keeping my side of the bargain.'

'I thought if you retired . . .'

'I decide when I'll retire. That's not up to you.'

Evie stood up. She could see she was never going to budge him.

Byron smiled as he opened the car door for her to get in.

'Told you so. Something's keeping him here. Bobby will have to let him get on with it.'

426

CHAPTER TWENTY-FOUR

February 1939

Evie was sitting at her dressing table, dusting her cheeks with face powder. It was her forty-seventh birthday, a fact that was making her take stock of herself.

There were lines fanning out from the corners of her eyes now, but they were only noticeable when she smiled. Her hair had lost some of its colour but she wore it fashionably short and waved close to her head, and it suited her.

Her new red wool dress suited her too, with its long, swirling skirt. She wasn't as slim as she used to be, but she hadn't put on too much weight. She wasn't displeased with her reflection. She was wearing well. She pinned the cameo brooch, Byron's birthday gift, to her dress.

'You look more beautiful than ever,' he told her when she went down to the sitting room. It was a Sunday, and the scent of roasting beef was coming from the kitchen. The table was set for nine in the dining room. The children would be arriving any minute now.

Byron put a glass of sherry in her hand and raised his own to her. Evie was taking stock of her circumstances as she sipped it. She was very happy with Byron. They were rarely apart. She loved him dearly and couldn't imagine life without him.

Here, only the immediate family knew she wasn't his wife, and that made things easier. But it was the one thing she still wanted. She still wore Ned's wedding ring, but above everything else she wanted to wear one from Byron.

Apart from that, and the threat of war that was hanging over everyone, she thought that the thirties had been good to her.

Finding her mother's diaries had been traumatic. It had taken her some time to recover from the shock of learning the truth about her parents.

'I'm glad you haven't let it fill you with hate,' Byron said. 'Your father's an evil man, selfish beyond belief, depraved even. He wanted power over others but he's getting old, he no longer has his strength.'

'He fears others now. He even fears me. As if I'd harm him.'

'Ned helped you escape his influence while you were young. It was the best thing that could have happened to you. Living with a man who made demands like that was bound to increase your anxieties, but you got away before he did any lasting damage.'

Evie felt better now she knew the truth; she felt she'd laid the ghosts. She smiled sadly. 'But we still don't know everything. Did Bill Smith walk out on my mother? Such a cruel thing to do just when she needed him most. Or did Father . . . ?'

'You'll probably never know that.'

While Byron browsed through the Sunday papers, Evie reached for the field guide on birds which had been Daisy's gift to her. The garden here was full of them and she'd wanted to put a name to the species she could see.

Dear Daisy, thought Evie fondly. She was enjoying her third child. She'd been so much easier to cope with than the older two. Daisy was always happy. When she was seventeen and still at school, she'd announced her intention of training to be a chemist.

'There's a turn-up for the books,' Byron had chuckled. He adored Daisy too. 'It must be in your blood. You take after your mother's family. You'll be wanting to take over the pharmacy when your grandfather retires?'

'Not necessarily.' Daisy had smiled. 'Pharmacy's just something I want to do.'

She'd been training at Boots for some time. She was outside now, washing the Austin Seven they'd given her for Christmas, so that she could drive herself to work.

Evie heard another car pull into the drive and knew Queenie and Norman had arrived. It was a few moments before the bell rang. She could see them talking to Daisy. Byron went to let them in.

'Hello, Mam, happy birthday.' Queenie's kiss was a formal peck. Evie didn't feel as close to her as she would have liked. Queenie was very elegant these days, as well as being beautiful. She said she was happy, that she didn't care for children and didn't want any of her own; that she much preferred to manage the business. But there was a brittleness in her manner, and Evie wasn't totally convinced that that was so.

Norman followed three steps behind like a consort, with a ledger and a file under his arm. It was quite evident that Queenie was the driving force in the marriage. They came over every month or so, usually bringing the accounts of Henry Ball and Sons to show Byron, though he'd made the business over to them several years ago. They consulted him on major decisions and showed him the books regularly, and that pleased him. He still wanted to feel involved. He said that Queenie was making an excellent job of managing the firm, and generating more profit than he ever had.

Evie was unwrapping chocolates and champagne from them when Queenie said:

'We told you we were looking for a house in Oxton? We've found one we like. We'll be moving out of the flat.'

'We knew you would sooner or later,' Byron said. 'You've made no secret of that.'

Evie could hear Daisy coming in through the back door with Bobby and Sylvia. Bobby had two small sons now, Roger who was three and Paul who had recently had his first birthday. Bobby had bought a house in Heswall only some fifteen minutes' walk away. They often walked over with the children. Evie adored the little boys.

Bobby's cheek felt cold as he bent to kiss her. Evie couldn't get over how like Ned he was. He seemed very happy and very settled now, and was still working for the bank in Birkenhead.

Kitty came to tell them that dinner was ready. Evie led the way to the table. She really enjoyed having all her family round her.

Byron was worried by the steady approach of war. He knew only too well what it would do to the business of Henry Ball and Sons.

He talked to Norman and Queenie about how he expected exports to dry up as Britain's industries geared up for war. There'd still be imports if British ports could be kept open, but all shipping would run the gauntlet of the German navy. Imports would be cut to the basic essentials needed for survival. The business would shrink but staff would melt away too. They must be ready to expand again when the war was over.

Norman was likely to be called up. Byron tried to impress on Queenie that it would be up to her to see that the business survived.

War was declared at the beginning of September, and men of Norman's age were being called up even before that.

Things happened just as Byron had predicted. Norman got his call-up papers. His training gave him a commission and a desk job in the Pay Corps.

'He's lucky,' Evie told Queenie. 'He won't be in danger there.'

Norman was sent to Aldershot for nine months and was then posted to Chester. He didn't like army life. He bought himself an MG Midget and was able to get home regularly. Queenie found she could cope with the business.

As Evie had expected, Bobby was found to be medically unfit to serve in the forces. The old injury to his ankle had left him with a limp.

She was profoundly grateful now that he'd had that accident with Wilf Hutchins' bike. She felt it might well save his life. She couldn't forget that Ned and all his brothers had lost their lives in the last war. Sylvia whispered that she was relieved too.

Bobby said he wasn't pleased, but Evie knew he was torn in two. He didn't want to go away and leave his wife and young sons, but on the other hand it troubled him that he wasn't able to go and fight for his country. When he saw his colleagues and friends in uniform, he said he was afraid he'd be sent the white feather.

'You're no coward,' Evie told him.

Bobby enrolled with the Civil Defence and said he'd do as much as he could on the home front. He was soon involved in training, in building up resources and in enforcing precautions. After hearing Bobby's account of what he was doing, Byron decided he'd enrol in the Civil Defence and do his bit too. Evie, not to be outdone, joined the WRVS.

When the air raids started in earnest in the autumn of 1940, Evie was glad Queenie had moved out of the flat at the top of the Connaught Building. It was said that the enemy were aiming for the docks on both sides of the water, trying to put them out of action. Evie thought that Heswall, being on the River Dee, was much safer, and even Oxton was a lot less dangerous than central Liverpool.

The Connaught Building received minor damage almost immediately. Its windows were blown in. During the Christmas raids, there was damage to the roof. That had only just been repaired when in March, bomb blast weakened one corner and offices at the rear of the building were no longer usable. Bulwark Insurance moved out.

Then, in the May raids of 1941, the Connaught Building received a direct hit and a land mine devastated most of the rest of South Castle Street.

That news left Evie shaking. It was a night raid, and if Queenie had been living in the flat she'd have been killed. As it happened, the caretaker they'd installed had been so frightened by its position, and the fact that there were so few other people around at night, that she spent most nights with her daughter in Bootle and had therefore managed to survive too.

Although Evie saw Queenie and Norman every few weeks, and knew that the house they'd bought was close to Veronica's and that she took them out for a meal in a restaurant every Saturday evening, they never mentioned her when they came over. Byron had let them know that he didn't want news of her.

It came as something of a shock to find them on the doorstep very late one night. Evie was putting away her knitting before going up to bed. Norman's face was ghostly pale.

'It's Mother,' he said with an agonised catch in his voice. 'I thought you'd want to know.'

'What's happened?' Byron brought them to the fire. It had burned low. He tried to poke it into a blaze.

'She went to London,' Queenie told them. 'She said she needed to get away.'

'To London?' Byron sounded incredulous. 'Now, when it's being bombed?'

'She said we're being bombed here so what's the difference?' Norman took out his handkerchief and mopped his face anxiously.

'Everybody else goes to the country. Peaceful nights are what we all crave.'

'She said she was bored. She wanted to go to the London theatres and shops.' He blew his nose.

'She's been hurt?' Evie asked.

'She missing.' Norman sniffed into his handkerchief. 'I'm afraid she's been killed.'

Evie felt a flush run up her cheeks. Byron had told her years ago that Veronica had sneered at him: 'Don't set your mind on marrying your fancy woman, because you'll have to wait until I'm dead.'

Evie couldn't feel sorry now that it seemed she was, but Norman was upset. He'd been close to his mother. Byron got to his feet and poured some brandy for him.

'Veronica stays at her club,' Queenie explained. 'It's really just a place for women on their own. She's given up the luxury hotels. She went out one evening and never returned.'

'Where did she go?' Byron asked. 'That night?'

'To a show, they think. With another woman who was staying there. They left before dark and neither has ever come back. The first alert came early that evening, and there were very heavy casualties during the night. A direct hit on an air-raid shelter near Leicester Square, and two theatres badly damaged.' Queenie did not appear to be upset. Evie thought there'd never been much love lost between her and Veronica.

'When they hadn't returned to their club by the next day, the manager rang the police. The beds hadn't been slept in, all her clothes, her luggage was there. It seemed she meant to return.'

'They've been combing through those injured that night and admitted to hospitals.' Norman's hand trembled slightly as he reached again for the brandy. 'Mother isn't amongst them. It seems that many were killed that night who couldn't be identified.'

'Norman thought of going down to London,' Queenie added. 'But I've persuaded him not to. They've packed her belongings up and are sending her cases back.'

Byron poured himself a brandy when they'd gone. 'Trust Veronica to make things difficult. We don't really know, but I think we can safely presume she's been killed.'

By September 1940, Bobby felt he had plenty to do. During the day, he was kept busy in the bank because so many of the staff had been called up. During the hours of darkness, he had his Civil Defence duties. Air raids were often coming on consecutive nights. After a bad night, the little sleep he managed to get was in his office chair with his head on his desk. He washed in the staff cloakroom until the water mains were damaged and there was no more water.

The night the Argyle Theatre went on fire was terrifying. The bombers had been coming over in waves ever since nightfall. An air-raid shelter had received a direct hit, and he'd been doing what he could to dig out those who had survived. He felt sick with shock from that, and when his fellow workers pointed out a huge and growing fire in the night sky, and told him that incendiary bombs had fallen on the famous Argyle Theatre, he was relieved to hear that it was thought everybody had managed to get out.

He stood for a moment watching the theatre going up like a tinder box, and couldn't help thinking of all the good shows he'd seen there. Then it came to him that his pharmacy was only a short distance down the street and might have been damaged too.

Bobby knew that his mother had tried to persuade Joseph to move out, to get right away from the town centre. Mam asked him often if he'd been to see if the shop was all right. He knew it wasn't the shop that bothered her. If that was damaged by enemy action, he'd be given compensation.

He felt he had to check that his grandfather was all right. Argyll Street was busier than he'd ever seen it, teeming with fire crews, and the leaping flames were lighting up the street like day.

When Bobby reached the pharmacy, he saw that both shop windows had been blown in, and some of the upper windows too. There was glass everywhere, but he could see no other damage. He hammered on the door and had to wait an age for his grandfather to come. At last Joseph opened the door six inches.

'It's not safe here,' Bobby shouted. The blood was coursing through his veins. The blaze was awesome and there was chaos all round.

'You should be in a shelter. Get some shoes on and a warm coat, and I'll take you.'

The door opened another few inches, Joseph was wearing an old dressing grown over striped pyjamas, and seemed sleep-fuddled and confused.

Bobby had to draw the old man out on to the pavement to see the blazing inferno before he understood.

'Come on,' he urged. 'Quickly.'

'I can't, not with the windows gone. The place will be looted if I leave it.'

'I'll see it's boarded up. Made safe.'

'I'm not leaving. If I'm going to die I might as well do it in my own bed.'

'I'm ordering you to a shelter,' Bobby told him firmly. 'You've got to go, it isn't safe here. The place is lit up like day. The next wave of enemy aircraft will . . .'

Joseph stepped back and slammed the door before Bobby could stop him. That took his breath away. He hammered on the door again and shouted. Then he heard the bolts being slid home, and gave up.

The theatre was gutted, and what remained had to be pulled down to make it safe. There was a great empty space there afterwards. The pharmacy survived, and Joseph opened for business the next day.

As the months went on, Bobby felt there was no let-up. Even when there were no raids he had to take his turn on duty and be ready if he should be called out. He slept at home in his own bed when he could.

Christmas 1940 was a terrible time. The bombers came over every night. The building where Bobby worked was damaged, and although the bank continued to open for business, the window of his office was boarded up and he sometimes had to work by the light of a candle.

He felt stretched almost beyond his strength, but he had to keep going, do what he could for the hundreds who were buried beneath buildings that had collapsed and who needed urgent rescue. For him, it became commonplace to see the dead and the terribly injured and those who stared in numbed shock at homes and belongings that were reduced to rubble.

Every morning, after the all clear sounded, he went home to take a bath before going to the bank. Evie and Sylvia said they were fearful for him, being in the centre of Birkenhead and close to Cammel Laird's, the ship builders.

But he was equally fearful for their safety. He needed to see them and know that his own world was still safe.

January and February were not too bad on his side of the water, though he saw fire raging along the Liverpool skyline several times. Sometimes the flames were still visible twenty-four hours later. A ferry boat was sunk at her moorings. Other ships in the river and in the docks were damaged. Work went on tirelessly to keep the port open.

In March, the enemy bombers were coming over every night again. After the fifth very busy night Bobby felt exhausted.

When he heard the air-raid warning yet again on the sixth night, followed by the throb of enemy engines above, he felt he could bear no more. His eyes ached as he watched the searchlights cut swaths through the night sky, trying to track the enemy planes.

For Bobby that was the worst night of the blitz. Henry Street received a whole stick of high-explosive bombs. He'd been given charge of a rescue party and they worked for hours digging out people trapped under the rubble of their houses. He couldn't remember ever seeing so much carnage. His hands were sore with dragging at fallen beams, his eyes were prickly with grit and his mouth caked with dust. When there were no further signs of life beneath the debris and the last ambulance had departed, Bobby reclaimed the old bicycle he was using to get about.

The all clear had sounded. He was cycling along Argyle Street on the way back to his office. The road was filled with great chunks of masonry, plaster, bricks and broken glass. Debris of all kinds. After a heavy raid, there was a lot of clearing up to do.

He had to dismount to push his bike round the worst of it, and glanced up. He went cold when he saw the pharmacy. Much of the building had gone. It looked like a doll's house with the front folded back. On the ground floor, half the shop remained. On the first floor, it was possible to see into the living room and the kitchen behind it. The stairs were there, going up the wall. Above, he could see inside two bedrooms. He froze with fear, wondering which one his grandfather had been sleeping in.

A rescue party similar to the one he led was working its way towards the pharmacy. It was not Grandfather's shop alone that was damaged, but all the buildings along the side street.

He saw the body immediately. Somebody had covered it. He gritted his teeth and turned back one corner of the blanket. It was what remained of his grandfather. Bobby felt sick. It was so unnecessary. Joseph could have moved somewhere safer.

Mam would be shocked and upset, he knew. He glanced up at the open rooms above him, and for a moment thought he saw another person up against the wall. He looked more carefully; once there'd been a cupboard there. A soldier? Could that be a soldier? He was dressed in khaki. But no . . . Bobby caught his breath. He thought he knew what he was looking at. He could feel the sweat breaking out on his face.

He did something then he wouldn't normally have done. He knew he was endangering his own life. Somebody shouted that it wasn't safe to climb the stairs. He felt them swing beneath his weight. He was so weary he felt light-headed, but he had to find out. Mam wouldn't be able to rest until she knew for certain. He dragged himself up, sliding his back against the wall. He passed a keyboard with only one key hanging on it; a framed photograph hanging askew, showing Grandpa at the height of his boxing skill. Up again to the second floor and into the front bedroom.

The furniture had all slid to the ground, and the bare floor sloped down at an angle. It was unsupported on one side and swayed beneath Bobby's weight. He had to cling to the door frame to keep himself from falling. The cupboards had been blown off the wall. What he'd thought was a body looked very different from here.

Bobby didn't know what to make of it. He could go no nearer. It looked like some parody of Guy Fawkes. A soldier, an officer, with three pips on his shoulder and a Sam Browne belt. A captain then, in the uniform of long ago. The Boer War? The flesh had long since rotted; much of the cloth too. The bones remained, a skeleton that still wore shoes, the soles of which were separating into curling layers of leather.

Bobby felt everything swimming round him. His mother had shown him the diaries, told him the story of his grandmother. He'd found it hard to believe. Now he knew he'd stumbled on evidence of that final act. Evie would have the truth at last. Grandfather had killed Bill Smith and hidden his body in the cupboard being constructed at that time in his bedroom. Bobby knew now why Joseph wouldn't move out of the building.

A fireman had to bring Bobby down by ladder. He couldn't crawl back down those swinging stairs; he was paralysed by shock. Yet it all seemed unreal against the horrors of the night. Once down he vomited amongst the rubble and received a dressing-down for endangering his own life and that of the man who had rescued him.

It was a Sunday morning very early, hardly yet light. He went to Heswall then, straight to his mother's house.

It was the summer of 1942. Byron had taken Evie to

Windermere for their honeymoon. The wedding had been a discreet registry office affair, quieter than quiet. Only their children and their families had been present. He had booked a lunch table at the Adelphi for a party of seven adults and two children afterwards, and then he and Evie had driven up here.

Mrs Minto, who still kept house for them and their new friends in Heswall, thought they were having an ordinary holiday.

Byron felt they'd had a wonderfully peaceful morning walking in the hills. Now, after a lunch that was good considering rationing and all the shortages, they were sitting on the terrace, looking out over the shimmering lake.

He smiled at Evie. He could see here and there a gleam of silver in her dark hair. She was his wife at last. Her eyes were closed against the sun. He saw her smile faintly to herself.

'What are you thinking about?'

He reflected that you had to be truly close to a person to ask that with any hope of getting the truth.

Evie opened her eyes and looked at him gravely. 'That we never truly understand a different generation. My parents acted in a way I find unbelievable. When I think of what my father did, I go cold inside even now. Poor Mother, she had to put up with so much.'

'And as for our children . . .' She shook her head. 'I love them dearly. I admire Bobby and feel close to Daisy. Queenie's a beautiful girl, but . . .'

He laughed. 'The children do things that are no easier to understand?'

Her smile widened. 'I understand you, Byron.' It spread till it lit up her eyes, and the dimple he always watched for was plain to see.

Now you can buy any of these other bestselling
books from your bookshop or *direct
from the publisher*.

FREE P&P AND UK DELIVERY
(Overseas and Ireland £3.50 per book)

My Sister's Child	Lyn Andrews	£5.99
Liverpool Lies	Anne Baker	£5.99
The Whispering Years	Harry Bowling	£5.99
Ragamuffin Angel	Rita Bradshaw	£5.99
The Stationmaster's Daughter	Maggie Craig	£5.99
Our Kid	Billy Hopkins	£6.99
Dream a Little Dream	Joan Jonker	£5.99
For Love and Glory	Janet MacLeod Trotter	£5.99
In for a Penny	Lynda Page	£5.99
Goodnight Amy	Victor Pemberton	£5.99
My Dark-Eyed Girl	Wendy Robertson	£5.99
For the Love of a Soldier	June Tate	£5.99
Sorrows and Smiles	Dee Williams	£5.99

TO ORDER SIMPLY CALL THIS NUMBER

01235 400 414

or e-mail <u>orders@bookpoint.co.uk</u>

Prices and availability subject to change without notice.